PATHOLOGICAL

PATHOLOGICAL

Wang Jinkang

TRANSLATED BY JEREMY TIANG

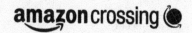

Text copyright © 2014 Wang Jinkang
Translation copyright © 2016 Jeremy Tiang

Previously published as 四级恐慌 by Wang Jinkang in China in 2014. Translated from Mandarin by Jeremy Tiang. First published in English by AmazonCrossing in 2016.

Published by AmazonCrossing, Seattle

www.apub.com

Amazon, the Amazon logo, and AmazonCrossing are trademarks of Amazon.com, Inc., or its affiliates.

ISBN-13: 9781503942059
ISBN-10: 1503942058

Cover design by Rex Bonomelli

Printed in the United States of America

PATHOLOGICAL

CHAPTER ONE
THE ULTIMATE VIRUS

September 1997—New Siberia, Russia

Kolya Stebushkin finished early that afternoon, and as usual headed to a little bar near his apartment to drown his sorrows in vodka. He worked at the State Research Center of Virology and Biotechnology, also known as the Vector Institute, which was still in a state of partial paralysis after the dissolution of the Soviet Union. Once superstars of the scientific world, its employees were now scarcely better off than beggars. The bulk of the tech staff had gone abroad for better opportunities, or else to the more European cities like Moscow or St. Petersburg, where conditions weren't as bad. Stebushkin had stayed behind, but his wife and their two kids were gone. In the six months since Natasha's departure, he'd sought comfort in the bottle, but his scientist's training kept a part of his mind permanently unclouded, so the pain never really left him. Director Chaadayeva, kind as always, advised, "Kolya, look on the bright side.

Luckily Natasha went to Moscow. If she'd ended up in Kiev or Minsk, she'd have turned into a foreigner overnight!"

That only made it worse. For people of his generation, everything had been smashed—family, life, ideals, ambitions—and could never be put back together again.

When he was almost to the bar, he saw a woman up ahead. Even from the back she was very attractive, her body swaying lightly as she walked. She wore trousers and a jacket the color of rice, her glossy black hair falling over the collar. It was early fall, and her clothes didn't look warm enough for Novosibirsk. She obviously didn't speak Russian, and was asking someone for directions, a plump old lady who studied the note in her hand and gestured that she should keep walking. As she turned, Stebushkin could study her profile—a silver-gray turtleneck tight against high breasts. She was twenty-six or -seven, Asian with delicate features. Stebushkin guessed she was Chinese. They weren't far from Xinjiang here, and it had become common to see people from western China on the streets of Novosibirsk—mostly profiteers. Of course, this woman was evidently no wheeler-dealer, but more likely a highly educated intellectual.

Several young skinheads brushed past Stebushkin, heading toward the woman. In an instant, they'd surrounded her, five switchblades waving before her eyes. Prey. A tall guy, presumably the leader, demanded in English that she hand over all her valuables. Stebushkin hesitated, uncertain whether he ought to step forward, a knight in shining armor.

The street was empty. The old lady lingered a moment, but finally shook her head and departed—she didn't dare provoke this gang. Stebushkin stayed put. As a gentleman, he could hardly stand by and watch as a woman was mistreated, but it would be risky to barge in. The skinheads weren't a political group, just a motley gang of racist hooligans. The targets of their violence were mainly people of color, but they were equally happy to raise their knives against anyone else who got in their way. The Chinese woman they now surrounded appeared calm and docile, frowning as she followed their instructions to take out her wallet. Just as she was about to fling the money to them, the leader snatched the whole thing. She called out in English, "Please leave my passport!"

The tall guy pulled out all the cash, then tossed the wallet and passport back to her. Stebushkin decided not to interfere. Giving up some money to avert disaster seemed reasonable, and they probably wouldn't have gotten that much anyway. The Chinese had a bad reputation here and were known for their scams, like trading fake goose-down coats and alcohol for genuine high-quality Russian fur and leather. They'd also brought over another bad habit from China—they'd use cash to smooth over any difficulties. The Russian police quickly learned to expect bribes from everyone, but especially from the Chinese. When they stopped a Chinese person on the street, they'd stretch out a hand for his or her wallet, without so much as an excuse. The police would always leave their victims enough to get a taxi home, though, which was more than the skinheads did. Most Chinese now knew not to carry too much cash on them.

These thugs, though, didn't stop with the money. The leader looked her up and down, then grinned. "You're a pretty girl. Wanna have some fun with us?" Knowing she wouldn't understand Russian, he repeated himself in English. The other four gang members laughed, and slowly closed in, until the woman was backed into a corner, screaming furiously in English, "Stop it! What do you think you're doing? I'm calling the police!"

The police were no threat to these guys. They pressed forward, wedging the woman in so she could no longer move. Stebushkin sighed; he'd have to step in now, never mind the risk. He wasn't about to let a foreign woman get raped on a Russian street. Dashing toward them, he yelled, "Freeze! Don't move!"

The five thugs had no intention of stopping. They glanced at him, and two of them peeled off casually to block his way. Seeing his scrawny frame and several days' growth of beard, they pegged him for a down-on-his-luck nerd, hardly worth taking seriously. They simply waved their blades threateningly, forcing him to stop. Meanwhile, the other three kept their knives on the woman, and were ordering her to take off her clothes. Watching this bunch of bastards, Stebushkin felt himself fill with rage. Was Russia doomed to become the realm of scum like this? He steeled himself. He would stop them, even if he got stabbed in the process. He wasn't just protecting this woman, he was defending the honor of the Russian people. But at this moment, the woman underwent an abrupt change. Her face, which had maintained a cool dignity, a plum blossom in snow, suddenly brightened with a seductive smile, as she said languorously, "I thought you just wanted to play? So what's with the knives? I'd like to sample some Russian studs. Take me somewhere we can be alone."

Stebushkin was taken aback—was she a hooker after all? She didn't look the part at all. The leader was the only one of the gang able to speak English, but her sultry smile transcended language. He quickly translated her words, and the others began chuckling, letting their knives fall to their sides. The woman took the initiative again, stepping forward and placing her hands caressingly on the necks of the tall guy and the one next to him, murmuring something in a low voice as she threw a glance at Stebushkin. The next instant Stebushkin heard the dull thud of heads crashing together. The woman shoved the two of them into a third, felling him too. In an instant, the gang of five had been reduced to two stunned individuals, their knives still pointed at Stebushkin, frozen as still as their unconscious friends. They weren't even panicked, they simply hadn't gotten a handle on this dramatic reversal. The woman's face was icy, her seductive smile gone. In a cold, hard voice, she said, "I'm Chinese. Want to try my kung fu?"

Her English was fluent, with a precise American accent. Seeing that the storm had suddenly calmed, Stebushkin let out a sigh of relief and admiration for this woman's resourcefulness and martial arts skill. The last two thugs stood like blocks of wood, unable to understand her, so Stebushkin helpfully translated into Russian. "This lady says she's from China. If you want to sample her Chinese kung fu, please feel free to go ahead. If not, then scram, and take your loser friends with you."

Dragging their injured comrades, the remaining hoodlums began scuttling away. The woman called after them, "Hang on, give me my money back!"

Stebushkin walked over and pulled the bundle of notes from the leader's pocket, handing it to the woman. It was a substantial amount—a few rubles, but mostly Chinese yuan and American dollars. As the thugs beat an inglorious retreat, she put the money back into her wallet and extended her hand to Stebushkin. "Thank you for risking yourself to save me." She smiled as they shook hands. "You've shown me what a real Russian man looks like."

"No need to thank me, I was just doing what a man ought to do. Those people"—he indicated the departing figures—"are the scum that rises when a country's in trouble. Don't think they represent Russia."

"I know. It's the same in China. When society opened up after years of repression, the dregs immediately floated to the top—like the lowlifes who turn up here selling counterfeit goods. Don't think of them as Chinese. When I see Russian shops put up signs—'Guaranteed no Chinese goods here'—I blush for my country. But never mind them. I really must thank you."

"What for? I didn't actually help—it was you who saved me. Your kung fu is excellent."

She laughed. "I just said that to scare them. The truth is, I spent two years in the States learning tae kwon do—I don't actually know any kung fu at all." She caught sight of the crucifix around Stebushkin's neck. "Perhaps you're the one I'm looking for? The virologist from the Vector Institute, Kolya Stebushkin, who lives at number thirty-two on this street."

Stebushkin's cross was identical to the one around her neck. So the Society had finally caught up with him. With a heavy heart, he nodded.

◆ ◆ ◆

Stebushkin's apartment was on the second floor of an old building. Flicking on the lights, he said, "Come in. Don't bother taking off your coat, the heating doesn't work."

The woman looked around. The room was large—about two thousand square feet—and gloomy. The high ceiling made the place feel spacious compared to Chinese apartments. The furniture was adorned with intricate wooden carvings in the Russian style. In the open-plan kitchen, a samovar sat on the counter, and empty bottles were accumulating in the corners. The TV set in the living room appeared to be a black-and-white model. Books were scattered everywhere, and all the furniture was covered with a fine layer of dust. The impression was of a once-upscale Russian household that had fallen into disrepair.

"Coffee or green tea?" Stebushkin asked his visitor.

"Plain water, please. That's all I usually drink."

He glanced at her in mild surprise, and filled a glass from the faucet.

"Where are your wife and kids?" she asked. Apparently she knew all about his life.

"We're divorced. After the country fell apart, she insisted on returning to Moscow, where her parents are." He smiled bitterly. "The children went with her. She said it was a better environment for them to grow up in, and I agreed."

The woman cradled her glass and studied him. "I'm sorry, I shouldn't have brought it up." Stebushkin waved her apology away. "But why didn't you go with her?"

"I'm already forty-three, it's too late for me to learn how to wait tables. Anyway, I didn't want to abandon my profession—I've spent half my life on it, and still believe it'll be important someday. By the way, I still don't know your name."

"My Chinese name is Mei Yin, Cassie Mei in English."

"You said you were from China earlier, but you sound completely American. I think English must be your first language?"

"I'm an American citizen. I was an orphan in China, originally from Harbin. My parents died of the plague when I was two, and I was adopted by an American couple at age ten. After that, I grew up and went to school in the States. After getting my master's, I returned to China, and I intend to stay there. Deep in my heart, I'm more Chinese than anything else. My American dad suggested I come back to China, and I wanted that too. I've been back nine years now."

Stebushkin nodded. "I see."

"You're right to say your profession will be important. I was in China during the Cultural Revolution, and even as a child, I saw and heard some terrible things. It was as great a calamity as the ending of the Soviet Union, yet China emerged from the wreckage. The Russian people are strong, I'm sure you won't languish. Novosibirsk might be remote, but it's still an important center of Russian science. A third of the country's research strength is here, with world-class scientists like yourself. I can guarantee that new life will be sprouting soon."

"That's good of you to say; I'll sleep easier tonight for your kind words. Now, you've come—I assume he asked you to get something for him?"

"Yes."

"The thing is," he said frankly, "I haven't decided yet whether to give it to you. True, I did promise the Godfather, but I regretted it right away. That makes me a coward and a liar, right? I imagine he'll punish me severely. No one who wears the crucifix has ever dared defy him."

Mei Yin seemed startled, but quickly regained her calm. "The Godfather leads the Society through farsightedness and force of personality alone. He'd never give out undeserved punishments. It makes me sad that you could say a thing like that."

Stebushkin blushed. His mood had been low ever since his wife and children left, and his words were often sharper than necessary. He knew it, but couldn't always control himself.

Mei Yin said gently, "In fact, before I set out, the Godfather said he understood what a difficult position you were in. He knows how hard it will be to make this decision, and the danger you'll be in afterward. After all, what he wants exists in Atlanta's CDC, but he has no way to get his hands on it."

Stebushkin chuckled humorlessly. "Whereas it's much easier in Russia, where all the systems have fallen apart, and it's chaos everywhere. As the saying goes, it's easier to steal fish from muddy waters."

Mei Yin answered levelly, "Yes, that's how it is. But our motives are pure and unselfish."

"I'm willing to believe that. Only . . . as I see it, Gorbachev was also a good person, and his motives were pure, but at the same time he's the villain responsible for Russia's downfall. And Western experts who insisted on economic shock therapy for the USSR, not only did they fail to cure the patient, they pushed her into a terminal condition. I believe the Western intellectuals acted from pure motives too, but that doesn't reduce their guilt."

Sounding displeased, Mei Yin said, "So you're saying, our operation is like . . ."

"I'm not saying anything. This isn't a straightforward comparison. No, what we're planning is even deeper than dissolving the USSR. This is the will of heaven we're setting in motion, it's no exaggeration to call it a wrestling match between humanity and God. I'm just an ordinary person, I'm not fit to judge right from wrong."

Mei Yin smiled abruptly. "So let's change the subject. It's time for dinner—can I trouble you for a meal? Smashing those two skinheads together has given me an appetite."

Stebushkin smacked his forehead. "How rude of me, I'm sorry—I completely forgot about dinner. I have to admit, after Natasha and the kids left, I've hardly ever bothered with a proper evening meal. Just a bottle of vodka at bedtime. Wait a moment, I'll rustle something up."

He went into the open-plan kitchen and got to work. Mei Yin stayed on the sofa, still holding her empty glass and staring into space. She hadn't expected this resistance. From what the Godfather had told her, Stebushkin had never expressed reluctance. The way he was talking now, she might well be going home empty-handed. But she wouldn't leave without trying her utmost to fulfill her mission.

Dinner was soon ready, a sumptuous spread by Russian standards: a green salad, smoked ham, carrot soup, potatoes and bread, and, finally, a pot of Indian green tea. During the meal, they deliberately avoided discussing Mei Yin's purpose in visiting him. Conversation ranged from Russian art and literature, to the history of Siberia, to the difference between the Eastern Orthodox Church and Catholicism.

"For one thing," Stebushkin replied, "look at all the varieties of crucifixes. The Catholics and Protestants wear a Latin cross, with a longer bottom arm, like the ones we wear. The Orthodox style, otherwise known as the Greek cross, has four arms of equal length."

"I know that much."

"Well, there's also the differences in doctrine, and traditions of thought."

"Such as?"

"The Orthodox Church is inflexible, it doesn't accept scientific advancement, nor adapt Christ's teachings to fit new discoveries. Catholicism, by contrast, has incorporated progress in human thought and science into its beliefs—eventually. I find the Eastern Orthodox Church far too rigid, lacking the ability of the Catholic or Protestant Church to renew itself." He smiled. "But then I seldom go to church, nor do most of the other scientists at the research center."

9

"You're right, rigidity leads to death. Christianity has accepted science—why hasn't science turned around and accepted God as well? Modern medicine's successes might be dazzling, but they can't shake the foundations of evolution, a path laid out by God four billion years ago."

After dinner, they returned to the couch, and Mei Yin returned to the point. "Kolya, you know the world's governments and scientists have urged that this substance be thoroughly destroyed—they fear that if this particular genie gets out of the bottle, no one will ever be able to put it back. But the Godfather has always argued humanity has no right to decide that any species is an enemy, and take away its right to exist in the natural world. The Godfather and many farsighted colleagues have done what they can to thwart calls for extinction from the medical field, but there's no guarantee they'll be successful next time. And so—no offense—the chaos of Russia might be our only chance; we'd regret not taking advantage of it."

Stebushkin started to interrupt, but Mei Yin stopped him. "Before I left, the Godfather said something I didn't fully understand at the time. 'Don't make him do anything he's not willing to do.' And so I'm not going to force you, nor will I urge the Godfather to punish you in any way. You'll have to decide for yourself. Although"—she smiled—"just now you said you hadn't made up your mind, so at least I have a glimmer of hope. I'd like to stay a few days, until you've made a final choice. You don't mind, do you? Don't worry, I promise not to pester you while I'm here. I'll be as quiet as a trout in the Volga."

Stebushkin smiled and nodded. He found this Chinese woman—American woman, he should say—quite enchanting. It would be a pleasure to have her around. "Do you have a place to stay?" he asked. "If you don't mind, you'd be very welcome to stay here."

Mei Yin was delighted. Looking round the spacious room, she said, "I was hoping you'd offer. I have nothing good to say about Russian hotels, and they charge something ridiculous, like two hundred American dollars per night. I don't mean to brag, but I'm a pretty good cook—both Western and Chinese cuisine. Perhaps I could pay my rent in dinners. Sound good to you?"

"It's a deal. But there's one thing I have to warn you about: the American spy novels got it right, Russian men really are sex maniacs." He laughed. "Of course, you've got nothing to worry about. You know Chinese kung fu."

Mei Yin laughed too. "Don't worry. I don't mind telling you: I've never done anything like that before. In China, we have a saying that even a rabbit will bite when it's cornered. Have you heard of Kochubey?"

"Kochubey? No. The name sounds familiar."

"Kochubey was a folk hero during the Russian civil war, and he was once captured by the White Guard and brought to trial. In the courtroom, he put his arms around two bailiffs and suddenly smashed their heads together, then escaped through a window. They made a movie about him that was once very popular in China. I watched it as a child, at an open-air screening in our village. I remember the wind was so strong that night it made the screen billow out, so Kochubey looked like he was pregnant. That's why it stuck in my mind. I remembered that scene just now and decided to try the maneuver!"

Stebushkin knew this couldn't be the whole truth. Whether or not she knew Chinese kung fu, she'd dared to strike while surrounded by five knife-wielding thugs. He chuckled. "All right, so now I know your secret. I'll be a bit bolder, then, if I try anything."

He straightened up his daughter's former bedroom for Mei Yin. They said good-night, and went to their separate rooms. Stebushkin lay in bed, eyes wide open, staring at the ceiling. The woman on the other side of the wall certainly knew what she was doing, and the more she remained "as quiet as a trout in the Volga," the harder he'd find it to turn her down. What ought he to do? Harden his heart and keep his promise to the Godfather, or harden his heart and break it?

◆ ◆ ◆

The next day, Stebushkin came home from work to be greeted by a smiling Mei Yin. "Back already? The ingredients are all prepared, I'll get dinner started now."

The apartment was completely transformed, everything put away and in order, the furniture dusted, the windows sparkling, and the empty bottles cleared away. He was particularly surprised to see that she'd dug out the family portraits from a drawer, and placed them back on the wall. There was Natasha, their two kids, and a younger version of him, all smiling in their frames. Stebushkin stared at the photographs in silence, then walked into the kitchen, which had undergone a similar metamorphosis. He'd suddenly acquired a wok and various Chinese condiments—soy sauce, vinegar, MSG, and so on. Mei Yin was shaking the wok with a practiced hand, sending delicious aromas into the air. "I had to walk for miles today before I found a Chinese grocery that had everything I needed, equipment and spices. Now you'll get a chance to admire my cooking."

But Stebushkin was admiring her: her movements burst with such energy he could barely restrain the urge to embrace her.

Soon, four platters appeared on the table. Mei Yin introduced them as kung pao chicken, steamed trout, tomatoes fried with eggs, and onion rings (this last dish was American). To go with them was a soup of lily buds and lotus seeds, and bottles of Tsingtao beer.

"How's the food?"

"Delicious! Looks, smells, and tastes great."

"You don't have to be polite, tell the truth."

"Honestly, I wasn't being polite. This really is superb."

Mei Yin beamed. "Then I'll cook for you every day—at least until you kick me out. And I promise you'll never taste the same dish twice."

"Of course I won't kick you out! But you're spoiling me. How will I cope once you've gone?"

"So come with me. Come live and work in Wuhan. You won't believe how good the food is there—you'll be amazed. Only thing is, the weather's hot. We call it the 'oven of China.' A polar bear like you might find it hard to get used to."

After dinner, he said, "It's the weekend tomorrow, so I'm going to my dacha to do a bit of farming. Everyone here does that, these days, planting a few vegetables to supplement their diet. Want to come? It's unspoiled nature out there, the scenery will be gorgeous."

"Of course I'll come." Mei Yin grinned. "I'd love to see unspoiled Russian nature."

The next day, they headed to the dacha in Stebushkin's broken-down old Lada. The dacha was about twenty-five miles from the city, and the road there seemed to be submerged in an ocean of trees. After an hour's slow progress along the rough road, they reached Stebushkin's dilapidated little cottage on the edge of the forest. All its windows were smashed, with wooden boards nailed over the frames. The interior was a jumble as well, with only one room in relative order, simply furnished and clean. Next to the building was a vegetable patch, fairly large but neglected, with a few carrots and potatoes surrounded by an abundant growth of weeds.

"What a lovely wild garden you have, Kolya," teased Mei Yin. "Pity some vegetables snuck in there to spoil it."

Stebushkin laughed too, embarrassed. He had limited leisure time, and very little skill or interest in gardening. Mei Yin pulled off her windbreaker and rolled up her sleeves, and they set to work. First to come up were the potatoes, which went into the trunk of the Lada. Next, they watered and weeded the ground around the carrots. It had been twenty years since Mei Yin had left the Chinese farming village where she was born, but her childhood skills returned to her quickly. At the end of the day, the garden was looking far more presentable.

Lunch and dinner were improvised meals of bread and beer. That evening Stebushkin said, "Come on, after a day's hard work, let's have a dip in the creek." He drove the Lada another six or so miles, into a boundless grassland with a stream running through it. The water here was calm and so clear you could see the emerald-green weeds undulating at the bottom. The banks were carpeted in grass, decorated with purple, blue, and bright yellow wildflowers.

Stebushkin stripped to his shorts, then turned to Mei Yin. "I brought Natasha's bathing suit, it's in the backseat of the car. Go change. Though the water's pretty cold this time of year, it might be too chilly for you."

He got a running start and plunged into the creek, shrieking from the icy cold, moving his arms frantically to warm up. He got to the other shore and turned back, then froze in shock. Mei Yin was in the water, but not wearing Natasha's swimsuit. She was completely nude. Her arms moved smoothly, her body fully displayed in the limpid water. She swam toward Stebushkin, and nonchalantly explained, "I got used to swimming naked in the States, but had to give that up when I got back to China—there isn't a single nude beach in the whole country. Seeing this Garden of Eden, I couldn't resist."

Stebushkin simply couldn't look away from her body. "Mei," he said lightly, "you know from last night that I'm a man with a great deal of self-control, but the temptation you're putting in front of me is simply too much."

"Then give in to it," she said lightly. "Pleasure between men and women is a gift from God, you shouldn't refuse it."

They thrashed about in the water for some time, until their bodies were warm, then Stebushkin held her as they made their way to shore. Setting her down on the soft grass, with her hands around his neck, he pulled her toward himself. Through the storm that followed, Stebushkin found himself wondering at how this liberal American woman seemed entirely unfamiliar with sexual matters. Her brow was furrowed, as if she were enduring great pain. She clutched Stebushkin hard, fingernails digging into the skin on his back. He soon understood the reason for this and rolled off.

"Mei Yin, I hadn't imagined you'd be a virgin."

"Yes." She laughed. "A thirty-year-old virgin. In today's world, that must be the rarest of species."

Stebushkin looked solemn. "Mei Yin, I swear I had no idea."

Annoyed, she said a little sharply, "What's with the long face? Afraid this virgin is entrapping you? Don't worry so much, I'm not a puritan. I've just been busy with my career all these years, and I never met a man I was attracted to."

Stebushkin sighed. "This poor specimen in front of you is surely not good enough either."

"No, you're exactly what I'm looking for, a real man—a bit shabby on the outside, sure, but full of masculine energy. Your eyes hold a little sadness, but they have depth. And the first time I saw you, you were taking the field like a knight, risking your life to rescue a fragile woman from danger." Her lightly mocking tone turned serious. "You're not just a knight, you're Prometheus, stealing fire from the gods."

When both of them were spent, they clutched each other tightly, and she slipped into a shallow sleep. Stebushkin remained wakeful, and troubled. He raised himself on one arm and silently studied Mei Yin. She was sleeping soundly. Out of his arms and probably feeling chilly, she was all curled up, moving a little and then huddling up again. Her naked, curved body was as smooth and shiny as an insect's carapace. For some reason, this put Stebushkin abruptly in mind of praying mantises, the female of the species turning around and eating the male's head after mating. For the male, then, sex must be closely linked to death—was this to be his fate too? But he felt no animosity toward the female praying mantis. As a biologist, he understood why the mantis's behavior was advantageous in perpetuating the species. It might seem cruel, and inhumane, but it was in keeping with natural law.

Likewise, he had been willing to prostrate himself before the Godfather, whose doctrines might be extreme, even cruel—certainly not humane—but were indeed in line with natural law.

He had startled her awake. She looked around blearily before coming to full consciousness. Laughing, she reached out to him, pulling herself upright, leaning back into his chest. Her spine and bottom were cool, her breasts as round and plump as apples, gleaming in the light. Surveying the landscape again, she murmured, "God, this place really is stunning. It's beautiful, in that solemn, tranquil way—not a glimpse of smoke, no sign of the ax. This is Eden, like in the Bible. You're Adam and I'm Eve, only we haven't had the chance to steal the forbidden fruit yet."

Stebushkin bent to kiss her breasts. "We haven't eaten the fruit, so we don't know it's shameful to be naked."

"No knowledge means no spiritual suffering."

"Please be careful of the tempting serpent, and avoid original sin!"

They burst out laughing. "I'll never forget this day," said Mei Yin. "When I retire, I'll live in seclusion here. Will you welcome me?"

"Of course, though I daren't get my hopes up."

Mei Yin turned to look at him. "That's after I've retired, let's not talk about that now. As for the present, I'm urging you to come with me. I'm serious. China's developing very fast, and our virology institutes need your abilities. Besides—you're the first man I've been with. I've told you, I'm basically an old-fashioned girl, and my 'first time' means a lot to me. Of course, if you and Natasha decide to give your marriage another chance, I'd have nothing to say except to wish you well. But if not, why not let me have my way?" She laughed. "Do I seem too desperate? It ought to be the man who proposes."

Stebushkin took her in his arms and kissed her. He was moved despite himself, but he was no innocent, and could see the situation all too clearly. A level-headed woman like Mei Yin wouldn't fall in love with a defeated man in just a couple of days. All this was in the service of a utilitarian motive. Such a marriage would be a castle built on sand.

Suddenly standing, he reached out a hand and pulled Mei Yin to her feet. "Come on, let's go home, right away! I'll give you what you came for—quick, before I change my mind."

Mei Yin gave him a long look, but said nothing. They hurriedly got dressed, returned to the dacha and locked it up, then got in the Lada. All the way home, Stebushkin was silent, his brow furrowed, his eyes burning into the distance. Mei Yin didn't say anything either, but kept one hand on his knee, gently stroking it. It was dark by the time they got home. Stebushkin parked next to his block, but instead of heading upstairs, he led her to a different building about a hundred yards away. They went into the basement, opened the door, and turned on the light, revealing a room full of fishing equipment, a broken-down motorcycle, several fishing rods, a folding tent—all covered in dust. Only a minifridge in one corner looked new, gleaming in the light, a stark contrast to the shabbiness of the clutter. A Japanese brand. Stebushkin pulled open the door. It was almost empty; he pulled out a small box that emanated frosty white mist. There were four red exclamation marks on its lid, the Vector Institute symbol for a Level-Four virus.

In the murky light, his eyes gleamed like a cat's. "Here, this is it. Actually, I got it ready as soon as the Godfather called, and for safety stored it near the apartment. But I wasn't sure if I should actually hand it over. And now . . . open it."

Mei Yin took the box and carefully pulled off the lid. The white mist grew thicker as the dry ice inside sublimated. Through the thick fog, she could see three tiny sealed glass vials.

"This is what the Godfather wanted, Satan's gift. During the Cold War, all scientists, including me, were forced to research these things, not in order to harm others, but to prevent them from harming us. And now I'm handing them to you, to pass to him. Of course, you know what they can do."

"I know," said Mei Yin softly. "Thank you, Kolya. I'm thanking you on behalf of the Godfather, and of—the future."

Stebushkin's expression grew forlorn. "The future? If only the people of the future will want to thank me, and not curse me. If only what I've done today is good and not evil. If only."

At last, Mei Yin had her hands on the three tightly sealed glass vials, and what slumbered within. They were extremely simple lives, perhaps only half lives, yet they were also extraordinarily resilient, God's most successful creation. Mei Yin tried to appear calm, but couldn't hide the exhilaration in her eyes. Stebushkin looked at her, conflicted. He envied her, but there was fear within the envy. Mei Yin's faith was much stronger than his. She seemed to lack the internal torments that had driven him close to madness.

That night, they lay again in each other's arms, but for a long time were unable to sleep, their attention fixed on the humming of the fridge. Mei Yin had retrieved the box from the basement. Since she'd learned of its existence, she hadn't let it out of her sight. The virus now rested in the apartment fridge, an old-style Soviet machine whose compressor sounded as loud as a tractor. Its insulation wasn't great either, which meant the racket started up frequently. Yet this rumbling sounded to Mei Yin as sweet as celestial music, leaving her secure and happy.

Having resigned himself to handing "Satan's gift" over to Mei Yin, Stebushkin no longer wanted to think about it. He didn't ask her which country she planned to bring the virus to. In any case, he thought, she (and the Godfather) wouldn't necessarily be willing to tell him. He only asked, out of concern, "How will you get through customs? The best thing would be to get the Godfather to come up with a clearance certificate from the WHO or CDC. Of course, you could just forge one."

"No, I don't want to leave a paper trail. Anyway, there's no need to bother with all that, I've already got in touch with a black market runner who's helping me find a way across the Russian, Kazakh, and Chinese borders. You know how slapdash customs officers are these days—it should be foolproof."

Her mention of the Chinese border was a hint that the virus would end up in China, perhaps even in her workplace, the Wuhan Institute of Virology, part of the Chinese Science Academy. This was the country's most influential virus research center, initially investigating agricultural viruses, but later moving into medical viruses and new diseases. Hearing Mei Yin mention "slapdash customs officers," Stebushkin was overcome by a flash of rage. "That black market contact you're talking about presumably doesn't know what he's trafficking, a little box that could kill a million people. As long as there's a tiny speck of profit to be made, he'll carry it for you with a clear conscience. It's just like you said, when a country's corrupt and confused, it's easy for us to reap the advantage. The Godfather was right to choose you for this job."

Hearing his anger, Mei Yin said in a conciliatory tone, "I believe that when we leave this world, we won't regret what we've done today."

Stebushkin remained silent. He had to admit that Mei Yin was taking just as big a risk as he was. He was merely a custodian turned thief, but she'd be guilty of smuggling the most dangerous Level-Four virus. If this were to get out, the two of them would be public enemies. And the truth would get out sooner or later, because Mei Yin surely had plans for the virus beyond keeping it in a fridge forever. Trying hard to slough off these dark thoughts, he smiled. "Fine, let's not speak of these things. I hope everything goes smoothly. Now let's continue where we left off—the pleasure God bestowed on Adam and Eve."

They remained entangled till dawn. Exhausted, they slept a little, and when they woke blearily resumed making love. Both knew this might be their last hurrah, and they might well be separated after this day. They gorged greedily on each other. When Stebushkin woke, he saw that she was up too, sitting cross-legged and staring at him with faintly sad eyes, as if trying to brand his image onto her retinas. Clothed in the bright light of dawn, her naked body glistened, the tiny hairs standing out on her neck. Stebushkin said, "Have you been up long?"

"Very long." She grinned. "I've just been looking at you."

"You're leaving after breakfast?"

"Yes."

"I'll take you to the border." A twinge went through his heart. "I can't bear to lose you. I'll never forget you."

"Me too. Kolya, you're the first man I've ever had, and for all I know you might be the last. I'll never forget you. And please remember my invitation, it was genuinely meant, and will remain open forever." Then she added, "Whatever you decide, I'll always wait for you."

Stebushkin didn't reply. Smiling, he pulled Mei Yin onto himself once more.

Mei Yin's return journey was uneventful. After passing through Russian and Kazakh Customs, she and Zhang Jun, her "black market contact," sat in the cab of a Steyr van. They'd set off from Aktogay in Kazakhstan, and passed through Druzhba to the Dzungarian Gate in China. Now they were waiting for the Chinese Customs official to wave them through. She'd met up with Zhang Jun the day before. While chatting, they'd discovered they were both from the northeast. He was from Shenyang, a short but sturdily built man, with a small, closely cropped head and broad shoulders. Given his line of work, he'd probably been involved in many illegal activities (such as tricking Russians with fake booze and down jackets), but he behaved himself with Mei Yin, and seemed honest and trustworthy. He said, "It's a small matter, transporting frozen thoroughbred horse sperm"—Mei Yin's cover story—"a little box no bigger than my palm, we'll get that across with no problem!"

Since they were from the same part of China, Zhang Jun said he'd waive his fee just this once—he was happy to have made a new friend. After all, even without her extra contraband, he'd still have to fork over the same amount in bribes. As he tucked the little box safely away in a truckload of Russian fur coats, military binoculars, and leather boots, Zhang Jun said half-jokingly, "As long as you can keep your cool crossing the border, your cargo could be an atom bomb and you'd be fine. If you break into a cold sweat the second a customs officer looks your way, you'll give yourself away."

Their officer was a hard-faced young woman clutching a clipboard. She didn't look Chinese—thick, joined eyebrows and a high nose—and her Mandarin was accented. She carefully studied everyone's passports, but when it came to their cargo, Zhang Jun murmured something to her, and she waved them on after a brief glance into the back of their vehicle. It was late when they left the border, the setting sun gleaming on the sign behind them: "Dzungarian Gate Chinese Border." Zhang Jun and the driver seemed in a hurry to get home, wanting to drive nonstop through the night, until they reached Urumqi at noon the next day. "Sister Mei, we did what you asked, lunch is on you! We're going to the Grand Mercure—that's a five-star joint."

Mei Yin, feeling relaxed, joked back. "No problem, and we won't stop till you're raging drunk. But don't expect me to join in, I can't hold my liquor at all."

The truck roared down the empty highway, until the sun was half-hidden below the horizon behind them. Mei Yin had let go of her anxiety about customs, but now she was beset with worry about Stebushkin. She'd picked up on many worrying signs over the last couple of days, particularly the way he'd made his decision: quickly, almost thoughtlessly, and only after they'd been intimate. It was the sudden certainty of someone who had decided to ignore a dilemma, not resolve it. He'd made a choice—but what choice, exactly?

As the sun fell completely out of sight, Mei Yin felt a sharp, shooting pain. She wasn't sure of its source—in the veins at her wrist, her temples, or her heart. But it was real, leaping through her nerves. Seeing her discomfort, Zhang Jun asked, "Sister Mei, is something wrong? Do you feel okay?"

Forcing a smile, she shook her head. "It's nothing. Just a bit dizzy—maybe I'm tired out from the last couple of days."

She leaned her head against the window, and drifted. She remembered when she was twelve, watching the great wildebeest migration with her adoptive father (not yet "the Godfather") in Africa. As the animals surged across the rushing river to the other shore, they'd always leave behind a few unfortunates: dragged into the water by crocodiles, throats ripped out by lions on the river banks, trampled by their own kind so their spines broke, falling and snapping their legs. The sight made her sad, but her father told her that as long as the species continued to flourish, individual sacrifices were always worthwhile, and unavoidable. Then he said one more thing that she'd remember for the rest of her life:

> The Lord loves only the group, not the individual. That is how vast his love is.

Kolya, the only man I've ever truly known, please forgive me.

The morning after seeing Mei off, Stebushkin phoned his in-laws' in Moscow, where Natasha was staying. After he'd chatted aimlessly with her and the kids for a while, she said, "The children need to leave for school, and I should be getting to work. Is there anything else?"

He hurriedly said, "Nothing, nothing at all. You'd better go." After she hung up, he sat mutely by the phone for a while, watching the second hand of the wall clock ticking along. When the lab opened, he phoned to say he'd decided to quit his job. He'd come in at some point to take care of the paperwork. So many people had resigned in the last two years that Director Chaadayeva had grown numb to it. She went through the motions of persuading him to stay, asked him what his plans were, sighed, and wished him good luck.

Stebushkin did nothing that whole morning, apart from pacing round the apartment he'd lived in for almost twenty years, examining the family portrait, the wall-to-wall shelves full of technical books, the wok and Chinese spices left behind by Mei Yin. After that he took a nap, sleeping right through lunch. He woke a little after four and drove to the dacha with the last couple of six packs of Mei Yin's Tsingtao beer. Once he got there, he drove past the dacha to a riverbank about six miles away. This was the grassy patch on which he and Mei had lain, their limbs entangled. Stripping to his shorts, he plunged into the icy water, swimming hard until his body had warmed up. Then he went back to shore and, his body still half-immersed, looked up at the sky, unhurriedly working his way through all twelve bottles of beer. His vision grew blurry, his blood pleasingly full of alcohol. Mei Yin's image fluttered before his eyes, flickering into being in the haze of the setting sun. Her voice seemed to drift by his ears, soft and magnetic.

A smile settled onto his lips. On the brink of ending his life, this connection with Mei Yin felt unbearably precious, a glimmer of light in the gray of his life, something to look back on from the other world. He removed the exquisite cross from around his neck and absently ran his fingers over it. Mei Yin's belief was definitely stronger than his, almost fanatical. The Godfather and his devotees might have everything planned out, but what if they took one step too far on the path of righteousness? A step too far, and they'd fall right off the cliff.

If that happened, then his sin would be the greatest, the first link in this chain of events.

He didn't want to think anymore; the alcohol had made him hazy. Letting out a long sigh, he held up the crucifix. In its center was a small diamond, actually a cunningly concealed catch. Pressing it with his thumb, he gently rotated it clockwise until it sprang open. With a little effort, he slid off the bottom arm—actually a sheath—to reveal a short double-edged knife. The blade was completely transparent, with an inky gleam to it, almost invisible to the naked eye. These specially designed crucifixes were the emblem of the Society. The Godfather personally placed one around the neck of each new member.

Of course, these crosses were only a symbol of their faith. The Godfather had never required adherents to kill themselves for the cause.

The sun slowly went down, beams of red light shooting through cracks in the clouds to stain the clear river water crimson and gold. Stebushkin held the upper arm of the crucifix—the dagger's handle—between the index finger and thumb of his left hand, and lightly drew the near-invisible blade over his right wrist. The knife was so sharp that he barely felt any resistance as it sliced open his flesh, as easily as passing through butter. There was hardly any pain at first. Stebushkin carefully replaced the sheath and fastened the catch. A researcher's habitual meticulousness. Next, he plunged his right hand into the river, so the bright red blood quickly spread through the gilded water, irregular scarlet eddies more vivid than the background color. His sight blurring, he watched these ripples as his body filled with a soothing exhaustion. Finally, his head slumped onto the riverbank, and he fell asleep forever.

September 2001—Pakistan-Afghanistan border

Walking single file, three people and a mule made the arduous trek up to the Ayal Pass. Although only the end of September, it was already extremely cold fifteen thousand feet above sea level. Along the highest mountain ridge, there wasn't a shred of greenery. The only vegetation lay beneath the snowline, dark green grass hugging the ground. After the pass was a sea of clouds, above which floated several snow-topped peaks, looking for all the world like desert islands in a wide ocean.

The leader of the trio was a short tour guide, Tamala, a Pashtun tribesman from the border regions. He wore knickerbockers, and beneath the rounded flaps of his leather coat was a Soviet-style Makarov pistol. Around his head was a *longga*, a traditional scarf. He spoke Pashto and Dari, as well as being able to stammer out a little French or Arabic, so he was in charge of speaking to anyone along the way (the visitor and other guide knew only Arabic).

The second guide brought up the rear, a tall man dressed in a sleeveless Kaffir jacket, a Kalashnikov rifle strapped diagonally to his chest. He was a foreigner, face like the blade of a knife and nose hooked like an eagle's beak, the prominent characteristics of the Bedouin people. Despite not being local, he'd fought here more than ten years before, in the resistance against the former Soviet Union's invasion during the eighties. He knew the area well, and was untroubled by the thin and icy air.

Between them was a more pathetic figure, dragging himself along by the mule's tail. This man, who called himself Mohammad Ahmed Segum, was of medium height, a little plump, and dressed in local Kaffir clothing that plainly did not fit his physique. The coarse, stiff fabric had rubbed his skin raw yet completely failed to keep the cold air out, driving him half mad. He was close to collapse, his mouth gaping wide as he panted, a rustling sound in his throat like a burst leather bag. Even so, he clung tightly to his briefcase, refusing to be parted from it. Three days earlier, as they'd ascended the first mountain pass, the taller guide had kindly offered to take the leather case, only to be firmly rejected. That was the end of the guide's sympathy toward him.

The travelers rested at a water hole, bowing four times in the direction of Mecca. The shorter guide produced some flatbread and cheese from his knapsack. This high above sea level, it was impossible to boil water, so they were reduced to dry rations. With effort, Mohammad chewed at the cold, hard bread and odd-tasting cheese, choking it down with difficulty, remembering with longing the delicacies he'd eaten in the past. The two guides ate in silence, quickly finishing their lunch. They didn't enjoy the food either, but were used to it. The taller guide said brusquely, in Arabic, "Eat faster. If you take your time, who knows when we'll get there!"

Mohammad glanced coldly at the tall guide and didn't reply, but chewed faster. All along the way, he'd sensed—not rationally, but in his gut—how correct his leader's tactics were. Let these people fight the war, these tattered, scrawny fellows with the fierce vitality of wolves. Surely they'd be much better off as martyrs, ascending to paradise rather than stuck here on earth. They'd probably clamor to die on the field as quickly as possible. As for himself, well, terribly sorry, but he'd rather forgo the glory of battle and escape to safety.

That afternoon, they reached the Nuristan Valley, where the roads became more navigable. The short guide let Mohammad mount the mule, and walked in front, leading it. He didn't think much of this pampered fellow either, but he was a guest of the organization. Besides, for all he knew, the leather briefcase the man refused to leave aside might contain $100 million. The chief had given instructions not to slow him down. As they descended, shrubs began appearing on the slopes, and then stubby oak trees. A clear stream emerged from a crack in the rocks, then disappeared behind the hills. They began to encounter other travelers, mostly Nuristani locals, plus a few Tajik people. Dilapidated wooden huts stood in the distance, little farmsteads interspersed between them. Compared to the mountain pass earlier, this place had the breath of humanity, but still lay far from civilization. There were no cars, roads, power lines, or TV antennas. These farmers seemed to be the remnants of some ancient dynasty.

Two people appeared up ahead, also dressed in local clothes, but their features and bearing indicated at a glance that they were Arabs. Rifles were slung diagonally over both their shoulders, one of them an old-fashioned British weapon. The two guides approached, the four men exchanging a brief greeting, like ants meeting and touching antennas. "They said the fighting will start soon," said the shorter guide. "Five American aircraft carriers have reached the Persian Gulf, plus more than seventy navy ships. By Hamza's calculations, it'll start in the next few days."

"Hamza" was Abu Faraj Hamza, third-in-command of al-Qaeda, and the person Mohammad was here to meet. Mohammad silently congratulated himself on arriving just in time. After seeing Hamza, he would return by a different route, east through Pakistan, and go home from there. Even if fighting began in a few days, he wouldn't be caught up in it.

That night, they stayed at a village called Leenah. The short guide bought quite a bit of food, and even managed to get hold of three fish from the nearby Mandol Lake. They boiled up a pot of fish soup, and for the first time in days, Mohammad ate his fill. He felt much better after that, and even the taller guide's disparaging gaze no longer irked him. The shorter guide said they'd reach Kandiwal Pass the next day, the highest point of their route. This would be a difficult trek, so Mohammad should get as much rest as possible. He was handed a duck-down sleeping bag from the mule's burden, then both guides tightened their clothes, wrapped themselves in straw mats, and quickly fell asleep. Mohammad placed the leather case beneath his head as a pillow and zipped himself into the sleeping bag. Yet he stayed awake, the fierce cold of night piercing through the thick duck down, chilling him to the bone.

He thought back to what he'd seen on his TV screen just ten days previously: the two airplanes, New York's World Trade Center, raging fire and thick clouds of smoke, people fleeing for their lives like ants from a trampled nest. Al-Qaeda's strike created terror, but it had also created anger, and the Americans were now gnashing their teeth and plotting revenge. According to a friend who was close to him, the leader had clapped his hands and cheered after the attack, but then fallen into silence for more than ten hours. Finally, he made an important decision: he would completely change their nation's direction, and bend the knee to the West.

To put it plainly, this would mean being traitors. That sounded bad, but they all understood the leader's choice. They weren't like al-Qaeda, who had no fixed abode and could flee in any direction. They were rooted to their country, they couldn't run.

But before they bent the knee, they could make one last contribution to the common cause. And so he was here.

The next morning, the guides made him get up early, saying they were in a hurry to get moving. It would be best to reach the mountain pass before noon, before it got too cold. After a simple breakfast, Mohammad mounted the mule and the trio set out. As they climbed, the temperature plummeted quickly, and the ground was entirely white. The mule's hooves kept skidding, and it snorted ferociously, forcing him to dismount. Clutching the mule's tail, and sandwiched between the other two men, he dragged himself up the twisty path with difficulty.

And now they'd climbed high up into the sea of clouds. Damp fog surrounded them on all sides, and they couldn't see any farther than a few dozen paces. The little path grew steeper and more slippery, so narrow the mule could barely fit on it. On one side was the hillside, on the other a sheer drop, and even though mist shrouded the bottom, just looking at the viciously sharp rocks along the way was enough to send a shiver through one's heart. The mule rebelled, stamping its hooves and refusing to continue. No matter how hard they pulled at its harness, it refused to move an inch. The tall guide, at the head of the procession, clapped Mohammad on the back and told him to move back, so he could push the mule instead. Just at that moment, the mule's back hooves skidded on the stony ground, and its whole rear half slipped off the cliff. The guide in front pulled hard on the harness, but as the mule began to slide over the edge, he was forced to let go or be pulled down after it. The mule's cries sounded all the way down as it crashed against the jagged sides. Finally, there was a weighty thud, and silence resumed in the canyon.

After a long time, the shorter man said, "It's a pity all our rations are gone too. We'll have to replenish when we get to the bottom. Let's go on."

They started walking, but Mohammad was rooted to the spot. The shorter guide looked inquiringly at him, while the taller one pushed him roughly. Mohammad pointed down with a shaky finger, and said in a trembling voice, "My briefcase." Then, pointing at the taller man, "He jostled me."

The leather case was on an outcrop about eleven yards down, and although that wasn't far, it wouldn't be easy retrieving it from such a steep surface. The tall guide stared viciously. "When did I jostle you? Anyway, that's your bag, if you want it, go get it yourself."

Mohammad lay flat on the ground, looking over the edge, but could see no way down that wouldn't end in a fatal plunge. He looked back beseechingly at the shorter guide, who'd been kinder to him along the way. The man was angry too, glaring first at Mohammad and then at his colleague. But finally he produced a length of fine rope and tied one end around his waist, fastening the other to a protruding rock. He instructed them, "You two, hold on tight to this. Whatever happens, don't let go!"

Mohammad rushed over and gripped the rope with the taller guide. The short man carefully climbed down, reaching the briefcase just as he was about to run out of rope. Bracing one leg against the cliff face, he turned his body sideways and stretched his arm as far as it would go, barely reaching the handle. He tied the suitcase to the end of the rope, then pulled himself up, hand over hand.

Mohammad shed tears of gratitude as he got the briefcase back unharmed. He wanted to fling himself to the ground and kiss the short man's tattered boots.

Before they knew it, they were out of the clouds, and a short while later, they could see sunlight on the ridge. The landscape transformed completely after that point. Bright sunshine spilled onto the snowy white slopes, each more than ten thousand feet high. The sun warmed the air, and the path grew more level. A day's walk brought them through the Kandiwal Valley. They only rested for a short while at noon, but had nothing to eat, and were ravenous by the time they reached a village that evening. The short guide negotiated with an old man in the Afghan language, renting them a broken-down old hut and a pile of food, plus a tattered woolen blanket for Mohammad. They were starving and exhausted, and after wolfing down their dinner, quickly fell asleep.

The next morning, after breakfast, the shorter guide produced a length of black cloth. "I'm sorry. From now on, you'll have to wear this blindfold."

Mohammad felt a stab of joy. They must be close to their destination, and this arduous trek would soon be at an end. He smiled. "Go ahead. But—won't it be hard for me to walk?"

"No problem, we've found you a horse. It's waiting outside."

Sure enough, there it was, a scrawny creature. Mohammad let them cover his eyes, then mounted it, and happily set forth.

They walked another whole day. To the man blindfolded on the horse, north, south, east, or west had no meaning, and he could only tell whether they were going uphill or down. If the air grew warm and he heard water, then they must be in a valley, while colder temperatures and the horse's breathing growing labored meant they were going through a mountain pass.

The next day, there were more people on the road. From their voices, it sounded like a Pashtun area. That night, someone helped him off the horse, then led him forward as he stumbled on stiff legs. The two guides exchanged a few words. They sounded more relaxed than before, so Mohammad knew they really had arrived. They brought him into what must have been a cave, because the guide sometimes pushed down on his head so he had to stoop. He heard voices up ahead, and the guides spoke to other people from time to time. This was quite a deep cavern. He guessed they'd walked two or three hundred yards before coming to a halt. The guides spoke in low voices for a bit, then someone else said in Arabic, "Remove his blindfold."

This accent was familiar, and Mohammad was certain the speaker came, like himself, from a North African country. When the cloth was removed, Mohammad blinked in the light. They were in a small alcove within a larger cave. On a ledge sat a man of about forty, with a long black beard. His head was wrapped in a kaffiyeh, his Arab-style robe an immaculate white, gleaming in the surrounding gloom. Two AK-47s, their barrels crossed, were mounted on the cave wall behind him. Also to his rear was a simple bedroll, spread on the stone floor, with a small table at its head, made of what looked like cardboard. On it were a copy of the Koran, an atlas, a gleaming IBM laptop, and a handheld video camera. These last two gadgets seemed at odds with their surroundings, and it wasn't apparent where they could be charged. Mohammad guessed they must have just finished shooting a broadcast, the sort that was always being shown on Al Jazeera. No wonder this man was so neatly dressed, the guns behind him a familiar backdrop. As for power, they must have a generator somewhere.

There was another person behind the first man, scrawny and wearing a Pashtun-style *longga*, also sporting a black beard. He was younger, somewhere between thirty and thirty-five. The light was too dim for Mohammad to make out his face.

The two guides silently withdrew from this inner cave. The man in the kaffiyeh pointed at the ground before him, indicating that the visitor should sit. There was a low ledge there, on which had been spread a straw mat. Mohammad walked over and sat cross-legged. Now he could see the man's face much more clearly, and looked carefully for signs that it was Hamza. Al-Qaeda's leaders were secretive in their movements, and there were no photographs in the outside world of the number three in command. The only reliable information was that he had vitiligo. Now Mohammad studied him closely, and sure enough, there were prominent white marks across his face and neck. What left him doubtful, though, was that this man had only one eye, and when he'd gestured for his visitor to be seated, he'd used not a hand but a silvery hook. Perhaps he'd only recently acquired these disabilities, and word hadn't gotten out yet? In order to be sure, he asked, "Is this person in front of me the honorable Mr. Abu Faraj Hamza?"

"Yes," said the man flatly. "Speak freely."

Mohammad paused to clear his mind, and Hamza continued. "I only agreed to see you because of someone we both respect and know to be trustworthy, a Pashto tribal elder. But he kept mum when it came to the question of where you're from. Of course, we can easily guess: the person who sent you is that odd creature, the one who loves riding camels, living in tents, and keeping female bodyguards?"

Mohammad pretended not to have heard these rude words. "As for where I've come from, that ought to be kept secret. This has to be the first condition of our talk today."

Hamza nodded. "We'll keep your secrets, you don't need to worry about that. Your master was once a great hero. His infamous airplane bombing made infidels all over the world quake in their boots. He had nothing to fear then! But now, he's no more than a pitiful lapdog, wagging his tail and begging for infidel scraps. Did you know, he actually spoke out against 9/11! What a knife in the back."

Mohammad smiled bitterly. "I know. That was already in the works before I set out." He could sense great enmity from Hamza, so decided on a different tactic. "You're quite right, we're a bunch of cowards. It's because we're a snail, with a shell on our backs, and we couldn't bear for it to be smashed by the Americans. Besides"—he indicated the crudely made bed—"I couldn't deal with such hardship. I wish I could, but I don't have it in me. So we had no choice but to bow to the Americans. But deep down, our beliefs haven't changed, and we hate the Western devils just as much as before. I've come here today to demonstrate our sincerity with a small gift."

He'd done such an efficient job of tearing himself down that Hamza was left with nothing to say. Instead, he smiled at the visitor. "All right, I won't give you a hard time. Anyway, it's not everyone who's brave enough to be a martyr. But here's a warning for you to give your master: he can wag his tail all he likes, but the Americans still might not let him off. When they've finished dealing with Afghanistan and Iraq, they might reach out and crush you too."

"I'll pass that on."

"Fine. Let's have a look at this gift."

Mohammad was at ease now. "I have a question first. Is this the virologist I asked you to bring along?"

The third man nodded, still silent. By way of introduction, Hamza said, "He graduated from Duke University, majoring in global health, with a focus on infectious disease. Good enough?"

"And you brought the cooler too?"

This time it was the young man who answered. "Yes."

Mohammad set the briefcase in front of him, and before opening it, he spoke: "As you know, biological warfare is the poor man's ideal weapon. Think about it. You don't need modern factories, expensive facilities, or funding, and you don't need to worry about a B-2 plane dropping a bomb on you. Bacteria and viruses proliferate in the human body, so your enemies are also your factories, a perfect example of waste recycling, no need for electricity, raw materials, or wages. If you're able to infect one, you're able to kill hundreds of thousands, even millions— far more than your human bombs could ever achieve! We've been at work for fifteen years now, creating these, though it's a shame we'll never get to use them. Our leader has given orders for the whole lot to be destroyed, both the weapon stocks and equipment. Of course, it'd be a pity to really destroy everything, so we've saved a few seeds, to give to those who might make use of them."

Hamza looked at the briefcase on Mohammad's lap, his smile a little suspicious.

"Honored Mr. Hamza, please don't doubt my sincerity. To be frank, we're doing this not just for your sake, but also for ours. Just as you said earlier, as long as you keep making life difficult for the Americans here, they won't have the capacity to deal with us. Is that honest enough?"

"All right, I don't doubt your sincerity. Hand it over."

Mohammad opened the case, and a plume of white mist emerged. Nestled among the remaining dry ice were three firmly sealed glass vials. Mohammad explained: "Here, these are three different biological agents, all viruses. The first is Lassa fever, a fierce sort of hemorrhagic fever. There's no inoculation for it to date. The only flaw is that it's more susceptible to antivirals, but we've bred this strain to be sufficiently resistant. The second is Ebola, an even more vicious hemorrhagic fever, transmittable through the air and by contact. No vaccine or treatment, with a death rate of over ninety percent. Its disadvantage is that it's not infectious enough. The third virus is smallpox, which should need no further introduction. It's extremely transmittable, with a high death rate, and has killed more people in history than any other virus. You could say it's the biggest murderer of humanity. The only problem is that the medical world has studied it more thoroughly, and there are strong, effective vaccines against it. Still, ever since the world stopped cowpox inoculation in 1978, immunity has all but vanished in the general population, and the current stocks of vaccine wouldn't be able to withstand a large-scale outbreak. The strain I'm giving you now is virulent, more than able to withstand current medical technology."

He closed the container and handed it over. "As for which of these you choose to press into service, or if you decide to use all three, that's up to you."

The young man behind Hamza came over and took the bag. "May I ask, did you take part in the research yourself?"

"Yes, I did. And I should mention that I, too, studied in the United States, at the UC Davis School of Medicine. You can imagine how much it hurt me when the order came to destroy my work. Oh yes, I almost forgot." He asked for the briefcase back, opened it, and found a velvet pouch in one corner. "This contains eight hundred South African diamonds, all high-quality white ones. Low carat, to make it easier for you to exchange them for cash on the black market. Their total value is more than eighty million American dollars; even on the black market, you should get more than sixty million. Just a token of our appreciation. Call it seed money for your biological warfare venture." Opening the pouch, he pulled out a couple of the stones. "And I have a personal request. Two days ago, there was an accident at the Kandiwal Pass, and this case almost fell off a cliff. My guide, Tamala, rescued it. I'd like to give him these two diamonds in thanks."

At first Hamza and the young man were quiet, making Mohammad feel ill at ease. After a stretch of chilly silence, Hamza gestured for the young man to fetch the shorter guide. Tamala came in, looking curiously at Hamza, and then at the visitor. Mohammad handed over the diamonds, repeating what he'd just said. He'd expected the guide to be overcome with gratitude—the diamonds were enough for him to live on for the rest of his life. Yet Tamala shook his head, stating flatly, "I have no use for these toys. The Americans will start their war soon, and for all I know, I'll be heading to paradise any day now."

Mohammad stood with the diamonds in his right hand, at a loss. Hamza nodded in satisfaction, and after the guide had left, said to his visitor, "I'll take those diamonds. Thank you for your generosity, particularly as we're aware your funds are limited. You'll be due to pay the infidels a huge sum in compensation, won't you? Two billion, seven hundred million American dollars."

Mohammad could hear the mockery in Hamza's voice, which added to his humiliation. Hamza added, "I accept both your gifts. Of course, this isn't charity. We're standing in for you, teaching them a 'lesson from above.' Don't worry, we'll keep your visit secret. Tomorrow, the same two guides will bring you to Chetallali in Pakistan." He smiled. "You've had a hard time, these last few days, but you'll be leaving this sea of troubles soon. Go have a rest now. The guides will show you where."

Mohammad hadn't expected such cold treatment after his arduous journey. Hamza watched him depart in awkwardness, and after he was gone, muttered, "Clown."

The young man, Zia Baj, said nothing, but carefully moved the three sealed glass vials to a new cooler, then buried them in dry ice. A long cry rose from outside—the evening call to prayers. The two men went out, and joined their comrades in bowing three times in the direction of Mecca. Mohammad was among the crowd, but they ignored him. Back in the cave, Hamza asked, "Baj, what do you think of this present?"

"The man has a point," replied Baj. "Biological weapons can be very effective, as much as any atom bomb. For us, they truly are the perfect means of attack."

Hamza sat cross-legged on the straw mat and was silent for a while. "Take the viruses with you, and the diamonds too," he said somberly. "You don't need me to tell you how bad the situation is. Our neighbor to the east has completely submitted to the Americans, sealing the Pakistan-Afghanistan border. To the west, Omar might surrender at the last moment, handing us over as a Christmas gift to the Americans.

Even if Omar remains loyal, the Taliban's rifles are no match for the West's precision bombs. I might be sent to paradise at any moment, or forced to flee this place, and lose contact with you. So don't wait for orders from here. I'm putting you completely in charge of organizing and executing this plan. Do a good job, and avenge our dead brothers! Take revenge for my hands and eye. You have to succeed, Baj. I believe in you."

"I won't let you down," said Zia Baj calmly.

Hamza smiled, and looked at the young man out of his remaining eye. He'd known Baj for five years now, ever since he'd attended Derunta training camp near Jalalabad in Afghanistan, where there'd been three Westerners: two British, and Baj from America. All three were university students, ethnically Pashtun, from families who'd settled abroad two generations ago and were now completely Westernized. Hamza had at first been skeptical of the trio, with their Western designer clothes and chewing gum, but after a month of training, he saw them become dependable warriors.

"When you leave tomorrow, you should also head back home via Pakistan. They might not be able to seal the border against us, but as time goes on, it will get harder and harder to pass. Are you going straight back to the States? You'll have to find some way to get this box through, US Customs is especially vigilant with travelers from Pakistan or Afghanistan."

"Don't worry, I have a plan."

"Good-bye, then, my son." Hamza rose and hugged Baj, kissing him on the cheeks before walking him to the cave entrance.

At dawn the next morning, a line of four people departed the cave. The two guides were in front, then a blindfolded Mohammad on the scrawny horse, and finally young Zia Baj, the cooler in his backpack. Weak winter sunlight spilled across the craggy, desolate mountain road. This would be Baj's path from now on. He said nothing along the way, remaining so silent that Mohammad wasn't even aware it was Baj behind him, only sensing from the footsteps that there was an extra person, but not daring to ask who, listening suspiciously. Two days later, before Mohammad's blindfold was removed, Baj quietly said good-bye to them. He went back to his father's ancestral home and stowed the box safely away, before returning to the States with two assistants he'd chosen for himself.

September 2002—Henan-Hubei provincial border, China

On Saturday morning, Jin Mingcheng and his wife slept late, as usual. They'd only been married a few weeks, and the novelty hadn't worn off yet. When Mei Yin phoned at nine o'clock, Jin was flustered. Ms. Mei said she was driving over from Wuhan that morning, and would arrive in Xinye County within half an hour. Jin put down the phone and shouted for his wife to get his special outfit ready, they were about to receive an important visitor. He quickly washed up and got dressed, then rushed out without eating anything. His wife said no matter how urgent his work was, he should still have some breakfast, and Jin replied, "Who has time for food? Let me tell you, if everything goes to plan today, your man is no longer going to be the deputy head—they'll drop the 'deputy' for sure. That's kind of a big deal, don't you think?"

Jin was the deputy head of the county government's chamber of commerce. It sounded like a lofty title, but in truth, the position was mostly a sinecure, and he didn't have much power. The former head, Old Qi, had put a lot of energy into creating a free-enterprise zone, pumping millions into it, and in the end failed to attract even a single company. Two days ago, a phone call came out of the blue, filling Deputy Head Jin with both joy and suspicion. Ms. Mei Yin introduced herself as a Chinese American currently working as a foreign expert in the Planning Department of the Wuhan Institute of Virology's Zhengdian Research

Laboratory. Her American father wanted to invest in China, placing a first installment of $10 million in a high-tech biology lab. The site had to be within half a day's drive of Wuhan, for easy access, while the costs of land and labor would need to be kept as low as possible. She felt Xinye County was very suitable for this, and so found his number through directory assistance and cold-called him. Jin had immediately launched into his spiel about all the many ways in which this was the perfect location for her. There was a little padding, but essentially he told her the truth. They weren't too far from Wuhan, property was cheap, and wages low. Besides, the county government was so focused on luring rich investors that conditions were extremely favorable. Ms. Mei seemed interested in his pitch, and said she'd arrange a site visit soon.

"Soon" turned out to be much sooner than he'd expected. Jin hadn't even had a chance to report the conversation to the county chief. It wasn't negligence on his part, but caution: he'd decided to investigate the situation further, waiting till he was at least half-confident before speaking to County Chief Liu. But now the woman was showing up on short notice, and if this opportunity was for real, he'd need the county chief to put in an appearance to welcome her and clinch the deal. Jin phoned Liu at home and quickly made his report, explaining why he'd hesitated to say anything before. The chief wasted no words. "I'm sending a car over at once, and at noon Secretary He and I will be there to receive her. Jin, don't worry about anything, let's just assume this is the real thing, and give her whatever she asks for. Better to get cheated a few times than miss out when the true God of Fortune arrives."

With this guarantee in his back pocket, Jin grew much bolder. Ten minutes later one of the county's drivers turned up in their best Nissan Lannia, and they rushed to the appointed meeting place just outside town. Soon, a Volkswagen Santana pulled up, and a beautiful woman emerged, smiling. "You must be Deputy Head Jin."

She was refined and elegant, in a jacket the color of rice, her long hair spilling over its collar, slim figured, a silver-gray turtleneck sweater tight across her high breasts, a silvery crucifix around her neck. Jin rushed over to shake her hand. "Welcome! If only you'd given us more notice. County Chief Liu wasn't able to be here in person, but he'll meet you later at the county office. You can have a rest there, and at noon he and Secretary He would like to host a banquet for you."

Mei Yin laughed. "What a lovely reception! No need for a banquet, though. Now let's have a look at this abandoned farmland you were telling me about."

Jin tried to insist on the banquet, but she wouldn't budge, and finally he had to call the chief on his cell to cancel. Mei Yin then suggested he send away the Lannia, and they could just go there in her car.

As they walked toward her car, he said politely, "Ms. Mei, you must be tired after coming all the way from Wuhan. Our driver could have taken over."

She misunderstood what he was getting at, and said breezily, "You take the wheel, then. Anyway, you know the way there."

Jin blushed. "I don't have a license."

"That's all right," said Mei Yin hastily. "I'm not tired at all. Just point me in the right direction."

The car turned around and headed south. In a short while, they came to a stretch of pitted, bumpy road. Jin explained in embarrassment that the way was only bad for a couple of miles, and they'd soon come to a new paved road, while the section they were on was due to be resurfaced soon. Silently, he cursed the Roadworks Department. If this bad road cost them a millionaire, he would personally castrate the man in charge. Fortunately, they soon reached the new road, all smooth and even, its newly laid surface still gleaming black. They passed a tractor now and then, and quite a few of the old villagers were using the road as a surface to dry peanuts in the sun, carving it up into little patches, though they left a space for cars to pass. Department Head Qi had fought for this road, though when the free-enterprise zone failed, it left him open to a wave of public criticism.

Mei Yin sped along, proclaiming happily, "This is the best kind of road to drive on."

Jin felt a moment of quiet gratitude to former Head Qi for leaving him an excellent present. His other thought was that he should hurry up and learn how to drive, even if he had to pay for lessons himself, before he was embarrassed like this again.

In half an hour they reached the site, a large patch of empty ground with several abandoned sheds in its center. Even from a distance, it was clear that they were missing windows and doors, and the walls were on the point of collapse. Farther on was a larger, more intact structure, the fence around it sprayed with slogans commonly seen in farming villages: "Shake a farmer's hand, make friends with the land"; "Have one child then stop, and you'll come out on top."

"This used to be a farm for Educated Youths during the Cultural Revolution," explained Jin. "About a hundred and seventy acres. After the Educated Youths went back to the cities, the land changed hands several times. It's been used for a chicken farm, a fishery, and a free-enterprise zone, but none of them were successful. Now it's privately rented."

"If I wanted to buy it, roughly what would that cost me?"

"About three hundred and twenty hundred yuan per acre." He added hastily, "But we can discuss that later. I'll be sure to get you the best price."

"Thank you very much."

In fact, the price Jin named had already been so low as to almost stun Mei Yin. She then asked what local wages were like, and again, they were astonishingly tiny. A few more questions about setting up a business here were also met with satisfactory answers. The road had been built, though she'd need to dig a well for water. That was fine. As for electricity, former Head Qi had installed wires to this point, with a 200 kVA transformer currently lying idle, waiting to be hooked up to the grid. The only downside was how remote this place was. It was on the border of two provinces, and the road went no farther. Funding issues had stopped it from linking up with Hubei, so it became a dead end. This was the main reason previous rounds of investment hadn't attracted anyone. Jin didn't realize that this was precisely what had attracted her to this out-of-the-way location.

Mei Yin said she wanted to have a look at the structure covered in slogans. They drove over and stopped at the front door, where an old lady emerged and invited them in. Inside was a crudely built two-story dwelling with more than thirty rooms, and the courtyard was sizable too, an emerald sea of chives and bok choy patches. Jin tried to chat with the old woman, but she just grinned, pointing at her ears. "These don't work at all. I'll get Shuan to talk to you. He's somewhere in the compound."

Mei Yin tried to protest, but the lady had already climbed nimbly up to the roof. Soon, a crisp bell sounded—she was probably striking an old plowshare. About ten minutes later, Shuan appeared, still carrying his shovel. He was in his early- to midtwenties, wearing a mourning armband. Although he was dressed as a student, his coarse skin made him look like a farmer. He smiled as broadly as his grandmother, and said several times what an honor it was to receive visitors. Without asking who they were, he told his granny to prepare lunch for them.

As they chatted over lunch, it turned out the a hundred and seventy acres of land wasn't all leased to farmers. Twenty-five acres, including this house and its surroundings, had been sold to this family two years previously. Jin blushed furiously to hear this. He'd spent all his time on chamber of commerce business and knew little about the particulars of the area. The young man was named Sun Jingshuan, and his grandfather had used his life savings to buy the surrounding land and the house, which he then restored brick by brick, preparing to plant quick-growing trees around it. He ran out of strength to finish his scheme, and so insisted his grandson—who'd graduated from an agricultural college—come back. When the old man died, Sun Jingshuan took over the place.

When the young man went to help in the kitchen, Jin whispered to Mei Yin, "Don't worry. If you decide to set up your facility here, the county will make sure we get back these twenty-five acres of land and the house." Afraid she wouldn't believe him, he added, "This isn't America. In China, the well-being of the group is more important than individual rights. There won't be any problems."

Lunch was splendid. The vegetables came from the yard, and the chicken was freshly slaughtered. The old woman kept lamenting what a terrible hostess she was: "Look at these simple dishes and coarse rice!" She seated her guests, then scooped some food into her bowl, squatting in the kitchen doorway to eat. Mei Yin and Jin urged her to join them at the table, but she wouldn't budge. Shuan said his grandmother had certain habits that she'd never change, and it was no use trying to force her.

During the meal, Mei Yin kept asking the grandson about his life. What had he studied at agricultural college? Biological engineering, he answered.

"Is it lonely here?" she asked. "All alone, so far from civilization, with only your grandmother for company, and even then she's deaf. Two of you rattling around so many rooms."

"Not at all," said the young man, smiling good-humoredly. "I've never been one for socializing."

Mei Yin asked, "Do you make use of what you learned in college?"

"Some of it, but not much."

"That's a pity," she said with a sigh.

The young man didn't respond, instead asking why the pair had come. Mei Yin replied, "Trying to find a suitable piece of land around here for a biological goods facility. Did you study cell engineering at college?"

"Yes, the cultivation of animal cells for use in vaccines and whatnot."

"So you must know what facilities are required for the industrial production of animal cells?"

"Essentially, you need a bioreactor. There are several methods of cultivation, such as floating, fixed-wall, stable, and so on. I think the best sort is a filling reactor, including those that use hollow fiber, glass or ceramic. I can't really remember. All I know is that China's a little behind in this area. Foreign cultivation models can produce almost three thousand gallons, while here we can only reach the double digits. At the highest level, we're still barely above fifty gallons."

Mei Yin laughed, and proclaimed, "I came to this place in order to attract American technology to build a bioreactor with a capacity of four thousand gallons, producing animal cells for medical use. This will be the largest such device in the world."

At her words, Shuan's eyes suddenly grew bright. He looked at Mei Yin, speechless, then lowered his head to continue eating. Mei Yin smiled as she studied him. She'd never expected to find a suitable candidate here. A young person like this—technical background, no social connections, isolated by preference—was exactly what Mei Yin had been searching for.

After the meal, the old lady took away their plates and bowls and asked how the meal was. She hoped it hadn't been too shabby. Mei Yin laughed loudly. "You're far too polite. Everything was delicious. Whenever I'm free again, I'll be sure to come visit for another meal."

The old woman understood what she was saying. "So it turned out well. We look forward to seeing you again."

Mei Yin turned to Shuan. "Could you show me the grounds? I know the Educated Youths had about a hundred and seventy acres of land, and I'd like to see where the borders are. Department Head Jin, why don't you take it easy here, you don't need to come with us."

Jin wasn't an idiot, he knew very well the two of them had something private to discuss. Probably Mei Yin was planning to ask Shuan about handing over his twenty-five acres. He had no objections—after all, if the two of them could negotiate directly with each other, that'd be less trouble for him. After a while, his cell phone rang. It was County Chief Liu, wanting to know how things were progressing. "The visitor and a young guy who lives here have gone out, leaving me with a deaf old woman. We haven't gotten to the point yet, but, Chief, going by my instincts, I think there's an eight in ten chance we've got it in the bag. This young woman is smart and strong-minded, and deals with everything quickly and cleanly. Not like the greasy old slimeballs we had to deal with the last few times."

"Then grab on to her and don't let go. Give her all the special treatment we can offer. If you let this deal slip out of your hands, I'll chop you up and feed you to the dogs."

"And if I succeed? Will you get rid of the 'deputy' in my job title?"

"Huh, and they say the shortsighted lack ambition."

The chief hung up. His final words of "criticism" set Jin's heart at ease. He heard footsteps, then Ms. Mei and Shuan appeared, looking delighted. Mei Yin said, "Thank you, Deputy Head—oh, forget it, let's not be so formal, I'll just call you Jin. So thank you, Jin, for helping me to find such an excellent location, as well as a brilliant general manager." Jin stared in shock at Shuan, who continued beaming happily. They must have settled it between them. "I've decided to invest ten million in setting up a plant here. The Sun family will exchange their land and house for shares in it, and I'll buy the other hundred-plus acres. Trees will be planted around the perimeter, and the facility will go in the center. Now why don't the three of us head into town and get this locked down? I'm returning to Wuhan tomorrow, and the day-to-day running of the place will be up to you two. How about it? It's Saturday. Will we be able to get hold of the relevant authorities?"

Jin was overjoyed. He'd bragged to the chief that this deal would probably go through, but he'd never expected it to happen so smoothly. It was scarcely believable! He confidently proclaimed, "No problem at all. The secretary and county chief are waiting for you in town. As for the Land Authority, the Environmental Agency, and so forth, I'll just snap my fingers and they'll come running."

They said good-bye to the deaf old lady. She said, "Shuan, boy, are you bringing our visitors into town?"

"Yes."

"Will you be back today? If you leave too late, the buses will stop running."

She still had no idea her grandson was now a general manager. He smiled. "Grandma, I won't be back tonight. I'll tell you all about it tomorrow!"

While Mei Yin got the car, Jin called the county chief and told him to gather the various heads of the departments, so they could wrap up the deal that evening. Chief Liu's excitement could barely be contained. He kept saying, "Good! Good work! You've done so well, Jin!"

When they got into town, the department heads were already waiting in the meeting room. The ensuing discussion went exceedingly well, both parties seeming to compete to make concessions—the county gave Mei Yin every incentive they had at their disposal, while she relinquished her claim to shares in the technology (which was essentially for the benefit of Sun Jingshuan). By ten that night, the negotiations were more or less over. Only the head of the Environmental Agency still had some doubts: "You're talking about cultivating viruses. How can you guarantee they won't get out?"

Mei Yin smiled and turned to Sun Jingshuan, who explained. "Director Mei has said that this facility will only produce animal cells, which will be sold to other institutions who require them, such as the Wuhan Institute of Virology, in order to cultivate viruses; or else they'll go to the inoculation industry to develop vaccines. That is to say, this site will have nothing to do with the actual production of viruses, so there's no danger of a leak."

The department head blushed bright red, muttering, "So sorry, this is all outside my area of expertise."

Mei Yin then produced a letter from her adoptive father, Walt Dickerson, authorizing her to act as his agent, and then signed the investment agreement in his name. She thought his plan to put money into a facility here was a smart one. Chinese laws and regulations were much simpler than in other places. For example, not one person (including Shuan, a supposed industry insider) had noted that the facility's output would include genetically modified cells, the production of which ought to be strictly regulated. Of course, the dangers of these modified cells were purely theoretical—or even philosophical—and there was no solid evidence of a threat. Her adoptive father had always held that these abstract worries were necessary, but scientists couldn't allow them to get in the way of decisive action.

And in China, it was much simpler to take action.

A decade previous, when Mei Yin got her master's in America, her adoptive father had urged her to expand into China. "The future of biology is in China," he would say. "A society that values collectivism is much closer to God's will than Western society with its reverence for the individual." He also believed that in China the teachings of his Crucifix Society would face much less resistance on ethical grounds. The ease with which this contract was signed could be a good omen.

The next morning at seven, Mei Yin knocked on Sun's door. "I'm leaving now. Something else to deal with in Nanyang. You have complete authority over everything here, but get in touch if there's a decision you can't make. When Jin gets here, tell him I'm sorry I had to leave without saying good-bye."

Sun knew the county had planned a whole follow-up agenda, a round of banquets hosted in turn by important government agencies, followed by visits to local scenic spots. This was all in keeping with local custom, the only way they knew how to express hospitality. Yet he knew it was precisely these rituals that Mei Yin wanted to avoid, and so didn't say anything, just nodded in agreement. While Mei Yin went to get her car, he dashed to the hotel restaurant and returned with a bowl of soy milk and several bean-paste buns. Mei Yin thanked him, drank the milk, tossed the buns into the passenger seat, and zoomed off.

She was rushing to Nanyang to check up on the preparations for another project she was planning there: the Sacred Heart Orphanage. She had already been through two rounds of negotiations with the city government and the Protestant "Three-Self Patriotic Movement" committee, who were in support of her plan. Two older women, Mother Liu and Mother Chen, were willing to join as her "mothers." This place was about forty miles from the site of the future facility, a half hour's drive, in the old part of Nanyang, where the roads were narrow, lined with stalls and hawkers. Mei Yin had to honk her horn and reverse quite a few times before she managed to get her car through. The building, a former church, had been freshly painted, including the Latin-style cross mounted on the roof. The rooms were spick-and-span, with neat little beds piled with all sorts of toys. None of this had cost her adoptive father a penny—she'd funded it all out of her own salary.

Hearing the car pull up, Mother Liu ran out joyously. "You're back, Director Mei! Look, even before our official opening, someone's already brought us a child. It's a baby girl, perfectly healthy. Isn't she beautiful?"

"Really? Let me see."

Mother Chen was inside, feeding the baby from a bottle. When she'd had her fill, she looked with her dark eyes at the grown-ups around her. She really was lovely: pale skin, large eyes, about a month old from the looks of her. Mother Chen said, "We've examined her carefully, and there's nothing wrong with her. Such a pretty child, in fine condition. How could the parents bear to get rid of her?"

Many people got rid of their girl babies, of course, hoping the next one would be a boy. Mei Yin scooped up the child, who stared with gorgeous eyes, her tiny hand gripping Mei Yin's finger, sending a shiver through her heart. Touching her tiny face, Mei Yin asked Mother Liu, "How did she arrive?"

"Late at night, left at our front door. She'd thrown off her blanket, and by the time we heard her crying and rushed out, she was lying there completely naked, legs and arms thrashing, out in the freezing cold for God knows how long. It's a miracle she didn't get pneumonia or even a cold. A strong child."

These words struck a chord in Mei Yin's memory, and she froze, an image flashing before her eyes: snow-covered ground, frosty air, two children about two or three years old—a boy and a girl—getting out of bed in the morning and running out naked into the courtyard for a snowball fight. She'd been an orphan herself, but it had happened so early she knew no sorrow, and happily ran around naked in the snow with the neighbor's son. Her adoptive father was at the time an expert with the World Health Organization, working to eliminate contagious diseases. He happened to see this scene and—he later told her—was utterly stunned. The strength of a poor child's life force, her joy in the midst of tragedy. This struck him with the force of a blow. From that instant, he decided to formally adopt her, but the Cultural Revolution had just begun, and the paperwork dragged on for eight years until, at the age of ten, she finally joined her new family.

Mother Chen brought her back to earth, reminding her that the child had arrived without a name, so would Director Mei please give her one. Still thinking of the frosty ground, Mei Yin said, "Let's call her Little Snow. As for her surname—she can be a Mei. Mei Xiaoxue, Little Snow."

"What a lovely name. Mei Xiaoxue. Mei Xiaoxue, you have a name now!" Mother Chen prodded her adorable tummy, and Little Snow gurgled. That night, Mei Yin hosted a simple dinner, to celebrate the orphanage's official opening. The guests were only three adults and a small child, and although Mei Xiaoxue wasn't able to partake of the food, she was unquestionably the most important person present. The

49

three adults clamored to hold and amuse her, and she played along, smiling and gurgling, staying awake till the very end of the party. And so this abandoned baby, Mei Xiaoxue, became the first formal member of the Sacred Heart Orphanage.

Late fall 2002—Payette National Forest, Idaho, USA

A fire had swept through Payette National Forest; the culprit wasn't a human being, but nature itself. The Forest Service did nothing to control the fire, and the flames surged for a week before burning themselves out. The next day, Forest Ranger Sam Hoskirk and Cornell geologist Bruce Malamud went into the hills together.

As they entered the remote mountain zone, they caught up with a Ford van, slowing as it prepared to turn into a smaller road. Sam and Bruce slowed down too as they overtook the vehicle, calling out a warm hello. The other driver waved and said hello back, but then quickly sped away. The rear window of the van was open, but the two backseat passengers remained rigid and expressionless. Sam found this a little odd. There weren't many vehicles around here, and it was normal to stop for a chat when you happened upon another car. "Maybe those two in the back were foreigners," Bruce surmised, "and don't speak English."

"The road they turned onto only leads to a small farm owned by my friend Moraine," Sam answered. "I wonder what those three want with old Moraine?"

They drove on to the end of the mountain road, locked the car securely, then headed into the hills with their equipment.

This year had seen the most wildfires of any year for half a century, 150 of them in a forest of more than two million acres, destroying a whole seventy thousand acres. This was the result of Bruce's theories and mathematical models, recently accepted by the Forest Service, which suggested it would be better not to attempt fire control, but to simply let them burn themselves out naturally. Today, the two men were there to study the aftermath.

It was a mixed forest: oak trees in the lower reaches, up above ponderosa pines, white pines and lodgepole pines, spruces, fir trees and western hemlock. Undergrowth flourished below the tall trees, the ground covered in piles of dried leaves. Great tits and northern cardinals chirped in the branches. The two men arrived at the site of the fire. The undergrowth had been burned away, as had the fallen leaves. All around were blackened branches and ash. The air still held the dry heat of the fire, and the ground was warm too. Yet the trees hadn't been too badly damaged, and while the bottoms of the trunks showed scorch marks, they hadn't been burned through, and the health of the trees had not been threatened. Their crowns were still perfectly healthy, all green leaves and branches. Sam noted that the damage caused by a fire depends on how long the flames lingered in one place. If they remained at the lower levels, then they'd quickly move on after consuming the fuel of fallen leaves and underbrush, leaving the trunks and branches untouched. The forest would recover quickly.

As they chatted, they continued to study and record the state of the site, measuring the highest extent of the scorch marks on the tree trunks, the height of the burned shrubbery, the density of insect corpses left by the flames. They also dug into the soil to examine how deep the effects of the fire extended, and particularly how it had affected buried seeds. After a while of this, Sam smiled. "Bruce, I really have to thank you."

"What for?"

"That computer game of yours. Those old men in the Forest Service wouldn't trust what I told them, a ranger of thirty years' experience, but they believed a simple computer game."

Bruce had created a forest-fire simulation game that convinced the higher-ups to adopt the tactics long suggested by Sam. The program placed trees and fallen branches at random places around a grid, allowing undergrowth and debris to accumulate at different rates. Next, it dropped flames onto the grid at unpredictable intervals, and modeled the results based on how much undergrowth had built up, how long the conflagration lasted, and how often it changed direction. After running the simulation several times, the final conclusion was that allowing low intensity, high frequency fires would reduce the amount of flammable material, creating a mosaic of clear spaces and reducing the destructive power of future incidents.

Sam was a little peeved. He'd been screaming about this for more than a decade, but the old fools in charge treated his arguments as the ravings of a lunatic. Then someone showed up with a computer game and suddenly it was "theory," and they believed it at once. How did that make sense!

They were a little tired, and it was lunchtime, anyway, so they found a clearing to sit in and have their bottled water and sandwiches. They continued their investigation after lunch, covering the entire site of the fire on foot. The federal government had issued a policy statement that year, acknowledging that "forest fires are a part of the ecological cycle," a historical shift as far as the Forest Service was concerned. The report that Sam and Bruce planned to present after their study would serve as proof of this new strategy. Having seen the site, Bruce had even more confidence in his theory—and in Sam's instincts.

Bruce said, "I was thinking—in the future, instead of just not putting out fires, perhaps we ought to set them at regular intervals, so we can control when and how they happen, and be prepared. What do you think of that?"

Sam was looking down to study an anthill. The creatures were busily storing food to get them through the winter. The inferno hadn't done any harm to the ants—they'd probably hidden deep within their nest while the fire raged. Whatever means they'd used to escape death, you couldn't help admiring God's arrangements for every species, as well as the resilience of life. Sam didn't answer Bruce at once, and only when Bruce had repeated the question did he say, "In theory, you have a point. But—"

"I want your honest opinion, Sam. I value your point of view."

"I don't have a clear idea, just a sense that there are times when scientists don't necessarily make better choices than God. You all are clever in a small way, and have a kind of 'short-term logic,' but the Lord's mighty intelligence is the ultimate logic." Sam chuckled. "But you don't need to go along with this. The Bible teaches that Christ is infinite, omnipotent and all-knowing, beyond human understanding. Apostle Paul warned that we have to beware of favoring human reason and logic over the teachings of God, lest we end up captive—and it seems to me that when he says to beware, the people he's talking about are scientists."

Bruce, an atheist, didn't want to get into an argument, so simply smiled. "God doesn't seem to mind having the Bible printed with modern technology, nor his teachings being spread on TV."

It was getting late. The two men made their way back downhill and got in the car. When they were almost at the junction, Sam suggested visiting Moraine's farm. He liked to pay his friend a visit whenever he was in the area. From a distance, they saw the Ford they'd passed earlier, parked at the start of the lane. The three passengers were prostrate, facing southeast as they bowed three times. Bruce recognized this as sunset prayers. Sam slowed down, partly to prepare for the turn, partly because he thought it would only be polite to say something to them. But even though the trio saw the car, they showed no inclination to chat, instead finishing their devotions quickly and hurrying back into their van. As the two vehicles passed each other, once again the driver waved, while the two people in the backseat remained rigidly inexpressive, still as painted idols. After the van had gone, Sam said, "You might be right. They're probably foreigners who haven't been in the country long, and don't know how to be polite."

Hearing the car arrive, old Mr. and Mrs. Moraine came out, beaming, hugging their visitors. Sam explained that they'd been held up and apologized for stopping by so late. Moraine insisted, "But that doesn't mean you have to go right away? That won't do at all. I insist you join us for dinner, and spend the night here. You can leave in the morning. Besides, Sam, this will be the last time I'm able to host you. I'm selling the farm."

"What? To who?"

"You probably bumped into them. They just left, the ones in the Ford van."

"Were they foreigners?"

"The one who signed the contract was called Zia Baj, an American. He works at the University of Idaho. The other two had just immigrated here from Central Asia, and didn't speak English."

Sam turned to Bruce. "Would you mind spending a night here?"

Bruce shrugged. "Up to you. I don't have anything urgent to do tomorrow."

Moraine was pleased to hear this, and urged his wife to prepare dinner quickly, while he took his guests to have a look at the farm. This was a small piece of land, about seventy acres. The courtyard was full of farming machinery, including a hand tractor, lawnmower, and harvester, all looking fairly old. In an enclosure were some cows and alpacas, about fifty in all. There were also a number of sheds, including simple greenhouses in which straw mushrooms, shiitake, and other fungi were grown. Moraine spoke, his voice full of affection for the place. "I took over this farm from my father, forty-five years ago. I can't bear to give it up, but I also can't go on like this. The place is too small, and too remote. I can't compete with the bigger establishments. Nancy and I are old, we can't keep doing this kind of labor." He sighed. "We've made a loss three years in a row. We really can't go on."

Sam tried to comfort him. "It's good to get it off your hands without any fuss. Now you can go back to the city and enjoy your retirement. How much did you get?"

"It was a good price, six hundred and eighty thousand. I'd thought six hundred grand would be as much as I could hope for. Now we'll be able to buy a nice place in the suburbs."

"That's great. Move in quickly, and I'll come for your housewarming."

Moraine asked what they'd been doing in the mountains. Sam told him about their new forest-fire theory. He briefly summed up the tactic of allowing fires to exhaust themselves, and mentioned that he and Bruce were debating if controlled burns would be the next step. When he asked Moraine for his opinion, the old man laughed. "I've never thought about it. But I'm sure there've been forests here for millions of years, and they've never been wiped out by infernos. So it seems that without man interfering, God manages the whole thing pretty well."

This was exactly what Sam thought. He turned smugly to Bruce. "You see? Another vote for me."

Bruce looked startled. "What? Oh, right, yes." His mind had been elsewhere.

Mrs. Moraine summoned them to dinner with a bell. The chatter continued merrily over the meal, only Bruce remaining sunk in thought. His hostess, a thoughtful woman, was the first to notice he seemed unsettled, and asked in a concerned tone, "Mr. Malamud, you didn't know you'd be spending the night here. Is there something you need to take care of at home?"

Bruce quickly answered, "Ah, no, no." He looked around the room. "But something is worrying me tonight. I'm suspicious about the three people who bought this place. I didn't say anything earlier in case you thought I was a racist or Christian extremist, but—Mr. Moraine, you've said your farm's been losing money, and yet they offered you a good price?"

"Yes. They didn't really bargain. I thought that was odd too. They didn't seem particularly concerned about how the farm was doing. All they asked was about the surroundings, and how many buildings there were."

"I wonder why they'd come all the way out here to buy a farm?"

"They saw the ad I placed. But this really is remote, most people wouldn't be interested."

"Hmm," Bruce said. "You must have seen those news reports: how some of the 9/11 terrorists rented a farmstead in the States, and turned it into a training camp for terrorists within the country. They even had a shooting range, with Westerners as the targets! I love this country, but I'd also hate to report a neighbor or colleague to the FBI. Yet . . ."

Old Moraine hesitated. His suspicions had no basis in fact, and he, like Bruce, loathed stool pigeons.

After they'd talked it over a while, Bruce said, "How about this: when Mr. Moraine hands the property over to the new owners, he can tell them that his old friend Sam Hoskirk often spends the night here when he's in the hills, and he hopes they'll be able to keep letting him stay. I think a neighborly farmer wouldn't refuse to help. Besides, they don't know anyone here, so why wouldn't they want another friend? Don't you think so? If they agree, then Sam can continue keeping an eye on them. But if they refuse to let Sam come, then—that'll be suspicious."

Everyone agreed that this was a sensible plan. Mr. Moraine added, "When they come back, I'll definitely speak to them. Sam, you should drop by a couple of times as well."

Someone changed the subject, and the conversation moved on.

A week later, the new owner of the farm, Zia Baj, arrived. Moraine asked if he'd continue hosting his friend, Forest Ranger Sam Hoskirk, to make things easier for him on his mountain expeditions. Mr. Baj froze for a moment, then reluctantly agreed. Moraine thanked him on behalf of Sam, then told Sam what had happened. A few days later, Sam decided to pay the farm a visit, even though he didn't actually have any official business there. He found the turn onto the small road barred by a gate, crudely nailed together from untreated wood. It was secured with an old-fashioned combination lock, and a sign proclaiming "Private Property, No Entry Please."

This was obviously meant for Sam. Even after Moraine's request, the new owner was determined to keep him out. Sam drove back to town. Instead of going home, he headed straight to the office of the Fremont County FBI dispatch center.

Senior agent Rosa Banbury, a twenty-five-year veteran of the FBI, was waiting for him. She listened patiently to his story, smiling as she encouraged him to tell the whole thing. He felt awkward, and kept emphasizing his lack of evidence even as he shared his suspicions. Finally, Rosa said, "Ranger Hoskirk, please don't worry, I'll be sure not to take my eyes off that farm. Of course, I hope they're innocent. No matter what happens, I'll keep you informed."

"That's great, thank you. That sets my mind at rest."

Back home, he told Moraine and Bruce what happened. After that, there was nothing to do but wait for Agent Banbury to get in touch.

CHAPTER TWO
AMERICAN MISFORTUNE

Early September 2016—Nanyang, Henan-Hubei provincial border, China

When school let out at noon, Mei Xiaoxue dashed back to the orphanage to find Mother Liu and Mother Chen preparing lunch. "Has Mother Mei arrived yet?"

"She's reached the county, and will be driving over from Wuhan, together with Uncle Xue Yu who came last time. They have some business down south, in Xinye, but they'll definitely be back for your birthdays this evening."

Thirteen-year-old Xiaoxue cheered, and so did her friends, twelve-year-old Mei Xiaokai, eleven-year-old Xue Yuanyuan, and a gaggle of girls aged two to six. Xiaoxue said, "Is Mother Mei's room ready for her?"

"Of course," said Mother Chen, then, knowing what she was hinting at, she added, "The door's not locked, if you want to go and give it a final sweep, go ahead. But don't forget lunch."

Mei Xiaoxue ran out joyfully, followed by several of the children. Mother Liu and Mother Chen watched her go, smiling. In its fourteenth year, the orphanage now housed thirty-two children, with Xiaoxue the oldest. These kids were more than usually thoughtful, and had formed a deep bond with Mother Mei. The director kept a small room here, furnished very simply, which was normally locked. She spent no more than a day or two here at a time. Before and after each visit, Xiaoxue would find all sorts of excuses to spend time in her room. Once, after Director Mei had gone, Mother Liu went to check on the room and found Xiaoxue hugging the pillow she'd used, breathing deeply. Seeing Mother Liu come in, she blushed bright red, and shyly explained that the pillow still had Mother Mei's "Mommy scent" that she liked to smell. All the orphans, not just Xiaoxue, had invested their affection in Mother Mei.

Out of thirty-two orphans, twenty-four were girls, a sign of Chinese society's preference for boys. None of them knew their birthdays for certain, but over the last decade, they'd started a tradition that on the first Sunday in September, at the height of fall, Director Mei would find some time to come visit and celebrate a group birthday. And so, on this day, the children were every bit as excited as on Chinese New Year.

Mother Liu and Mother Chen had met Director Mei for the first time fourteen years ago. Seeing the glittering crucifix around her neck, they'd assumed she too was a believer, and it was only later that they learned she wasn't a Christian. Still, her benevolence was every bit as real as the most devout person of faith. She'd never married, and lived very simply, spending all her money on the orphanage. The living expenses of all thirty-four residents (including the two custodians) were entirely covered by Director Mei, along with a small amount of government funding. Mothers Liu and Chen always said that it didn't matter about Director Mei not being a believer (the greatest regret of these two women was that such a good person should lack faith)—in a hundred years she'd certainly ascend to heaven.

Xiaoxue came back from Mother Mei's room. She was the oldest child of the orphanage, and often helped the two mothers with odd jobs—serving lunch, washing dishes, and so on. Now she rolled up her sleeves and prepared to work. At thirteen, she was extremely beautiful, with a pair of bright eyes and two rows of straight white teeth. Her skin was delicate, red blooming through the white, and very smooth. Her face nearly always wore a smile, along with its accompanying dimples. She was the prettiest girl in the orphanage, and indeed the town. Quite a few people murmured that if her parents had known how attractive she'd turn out to be, they'd never have abandoned her.

All thirty-two children were assembled in the dining room, on either side of a pale wood table. Mother Liu led them in prayer. "Give us this day our daily bread . . ." Although this wasn't really a Christian orphanage (the Church had only provided the land), both mothers were believers, and naturally wanted the children to say grace. Mei Yin hadn't initially approved of this, but neither had she explicitly forbidden it, and so they continued. Four of the children were young enough that they needed to be fed. The two mothers took one each, while the oldest children, Xiaoxue and Xiaokai, took care of the other two. Xiaoxue was feeding Little Niu, while her own meal was placed nearby, so she could shovel in a few mouthfuls whenever she had a moment. All the kids were thrilled at the news of Mother Mei's imminent arrival, chattering away about it. Little Niu asked, "Sister Xiaoxue, does Mommy Mei have a mommy and daddy?"

"Mother Mei's mommy and daddy died of an illness, so she's an orphan, just like us. But she has a mommy and daddy in America—no, just a daddy, her mommy died last year."

"Is her American father named Mei, too?"

Xiaoxue smiled. "Of course not! This granddad's name is Dickerson. He's a scientist too."

"Mother Mei, and Grandfather Dickerson, they're the best scientists in the world. Just like Jesus, and the Virgin Mary. Isn't that right?"

Xiaoxue had no answer to that. Jesus and the Virgin Mary she knew about—the two mothers had seen to that. But it was the first she'd heard them compared to scientists. Mother Chen said threateningly, "You little rascal! No more talking, sit down and eat your lunch. If anyone of you misbehaves, you won't get to eat Mother Mei's birthday cake tonight."

Little Niu immediately shut his mouth, and obediently finished his meal.

After they'd done the dishes, Xiaoxue quietly asked, "Mother Liu, what time is Mommy Mei arriving? I only have gym class this afternoon, I can ask to skip."

Knowing she wanted to spend as much time with Mother Mei as possible, Mother Liu replied, "She phoned to say she'd be here after four." Then she teased, "Xiaoxue, Mother Chen and I are very sad, you know, because you only think of Mommy Mei."

Xiaoxue blushed a little, and replied sweetly, "Who says? I love all three of my mothers, it's just that Mommy Mei is only here for such a short time." And with that, she ran off to school.

A little after nine that morning, Mei Yin and Xue Yu arrived at the road to the main town in Xinye County. There, they met County Chief Jin, standing in front of a top-of-the-line Lifan car. Afraid they wouldn't see him, Jin flagged them down vigorously. Mei Yin quickly asked Xue Yu to stop and leaped from the vehicle, smiling. "Hey, Jin, how did you know we were coming back today? Look at you, blocking our way like the king of the hill. What's the matter?"

"What's the matter?" said the county chief with mock outrage. "All I want is for Ms. Mei Yin, director of Heavenly Corp., to do me the honor of allowing me to host her this once, a wish I've cherished for fourteen years. As for how I knew you were coming today—I have a spy!

I'm kidding . . . I knew you had set up an orphanage in Nanyang, and that you come back on the first Sunday of every September to celebrate all their birthdays. So I knew you'd likely be passing this way, and came here early like a hunter in front of a rabbit hole. I'd like to throw you a banquet at noon. You'll still be in time for the kids' birthdays."

"Forgive my bluntness, but I've been back in China more than twenty years now, and I'm still not used to all this government entertainment. I think if everyone stopped wasting time and money on official banquets, the country would develop a lot faster."

"It's not an official banquet, I'm planning to host you myself. Just a few of us, for a private chat. Though I admit this car behind me was bought with government funds—and it's for you, a reward for the part you've played in Xinye's economic development. I insist you accept it. You've had your Santana so many years, it ought to have been scrapped years ago. I know your finances are tight, and you've never awarded yourself a bonus at Heavenly, plus most of your salary goes straight into the orphanage."

He was clearly moved as he got to the last sentence. Mei Yin thought about it, then happily accepted the car. County Chief Jin called over the Lifan's driver, and told him to bring the Santana to the county hall, while he took the wheel of the Lifan himself. "Please get in, Sister Mei, and this comrade as well." He glanced over at the tall, thin young man, who exuded an air of competence. "Is it Mr. Xue? You were here last time."

"Yes, I'm one of Professor Mei's doctoral students. I met you a year ago, sir."

"Please get in, both of you. I'll take you to Heavenly Corp. first, so you can take care of official business, then to your party."

Mei Yin joked to Xue Yu, "Does this seem like a kidnapping to you?" Feeling helpless, she got in the car.

The Lifan sped toward Heavenly Corp. Along the way, County Chief Jin pointed out the car's many features: car-mounted computer,

GPS positioning, big-screen navigation, and genuine-leather, heated massage seats. Not to mention the standard rearview monitor, double safety air bags, and so on. He bragged that this vehicle was well made yet inexpensive, less than a hundred and fifty thousand, and every bit as good as a BMW, apart from the lack of a car phone.

The road was different now than a decade before. It was no wider than before, but it had been resurfaced, and there were now pedestrian crossings, flower beds along the side, and traffic lights. The riot of beautiful blossoms, together with artistically designed street lamps, stretched the whole length of the road. The refurbishment of this road was Jin's first act after becoming county chief. Mei Yin admired the scenery on both sides, thinking how fourteen years ago, when she'd chosen this abandoned farmland as the site for her facility, the main reason had been its unobtrusive remoteness. But as the saying goes, tall trees catch the wind; Heavenly Corp. now had an output value of two billion, and would have attracted notice whatever she did.

County Chief Jin said, "This is my first time hosting you in Xinye, and it may also be my last—I'm being transferred to Nanyang, to be their deputy mayor."

"Ah, that's good news," beamed Mei Yin. "Jin, you're a rising star, and there's no limit to what you'll achieve. You must be the youngest deputy mayor the city has ever had?"

"It's all thanks to you," he said, truly grateful to Mei Yin. His successful career had begun with the deal they'd struck fourteen years before. "This is just a temporary position. The official appointment won't take place until the next People's Congress."

"That's just a formality, of course you'll be confirmed, unless you make some terrible error in the meantime. But I know our Jin isn't corrupt and doesn't womanize, so what could possibly go wrong?"

"It's hard to say. Government is like a battlefield—being in politics is the most dangerous job, even worse than being a Hollywood stuntman."

They laughed and chatted till they reached the Heavenly Corp. building, which still kept up its low-key exterior, surrounded by a large grove of pine trees, planted fourteen years ago and now fully grown, so lush they turned the day green. An unremarkable cement road led through the pines, only wide enough for two cars to pass, not at all resembling the entrance to a large work site. The woods were very still. Occasionally, the red roof flashed into view. There were no slogans or flags on the outside of the building, not even the company's name or road signs pointing to it. When they got to the office, General Manager Sun Jingshuan welcomed them without much fanfare. Seeing County Chief Jin, he was stunned for a moment, then smiled. "I'd said the magpies were chirping a lot today. Turns out it was because of our important visitor!"

County Chief Jin said, "No need to praise me. When I asked you when Director Mei was coming, you kept your mouth sealed. But didn't you say, 'You might be the county chief, but you're no chief here; you might be a high official, but this is my domain.'"

Sun laughed. "Oh no, I'm done for, I've offended Mighty Lord Jin. In all your vast territories, I'll have nowhere to shelter from your wrath!"

He ushered them into seats as he spoke. County Chief Jin said, "Enough of that. You two have business to discuss. Do that, and get someone to show me around the facility. I haven't been here in five or six years."

General Manager Sun exchanged an unobtrusive glance with Director Mei. As the brightest star in the county's sky, their business had naturally attracted its share of officials wanting to take a tour—but they usually refused diplomatically. County Chief Jin knew they had a firm rule that unless it was a compulsory inspection, no one was allowed to disturb the workplace. Yet he'd asked directly, and it would be rude to turn him down, so Mei Yin said breezily, "Of course. I didn't come here to talk business today, I'll give you a tour myself. Xue Yu, you can come have a look too. Sun, you don't need to come, stay here and take care of your own work."

The forest of pines wrapped around the workshop like a shell. These buildings were all a pleasing sky blue, and it was quiet here, with none of the commotion you'd hear in any other facility. Along the roads were orderly lines of boxwood and holly hedges, all neatly trimmed, not a scrap of trash in sight. Xue Yu complimented Sun Jingshuan, saying his management of the area alone showed his caliber. Mei Yin smiled, replying, "Not only does he keep everything running smoothly, he also has a great aptitude for technology. After more than a decade here, he's been responsible for quite a few innovations in animal cell cultivation."

First they went to the preparation lab, which mainly focused on preparing blood serum–free cultures and consisted of rows of containers and pipes in a variety of sizes. All the workers were in clean white lab coats and smiled in recognition at the sight of Mei Yin, before burying their heads back in their work.

Next was the main laboratory, which contained neat rows of a dozen or more large tubes. Xue Yu explained that they were the world's most advanced hollow-fiber biological reactors. Each contained tens of thousands of hollow fibers, creating separate reactor chambers inside and outside the tubes. The cells grew on the tubes, unable to enter the inner chamber, their secretions similarly kept out, including macromolecules such as monoclonal antibodies. Blood serum–free culture circulated through the inner chamber, oozing out, while waste products leaked back in and were carried away by the movement of the culture. Within this system, cells could proliferate in three dimensions at a density as high as 109/mL.

Mei Yin explained, "We're number one internationally in terms of density of cell cultivation."

After visiting several more auxiliary labs, Mei Yin said, "That's everything we need to look at. Shall we return to the office?"

Jin halted. "Isn't there one more new lab? The one we invested in last year."

Xue Yu glanced at Mei Yin—he hadn't heard of any new lab. She nodded. "Right, I forgot about that. Come on, I'll show you."

They followed a small path into the woods. Another building appeared from behind the trees, sky blue like the others. This was County Chief Jin's main reason for that day's visit. Heavenly Corp. was very dear to him, and he was very protective of it, preventing other government departments from causing them any trouble. But he'd heard about a new heavily sealed laboratory on the premises, and it made him uneasy. Director Mei had said the facility would only produce animal cells, nothing at all to do with viruses, and there was no possibility of viral contamination—so what were all the precautions for? If some accident were to happen, his job would be in danger. His professional success had started with this company; he hoped it wouldn't also end here.

The lab was in regular operation, but the entrance was firmly locked. Mei Yin let them in with a magnetic card. At first glance, it looked no different from the other workshops, just rows of large bioreactors. Mei Yin explained that their interior construction was different. "The techniques used in this lab weren't our innovation, but a mature technology purchased from the Mérieux Research Center in France, which produces a new kind of rabies vaccine. With all the new pet owners in China, the market for this vaccine looks very strong.

"I made a promise to you that this facility would have nothing to do with viruses, and that promise is still in effect. The rabies vaccine consists of the attenuated virus, curative rather than pathogenic. No danger there. We keep a tight rein on this lab only to prevent industrial secrets leaking out."

County Chief Jin stopped worrying. While entry to the building was restricted, the workers were dressed in ordinary lab coats and masks, no special protective gear.

After they finished their tour and went back out, they came upon a medium-size lab. The door was locked, and when they looked through the window, there was no one inside. Mei Yin said, "This is an auxiliary lab, not in use yet. I'll phone for the guard to open the door." After making the call, she reported, "Sun says the guard will be here in half an hour at the most."

"Forget it," Jin said. "No need to go in."

"If you're sure, I'll tell Sun not to bother, then."

Xue Yu looked through the window. The lab contained three completely sealed negative-pressure ultraclean workstations. He had no idea why a vaccine lab would require such a facility, but didn't ask.

The trio returned to General Manager Sun's office. County Chief Jin offered to whisk them off to the government hotel in the town, where a banquet was waiting for them. Sun laughed. "County Chief, there's no need for that. You're on our territory now, how could we let you play host? Come on, we're going to my home. A regular farmer's meal."

Granny Sun was still healthy, and as the visitors arrived, she rushed out to welcome them. Her white hair was dazzling, her body still sturdy, and her memory extraordinary. She cried out, "Jin, you're here—it's such an honor. It's been twelve, no, fourteen years since you were last here." Her grandson roared into her ear, "He's the county chief now! Lording over us all!" Jin cut in. "Manager Sun, you should scold me instead. In front of your grandmother, I'm always going to be junior— she should lord it over me instead!"

It truly was a farmer's meal: steamed chrysanthemum greens, stewed vegetables, twice-cooked pork, mutton noodle soup. Granny Sun's habit of eating her food while squatting at the kitchen door hadn't changed, and she wouldn't move no matter how they tried to drag her to the table. Instead, they had to respect her wishes. The three visitors had almost finished their meal when she broke in from her perch, smiling.

"Jin, and Sister Mei, it's good that you're here. After the meal, you can help me deal with an important matter."

Both Jin and Mei Yin said, "Whatever it is, just ask." Granny said, "You have to urge this grandson of mine to hurry up and find a wife. He's thirty-six this year! Sister Mei, try to reason with him. I know he respects you more than anyone in the world. You're sure to sway him."

Before Mei Yin even opened her mouth, Sun Jingshuan blurted out, "Granny, there's no point asking Sister Mei to persuade me. You're barking up the wrong tree there—she's not married herself. In fact, I'm just following her example—I've made up my mind that I won't get married until Mei Yin does."

This last line might have sounded like a joke, but Jin could feel a deeper meaning behind it. He figured that Director Mei must be in her forties, quite a bit older than General Manager Sun. But then, she looked young with her simple clothes and slender figure, and would be a good match for Sun. Without knowing how Mei Yin felt, though, it seemed best if he pretended not to notice. Laughing, Mei Yin proclaimed loudly to the old woman, "Don't worry about it, I'll be sure to advise him when I have the time!"

After the meal, Jin said he had to return to the city for an afternoon meeting. The other three walked Jin to the door, and after they'd said good-bye, the county chief walked down the gravel path back to the facility entrance. As he went, Xue Yu suddenly called out, "County Chief Jin, I'll walk you out. I have something to discuss with you."

He caught up, and the two men strolled along the path, wild grass and dried twigs snapping beneath their feet. Jin said, "Xue, what's up?"

Xue Yu smiled. "Nothing's up. I just wanted to leave the two of them alone."

◆ ◆ ◆

Meanwhile, after saying good-bye to Jin and heading back inside, Mei Yin had tried to help Granny Sun with the dishes, which alarmed the elderly woman. "What's this? This won't do! How could I allow an honored guest to do any housework!" She insisted on chasing Mei Yin and her grandson into the living room, while she busied herself in the kitchen. Sun Jingshuan poured Mei Yin some tea, then sat opposite, silently gazing at her. "Sister Mei," he said, "don't listen to my grandmother. I've made up my mind, and unless you're willing to get married, I'll stay single my whole life."

Mei Yin sighed and said nothing, watching the steam rise from her cup. Sun went on. "The age difference simply isn't a problem. It's not like we're that far apart. I think that's a kind of destiny."

Mei Yin shook her head. "I don't mind about our ages. That's not the problem."

"Then what is? Can you tell me?"

She was silent for a moment. "I'm afraid that I'm an unlucky lizard."

"Lizard?"

"There's a Russian legend about a goddess who protects copper mines and malachite, I can't remember her name, but her true form is a lizard. She lures young miners into falling in love with her, but brings them only bad fortune—even though that's not her intention."

Sun Jingshuan laughed. "I'm Chinese, I don't believe in these Russian superstitions. Actually, ever since I joined the Crucifix Society, I've been prepared for bad fortune." He looked straight at her. "Sister Mei, I know you've got something on your mind."

Mei Yin had intended to keep silent, but with Sun's gaze fixed on her, she found words spilling out. "When I was thirty, the year before I opened the facility here, I fell in love. He was a Russian, and even though we never formally married, I've always regarded him as my husband. Later he killed himself and—his suicide had something to do with me. Since that time, I've been unable to get close to any other man emotionally."

"Sister Mei," he answered tenderly. "I guessed long ago that you must have had your heart broken before. It doesn't matter, I'll put it back together again very carefully. You know how good I am at fixing things."

Mei Yin silently watched this young man, saying nothing, but she had been warmed by his words. If she could have a man by her side, a shoulder to rest on when she grew weary, it would surely lighten the burden placed on her by the Godfather. Sensing the slight change in her attitude, Jingshuan plucked up his courage. He walked to her, sat beside her, and put his arm across her shoulders.

Mei Yin didn't stir from his embrace, so he went on to boldly kiss her. She let him, placidly kissing him back, and soon their blood was boiling. His lips awakened urges in her that she'd forced into hibernation for many years now, and they stayed locked in their embrace for quite some time. It was Mei Yin who first calmed down and gently pushed him aside, ruffling his hair and saying, "Jingshuan, I know how you feel, but please give me some time to think it over, and we'll talk about it the next time I visit. Is that all right?"

"Of course."

"I should go now. The children at the orphanage are waiting for me. Where's Xue? Is he back yet?"

"I'm afraid he might be leaving us alone on purpose. He's rather sneaky."

Mei Yin smiled and nodded. Just as she pulled out her cell phone to call him, it rang—an American number. After hearing what the caller had to say, she answered heavily in English, "All right, I'll be there tomorrow."

Hanging up, she turned to Jingshuan. "That was my adoptive father's personal physician. His heart disease is acting up again, and he's just gone back into the hospital."

"Is his life in danger?"

"He said they discovered it early, so he shouldn't be at risk. But then my father's eighty-six, so it's hard to say." She sank into thought for a minute. "Get the office to arrange a plane ticket as quickly as possible. If I hurry to Zhengzhou now, I'll be able to get the next flight to Shanghai, and from there to San Francisco."

Xue Yu knew Ms. Mei would be anxious, so he drove as fast as possible. When they were almost at Nanyang, Mei Yin said, "I think we still have time to stop at the orphanage. The children know I'm coming to Nanyang, and they'll be waiting to see me."

"All right, but we mustn't stay too long. Better to be a little early to the airport than a little late."

The car wound its way through the narrow alleys before finally reaching the orphanage. Hearing the horn, Mother Liu and Mother Chen bustled out, but Xiaoxue was ahead of them, the first to reach the car and fling herself into Mei Yin's arms the instant she stepped out, shouting, "Mommy Mei, Mommy Mei, you're back! Mommy Mei, I missed you so much."

Mei Yin held her and stroked her face. "I missed my daughter Xiaoxue too." They snuggled for a bit, then she said, "Say hello to your Uncle Xue."

Mei Xiaoxue stared up and said curiously, "Uncle Xue, hello. Do you have the same name as me? I can be Little Snow, and you can be Big Snow."

Xue Yu tweaked her nose. "Silly child, not 'Xue' as in snow. Xue is my surname. I'm called Xue Yu."

Xiaoxue smiled awkwardly and hid behind her Mommy Mei. A dozen or so of the younger orphans who weren't at school yet came surging out then, clustering tightly around her, babbling loudly like a nest of sparrows. Mei Yin's face lit up and she hugged every child, then greeted the two mothers. Mother Liu said, "Director Mei, the children have longed for you so much, especially Xiaoxue. Today she specially asked to stay home, and she's been running in and out the whole day."

"I'm so sorry I can't stay longer," said Mei Yin. "I got a phone call an hour ago saying my father's very ill, so I need to hurry back to America. I won't be able to see the kids who're at school now, and I won't be around for the birthday celebration either. Please explain this to the children for me. I'll make it up to them. The birthday cake for today's been ordered, so you should enjoy that, and when I get back from the States I'll get an even bigger one."

Hearing that she was leaving right away, the children stopped smiling. Xiaoxue's tears began flowing. Mei Yin quickly pulled the girl to her and scolded her. "Xiaoxue, look at you! You're the oldest of all the children, and I was hoping you'd help me to comfort them. Instead, you're the first one to start crying. Don't be sad, I'll be back in two weeks at the most. I won't go to Wuhan then, I'll come straight here and celebrate your birthdays with you. How about that?"

Mei Yin hugged them all again, said good-bye, and hurried away. As he started the engine, Xue Yu noticed Xiaoxue by the entrance, waving, her eyes once more full of tears.

The car sped onto the expressway. "Xue," said Mei Yin. "You're good with children. Thanks for stepping in earlier."

"I'm like the king of the children, wherever I go—I always end up having fun with the kids. Ms. Mei, you can tell that these kids feel very close to you, maybe even more than a birth mother."

Mei Yin sighed lightly. "Yes. These thirty-two children bring me a lot of happiness. Whenever anything clouds my horizons, I just come here and the bad mood vanishes right away."

"That girl, Xiaoxue, seems especially close to you."

"She was the first orphan we took in, even before the orphanage opened. I've seen the most of her, so our relationship naturally runs deeper."

Mei Yin's phone rang at that moment. It was General Manager Sun. "Sister Mei, the connecting flight has been arranged, you'll be in San Francisco by morning the day after tomorrow. Li from the Zhengzhou office admin department will meet you at the airport. Have a good trip, Mei Yin. I'll wait for you to come back," he said, his meaning clear to Mei Yin.

"All right. Thank you."

Mei Yin didn't say a word for the rest of the trip, as her anxiety for her adoptive father grew. In the more than twenty years since she'd left him, she'd only seen him twice. He was an old man. Besides the story he'd told her, of the first time he'd seen her, the memory that was burned deepest into her mind was in Africa, the year she turned twelve, when he brought her there to see the wildlife, the wildebeest herds so vast they blotted out the sun, murderous crocodiles in the rivers, lions glaring at their prey from the grass, vultures shuffling along the ground, not to mention the terrible epidemic in the Yambio region of the Sudan . . . It was after this trip to Africa that her adoptive father became the Godfather.

Three hours later, they'd arrived at Zhengzhou Airport, where they found young Miss Li waiting for them at the entrance. She handed over the tickets and a little leather case, saying, "General Manager Sun said to get you a change of clothes and some toiletries. It was a rush, but I did the best I could. I hope Director Mei will understand."

Mei Yin thanked her. After saying good-bye to everyone, she walked through security with her new leather suitcase.

September 2016—San Francisco, USA

Mei Yin arrived in San Francisco on the morning of the third day, where her father's personal physician, Dr. Kenrick, met her at the airport. The doctor said old Walt had been in grave danger; his heart had experienced tissue death, nearly costing him his life. He was recovering reasonably well, and while he couldn't be discharged yet, he was no longer at risk. Mei Yin finally allowed herself to stop worrying. Before working at the CDC, her father had taught at the University of San Francisco, so he and his wife had chosen to live here after retirement, in a seaside home by the Pacific. They once joked, "Living here, it feels as if we're closer to our Chinese daughter."

Mei Yin and the doctor sped along Bayshore Freeway to the UCSF Medical Center, where they found Walt still hooked up to a drip, his heart monitor emitting a low, monotonous beep. He was in good spirits, though, propped up in his raised bed. When he saw his daughter come in, he spread his arms wide and grinned. "My little Cassie's come back!"

Mei Yin ran to him and gently pushed down his left arm, which had a drip tube coming out of it, before hugging him. "Dad, you scared me. I thought I'd never see you again." She was a little choked up, but still smiled. "But I was sure you wouldn't be beaten so easily."

Walt smiled back. "I'll be beaten in the end. No one can overpower the will of God, and I'm an old man of eighty-six. If you don't get to see me next time you're back, you shouldn't be sad."

Dr. Kenrick said he'd leave them alone to chat. Mei Yin said good-bye to him and came back to the bedside, where she studied her adoptive father. Although they often saw each other over the Internet, it was only now that she truly realized how old he'd gotten, with sparse white hair and age spots on his face and the backs of his hands. His skin was withered, and his collarbones formed deep hollows. She sighed. "Dad, I shouldn't have left you, especially after Mom died."

Walt waved this away reproachfully. "Don't say that, there's nothing wrong with you making your way in China. That was definitely a good move. See how well Heavenly Corp. is doing, the thirty million the Society invested has already increased to one billion. The tens of millions we get in dividends every year is an important source of funds for us."

"That's mostly the work of our general manager—that young man's done really well. I've brought him into the Crucifix Society. He was one of eleven new members. I'll give you the list later. I hope to have their crosses inscribed by the time I head back to China."

"No problem. Of all the countries in the world, we're expanding the fastest in yours."

"It might be as you said, China's collectivist ideology is well suited to our teachings."

Walt gripped his daughter's hand and asked tenderly, "And your marriage? In your last letter, you said you might be making a decision."

"Yes. It's the manager I just mentioned, Sun Jingshuan. He's proposed three times now. He's thirty-six years old, so by the Chinese zodiac, he's a full cycle younger than me—we're both born in the year of the tiger. I've never dared to say yes, because according to Chinese superstition, one hill can't hold two tigers, and the marriage would be doomed!" She burst into laughter.

"Well then, why not make the decision now? The age difference isn't an issue."

"True, it's not. But if I agree, I'll have to have at least one child, despite my age, otherwise his granny would die of sadness. After she married into the Sun family, you could say she practically forgot her own surname. Now all she longs for is for the Sun family name to continue. She's stubborn about it—it's hard for a Westerner to understand. Even young people in China don't understand, they think it's just outdated rubbish. But the way I see it, this too might be in keeping with God's morality—focusing on the continuation of the species rather than the life or death of any individual."

After a moment, she went on. "She's a good woman, and I respect her a lot. If I decide to accept her grandson's proposal—or, to put it the Chinese way, to marry into the Sun household—then I couldn't bear to disappoint her. That's my only hesitation."

"Having a baby in your forties isn't a problem at all. The oldest mother in the world was around sixty-seven, I think."

"I know. I think I'll make my decision before going back to China."

"Child," said Walt, smiling, "you're deciding to have a baby because of an old granny who wants a great-grandchild. You may have lived in the States for more than a decade, but you're fundamentally still Chinese. An American woman would never take all that into consideration."

"Yes, that's true. I didn't used to think this way, but living in China, there's a sort of weight in the air that you can't resist."

She continued. "Now, no more talking. Close your eyes and have a rest. You mustn't tire yourself out or get too excited, it's bad for your heart."

Before he shut his eyes, Walt said, "This talk of God's morality reminds me of something. In the last few years, an independent forum called 'God is Here with Me' has sprung up. It's heavy on philosophy, and its viewpoints are mostly quite extreme, but some of the content is brilliant. Everyone posts on the website, though there's also a regular meeting at a college, once per season, and quite a few people come from abroad to attend. I've been a part of it ever since it was founded, trying to find like-minded people, and sure enough, a few have come my way. Why don't you go on my behalf this time? You can expand on the point about traditional morality for your speech. The gathering is tomorrow, at the UCSF School of Medicine."

"All right."

He closed his eyes, but said after a moment, "I have another reason for wanting you to go. While you're there, look out for someone called Zia Baj. He was a student of mine more than ten years ago, an extremely talented virologist, Afghan or Pakistani, I can't remember, a Pashtun tribal leader's son from the border region. Anyway, I didn't stay in touch with him after I retired, but I ran into him a few months ago at one of these meetings. After more than a decade, he'd changed a great deal. His words were—how can I put it? All the speeches at the meetings are very extreme, even heretical, but he seemed to have a sort of bloodlust, too. Keep an eye on him."

"You mean . . ."

"I'm not sure yet. I think this man might be of use to us. Let's see."

The next morning, Mei Yin headed to a conference room at the UC San Francisco School of Medicine. The room held an oval table, with places around it for more than forty people, most of which were taken. Mei Yin found an empty seat, and was greeted politely by those around her. In front of each person was a bottle of mineral water, and in the middle of the table were several inexpensive potted plants. An electronic blackboard stood at one end, and on the lectern was a bow-shaped mask that covered each speaker's eyes. Her father had explained that this was one of their little rituals. Before speaking, everyone had to disclose their real identity, to show that each speaker was taking responsibility for his or her words. Next, they'd put on the mask, symbolizing a moving away from the subjective, taking an objective standpoint, which is to say, a godly one.

The current speaker was a Russian man, a professor at St. Petersburg University. His English wasn't very good, and he frequently had to stop to find the right word, but everyone listened intently. His topic was "Energy Sources in the Next Century." Mei Yin had little grounding in physics, but the man seemed to be proposing the use of micro black holes to consume trash and other "waste matter produced by societal metabolism." It sounded a bit like science fiction to her, and indeed, at the end of the speech, another participant raised his hand to challenge him, asking how he proposed to keep these black holes under control.

Mei Yin didn't hear the answer because an old man who looked Chinese came in then. Sweeping his eyes across the room, he noticed Mei Yin and cheerfully walked over, pulling up a chair to sit beside her.

Leaning over, he whispered in Mandarin, "It's a small world, Ms. Mei. I didn't expect to see you here." Seeing her confusion, he added, "Xue Yu's uncle. I met you in Wuhan last year, while visiting him."

Now Mei Yin remembered. His name was Zhao Yuzhou, a retired professor of Tsinghua University, a neurotic, bigoted old man. She'd met him only once, on a staircase at the Wuhan Institute of Virology's Zhengdian Research Laboratory.

"Ah yes, Mr. Zhao. What a coincidence. I didn't expect to see you in America either."

"Are you visiting relatives?"

"Yes, my adoptive father's heart disease took a bad turn. And you? Is this a family visit or a work trip?"

"Neither, I came specially to attend this gathering. Self-funded. There's no help for it, I've always been stubborn, and my sense of social duty is just too strong. I'm sick of reading online about these Western thinkers, their religiosity, their so-called 'be in awe of nature,' all that old rubbish. I came to have a go face-to-face with these people. This antiscience rhetoric is like opium, poisoning our young."

Mei Yin smiled and wondered how Mr. Zhao would respond if he knew she was wearing a crucifix with the very words *Be in awe of nature* inscribed on it. Hearing that this was her first meeting, Mr. Zhao seemed to feel a need to take care of her, and began explaining the setting, chiefly what sort of people were attending, what sorts of opinions were expressed on the website, which people were "anti," and so on. Mei Yin felt it was rude to talk about these folks behind their backs, and looked for a way to stop him politely. Just as she opened her mouth, Mr. Zhao fell silent, turning his ears to the speaker. A different person was behind the lectern now, introducing himself as coming from the Santa Fe Institute, which was famous for its studies of complexity, though he was speaking on medical issues.

Mei Yin stopped paying attention to his presentation, and began keeping an eye out for Zia Baj. Going by the description her father had given her, he was probably the man at the far end of the table, around forty, dark skinned, his features and clothes ordinary, of medium height, a little thin, unlikely to draw attention in a crowd. It was only something about his gaze, which was icy, hard, and unyielding—not meeting anyone else's eyes, as if keeping himself locked away. Mei Yin's guess was right, and when this person stepped up to the lectern, he introduced himself as Zia Baj, a virologist from the University of Idaho's Biology Department. His topic was "The Fundamental Nature of Genes."

"Before taking part in this forum, I said good-bye to three Native American friends, who were planning to retrace the Trail of Tears, a peaceful protest to remind white Americans of their historical sins. Thanksgiving began when America's earliest pilgrims were taught by Pocahontas, the daughter of a Native American chief, to plant tobacco, potatoes, and corn, and to survive the winter. Two hundred years later, they showed their gratitude in concrete ways! In 1836, white people forced the native populations out of the fertile plains, corralling them in the barren hill regions to the west. A majority of the Indians never made it to their destination, but died on the harsh journey there. This was the notorious Trail of Tears. Below the foundations of American history are buried 1.1 million Native American corpses, eighty percent of the native population at the time! Today, Americans despise Hitler for his massacre of the Jews, but actually Hitler's behavior wasn't as bad as theirs. And another historical fact we shouldn't forget: earlier in the eighteenth century, the powerful commander-in-chief of North America, Lord Amherst, had the idea of using smallpox to eliminate natives, thus becoming a pioneer of biological warfare. On January 24, 1763, a commander of the combined forces, Captain Ecuyer, deliberately distributed blankets used by smallpox victims among the North American Indian settlements. He didn't see a need to conceal his evil deeds, instead recording them proudly in his journal."

His voice remained absolutely steady as he continued to recite more bloodstained events, as if he were a robot reading from a history book. "The British biologist Richard Dawkins said that genes are selfish, and he was completely right. Those three Native American friends of mine are at this moment undertaking a peaceful protest, but what good will that do? Will it chase the white people out of North America, and return the land to the Indians? Pocahontas's kindness was rewarded with the near extermination of future generations of her tribe. As for the English settlers, they neatly accomplished the task of spreading Anglo genes far and wide, expanding their lebensraum, and now not only are they the owners of North America, they rule the world. They can wash the blood from their hands, pull on white gloves, and bestow democracy, human rights, charity, and good works upon the weaker peoples of the world. But actually, we shouldn't just blame the Americans. The history of humankind is, on the whole, a chronicle of murder. Those of us alive today are all the descendants of killers."

The next few minutes were set aside for questions, but no one raised their hand. His words had obviously incurred the anger of the audience—not that he'd spoken nonsense, no, his historical examples were all accurate, but true history doesn't necessarily lead to true conclusions. Taking one step past the truth leads to error, and he seemed to be publicly advocating racism and genocide, while cloaking himself in a veneer of rationalism.

Yet Mei Yin was confused. What was the point of coming to this forum and making such a speech? And what had her father meant about him being of use?

The mood of the room was restrained, and although this man's speech had aroused their ire, no one stepped forward to attack him. Zia Baj walked calmly back to his seat amid the audience's stony silence. A few more people spoke after that, and Mei Yin said a few words too. After the meeting, those who knew each other left together, chatting, and no one paid any attention to Zia Baj except Mr. Zhao, who beckoned him over. Mei Yin overhead him praising Zia's speech. ". . . your points were so sharp, ripping open these Westerners' old wounds, the syphilitic sores they're trying to conceal! It was cathartic to hear you speak, but I have to warn you, your final conclusion was too extreme . . ."

Zia watched expressionlessly as Zhao prattled on. Mei Yin shook her head at his pedantic tone. He was a born teacher, but you had to consider the aptitude of your students. How likely was Zia to be talked out of his viewpoints? Seeing that Mr. Zhao was just getting started, and not wanting to say good-bye to him, she slipped away behind his back. It was Zia Baj who spotted her and, cutting Mr. Zhao off, went over to say hello.

"You're here representing Walt Dickerson, I take it. You were sitting in his usual place, and I know he has a Chinese daughter."

"Really? I didn't know that was his seat, I just sat there because it was empty. But yes, I'm here in place of my adoptive father. He's not well, and I'm visiting from China."

"He was a good teacher. I learned many useful things from him. Please pass on my best wishes and gratitude."

"Thank you—he mentioned you too. When he's out of the hospital, please come visit us at home. His condition has stabilized."

Zia shook his head. "There won't be time, I've already decided to go back to my country, and will leave at once. This was my last social engagement in America. In fact, my plane ticket is for this afternoon."

He waved good-bye to Mei Yin and departed, leaving behind Mr. Zhao, who had lingered in the hopes of imparting more of his wisdom.

September 2016—Fremont County, Idaho

Agent Rosa Banbury of Idaho's Fremont County FBI dispatch center had been busy all day, and got home very late. It was the fifteenth

anniversary of 9/11, and several terrorist outfits had been creating
trouble on the Net, talking about commemorating the day with blood
and fire, as a result of which every intelligence organization in America
had been on red alert. Yet the actual day turned out to be perfectly calm,
with not a single attack on American soil.

Her husband, John, and granddaughter, Emily, were watching
television. John asked if she'd eaten, and Rosa wearily answered yes,
she'd grabbed a quick bite at her desk, so she was going to head straight
to bed. After quickly washing up, she changed into her pajamas. Emily
was happily watching TV, laughing to herself. Their son and daughter-
in-law had just left for India to set up a software company, leaving their
seven-year-old daughter behind, saying they'd send for Emily when
they were settled. Emily was adorable, a lively, playful child. When the
time came to send her away, she and John would miss her. Now Emily
pointed at the screen and cried, "Look, Granny, three Indians are doing
the sun dance!"

The TV news was reporting on the three Native Americans and
their tour of remembrance. Only the Idaho local news was reporting
regularly on them; the national news seemed uninterested. They'd begun
three days ago, driving a Ford station wagon, traveling the Trail of Tears
and making speeches at various locations along the way. They said they'd
organized this tour of remembrance not to revisit old grudges, but as a
gesture of reconciliation, symbolizing the hope Native Americans held
for the future. They visited many elementary schools along the way,
performing for the kids with puppets and jokes.

Now they were on an Indian reservation, with its scattered wooden
houses containing wooden beds, low tables, benches, fire pits, and water
tanks, with wooden-handled hoes hanging from the walls, the entire
area surrounded by a wooden fence. There weren't many people on the
reservation, the young people having long departed for the big cities.
The few remaining Native Americans clustered around the car, smiling
as they listened to "Big Chief Sealth" speak.

The sides of the station wagon were colorfully decorated with all the totem animals worshiped by the various tribes. On its front was a Gamma symbol, to represent a century-old prophecy from Wakan Tanka to the Hopi tribe, about a "Great Purification," which stated that a purge would destroy the whole earth, including the white people, but that afterward the white man and the native would both gain new life in a harmonious new world. The trio in the car wore traditional garb. Their leader was dressed like Chief Sealth: straight black hair, a high feathered headdress, bare torso, scarlet and brown diagonal lines painted across his face and chest, and around his neck a bone necklace with silver and turquoise ornaments and a jade pendant. The other two were similarly clothed, but their headdresses were simpler and they wore bows and arrows slung across their backs, and held long spears. The trunk contained several objects made of bison hide, used for ceremonial worship, including drums, insignias, scabbards, and so on. The camera turned away to show a sixteen-foot-high half-body statue of an Indian chief at the village entrance, his head lowered in thought. A close-up showed exaggerated teardrops running down his cheeks. Needless to say, this wooden figure had been created to mark the Trail of Tears.

On Chief Sealth's face, though, there were no tears, only a joyful smile. The drums were beating wildly, and the other two travelers were executing a wild sun dance, which, according to legend, was taught to the Indian people by the great spirit Wakan Tanka, and had been popular among the tribes in the nineteenth century as an expression of rebellion against the white man. At that time, the officials appointed by the American government to herd the Indians into reservations had two important duties: first, to prevent anyone from doing the sun dance, and second, to prevent their children from speaking native languages. "Infractions" were severely punished.

These two didn't seem especially practiced at the dance, but they were throwing themselves wholeheartedly into it, staring up at the sun, their entire bodies shaking vigorously, as if intoxicated or mad.

"Sealth" didn't dance, but looked on smiling, speaking in English to the Native Americans surrounding the car. "My fellow tribespeople, do you acknowledge me as your big chief?"

His audience smiled, and answered raggedly, "Yes!" "We do!"

"Very good, tomorrow I'll represent all the native people in the United States—the Navajo, the Iroquois, the northwestern tribes . . . and I'll parlay with the American government, asking them to sell us the land that belonged to us, the entire country, for a good price! Do you believe me?"

"Yes!"

"Good, we're off now. May Wakan Tanka protect you!"

He waved, and his two companions stopped their dance. One of them leaped off the roof and got into the driver's seat, and the station wagon slowly moved off. When they were out of sight, the camera turned to a white woman of about thirty, who smiled at her viewers.

"This is Elizabeth Ginsburg, continuing our report from the Lakota reservation. Tomorrow, Big Chief Sealth will continue on to Fremont County, where in 1877, Joseph of the Nez Percé tribe led an uprising. In this significant location, Chief Sealth will formally demand reparations from the federal government. What astronomical sum will he ask for? Tune in tomorrow to find out."

The TV crew's vehicle went off in the same direction as the Ford, and from the jostling interior of the news van, the reporter gave out more background information. The man dressed as Chief Sealth was Robert Thomas, an employee of United Mutual and member of the northwestern Tlingit tribe, though he'd always lived in the city, and didn't speak any native languages. The other two men had remained silent and refused all interviews, so their real names and tribal affiliations were not known.

After the report, a commercial came on. Emily turned to her grandfather, exuberant. "They'll be here tomorrow. Will they come to my school?"

"Maybe. We'll see."

"I like Big Chief Sealth. He's handsome and looks friendly. Don't you think so, Granny?"

On the sofa, Rosa had been drowsing off. "What? Oh, yes, he does look nice."

It was getting late, so they sent Emily up to bed and came to tuck her in. After saying good-night, the child suddenly asked, "Is it true, what they said?"

"Is what true?"

"The American land—that we white people stole it from them?"

John and Rosa exchanged glances. Rosa said, "From a historical angle, it's true. But history is very complicated, it's not black and white. You're young. You'll understand, bit by bit, as you get older."

Emily snuggled beneath the covers and stared at the ceiling. The adults kissed her good-night, then as they were leaving, they heard the child mumble to herself. "Weren't our ancestors the worst people in the world? They stole the Indians' land and killed a million of them, then captured all those black people from Africa as slaves."

The couple's hearts lurched. These were surprising things to hear from a seven-year-old girl—impossible to explain, but impossible to deny . . . Instead of responding to Emily, they slunk away quietly.

That night, hearing his wife stir, John asked, "Can't sleep? Is it because of what Emily said?"

Rosa rolled over. "No. I was thinking of the three Native Americans on the TV—two of them looked very familiar, the two who didn't speak. But where have I seen them before? I simply can't recall."

"Maybe they're not Native American at all."

He was teasing, but this touched off something in Rosa. The two men had black hair, but didn't otherwise seem particularly Native American. The paint on their bodies and faces almost completely obscured their actual skin, but where it showed, it was darker than that of their chief. Their eyes were sunken, their noses high, neither of which were typical of indigenous faces. Now she imagined them without their native markings, trying to ferret out their original appearance, and felt they must be Central Asian or South Asian. So where had she seen them?

John was asleep, his breathing level. Rosa abruptly bolted upright, startling him awake. "What is it?" he cried out.

"I remember. I know where I've seen them before. A small farmstead near the entrance to Payette National Forest. They're not Indian at all, they're a pair of Pashtun brothers from Afghanistan."

"You mean . . . those two men you investigated fourteen years ago?"

"Yes, they were under surveillance for two or three years, but nothing suspicious ever came up, so the investigation was called off."

"It's been fourteen years. Are you sure it's them?"

"There's too much greasepaint on their faces to be sure. But—I'm fairly certain. Let's leave it. I'll get to the bottom of it tomorrow."

"All right."

Her husband rolled over and was soon asleep again, but Rosa tossed and turned. Afraid of waking him, she slipped away to another room, cradling her head in her arms as she thought back to the past. Fourteen years ago, the day after seeing Mr. Hoskirk, she'd paid a secret visit to the farm he'd described. She found the gate locked, and dialing the number he'd given her, she said she was there for a termite inspection. The person who answered the phone didn't seem to understand what she was saying, and in a heavy accent insisted, "If there's a problem, please call Mr. Zia Baj." He then gave her a number in Moscow, Idaho. When she phoned that other number, she spoke to someone with perfect American English, who said he was the titular owner of the farm, but had always worked at the University of Idaho in Moscow. Only a couple of workers usually lived on the farm, his cousins from Afghanistan.

"After 9/11 and before the Afghanistan War, they fled to the United States to avoid the fighting. My uncle, a Pashtun tribal leader, gave me a sum of money to buy this farm for them to live on. They haven't managed to learn English, so if there's a problem it'll have to wait till I'm back for a visit."

Rosa insisted on carrying out her inspection, and the man said to wait a moment, he'd talk to his cousins. He called again a few minutes later. "All right, you can go in. The gate has a combination lock, just enter the code 219. Someone will be waiting at the entrance to show you around all the areas you need to see. If you need to speak to them during your inspection, give me another call."

She entered the code as directed, and drove into the farm. A Central Asian man around thirty-six or thirty-seven was waiting for her, dark skinned and wearing a scarf, in a long garment that reached to his knees. He remained expressionless and silent as he showed her around the grounds. Rosa made a big show of inspecting for termites, though actually she was studying everything on the premises. By the time they'd made a complete round, she hadn't detected anything suspicious, just sturdy stalks of corn, dairy cows and alpacas mooing in their pens, edible fungi in hothouses. A perfectly normal farm. In the courtyard, another dark-skinned man was learning how to drive a tractor. He didn't seem very confident, and the vehicle kept swerving here and there. Rosa signaled for him to stop and come down from the cab, then proceeded to show him how to do it. He practiced for a while and thanked her in ungainly English.

Finally, they went to the living room, which had been set up as a place of worship, with rush mats on the floor and a crescent moon above the altar. Zia Baj called again to ask if there was anything else he needed to communicate. Rosa answered that the inspection was over, and she hadn't found any termites, but thanked him for their cooperation. They exchanged a couple more pleasantries before hanging up. It was lunchtime, and there were no restaurants within dozens of miles of this remote location, but neither Zia nor the two men asked her to stay. Silently, they saw her to the gate.

After that search, Rosa abandoned her suspicions of the farm. It might have been unreasonable of the two men to refuse Hoskirk's visit, but on the other hand it made sense that two newly arrived non-English-speaking immigrants might withdraw into themselves. Back home, she looked into the two men's immigration status, and found all the paperwork in order. Zia Baj had personally brought them over before the war in Afghanistan. Baj was an accomplished virologist at the University of Idaho's Biology Department, a second-generation Afghan American. As for Hoskirk's other suspicion: Why were the three buyers of the farm so unconcerned about its business prospects? She could understand that better now—Zia Baj himself knew nothing about agriculture, and had just bought the place on his uncle's instruction, with the aim of supporting his two cousins rather than of making a profit.

Nevertheless, she continued keeping an eye on this place. The following year, and the year after that, she visited again with the same excuse, and again found nothing suspicious. By her third visit, the two Afghans had switched to American-style clothes, and had a basic grasp of English. They seemed comfortable driving the tractor and with the farm chores. In other words, they appeared to be content to keep their heads down, settle in, and farm. She called Hoskirk to explain this to him, then turned her attention away from the farm.

Yet now, lying in bed again, clouds of doubt appeared on the horizon. She was more or less certain that the two silent "Indians" on TV were in fact the Afghan farm workers. If she was right about that, then why were they dressed as Native Americans? Surely not just for fun? But then, she might be wrong. After all, it had been seven years since her last sight of them. Drifting in and out of sleep, her thoughts roamed freely, and three numbers jumped up from the murk: 219, 219 . . . the gate code, still clear in her mind. Suddenly, her heart jolted. Reverse that number and you got—912. The day after 9/11. And tomorrow, the day the three "Native Americans" would seek reparations from the American government, just happened to be September 12!

What if all of this—the gate code, and the date of the tour of remembrance—wasn't a coincidence, but had been chosen for a particular reason, with a very clear message?

What if this was the sequel to 9/11?

If her guess was right, then their plan for revenge had been underway as early as ten years ago, when they'd set 219 as the code on their gate. She didn't sleep that night, and the next day, after sending Emily to school, she hurried to the office and dug out her records from that year, searching for the phone number of the farm. No one answered when she called, the monotonous ringtone like an ill omen. Next, she found Zia Baj's number. An unfamiliar man's voice answered. "University of Idaho, Biology Department. How can I help?"

"I'm looking for Mr. Zia Baj, in your department."

"Professor Baj has resigned and gone back to Afghanistan. He left two days ago."

"Did he leave any contact details?"

"I'm afraid not. He said he'd be in touch once he was settled back home."

Rosa hung up, a chill sweeping over her heart. Zia Baj just happened to have left the country. It was hard to see that as another coincidence. All these little indications were innocuous on their own, but pieced together, they traced a clear and ominous outline. Without hesitation, she drove straight to the farm. Already she had a bad sense that, if her conjectures were right, this was where she would find proof.

At nine in the morning, the colorful "Tour of Remembrance" Ford station wagon pulled into East Fremont Elementary, with a local news van behind it. Instead of stopping at the gates of the school, the station wagon went straight in. Still filming, Elizabeth Ginsburg gasped. "They've driven right in! School is in session, and they're not supposed to disturb the kids. Now someone's running out of the office, probably the principal. She's gone around the front of the car to stop them from going any . . . Oh my God!"

Elizabeth's cry of alarm was broadcast across the whole of Idaho, heard by all her viewers, as well as the county FBI office. That cry was followed by her urgent narration of events as they unfolded: "Two of the three Native Americans have jumped from the station wagon, holding M16s. No idea where those could have come from. They're threatening the principal, forcing her toward the classroom . . . Big Chief Sealth is following them, holding a traditional long spear . . . Now he's looking back, flashing a victory sign at the camera. How could he grin at a time like this! They're herding all the children into one classroom." The reporter's voice trembled with anger and fear. "These three men seem to be terrorists, and now they've taken dozens of children hostage! Viewers, or someone at the station, call the police right now! We'll remain here and keep reporting, for as long as we can."

The classroom door shut, and they could no longer see what was happening inside. The school yard was quiet again, now with the eerie stillness of a graveyard. Within half an hour, Fremont County, the whole of Idaho, and indeed the entire country had stirred into action. The relevant reports had been sent to Homeland Security in Fremont County and the state governor's office, as well as Homeland Security's Rapid Response Unit, and to the president himself. In Fremont, a few family members happened to be watching TV and learned about the situation right away, then drove to the school in a panic. One of them was Emily's grandfather, John.

After a nail-biting bout of silence, Big Chief Sealth emerged, and the camera immediately turned to him. He was smiling broadly, beckoning warmly at Elizabeth. She said dubiously to the camera, "He seems to be telling us to come in!" In a low voice, she asked the cameraman,

Francis, for his opinion. Francis nodded, and Elizabeth told her viewers, "We can't be sure this won't put us in danger, but we've decided to take the risk, and while we're in there we'll keep you updated. We're going in now. It's unclear how the situation will develop, and our reporting might be interrupted."

She and the cameraman got out of their vehicle and, still filming, walked toward the classroom. A piercing siren started up, and a dozen police cars appeared, stopping outside the school. Police officers in dark blue uniforms and the National Guard in camouflage scattered and took up strategic positions as they'd been trained to do, the silhouettes of marksmen appearing a few moments later in the windows of surrounding buildings, while other snipers fixed their sights on the classroom. Elizabeth's cell phone rang, and a deep male voice spoke. "Good morning, Ms. Ginsburg. This is Agent Hoffman from Homeland Security. I'm at the scene, behind the police vehicle by the school gate. You can go in, but please don't hang up, keep the line open. Be careful. Thank you!"

Elizabeth relaxed a little and walked into the classroom. Inside, she froze for a moment. The scene that greeted her was not at all what she'd expected: the children laughing and talking cheerfully, the "terrorists" laughing too, even as they strapped explosive vests onto the kids, although the bomb pouches were so small that they were obviously just toys. The children were having a great time, and those who hadn't yet had their turn cried out, "Mister, I want one too!" Elizabeth stared at them in relief, unable to believe her eyes, whispering into her phone, "They may not be terrorists, this might just be a prank. Agent Hoffman?"

Outside, Agent Hoffman saw what was happening on the screen, and was equally confused. After a brief silence, he said, "We can't be sure, keep observing them." Into his other speaker, he said, "The situation is unclear. I suggest we don't report to the president for the time being."

In the classroom, only the principal was outraged, sternly scolding all three men for going too far, demanding that they leave the classroom at once. Big Chief Sealth was all smiles as he cajoled her, while the other two Native American men finished putting explosive vests on all the students. At last they approached the principal, waving their guns at her, and she reluctantly shut her mouth. Big Chief Sealth smiled, and motioned for the children to be silent. They obediently quietened down, and Sealth signaled for Elizabeth to direct her microphone and camera at him.

As the events in the classroom were beamed out via electromagnetic waves, TV viewers were dazed for a moment, uncertain whether they were watching a terrorist attack or some kind of comic performance. Hearts in their mouths, they kept watching.

Big Chief Sealth put on a look of exaggerated rage, shook his head at the camera, and proclaimed, "Yesterday, I said I would begin negotiations with the government today on behalf of all Native Americans. At the moment, I have seventy-six hostages at my disposal, which I believe greatly increases the weight of what I have to say. I do hope the president won't dismiss us! Right now, I have a final diplomatic dispatch for the American government: four hundred years after your despicable occupation of America, you must pay the Native Americans transfer fees for all that land, plus four hundred years of interest. I am going to announce the amount of these reparations, which is not up for negotiation, so don't try to bargain. And the price is"—he let the pause hang for a moment before proclaiming—"a bison skin!"

A burst of laughter rose from the children. Those watching on TV smiled too. They began to relax a bit—was this a farce? An elaborate prank to make a point; an expression of four centuries of accumulated grievance? Even the stern-faced chief couldn't help cracking a smile, though he immediately wiped it off his face and barked, "No laughing! All of you—" He pointed at the children. "No laughing!"

The children's laughter grew even louder. Big Chief Sealth, suppressing a giggle himself, turned to the camera and screamed, "No one laugh, I'm serious! This is a warning. The United States government must agree to my demands at once, or I'll release one hostage every hour!"

Elizabeth Ginsburg thought she must have heard wrongly, and quickly thrust the microphone forward. "What was that? Could you say that again, please?"

Big Chief Sealth repeated, with emphasis, "Until the United States government agrees to my demands, I'll let one child walk free every hour, until they're all gone." He nodded at the reporter. "That's right, sweetie, you didn't hear wrong. I said 'release,' not 'kill.' But, when all the hostages are free, this offer will come off the table, and the government will be in trouble then! It'll lose the best deal it'll ever be offered. A bison skin for the entire country? That's a much better bargain than back in the day, when seven point two million was enough to buy Alaska from Russia. Think about it. With just a symbolic payment of one animal hide, you can proudly proclaim yourselves eternal rulers of America, and no one will ever be able to blame you again. No more guilt. Is that a great deal, or what!"

He chortled again, and so did all the kids, but Elizabeth and the viewers at home couldn't bring themselves to laugh. There was a hidden barb in his words, aimed directly at the hearts of all Americans—or at least the white ones. At that moment, a little girl in a vest squeezed her way over to the big chief and asked shyly, "Mr. Sealth, how much is a bison skin worth?"

He looked down at her. "At today's prices, about thirty or forty dollars."

"Then I'll pay for it," she proclaimed happily. "I have more than a hundred dollars in my piggy bank."

Big Chief Sealth laughed, ruffling the girl's hair. "What's your name, child?"

"I'm Emily."

"Thank you, Emily. But I can't accept your money. We couldn't possibly take money from children. We're after the ones who really owe this debt." He straightened up and looked directly at the camera. "In order to show the seriousness of our threat . . . Hey!" he shouted at his two companions. "Fire on the crowd! Detonate this girl's vest!"

Their hearts froze. The two men raised their rifles, and without another word, aimed them at the kids. Elizabeth and her TV audience instinctively closed their eyes, unable to watch, yet there were no gunshots, no blood-spattered scenes, only an enormous burst of childish laughter. What exploded from the barrels of the guns was not bullets, but soap bubbles, dancing colorfully in the air. The kids giggled and jumped up and down, reaching up for the bubbles bobbing overhead. Elizabeth studied the rifles and exclaimed quietly, "These M16s are toy guns! These bastards. They tricked us."

Emily was snatching at the bubbles too, when Sealth pulled her in front of the camera and made a big show of pressing a remote control, causing her vest to explode with a bang, shooting out colored smoke and confetti, showering the chief and reporter, not to mention the girl herself. The other kids got even more worked up, running over and surrounding the chief, begging to have their own vests set off too. The big chief squeezed his way out of the crowd, bringing Emily with him, and said to the camera, "This is the first child to be released. Emily, go on, tell your government to hurry up and fulfill our demands. It'll take three days and four hours to release all seventy-six children, that is to say, at two in the afternoon, three days from now, the offer comes off the table. If the American government doesn't take this opportunity, they'll be sure to regret it."

As he finished speaking, his two companions grabbed at him, pointing at their own waists, pulling up their shirts to reveal their own explosive vests. These vests looked a little more substantial than the children's. The chief smiled and added, "Oh, that's right, I forgot one last thing: before all the hostages are set free, the reporter and her cameraman are free to stay here, but the police aren't allowed in. Otherwise—these two brothers will blow their own vests!"

He pushed Emily outside. She didn't want to go, but reluctantly walked out. When she got to the school gate, her grandfather rushed over and snatched her up. Several police officers came too, examining her exploded vest to make sure there was no TNT or shrapnel there, but it really was just a few expended confetti cannons. The girl was unhurt. A bit calmer, John thought he should let his wife know all was well. Rosa hadn't been aware of the news, and sounded stunned at his phone call.

"They really went to Emily's school?"

"Yes. And now Emily's the first one to be released."

He described the whole tense scene to his wife, like a play, with all the unexpected developments. Emily grabbed the cell phone. "Granny, it was so exciting today! So much fun! I wanted to help the government buy a bison skin, but Chief Sealth wouldn't let me. Where are you? Why don't you come see?"

"I'm on a farm a hundred miles away. Emily, give the phone back to your grandfather."

John took the phone back and asked what was wrong. After a moment, she said, "Forget it, I'll talk to you after I'm done inspecting this farm. Stay close to Emily. Don't leave her, and wait for my call. You hear? Be ready to answer when I call."

She sounded deadly serious. John hung up and muttered, "What does this mean? Your granny's on edge about something."

Big Chief Sealth had arranged for the police to deliver food, drink, and toys to the classroom, and now told them to prepare bedding for that night. He organized games for the children, and set one of them free every hour. The kids were so thrilled that those picked for release pouted and went unwillingly. The chief had to urge them to do as they were told, in order for the show to go on as planned. He only got them to go by agreeing to set off their vests as they left. Elizabeth took this time to interview the two Native American escorts, who still hadn't revealed their true identities. Neither would say a word, and both refused her questions as they'd done for the last few days. The reporter could only turn from them in frustration, and talk to the children instead. Francis looked at the silent men with misgivings, before turning his camera on the kids.

A soft tone sounded from her cell phone. Elizabeth couldn't risk Hoffman's words being broadcast, so she quietly turned off her microphone. Hoffman whispered, "Have a closer look. Do those Indians have real bombs?"

"Looks like it," she whispered back. "I see wires and flashing red lights. Do you still think they're terrorists?"

Despite her precautions, one of the silent companions noticed she was speaking into her cell phone, not her reporter's mic, and quickly strode over and snatched the phone from her, violently smashing it on the ground. Elizabeth hadn't expected such violence—wasn't this meant to be a light-hearted farce? Some of the smiling children immediately looked fearful at this sight. The chief saw it too, and angrily dragged the man to one side, snapping at him. The man reluctantly nodded. Then Big Chief Sealth walked up to Elizabeth and apologized. "I'm so sorry, he's a thug. He's not actually Native American, just someone a friend found to help. I had no idea he'd be so rough."

"He's not Native American?"

"Of course not. But don't worry, I've spoken to him."

During their quiet exchange, Francis kept the camera pointed at them, so these silent scenes made it onto TV. Outside the school gate, Hoffman had been watching on a portable screen when he made the call. At this point, he grew much more alert. So a tour of remembrance had suddenly morphed into a terrorist attack, but then turned out to be some sort of publicity stunt, a roller coaster of emotion for the viewers. Only Hoffman had kept his guard up all along, and with an old spy's nose for trouble, sniffed out something rotten behind this jolly gathering. Big Chief Sealth's identity had been verified, and he was, as he said, an employee of United Mutual in Idaho, a cheerful man with no criminal record, who was well regarded by his colleagues. As for his two companions, no one had been found who'd admit to knowing them, and they remained ciphers. Their tense silence was at odds with the chief's open demeanor, like two images of different color schemes placed side by side. He couldn't help but feel uneasy. And now this outburst of violence had shown a rift between the chief and his silent escorts, leaving Hoffman ten times more worried than before.

He'd already asked Homeland Security technicians to compare the two men's faces against their database in an effort to verify their identities. And now the results were in, displayed on his laptop, but they'd hit four or five matches each, a total of nine mug shots and names neatly arrayed before him. Hoffman studied them, guessing which were the most likely matches. Just then, a subordinate ran over and reported, "Two priority calls came in! Both said they had urgent information about the terrorists. One from a Walt Dickerson, a retired senior figure in the CDC, the other from a Fremont FBI agent, Rosa Banbury."

Hoffman, no stranger to these situations, felt a wave of giddiness, and his heart beat faster. Even without having taken the calls, he knew his premonitions were about to be validated. Calming himself, he rasped, "Patch them to me, Dickerson first . . . Hello, Mr. Dickerson. Agent Hoffman speaking."

A woman's voice. "Mr. Hoffman, my father is recovering from heart disease, so I'll speak on his behalf. A few days ago, we observed a few strange things. Nothing concrete, so we can only ask you to watch closely. There's a possibility you're facing a biological weapon attack, possibly arranged by an Afghan American virologist who left the country yesterday. If you'd like a more detailed explanation, please send someone to visit us. That's all I have to say."

Hoffman got her address. "Thank you, Ms. Mei. I'll dispatch someone right away." Hanging up, he turned to his subordinate. "Officer, I'll take the Banbury call next . . . Hello, Agent Banbury, Agent Hoffman speaking."

She was an experienced operative, who came straight to the point. "Hoffman, I'm on a farm near the entrance to Payette National Forest. I can verify the identities of the two Native Americans. They're Afghans who have been living on this farm. I've found something here that you'll want to see right away. And make sure whoever you send wears a hazmat suit—this may be a biological attack."

"Thank you. I'll dispatch someone now."

Another child was released then, bounding from the classroom to the school gate. A dozen or so people had gone up to the child when the vest went off, showering them in smoke and confetti, setting off another bout of laughter.

There was such a strong contrast between the children's joy and the bizarre nature of the situation—but it seemed that only Hoffman could feel it. If this bizarre party turned out to be a covert biological attack, if the bubbles, smoke, and confetti were in fact impregnated with Ebola or smallpox . . . What if the terrorists' attack had begun four days ago, at the start of their tour of remembrance? How many would have been infected? And how many would they have infected in turn? Hoffman was an old hand, and had gone through many simulated biological attacks in his training, but he found himself breaking out in a cold sweat.

He hesitated no longer, and gave the order. "Report to Homeland Security and the president immediately. Strongly urge activating anti-biological-attack measures!"

◆ ◆ ◆

Earlier that morning, Rosa Banbury had sped along as fast as the rough forest service roads would allow, hurrying to the farm. It was 9:40 a.m. by the time she got to the junction. The gate remained locked, and the "Private Property, No Entry Please" sign was still up, though looking somewhat worn. She entered 219 into the lock, but nothing happened. The code had been changed. She called the farm again. No answer. No time to waste, and never mind if she'd be guilty of trespass—she got a hammer from the trunk and prepared to smash the lock, but a thought struck her just as she was about to bring it down. Putting aside the hammer, she tried 912, and the lock clicked open.

At that moment, she knew her suspicions were correct: 9/12—the sequel to 9/11. Zia Baj and the two men on the farm were determined to follow in the footsteps of al-Qaeda. A decade ago, when they'd set the combination to 219, they must already have been preparing for this day.

Her phone rang—her husband. He sounded agitated, quickly recapping the events of that morning: We've been in the middle of a hostage situation, only it turned out to be a hoax, now everything's fine, Emily was the first to be released, she's standing next to me now, don't you worry about a thing. Rosa was, in fact, extremely worried. It was hard to say whether Emily was safe, even at this moment, but she didn't want to alarm her husband before finding out the truth, so said she'd call him back after she'd finished inspecting the farm. She hung up, and drove into the site.

There was no one on the premises. The cows and alpacas were frantic, butting against their enclosure, obviously starving. This increased Rosa's sense of danger—real farmers wouldn't just abandon their livestock like this. Rosa didn't have time to tend to them, and instead ran around the place, looking for anything unusual. Everything looked the same as before, apart from the large fungi cultivation room, which was completely transformed. The wooden racks and dried wood for growing mushrooms were gone, replaced by a round metal structure, about twice the length of her Chrysler, all sorts of pipes coming out of it. Her training enabled her to recognize this as a biological reactor for the cultivation of animal cells and viruses. She'd feared this most of all. Those bubbles her granddaughter Emily was covered in were very possibly filled with whatever came out of this machine!

She didn't know when this thing had been bought or installed, having ceased her surveillance of the farm in recent years. From its appearance, it had probably arrived within the last two years. The other facilities were shabby looking, with only one ultraclean workbench and a sterilizer looking like they were recent additions. A bookshelf held a jumble of various medicines, and there were basins full of petri dishes. This was all any terrorist needed for the production of biological weapons.

Rosa went into the main room, where there'd been some changes. An arched niche had appeared in one wall, its edges decorated with shell shapes and scalloped edges, verses from the Koran carved into it. This was where they prayed. Rosa felt guilty for letting her guard down, for disregarding Mr. Hoskirk's alertness and sense of duty. This was a suicide attack. The two Afghan brothers carrying out the operation surely didn't plan to survive it. The mastermind, Zia Baj, hadn't shown up, and might in fact actually have left the country, escaping before the attack. The only thing she wasn't sure about was what role Big Chief Sealth played in the plan.

Rosa had no time to dwell on this. It was September 12, and the climax of the attack would surely take place today. Emily and the other children were in severe danger. Time was of the essence: First, she called the local station to get Agent Hoffman's cell number, so she could tell him what she'd discovered. Next, she reported to her superiors in the FBI. "I'll have to quarantine myself on this farm," she said, with a mirthless laugh. "I came into contact with the biological reactor earlier, and might already be infected with Ebola, or smallpox, or whatever evil they've cooked up. Send someone quick to seal up the place, and investigate what sort of viruses these were, then put me in a hazmat suit and send me to an isolation ward. I'll wait here for help to arrive, but before you come for me, go save those East Fremont Elementary students. My granddaughter Emily's one of them."

She hung up, went to the animal pens, and flung some straw over the walls. The starved cows and alpacas stampeded toward it. Rosa smiled grimly. Better to be a beast, she thought, at least that was more secure—animals don't become terrorists and hurt others of their own species, nor do they have weapons that can do each other such grievous harm.

A few hundred miles away, in his room at the UCSF Medical Center, Walt Dickerson watched a TV news report about the East Fremont Elementary students in Idaho. Mei Yin was hurriedly packing her bags. Her father's health hadn't completely stabilized, and the events of the day had agitated him, so his condition had worsened. She wanted to stay and look after him, but Walt had insisted that she go at once. He said the government would soon be setting their anti-biological-weapon rapid-response plan into action, and the nation might well be put under a state of emergency. Other countries might subject American travelers to increased scrutiny, or even quarantine them. If she didn't go now, she might be trapped in the United States for some time.

She deeply admired her adoptive father, whose mind was as nimble as ever, even at the age of eighty-six. The task she had to accomplish when she got back to China was time sensitive, and she definitely couldn't miss her opportunity. Her plane would leave soon, but she still had a moment to spend with her father. Putting aside her packed suitcase, she sat by his bed, glanced at the TV screen, and asked, "Any new developments?"

"No. Everything seems calm."

The TV was alternating between two scenes, the first inside the classroom with Elizabeth Ginsburg, the second outside, with a male reporter from the regional bureau who'd turned up in a second van after the incident broke. The children and the three "Native Americans" now looked a little tired, and had settled onto the floor for a nap. One of the men would raise his rifle from time to time and send a plume of bubbles into the air, but the kids seemed too tired to stir, only lethargically reaching for a bubble. Dickerson muted the TV and said, "They'll probably want to keep things quiet for a bit longer. Anything else before you go?"

"I'm sorry to leave in such a hurry," said Mei Yin with disappointment. "I haven't been back to our home by the sea, or to Mom's grave."

"I'll tell her you said hi. Your mom would understand."

"Could you also tell her that I've decided to marry Sun Jingshuan as soon as I get back to China? Before I . . . It'd be best if I could give the Sun family a child." She shook her head. "Am I even still American? I feel I'm going too far."

"Americans are the same, anyway, always clamoring for grandchildren. The day before, a doctor told me I'd live to a hundred, and of course he was just saying that, but I do want to live until—until the day I can bring my grandson to Africa to see the wildebeests and cheetahs."

Mei Yin sighed. "It doesn't seem that long ago that you brought me to Africa, and in the blink of an eye I'm almost fifty."

"Cassie," said Dickerson, looking straight at her. "This isn't what a father ought to say when his daughter's saying good-bye, but I want you to know: I'm in fine health, and if anything were to happen to you or your husband, I'd take care of your child."

Mei Yin didn't brush away these ill-omened words, but neither did she agree right away. Instead, she smiled. "That will never do. What about Granny Sun? She'd never send her grandson so far away."

Father and daughter were silent, gazing at each other, their eyes full of mutual understanding. Finally, Walt Dickerson said, "Let's not talk about this anymore. You should go now. Your plane leaves soon."

Mei Yin stood and kissed him good-bye. He was both her adoptive father and also the Godfather, the man who'd guided her on her path. This parting might be farewell forever. Her eyes were moist as she looked at the old man, whose eyes were teary too. Neither would express their sadness, but they hugged a little more tightly than usual. Then Mei Yin took up her small bag and walked out of the ward without looking back. Her cab driver, who'd been waiting for some time, quickly started up his engine.

Late September 2016, Nanyang, Henan-Hubei provincial border, China

With a hundred things on her mind, Mei Yin had forgotten to let Sun Jingshuan know she was returning to China. It was midnight when she drove up the weed-stricken lane to the courtyard gate of the Sun household and honked twice. Before the sound had faded, a window lit, and soon there was a clatter of footsteps, and the front door swung open. Wearing only briefs and a jacket, Sun Jingshuan exclaimed joyfully, "I knew it would be you! Must be telepathy." Then he corrected himself. "Or rather, I should say it was deduction. When I heard what was happening in America, I knew you'd come straight back to China. Quick, come in. Sorry about my clothes, I'll go get dressed."

Mei Yin stepped out of the car, and without a word, hugged him tight, pressing her face to his naked chest. A shiver went through Jingshuan's body, and he knew she'd made her decision. He embraced her in return, lightly ruffling her hair. They stood amid the pine forest, caught like statues in the car's snow-bright headlamps. From within the courtyard came Granny Sun's voice. "Shuan! Who's here? Has something happened at the facility?"

Jingshuan killed the engine and locked the courtyard gate, bundling his lover into the house. He called out, "I'm already up, Granny. You stay in bed!"

Whether or not the old woman heard him, she said nothing further. The couple went into Sun's bedroom and began kissing passionately, until the earth seemed to stop moving around them. After a while, Mei Yin pushed him aside. "Get dressed. I wouldn't want you to catch a cold."

Pulling on a sweater and long johns, Jingshuan asked, "Did you see the latest news?"

"Only on the plane, news from the day before."

He sat her in front of his computer, and moved the mouse. "You should see this. I'm sure it'll have something to do with you."

Almost all the headlines were about the incident:

Nightmare Comes True! Homeland Security Confirms 9/12 Incident Is a Smallpox Attack!

Infection Zone Has Been Sealed Off!

"Big Chief Sealth" and Two Terrorists Are Infected, Pox Marks Have Appeared on Their Faces!

Terrorist Mastermind Zia Baj Has Vanished!

American President Declares State of Emergency, All Flights Suspended!

Government Begins Smallpox Inoculation Program in Idaho and Neighboring States!

Countries Worldwide Condemn Biological Warfare!

WHO Spokesperson Urges All Nations to Act Together Quickly to Squash the Epidemic!

Mei Yin clicked through to the full reports. She'd left America only two days ago, but the situation had developed rapidly. No surprise there: the tour of remembrance had started six or seven days ago, which was about the incubation period of smallpox. Everything would move very fast from now on.

Jingshuan asked, "How did you know Zia Baj was the mastermind?"

"He used to be the Godfather's student. A few days ago, I met him at a forum in America. His speech was so bloodthirsty, it aroused my suspicions."

Reaching around her, Jingshuan took the mouse and started a video. His voice full of pity, he said, "It seems that, of the three, Big Chief Sealth wasn't actually a terrorist, just a gullible victim. Unlucky guy. Watch this, I think he's telling the truth."

The clip was shot in the evening, the setting sun like blood. The pox marks on Sealth's face were now very obvious, and he'd been so tormented by high fever and fits of shivering that he had barely any energy left. His mind was lucid, though, and he stammered into the camera. ". . . a friend, Zia Baj, came up with the idea for the tour of remembrance. I thought it was a good plan, and agreed. Baj even funded it generously, and hired two assistants, providing everything we needed . . . I wanted to stand up for the First Peoples, to show white Americans their historical guilt, to bring true understanding to these two communities, with a single bison skin . . . But I didn't know what devils they were. They told me we all have smallpox now, and the bubbles we were blowing at the kids . . . they contained the virus too!" His breath grew ragged. "My carelessness is unforgivable . . . I'm willing to die for what I did. I ask only that my mistakes don't cause greater hatred between the white people and Native Americans. May God forgive me."

The camera panned to the other two men, who were standing in the doorway, bare chested, bombs strapped to their torsos. Behind them were dozens of terrified students, some already showing symptoms. The two false Native Americans also looked feverish, their faces flushed, covered in blisters, their symptoms more advanced than Sealth's. One of them, even at the edge of exhaustion, growled fiercely, "We'll keep our promise, and will release one student every hour, until they're all gone. Before that, no one may enter the classroom! If the police try anything, we'll detonate our explosives!"

Mei Yin said, "They're trying to delay as long as they possibly can, to worsen the infection. At this point, they're still holding a couple dozen children hostages, poor things."

"That Zia Baj is an evil genius. The way he's organized this is absolutely flawless." Jingshuan let out a string of curse words. "That bastard! He's surely hiding in some cave in Afghanistan, laughing at us all."

"Yes, that's what Dickerson thinks too. He excels at using innocent pawns to put his plans into action, and manipulating white people's guilt toward the Native Americans. After the tour of remembrance started, people let their guard down, so he was able to merrily scatter smallpox along the way. They're estimating that at least a hundred thousand have been infected."

"Fortunately they caught it early. We're lucky that you and that agent alerted the authorities. America has three hundred million doses of the vaccine. I believe it can still be brought under control."

"It should be. We'll also have to see if governments in other countries are able to cut off transmission vectors in time. Now that flights in and out have been stopped, they ought to be able to limit it."

"Oh, that's right." Jingshuan opened the browser again and brought up an English article. "Speaking of Zia Baj being an evil genius, this piece says the same thing."

Mei Yin skimmed through it.

". . . Zia Baj is both talented and demented, yes, but the success of this attack wasn't his, but rather belongs to a sinister god. The Lord hates perfection. He does not allow any species complete dominion over earth. And so, in his unfathomable wisdom, he left humanity with an Achilles' heel. Even the most advanced fire-fighting methods can't eliminate the forest fires at Yellowstone Park. The most sophisticated security software can't completely wipe out computer viruses. And the strongest anti-terror measures can't rid us of terrorism. The rules laid down by God dictate that terrorism (or forest fires, or computer viruses) might theoretically be eradicated, but the costs would be too high, and the system wouldn't be able to withstand it.

"And so highly civilized and prosperous societies will never be free of low-cost terrorism. Our various protective measures must always take this pragmatic calculus into consideration. Which is to say, the historical elimination of smallpox might well have been wasted effort. The disappearance of smallpox from the world created a dangerous vacuum, one that could be filled with only a little effort, creating disproportionately greater damage. Zia Baj discovered and exploited this point. The hard work that medical and health professionals around the world once expended in the fight against smallpox only provided fertile soil for low-cost terrorism. Zia Baj must be grateful to them. Wiping out smallpox, or other viruses and bacteria, can only be a waste of man power and resources, creating a medical Maginot Line, Bar Lev Line, or Great Wall of China: showy but ultimately useless barriers.

"The Chinese say: Good fortune is the crutch of disaster, catastrophe is the foundation of luck. Taking the long view, Zia Baj's smallpox attack has breached this viral vacuum, and that can be counted as a good thing."

The essay was signed with a pseudonym. Jingshuan said, "It's insightful, but the conclusion is a bit callous."

Mei Yin had guessed right away that her adoptive father was the author, but said nothing. Instead, she said levelly, "It is a little cruel, but truth knows no tenderness."

Jingshuan shut down the computer. "Go have a shower, then head to bed. You must be exhausted. Why don't you sleep in this room? I'll get you clean sheets. I can take the sofa. The other bedrooms haven't been used for so long, they're cold and damp."

"No need for that. We can both sleep here. I've made my decision, and I'm not going to waste a single day. That'll make your granny happy! And who knows what will happen tomorrow."

Jingshuan hugged her tight. Mei Yin thought of something and pushed him aside, rifling through her bag for the eleven crucifixes. Picking out the one with his name on it, she hung it round his neck. "Maybe I was wrong to bring you into the Society. If you stick with me, you'll know no real peace in this life. Remember that Russian folktale? I'm the unlucky lizard."

Jingshuan held the cross up and studied it intently. "You did the right thing. I don't regret it either. I'd marry you even if you were a lizard! Let's not talk about that. Go shower. I can't wait."

Mei Yin had a quick shower, then burrowed naked into her lover's arms. Since saying good-bye to Stebushkin, she hadn't been with a man, and so was a little awkward to start, but with Jingshuan's kind caresses she gradually slipped into the right zone, and roused the passions that had lain dormant so many years. Afterward, Mei Yin lay in the bend of her fiancé's arm, neither of them the least bit sleepy, talking about this and that, listening to the dawn chorus among the pine trees. Mei Yin suddenly thought of something, and lifted her head to tell Jingshuan. "In the morning, go see your granny as soon as you're up, tell her we've got our marriage certificate already. You know I don't care about these proprieties, but she can be very particular."

"That's fine, it'll keep her happy. We can go to the registry tomorrow morning. Or, I guess, this morning."

"Tomorrow night—no, tonight—I'll need to be at the orphanage, to make up for that birthday party I missed . . ."

Jingshuan turned to stare at her. "Is it really starting?"

Mei Yin nodded.

". . . all right, so it's starting."

For a long time, neither of them said a word. They'd been preparing for this day for more than ten years now, but with the actual event close at hand, they were a little fearful. After all, there were so many uncertainties about the outcome, so many ideological and emotional contradictions.

Eventually, Mei Yin finished her previous sentence. ". . . and you should come too, so this birthday party can also be our wedding celebration. I want to keep it low-key."

"All right, we'll do as you say."

"Will Granny be all right with this arrangement?"

"She won't be happy about it, but I'll find a way to explain it to her. Besides, she likes you. She'll be so happy to have such a beautiful and sensible granddaughter-in-law, the respected Director Mei, that she'll loosen the old regulations around marriage."

Mei Yin chuckled, then suddenly jumped out of bed. "Come on, let's go to our lab."

"Now?" He stared at the clock. "It's four-forty. But fine, let's go, I won't get to sleep anyway."

They got dressed and slipped out the door, walking down the weed-choked road out of the pine forest to the facility gate. The night guard hurried to welcome the chairperson and general manager, but Jingshuan stopped him with a raised finger. They used their keycards to get through both sets of doors, then opened up the lab, and went into the empty space. The room was fitted with negative-pressure workstations, three small bioreactors, and a dozen or so other machines. This was where Mei Yin had taught Jingshuan to cultivate the smallpox virus, where he'd successfully created the RYM and RNM cell lines, initially designed as hosts for the smallpox. Nineteen years ago, Stebushkin had given her three small vials of the virus, containing the West African, Asian, and South American varieties. They'd bred many generations of them, hundreds of pounds' worth. The viruses slumbered quietly in their baths of liquid nitrogen. The three small biological reactors were always working away, each containing a smallpox variant, endlessly reproducing, keeping the virus active. To ensure secrecy, most of the work was done by Jingshuan and Mei Yin themselves, with a few lab assistants to deal with manual labor. When Mei Yin wasn't in Xinye, it was hard on Jingshuan, who had to carry out this work on top of his duties as general manager.

They gazed in silence at the liquid nitrogen tanks and biological reactors. Mei Yin said, "The last few years have been hard on you."

"Not at all. I'm happy to work hard for my lizard goddess." He smiled. "I'm in good health, it won't hurt me to burn the midnight oil now and then."

"The smallpox demon is reborn in America, and we won't be able to keep our secret much longer. Remember what we decided: if anything goes wrong, insist that this was all my handiwork."

"I'll keep my word."

"If this gets out, it could even put Jin's position in danger. He's a good official, business minded, steadfast, and honest. I'd feel bad if he was affected."

"We'll keep this as far from him as we can."

"And also, this young fellow, Xue Yu, isn't bad. He's down-to-earth, fairly mature, knows when to keep his mouth shut, and he's quite sharp on the technological side too. I want to bring him on board, to take over your work in this lab. You're too busy with all your other duties. Oh, by the way, I met his uncle in America. The old man was so pedantic, it was ridiculous. He even tried to teach Zia Baj a lesson."

"That's fine. I have a good impression of Xue Yu too."

Mei Yin smiled. "I'm in an odd frame of mind today; it feels like I'm preparing for my own death. Maybe everything will go smoothly, and we won't need any of this."

"Let's hope so."

She waved the unhappy mood away. "Enough. Starting today, we're on our honeymoon!"

That morning, they told Granny Sun that they were going to buy some things for the wedding, but first had to go to the register at the local government office. The official there didn't recognize them, but seeing their names, exclaimed, "Mei Yin! Sun Jingshuan! You're celebrities in Xinye!"

Jingshuan laughed. "My wife hates being famous, so we're trying to keep our wedding as quiet as possible. Please don't make a fuss."

Mei Yin phoned the Sacred Heart to let Mother Liu know that she was back in the country, and that she'd be at the orphanage before dinner to celebrate the group birthday she'd missed, so could Mother Liu please buy a cake. Mother Liu crowed, "That's wonderful! The children have been missing you so much they're almost mad, especially Xiaoxue!" She abruptly changed the subject. "Director Mei, the American children have all been rescued! It was just on the news."

"Really? That's excellent. How were they saved?"

"They used a powerful tranquilizer to knock out everyone in the room. When they were snoring, police in protective gear sneaked in, cut the wires on the terrorists' bombs, put them in handcuffs, and took them away. Then they were able to rescue the children. Director Mei, do you think those poor children will be left scarred?"

Mei Yin hesitated. It had been three days since the children first came into contact with a highly concentrated dose of smallpox. They would now receive the very best treatment, but that was only a dose of vaccine, probably too late to be effective. Most of the children would succumb to the sickness and be left pockmarked, or even die. The people who'd been infected earlier on, such as those on the Lakota reservation, were probably already ill. She said to Mother Liu, simply, "I imagine the children will be very sick."

"What black-hearted terrorists, making children sick. The Lord won't forgive them!"

Mei Yin told her that she had married Sun Jingshuan from Heavenly Corp. in Xinye, but given the ongoing tragedy, she wanted no great festivities or formal ceremony. At that evening's birthday celebration with the children, they'd give out some wedding candy too, and that would be enough to mark the occasion. Mother Liu was delighted, although she felt the arrangements weren't fair to Mei Yin. But when the director insisted, she agreed.

Next, Mei Yin called Xue Yu in Wuhan to let him know she was back in the country, though she wouldn't be coming in to the research center for a while because she was on her honeymoon. She told him to pass all that on to the center. "So you finally married General Manager Sun?" Xue Yu asked, the pleasure evident in his voice. "I'll arrive as soon as I can; I wouldn't miss it."

"All right, come, then. Just bring some flowers, no need for a proper gift."

Xue Yu laughed. "Don't you worry about that."

After she hung up, Jingshuan asked, "Have you decided not to tell County Chief Jin—or I should say, Deputy Mayor Jin? He'll be offended if he finds out."

"No, we ought to keep our distance from him. He'll understand why, in the end."

After lunch, the orphans heard that Mommy Mei was coming to visit, and a wave of cheers rose from around the table. Mother Liu had another piece of good news: Mommy Mei was married, and the groom was General Manager Sun from Heavenly Corp. in Xinye. The children were even happier at this—only Mei Xiaoxue felt something a little more complex. She was happy for Mommy Mei, of course, but also a little—melancholy. Xiaoxue had always felt that she was the favorite, that she held a special place in Mommy Mei's heart. At times she'd even daydream that she might be Mommy Mei's real daughter, and that her daddy was a very good man, it was just fate that kept him from being together with Mommy Mei. Unable to part from her, but obliged to keep the true nature of their relationship secret, Mommy Mei had set up this orphanage. Perhaps, one day, Mommy Mei would take Xiaoxue away from here. But now Mommy Mei was getting married, and General Manager Sun was definitely not her real father (he was far too young), so when Mommy Mei did decide to bring her home, would General Manager Sun be unhappy about that?

She knew she was just daydreaming, but a dream repeated over years can come to seem real.

That afternoon, she practically flew home after school, and was thrilled to see Mommy Mei's black car in the courtyard. Mommy Mei embraced her and touched her cheek, saying, "Xiaoxue, this is Uncle Sun."

Xiaoxue studied the man standing next to Mommy, and relaxed. He was smiling broadly, with an open gaze, and was clearly a warmhearted, good person—not that Mommy Mei would ever have married a bad one. Playfully, she said, "Not Uncle Sun, it's Daddy Sun. Hello, Daddy Sun!"

Standing to one side, Mother Liu and Mother Chen laughed too—Xiaoxue could be very sweet! Jingshuan hugged her and kissed her cheek. Then a rental car drove into the courtyard, honking its horn, and Xue Yu leaped out, bearing a bouquet of flowers and a wrapped gift. Hurrying over, he said, "It was quite a dash, but at least I made it in time for the evening celebration. Ms. Mei, Manager Sun, this is for you. Ah, but I don't know what to call you now. Ms. Mei was my teacher, maybe I ought to call you Mr. Mei?"

Everyone burst into laughter.

Xue Yu asked about the situation in the States, adding, "After this terrorist attack, I'm thinking you were right in what you said before, that leaving a vacuum where viruses should be is like hanging the sword of Damocles over humanity. It wouldn't cost the terrorists much to cut the hair holding up the sword."

"I met your uncle in America. He'd made a special trip to attend an independent forum."

Xue Yu laughed. "Did the old busybody say anything bigoted? I know he's heavily into scientism. He believes that scientists will be able to use mathematical formulas to design human thought, and that it will eventually be possible to mass produce human beings in factories."

Mei Yin chuckled, but didn't express an opinion.

Half an hour later, at the communal dining table, Mother Liu led the children in saying grace, then put the lights out. Mother Chen appeared from the kitchen with an enormous cake, thirty-two little candles around its rim, one for each of the orphans, and two larger ones in the center, representing the newlyweds. The thirty-four candles emitted a warm, golden-yellow glow. When it was placed on the table, they could see the cake was covered in brightly colored buttercream icing, with the words *Happy Birthday* and *Joyful Marriage* across it.

Xue Yu had appointed himself emcee for the evening, and now laughingly proclaimed, "This is the wedding day of Mr. Sun Jingshuan and Ms. Mei Yin, as well as the collective birthday of their thirty-two children. I daresay this is the first time someone has gone into a marriage with thirty-two children in tow; it ought to be in the *Guinness Book of Records*. And now, would you please shut your eyes and make a wish?"

Everyone closed their eyes and thought seriously about their wish, including Mei Yin and Jingshuan. Then thirty-seven mouths blew out the candles together, and Xue Yu wielded the knife.

As he passed slices of cake to Mothers Liu and Chen, and the thirty-two children, he kept an eye on Mei Xiaoxue, with a catch in his heart. She was an especially sensitive girl, and the whole evening she hadn't taken her eyes off Mommy Mei, her gaze full of love, almost besotted. During the party, Mei Yin announced that before setting off on their honeymoon, she'd stay in Nanyang for a few days, spending her days at the Sun family home in Xinye, sitting with Granny Sun, and her nights—as far as possible—at the orphanage. "This is a rare opportunity, so I want to spend as much time with you as possible. It's been a busy few years, and I haven't been around as much as I would have liked." The children cheered, of course, particularly Xiaoxue.

The party went on till ten at night, then everyone saw the newlyweds to their simple bedroom. Mother Liu hadn't allowed Xue Yu to book a hotel room, insisting that she and Mother Chen could share for the night, and he could have her room. The bedrooms didn't have attached bathrooms, so after Xue Yu made his bed, he went to the courtyard bathroom. Passing by the newlyweds' room, he noticed the lights were already out. A little silhouette huddled by the entrance, behind the Lifan car. It was Xiaoxue. Curious, Xue Yu went over and quietly asked, "What are you doing here, Xue?"

She whispered back, "Big Xue, I'm standing guard for Mommy Mei. Just now, Mei Xiaokai, Xue Yuanyuan, and a few of the others were trying to eavesdrop. I chased them away."

"But why?" Xue Yu asked. "It's normal to tease the newlyweds and eavesdrop on them. That's part of our wedding night tradition."

Xiaoxue replied awkwardly, "I thought because Mommy Mei's age is . . . not small, if there's too much mischief, she might feel embarrassed."

Xue Yu dragged her away from her post and patted her on the head. "You complicated child, you should go back, it's late, and no one else is going to turn up to eavesdrop. You love Mommy Mei best, don't you?"

"Of course! She's the best person in the world. I think she's like Mother Teresa in India."

Xue Yu laughed and shook his head. "Your Mommy Mei isn't a nun. She might wear a crucifix, but she doesn't believe in God."

"So what? We might say grace at every meal, but none of us believe either. Let me tell you, even Mother Liu might not believe. The other day, I asked her if there really was a God in heaven. She said God was a good person that human beings had imagined, sitting high above us to make sure we didn't do bad things. As long as people had this fear in their hearts, they wouldn't dare do anything wicked. As for whether or not there actually was a God, she didn't say."

"Xiaoxue, have you ever done anything bad?"

"No."

"Really, no? Not even once?"

"Truly." Looking at Xue Yu, she said stoutly, "What's so strange about that? Mommy Mei's been alive forty-nine years, and I'm sure she hasn't done anything bad either."

Xue Yu paused, moved by Xiaoxue's purity, and by her faith in Mommy Mei. He said it was getting late, and she should go to bed. Xiaoxue said good-night and skipped away.

Xue Yu watched as her little shadow disappeared, then shook his head and went back to his own room. For a very long time after that, this combined birthday and wedding celebration, and afterward his idle chat with Xiaoxue, remained carved in his memory. The mind plays tricks, though, and in the version he remembered, it was not moonlight or electric lamps that hung behind them, but golden-yellow candlelight, swirling gently through the air. Later, when the black wing of catastrophe dipped down to brush the orphanage, and tarred Xiaoxue's beautiful, adorable soul; when he had to harden his heart and denounce his beloved Ms. Mei to the government; when Mei Xiaoxue vanished and he went in search of her throughout the wide world—this golden scenario still shone in his mind from time to time. By then, though, it was no longer a lingering moment of happiness, but had become an instrument of torture.

December 2016—Tokyo, Japan

The hostess slid open the door, her face wreathed with smiles, and bowed to Akiji Nakamura and Omar Nasri. "Honored guests, welcome, please come in."

As the two men entered, she retreated, still on her knees, shutting the door behind her. The room was simply decorated, with an old-fashioned paper sliding door facing a bamboo woven screen, in front of which was a bonsai tree with gnarled branches, and an ancient Chinese ink painting on the wall. There was a mild, springlike warmth in the room, in contrast to the icy snow outside. Even so, the temperature wasn't too high—it was kept low enough to prevent the geishas from perspiring. Due to the special nature of the *nyotaimori* service, sweat was absolutely out of the question.

The geisha serving them had been prepared: she was completely naked apart from flower petals covering her nipples and crotch, lying flat on the dining table—in fact, she *was* the dining table—with an unvarnished wooden boat-shaped structure beneath her. Her hair fanned out elegantly, with more petals elegantly strewn across it. Her eyes stared at the ceiling, a smile fixed on her face. This posture was a strict requirement in nyotaimori work, which is why her smile was a little stiff. It wasn't unusual, in these kinds of banquets, for geishas to be used as props.

The two visitors, dressed in traditional bathrobes, sat cross-legged beside her. The sushi hadn't yet been placed on her body, but the man named Omar was already wide-eyed. The elegant body before him was good enough to eat—you could even say she was the main course. Nyotaimori geishas need to keep their bodies in good shape, and as these were special guests, they'd chosen the very best. Her breasts and buttocks were full and firm, her waist slender, and her skin as smooth and soft as butter, almost transparent, so clear you could see the blood vessels beneath. And as for the parts half-concealed beneath three flower petals, enough was visible to inflame the male imagination.

Playing the host, Akiji Nakamura explained that in Japan, nyotaimori geishas faced stringent requirements, and had to be virgins with excellent posture. The process of cleaning their bodies before service was very strict. First, they had to get rid of any hair on their legs, armpits, and crotch, then ladle warm water over their entire bodies, after which they'd rub unscented soap over a sponge and wipe themselves with it. Next, they'd rub every inch of skin with a little hemp sack full of wheat bran, to get rid of dead skin. Then they'd soak in hot water, scrubbing with a loofah. And finally, a cold shower, to prevent sweating. Perfume was forbidden, as it would affect the taste of the sushi.

"What do you think?" chuckled Nakamura. "This is the finest embodiment of Japan, as well as an exquisite art form."

"Not bad." Omar smiled. "But why must those petals be there?"

Nakamura laughed. "I admire your directness! But these three petals are the reason we can call it art. If we got rid of them, only naked lust and sex would remain."

"I admire the Japanese, by which I mean Japanese men. They have such imagination. To treat women's bodies like this, turning them into an immortal artwork. I take my hat off to them."

The two men then went on to discuss this particular body, debating whether the breasts, buttocks, or crotch were most beautiful, picking out small imperfections. The fixed smile remained on the geisha's face, as if they were talking about someone else altogether. Then a server came in kneeling, and with practiced movements deposited a tray of sushi on her body. Nakamura said, "Please eat. Sushi tastes best when it's fresh."

Omar imitated him, picking up his chopsticks. He was clumsy at first, but got used to it after a while. Tasting the delicious sushi, sampling some Japanese sake, admiring the beautiful naked woman before him, Omar couldn't help thinking how different this was to his miserable existence ten years ago, suffering in that awful place on the Pakistan-Afghanistan border. He was much better off here.

On this occasion, he'd come to Japan as a sort of advance party on behalf of his superiors. He always enjoyed being a secret emissary: no need to put on a big show of diplomacy, no need to deal with reporters, and often a little something on the side for him too. At the very least he got to see a bit of the world, satisfying his bodily desires. On the whole, these secret duties fell to discreet individuals, not like those holding public office who only knew how to play a role and behave professionally. This time, for instance, he'd been the one to suggest sampling nyotaimori, prompting his host Mr. Nakamura to joke, "But doesn't that go against your religion?"

Then he'd happily arranged the meal, and of course Omar didn't have to reach for his wallet.

Ten years ago, Mohammad, as Omar was then known, had undertaken a difficult mission—delivering a final gift for an old friend of al-Qaeda. During that journey, he'd had a gut instinct that his leader was right to decide they would be "traitors." They'd enjoyed too good a life, and couldn't now go back to a hardscrabble existence, especially Omar himself, who from a young age had enjoyed a Western lifestyle, and was definitely incapable of living like Hamza: sleeping in a cave, living off basic rations, never having any female company. Here in Tokyo, with a nyotaimori feast before him, he felt in every one of his senses (his gut, his eyes, his nose, his skin . . .) the wisdom of the leader.

119

The meal lasted five or six hours, and now it was midnight. The geisha had been well trained, and remained motionless throughout, in the same posture from start to finish. The server brought fresh sushi from time to time, including marlin, tuna, cuttlefish, scallop, swordfish, and eel. The sake wasn't very strong, but Omar still found himself quite tipsy, and soon he'd whisked away the three concealing petals, and was staring lustfully at the forbidden zones, his conversation increasingly erratic, his hands roving. Nakamura was quite drunk himself, and chose not to see the offending behavior, though there was alertness deep in his eyes. Glancing at his watch, he suddenly said, "Oh, I forgot to tell you, an old friend said he'd come find you here."

"An old friend? Who?"

Without waiting for permission, Nakamura had stood to slide the door open, and a white man entered, also wearing a Japanese bathrobe, though he was tall enough that it only reached his thighs. Next to the slight Mr. Nakamura, he looked like Tarzan. Strolling over, he sat cross-legged opposite Omar, looking calmly at him.

"An old friend? You are . . ." Omar searched hard through his intoxicated brain.

"You don't know me. But we have a friend in common, and he asked me to say hello."

He pushed over a photograph of a slightly older man, one-eyed, with a full white beard, dressed in a prison uniform, looking downcast. Omar wasn't sober enough to immediately recognize him. It was only when he saw the two metal hooks protruding from the sleeves that he realized, and the alcohol in his body instantly evaporated in a cold sweat.

"Know who that is?" said the white man mockingly. "From your expression, I'd say you did."

Omar glared at him, then shot a look at Nakamura, who smiled back, the picture of innocence. Looking down, he tried a flat denial. "Who is that? Captain Hook? I've never seen him before."

"You don't know this al-Qaeda chief named Abu Faraj Hamza?"

"Of course not. I haven't had the honor."

"And you didn't make a special trip ten years ago to the Pakistan-Afghanistan border to give him Satan's present?"

"That's right, I didn't. I have no idea what you're talking about. Perhaps," he said sarcastically, "you're planning to kidnap me and bring me to the States for a lie detector test? Or to Guantánamo for a spell of incarceration and torture? That's right, 'torture' is too coarse a word, I know American government documents prefer a more diplomatic turn of phrase, like 'interrogation by other means' or 'bodily persuasion.' Mr. Nakamura, will you be helping him 'persuade' me?"

Nakamura had taken on the otherworldly expression of an old monk, a smile fixed on his face, his eyelids barely raised. The white man's face turned serious, and his eyes now held the sharpness of a razor.

"Here are some facts and figures, Mr. Mohammad Ahmed Segum, alias Mr. Omar Nasri. Three months ago, between the sixth and the twelfth of September, a terrorist named Zia Baj cleverly orchestrated the biological attack on Idaho. A total of 100,481 people were infected with smallpox, with 34,545 receiving a confirmed diagnosis—over thirty thousand! Fortunately America has a strong vaccine program, and the attack took place in a rural area, so the epidemic was quickly dealt with, and didn't spread to the rest of the country or beyond. Only China subsequently suffered an outbreak. Even so, a hundred and forty-three people died in America, and more than ten thousand were permanently disfigured, their faces pockmarked for the rest of their lives. We haven't yet finished calculating the total damage to the economy from this disaster, but it's estimated to be more than fifty billion dollars. Having heard these numbers, in your view, would we treat the perpetrators of this outrage with kindness? Or do you think you're out of America's reach?"

Omar felt cold sweat pouring down his back. This man wasn't making empty threats. If he was here to carry out a black op, Omar's diplomatic status wouldn't do him any good, and the friendly Mr. Nakamura wouldn't even furrow his brow while handing him over. He didn't dare say a word, and the man continued. "You might already know that Hamza was captured at the end of August, and he hasn't exactly kept his mouth shut, but unfortunately his confession came too late, so we weren't able to prevent this attack."

Omar worked to calm himself. He'd been very careful throughout this whole affair, and definitely hadn't left any physical evidence. If all they had was Hamza's testimony, the United States wouldn't be able to put a whole country in the defendant's chair—ten years ago, the false reports about Iraq had more or less destroyed America's reputation. Besides, if that really was their intention, this meeting wouldn't be taking place in such a clandestine setting. Thinking of this, he relaxed and smiled, then pressed the bell to summon the hostess. "Please bring some chopsticks for this gentleman," he said politely. "We'll keep talking as we eat, if that's all right? Please, help yourself. Your accusation is very interesting. Do go on."

The man batted a hand in refusal, and waited for the hostess to leave before smiling coldly. "No need to worry, we have no wish to create a big fuss. After all, your leader has been set up by the West as a model example of a reformed character, the only one we have, so it's still useful for us to leave him on display. We wouldn't want to force his hand."

Omar relaxed even more, and pricked up his ears.

"We came looking for you for two reasons. I'll get them over with, then I'll go. Firstly, could you confirm whether you saw the virologist Zia Baj in the presence of Hamza?"

He pushed over another photograph. This man was quite a bit younger than Hamza, with a thin face and dark skin, a cold expression and sharp eyes. Omar studied the picture awhile, then said nothing (he didn't know whether he was being secretly recorded), but nodded gently.

"Very good, thank you for your cooperation. Secondly, America has suffered a great loss during this catastrophe, and your leader has in the past shown himself very happy to do good works. Perhaps he'd be able, under whatever name, to donate five billion to the victims? This would be a drop in the bucket in terms of paying for your sins, but it's better than nothing. When you get back, please pass on this message to your leader. He's a clever man, he'll know what to do. I don't think he'd trouble me to press him further."

The man stood to leave, then paused and pointed at the geisha. "I imagine this young lady has trouble with her ears."

Nakamura nodded. "Don't worry, she won't have heard a thing."

After the man left, the smile automatically came back to Nakamura's face, and he said sincerely, "I apologize for arranging this meeting without your permission. As you know, such things are impossible to prevent. Now that you've both talked through this matter, I'm sure the situation's better for you."

Omar couldn't be bothered to bawl out Nakamura, and besides, he had a point. His face darkening, he wondered how he'd report this to the leader when he got back. He'd been following orders in carrying out this mission, so there was nothing to fear on that score, and he wouldn't be on the hook for any of the $5 billion. It was just . . . so humiliating. If he'd known this might happen, he'd never have come to Japan. Now Nakamura asked politely if he was done, or if they should order more food. Omar snapped a refusal, then started screaming, "Idiot! You hog-ignorant bastard!" This was directed at Zia Baj. "You only killed one hundred and forty-three people! That's less than if you'd put a bomb on a plane. You wasted my gift!"

Nakamura looked affronted, but Omar didn't feel like explaining himself. He'd finished his official business, and the next day would leave for home.

A few days later, Akiji Nakamura received a diplomatic message, saying the leader needed to cancel a planned official visit for "health reasons." The same day the message arrived, the TV news reported that a middle-aged man had barged into an American embassy, and the normally strict sentries seemed to put up only token resistance before letting him in. A security guard came forward to stop and question him, but without a word, the intruder pulled out a handgun and fired cleanly into his own mouth. The dead man hadn't been identified, nor was his motive for breaking into the embassy in order to commit suicide known.

Seeing Omar's blood-spattered face on his TV screen, Nakamura gave a bitter laugh. The American government naturally knew this person's identity and motive. They'd know that better than anyone else, but could only play dumb. Nakamura sincerely respected Omar's leader, and thought the United States might be no match for him when it came to dirty tricks. Without question, Omar's suicide was a forced one, and one possible scenario Nakamura considered was that Omar had gotten back to his country but didn't dare to tell his leader about the five-billion-dollar extortion, and with no other option, had killed himself. A gunshot to the mouth was a silent protest—he'd sealed his own mouth. And as the leader therefore never heard of this demand, there was of course no need to pay it. As for the American government, they'd have no way to take this matter up with him directly.

After this, Nakamura paid attention to any large sums transferred from the leader's country to America. A year later, there was a donation to an Indian reservation in Idaho, to fund research into Native American history, a sum of $14.3 million (Nakamura's mind immediately sprang to the 143 people killed by the epidemic). Apart from this, there were no other major movements of money, though Nakamura had no way of knowing whether there'd been any further covert engagement between the two countries.

CHAPTER THREE
THE PLAGUE SOURCE

Fall 2016—Nanyang, Henan-Hubei provincial border, China

After the joint birthday and wedding celebration, Xue Yu stayed another day in Nanyang. The following afternoon, Ms. Mei invited him to the facility, to see the lab he hadn't entered on his previous visit. Opening the door with her keycard, she said, "Please go in. This is the lab General Manager Sun built for me. You could say it's for my sole personal use."

Xue Yu smiled. "You have the keycard for this door? Last time you told County Chief Jin . . ."

Mei Yin smiled back. "I was lying. I needed to keep him out; it wouldn't do him any good to see what's in here."

"All right, Ms. Mei, you . . ." He'd been about to say, *You lie like a pro*, but thought that might be impolite, and in the end opted for "You're quite a good actress."

He studied the room carefully. Not a bad setup, almost as good as the one at the Zhengdian Research Laboratory at the Wuhan Institute of Virology, though of course much smaller. It was clean and tidy, flawlessly maintained. There were all the facilities you'd need. Apart from the negative-pressure workstations he'd noticed before, there were also electron microscopes, multifunction high-performance liquid chromatographs, gas chromatographs, super centrifuges, DNA/RNA synthesizers, PCR amplifiers, and so forth. In an alcove were three small biological reactors, currently in use, humming quietly, indicator lights on.

Xue Yu asked, "What are you doing here?"

"This is my personal research project. I'm investigating the white pox virus, a mutation of monkeypox. It's very similar to smallpox, impossible to differentiate under lab conditions, yet harmless to humans. I think you must have come across data on this."

"Yes, I read a report. It came from the kidneys of African wild monkeys in 1972, and is scientifically known as the Herpes B virus. Is that right?"

"That's the one. Everyone knows that evolution is a random process, and generally speaking, organisms will never repeat mutations that have already taken place—the odds are simply too high. But viruses are an exception. Their structure is so simple, it's possible to list all the potential permutations. Which is to say, this white pox could perhaps naturally mutate once more into the smallpox virus, as they're so similar. All of that is conjecture, and as for the practice . . . How can I put it—I suspect the conclusion that 'white pox can't affect humans' might not be accurate, and I'm looking into this question. Of course, this is quite difficult, and I can't use human subjects—except myself."

Xue Yu couldn't help looking around this open-plan lab, and saying anxiously, "But if your guess is correct . . . that's terribly dangerous."

"There is some danger. But given that the risk already exists in the natural world, it's essential that this research gets done, so we have a warning."

Xue Yu had nothing to say to that. Ms. Mei was farsighted, but this didn't make him less worried. The main problem was the notoriety of smallpox. Anything connected with that disease came with an aura of terror. On the other side of the earth, tens of thousands were currently being tormented by this demon. No wonder she hadn't allowed County Chief Jin to enter the lab.

Mei Yin turned to look at him. "I hope you'll take over this project. How about it? The salary and benefits will definitely satisfy you. It's just that this research is a little far out, and I can't guarantee when it'll produce results. If you take over, you'd have to be able to endure loneliness, like General Manager Sun. Before you succeed, you might have to sit here silently for a decade. Think about it, and give me your answer within a month."

Xue Yu pondered the offer, and was inclined to say no. The project had a certain element of risk, which didn't necessarily mean he wouldn't do it, but it was something that ought to be openly debated in the world of science, with approval from the relevant authorities, not carried out in a private lab. For the sake of politeness, he didn't turn her down right away, but said, "All right, I'll think about it."

General Manager Sun and his wife would soon leave on their honeymoon. Before that, he made sure to delegate all his duties at the facility. In the evening, the couple returned to the Nanyang orphanage, ready to say good-bye to the children before setting out on their journey. Xue Yu went along with them; the next day, he'd take the train from Nanyang to Wuhan. After dinner, he played with the kids in the dining hall, while the TV showed a news report about the smallpox epidemic. Those who'd gotten treatment early, such as little Emily, had been fortunate enough to escape full-blown infection. Her grandmother Rosa was even luckier, and hadn't been infected at all during her time on the farm; she was back home now. Those who'd been exposed earlier, or treated later, couldn't be helped by the vaccine, and at this point, forty-three of them had developed hemorrhagic smallpox and died of lung infection, septicemia, or total organ failure. More than a hundred more weren't out of danger yet, including Elizabeth Ginsburg and her cameraman, Francis. The two terrorists and the gullible Big Chief Sealth were close to death, and probably couldn't be saved. Still more people had less severe cases, but were in a great deal of pain, with high fever, chills, fainting fits, and blisters all over their heads and limbs. The news reports blurred the more distressing images, but the atmosphere of despair in the hospital wards was still palpable. Xiaoxue said, sadly, "Those sick people are so pitiful. Those wicked men ought to be cut to pieces!"

Mother Chen forgot her Christian obligation to be forgiving, and added viciously, "Send them down to the eighteenth level of hell, where they'll be fried alive, or burned at the stake!"

Mei Xiaokai asked, "Mommy Mei, isn't the smallpox virus supposed to be extinct? Where did they get it?"

"In the whole world, there are still two research labs with samples of the smallpox virus, the Vector Institute in Russia and the CDC in America. But the terrorists might not have gotten their supplies from either of those places. It's possible that they found the virus in the wild, by chance. Although the WHO has declared it extinct, we can't guarantee it's been completely wiped out in the natural world, nor that some rogue country secretly held on to some."

After the news report, the kids began clamoring for a cartoon. "Quick, Mother Chen, change the channel!" The kids already in middle school usually had to study in the evenings, and the elementary school students also had homework to do, and weren't allowed to watch TV except for cartoons on Saturday, their favorite treat. Not even a disaster on the other side of the world could distract them. Mother Chen turned to the kids' channel and sat with them as the other adults headed outside to chat beneath the garden trellis. Xiaoxue slipped out too. Seeing her, Mei Yin asked, "Don't you want to watch a cartoon?"

Xiaoxue scoffed, "No way, those are for little kids."

"Ha, our Xiaoxue's a big girl now," said Mother Liu. "I know you just want to spend a bit more time with your Mommy Mei."

It was early fall, and there was already a chill in the air. Xiaoxue sat in Mei Yin's lap, and Mei Yin wrapped both arms round her shoulders. Xiaoxue leaned back, basking in her mother's warmth, inhaling that "Mommy scent," listening to the grown-ups chitchat, and felt peace in her heart. They were talking about something quite profound, and she didn't completely understand, but she was happy as long as she could be here, close to her Mommy Mei.

"Ms. Mei," Xue Yu said, "yesterday my uncle was interviewed on Channel Ten, did you see that? He said he's an optimist, and believes that medical science will advance to the point it will get rid of illness altogether, and in the future, human beings will live in an Elysium of perfect health. A ridiculously infantile mind-set. Channel Ten actually broadcast it without a counterpoint, so they're infantile too."

"Human civilization is still young," Mei Yin replied. "We ought to allow it a little unrealistic fantasy."

"Ms. Mei, I may be a virologist, but I don't have the least idea where viruses came from. Evolution moves from the simple to the complex, and viruses are the simplest organisms. You could even say they're the transition point between life and non-life, but they definitely came into existence later than single-cell organisms, because they require living cells to exist. How can we explain this contradiction?"

"Science doesn't have a single answer about the origin of viruses. Perhaps they degenerated from single-cell organisms—after all, degeneration is a form of evolution too. Another possibility is that viruses escaped from the DNA of multi-cell organisms, a little segment of DNA that finally managed to become an independent form of life. That's possible with DNA viruses, anyway. It's even harder to explain RNA ones."

Xue Yu joked, "God really is unfathomable. He created exquisite, wonderful humanity, cheetahs, tuna, and swifts, so why also make viruses and bacteria to harm them all? What a cruel joke. Twisted, even."

Mei Yin looked at Mother Liu, concerned that Xue Yu's words might have hurt her feelings. Jingshuan had thought of this too, and nudged Xue Yu with his arm. Noticing this, Mother Liu laughed. "Director Mei, you don't need to worry about me. I've thought about all this long ago. I'd never dare say this in front of Mother Chen. We're both believers, but after learning a bit about viruses from you, I'm no longer certain if there is a God in heaven. If there really is a God, and he loves his lambs, why would he make viruses along with the rest of creation? He created viruses, then he kept us in the dark, and didn't mention them in the scriptures, so we had to suffer so much, groping for clues, only discovering them after so many millions of deaths. How could a heavenly father be so cruel? It doesn't make sense."

Xiaoxue listened with interest, giggling. Mei Yin laughed too, and said levelly, "Mother Liu, you can understand it in this way: there is indeed a God, but he's not just the God of humans, but also of all living things. He doesn't love human beings or antelopes more, nor is he fonder of viruses or houseflies. He just laid down several rules, and then let the various forms of life fight it out among themselves, and whoever survives is the winner."

"That may be. But—that means it doesn't matter whether or not we believe in God, because he isn't going to give us special treatment."

Xue Yu howled with laughter. He'd never imagined that Mother Liu, after being steeped in the gospel for twenty years, could still be so open-minded and so clearheaded. Mei Yin laughed too, then added, "Actually, I'm an optimist too, but in a completely different way to Xue Yu's uncle."

"Different how?"

"The growth of human civilization has always gone hand in hand with 'harmony,' increasing layer by layer, and I believe this harmony will expand from humanity to the animals. Some animals used to be our enemies, such as tigers or wolves, and now they have our protection. That's not all: I think this circle will sooner or later expand to include pathogens too. They're part of the natural world, and as far as God is concerned, have civil rights too, and the right to exist."

Xiaoxue looked up from her lap, and asked doubtfully, "Including the smallpox virus? That wicked thing?"

"Viruses don't set out to be our enemies. They're only concerned about their own existence. If they could live in harmony with their hosts, that would be even more advantageous for them. Think about it: once their hosts die, they have nowhere to live. In the long term, the antagonistic relationship of pathogens and hosts will become more temperate. This has been the case with the common cold, with syphilis, and even with smallpox. For instance, the settlers to the New World were far more resistant to smallpox and colds than the natives. I believe that rabies, Ebola, and AIDS will go the same way too, though naturally that will take longer. If scientists can take advantage of certain shortcuts, they might make the process quicker." She turned to Xue Yu. "Here's where I part ways with your uncle. I think humankind can't fight nature. Science can only speed things along, not change their direction. His idea of eliminating pathogens altogether goes against nature, and it will never happen."

Xue Yu asked, "What do you mean, take advantage of certain shortcuts?"

Mei Yin exchanged glances with her husband, and smiled. "Human civilization hasn't gotten to that point yet, and if you try to put it into practice, you'd run into all kinds of roadblocks. So at the moment, it's just talk."

Jingshuan said, "Let's change the subject. Look, Xiaoxue thinks this topic's boring, she's almost asleep. Aren't you, Xiaoxue?"

Xiaoxue did look a little groggy, but her reflexes were quick, and she jerked upright from Mommy Mei's lap. "Who says I'm asleep? I heard everything you said."

Mei Yin said it was getting late, and Xiaoxue had school the next day—she and Jingshuan also had to leave early. Xiaoxue held her mother's hand as they went back into the dorm building, and said good-night.

She'd heard about half the grown-ups' conversation as she'd drowsed. The strange thing was, thirteen years later (by which point she'd be the mother of a six-year-old child), when she recalled this evening, she found herself able to remember everything that had been said. Unfortunately, it was only then that she understood the deeper meaning of their words, and the cruelty contained within them.

After breakfast the next day, the newlyweds set off in the Lifan. Xiaoxue saw them to the door, reluctant to let them go. Mei Yin folded the girl into her arms. "Your Uncle Sun is normally far too busy, but now for once he'll be able to take a break. We're going to all kinds of places, and should return in two or three weeks. We'll spend another day in the orphanage after we're back. How about that? Xiaoxue, that's enough good-byes, you should get to school now."

"No, I want to see you off before I go. There's enough time, I won't be late."

Jingshuan called for her to get in the car, then waved at Xiaoxue, Mother Liu, Mother Chen, and the group of kids who'd come to see them off. The car got as far as the alleyway when a black Audi blocked its way. Deputy Mayor Jin stepped from the driver's seat, his face so clouded it looked ready to rain.

"Are the two of you off on your honeymoon? You kept that secret very well."

Jingshuan and Mei Yin quickly got out and began awkwardly explaining that they'd wanted to keep the wedding low-key, so they hadn't told anyone, and especially didn't want anyone official to know.

Jin said brusquely, "I'm not an official, I'm your friend. Yet I had to hear the news of your wedding from someone else. Do you think I'm not good enough for you?"

The couple couldn't think of a single word to say, and stared at him in mortification. There was no way they could explain their difficult position to Jin, but they'd had very good reasons to keep the marriage from him. Fortunately, Jin didn't let the moment linger. His face softened, and he produced a thousand yuan. "I was in such a rush I couldn't even get my hands on a red packet. Please take this cash as my gift."

Mei Yin didn't try to push it away, but quickly accepted, saying, "We'll make it up to you when we get back." Sun Jingshuan smiled, adding, "Yes, we'll humbly apologize at a banquet for you." Deputy Mayor Jin snorted and said he had official business to take care of and couldn't hang around. He painstakingly reversed out of the alleyway, waved good-bye from the window, and sped off in a cloud of smoke. Mei Yin and Sun Jingshuan didn't get back in the car right away, but looked back at the orphanage. They were going to spend a stretch of time away from this place—the honeymoon was just a cover story. Although the plan had been laid long ago, now that they were actually putting it into motion, they couldn't help feeling a little heavyhearted. Mei Yin sighed softly. "Jingshuan, I really can't bear to leave now."

Her husband didn't say anything, knowing she didn't need his encouragement. After a while, she roused herself and said decisively, "Let's go! As the ancients said, you can't control an army with kindness!"

Mei Xiaoxue got sick ten days after Mommy Mei's departure. At noon, she was helping the two mothers to serve lunch when Mother Liu said, "Xiaoxue, are you unwell? Your eyes are all wet, and sunken."

Whenever Xiaoxue got ill, her eyes became dark and sunken, and the two mothers had once joked that she got more beautiful the less well she was. Xiaoxue forced a smile and admitted that she had a slight headache, nothing serious. As usual, she fed Little Niu, then quickly gobbled her own meal before helping the mothers tidy up and heading off to school. That night she became feverish, and tried to push through it herself by drinking several bowls of hot water rather than alarming the mothers. The next morning, she really couldn't hold up, and asked to go home sick from school. Seeing her little face flushed red, Mother Liu touched her forehead and shrieked, "Ah! You're boiling! Quick, let's get you to the clinic!"

The kids from the orphanage all went to the Jianqiang Clinic at the end of the alleyway when they were unwell. It was run by Dr. Ma, a retired physician who was in his seventies and skilled at both Chinese and Western medicine. He was very experienced but didn't charge them much. He had always understood their constrained circumstances, and tried his best to rely on his experience instead of ordering up a bunch of expensive tests, like the bigger hospitals did. After taking Xiaoxue's pulse and temperature, he pushed back her hair to look at the backs of her ears and her hairline, then said, "Not to worry, the child has chicken pox, a small problem. Her temperature's on the high side, so I'll prescribe some cimetidine and we'll put her on a drip for a couple of days. Mother Liu, keep an eye on her. If her temperature spikes, come find me again, or take her to the hospital."

"Is it infectious?"

"Yes. When children get infected with the shingles virus, it develops into chicken pox, which will sort itself out after a week. But this isn't the full infection, and the virus will lie dormant in the body, and might activate again in adulthood, this time causing shingles, which we also call snake-egg pox or dragon-round-the-waist, a rather troublesome illness. After recovering from that, though, there'll be full immunity."

"Should we quarantine her?"

"Yes, especially with so many children on the premises."

This was difficult because the children all lived in dorms, and there were a limited number of rooms. She left Xiaoxue at the clinic to be hydrated, and went back to arrange her separate accommodation. Jianqiang Clinic was a threadbare establishment without a bed, so patients had to sit upright while on a drip. No one was waiting, so Dr. Ma sat next to Xiaoxue and chatted with her. "Don't worry, Xiaoxue, chicken pox isn't a major illness, it'll get better on its own and it won't leave any scars, so our Xiaoxue will be just as beautiful as ever. Oh, I saw two cars come and go this morning. Was that Director Mei coming back?"

Xiaoxue was quite uncomfortable, but still answered politely. "No, that must have been someone else. Director Mei just got married. She and her husband are still on their honeymoon."

Dr. Ma sighed. "What a good person she is, to have funded the orphanage herself. It's been ten years. I remember before I retired, when she first came to Nanyang to set this place up and raise all of you. It hasn't been easy."

After she'd spent enough time on the drip, Xiaoxue walked back on her own. Mother Liu and Mother Chen had decided to let Xiaoxue stay in Director Mei's new room, even though using the newlyweds' room as a sick room seemed like an ill omen. They knew Director Mei would think nothing of it.

Mother Liu prepared some chicken soup, and Xiaoxue managed to eat a bowlful before falling asleep. Her temperature was still too high, her whole body ached—especially her head and back—and her limbs were so heavy there seemed nowhere to put them. The two mothers had to take care of thirty-two children alone. Previously, Xiaoxue had practically been half an adult, and without her to help, they were much busier.

Stuck alone in the room, moaning from the high fever, Xiaoxue drowsily looked around her: the "happiness" character on the wall, the pot of flowers on the table (she thought, *Don't forget to water those for Mommy Mei every day*), the simple bookshelf, the rack hung with Mommy Mei's clothes, the pillows that still smelled like her. After thirteen years she'd all but forgotten she was an orphan, but in times of illness, she felt all over again what it meant to be alone. She longed to be like her classmates, able to burrow into their mother's arms when they were in pain, able to fuss or even have a little tantrum, so their fathers and mothers would coo and try to soothe them. She wept quietly, her tears soaking through the pillowcase.

After two days on the drip, her fever went down a little, but more and more blisters appeared all over her body, even inside her mouth. Another six or seven kids in the orphanage also came down with a fever. Mother Liu panicked, and quickly took Xiaoxue back to see Dr. Ma, who examined her solemnly. Trembling with fear, Mother Liu said, "Dr. Ma, do you think it could be . . . it could be . . . that disease they had in America?"

She couldn't bring herself to say the word *smallpox*—even pronouncing it seemed to invite infection. Just think of the tragic scenes in the American infection zone. She shuddered to imagine such a catastrophe taking place here. She and Mother Chen would be fine—they'd both survived cowpox as young girls—but what about the orphans? Dr. Ma had been having doubts of his own. Xiaoxue's blisters were clustered around her head, which was a symptom of smallpox (whereas chicken pox blisters tended to be on the torso). Yet smallpox blisters ought to be larger and deeper, and usually sunken in the center, like craters, while Xiaoxue's were smaller and shallow. The two illnesses could be difficult to tell apart at this stage. But smallpox had been eliminated long ago, and he'd not come across a single case in his forty years of being a doctor. Smallpox had even been taken out of all the medical textbooks, a decision that wouldn't have been taken lightly. The epidemic in America was caused by terrorists, a special case, and on TV it said they detected it early, managing to cut off the infection, and it hadn't spread any farther. How could it have come all the way to Nanyang, the middle of nowhere . . . Then, with a jolt, he remembered that Director Mei was Chinese American, and quickly asked, "Has your Director Mei been to America recently?"

Mother Liu almost sobbed out loud. She'd already thought of this, but still couldn't get the words out—it would seem too much like blaming Director Mei. But it wasn't something that could be kept hidden, and so she wept. "Thirteen, no, fourteen days ago, Director Mei got back from America. She didn't go to Wuhan, but came straight to the orphanage. But she left the States before the epidemic struck. And she said she wasn't anywhere near the infected part, Ida-something, and she didn't look ill . . ."

Dr. Ma felt a sharp stab of regret at his carelessness the day he first saw Xiaoxue—he'd neglected to ask who the patient had come into contact with. Fourteen days, precisely within the incubation period of smallpox. "You said Director Mei wasn't ill, but that doesn't mean anything. Some people are naturally immune, but could still be carriers. According to the law, anyone suspecting a smallpox case has to report it to the CDC within six hours. I'm making the call right now."

Mei Xiaoxue stared blankly at Mother Liu, muttering, "What did Grandpa Ma say? Small . . . pox?"

Mother Liu could no longer hold back her tears, but hugged Xiaoxue tightly and wept.

Dr. Ma's phone call put a national operation in motion. At the Municipal Health and Anti-Infection Unit (a sister organization of the CDC), Xiao, from the Epidemic Department, picked up the phone, and with a start, her eyes wide, turned and called, "Department Head, smallpox!"

Department Head Yang Jicun felt his mouth go dry—the catastrophe he'd been worrying about for days had really arrived. He'd heard about the outbreak in America, and although the official line was that all transmission routes were successfully closed off, he'd instinctively mistrusted this. With transport so highly developed these days, so many people went back and forth between China and America that it would hardly be possible to completely cut off all these corridors. That was the unfortunate thing about biological warfare: as long as one person slipped through the net, the entire barrier became useless. A single spark could ignite a forest fire.

Yang Jicun was thirty-two, a PhD accomplished in the field of epidemiology, and knew better than his colleagues what they were facing. Over thousands of years, smallpox had caused more destruction to human civilization than any other contagion, including the Black Death. In Egypt, the mummy of Ramses V, from 1200 BC, showed traces of smallpox. Records from the sixth century BC in India mentioned smallpox. The virus was now classified as Level Four, the most dangerous tier. In ancient times, China, Persia, and Turkey all experimented with using the scabs or pus of victims as a preventative inoculation, but it was risky. In 1796, the Englishman Edward Jenner produced an inoculation, after which smallpox infections gradually diminished until, in October 1977, the final case took place in Somalia. It was the greatest victory in the war of human beings against pathogens.

The question was whether the victory was *too* complete. Most people, including the older generation who'd been inoculated, would have lost their immunity. For historical reasons, the Han Chinese had a stronger natural resistance to smallpox, but after several decades of the smallpox vacuum, the resistance of the Han Chinese would also have begun retreating back to zero. If the evil spirit of smallpox was really once again descending on Cathay, they would find it hard to cope with a large-scale outbreak: China's anti-epidemic infrastructure was nowhere near as effective as America's, though at least, after the

American incident, they had quickly bought a million doses of vaccine from Europe. There was no effective treatment for smallpox apart from the vaccine, which had to be applied within four to six days after infection to work. The government had focused on infectious-disease prevention in recent years, with good policies and funding—for instance, you could be tested for AIDS inside Nanyang. The problem was that this focus hadn't included smallpox! After all, smallpox had already been eliminated!

An earth-shaking catastrophe. During the Jin dynasty, Ge Hong recorded in *A Handbook of Prescriptions for Emergencies* that smallpox "was acquired during the Jianwu era from invading barbarians in Nanyang, and is also called the barbarian pox." The Jianwu era mentioned in the book was probably during the Yuan emperor's reign in the Eastern Jin—approximately AD 495. So Nanyang was already a site of smallpox infection over fifteen hundred years ago. Could history be repeating itself?

He grabbed the phone from Xiao. Fortunately, after the 9/12 incident in America, he'd reviewed all the literature about smallpox diagnoses, and at least felt a little more confident in his knowledge. The new textbooks no longer contained a smallpox chapter, and he'd had to go back to the 1979 edition of *Epidemiology Studies*, edited by Di Guanyi. Dr. Ma described the symptoms once again, and they did sound like smallpox. Department Head Yang asked, "Have you tried pricking the blisters? If you stick a needle in a blister, whether or not it deflates is the main difference between chicken pox and smallpox."

An awkward pause. "Ah, I forgot that one. Let me try it now—ah, I don't remember which it is: Smallpox blisters don't collapse?"

"That's right."

Rustling noises. "I stuck a needle in and the blister didn't collapse. It's smallpox!"

"All right. Keep the patient isolated. I'll send someone at once to take a sample, and we'll run some lab tests to be sure."

Yang Jicun then asked about the source of the infection, and as he listened he began imagining the outline of the infection zone. The orphanage was fine, that was a relatively easy area to seal off. The problem was that kids from the orphanage had been to school, so there were an elementary and a middle school to deal with, which then affected their classmates, teachers, everyone's families, and suddenly the circle was a lot bigger. They'd probably have to quarantine the entire town. That was still possible. The most terrifying thing was the first carrier who'd come back from America, Mei Yin, was currently with her husband on their honeymoon. They'd set out ten days ago. Where might they have gone in those ten days? How many people had they been in contact with? How many would they meet after this?

He tried hard to remain calm, but the scenario before him was utterly terrifying. He couldn't stop waves of darkness from falling in front of his eyes. Hanging up, he immediately reported to Unit Head Lin and Secretary Chen, and then set out with Xiao to collect the specimens in person. Lin and Chen decided to first call Deputy Mayor Jin, who was in charge of Culture and Public Health. Once they were connected, Lin hurriedly explained the situation, and said, "We've only just learned about this infection, so it's not verified yet. I just wanted to give you a heads-up, seeing as you've just come into the post and might not be familiar with the situation. Ever since the smallpox outbreak in America, the Anti-Infection Unit has been prepared to take preventative measures here. This will be difficult, but we will deal with it. The biggest problem is the original carrier, the benefactor of the orphanage, who's presently on her honeymoon."

Jin's grim smile was almost audible on the phone. "That's Mei Yin, I know her. She's a famous virologist herself. Have you been in touch with her? You should isolate the two of them right away."

"Yes. I'll call her immediately."

"Forget it, I'll call her myself. I have her cell number."

Deputy Mayor Jin hung up, his face dark as he sat, sunk in thought. Destiny must really love him. He suddenly recalled a month previous, when he'd made a special trip to inspect Mei Yin's facility. He'd been worried at the time that the workshops might contain some secret that might damage him professionally. Maybe that was some sixth sense warning him of today's disaster? And now look, while his original fears hadn't yet been realized, the source of the catastrophe was still Mei Yin.

When she answered the phone, he heard a lot of background noise, and her cheerful voice. "Jin? What's up?—Hey, Jingshuan, close the windows, the wind's too loud." Most of the noise cut out. "Jin, are you in such a hurry to celebrate with us? Don't worry, we haven't forgotten. We're hurrying back now from Jiuzhaigou, should be back in two days at the most. The scenery in the highlands is breathtaking! Mighty and desolate. We're floating above a sea of clouds right now . . . Hey, Jin, if there's anything to say you'd better tell me quick, my phone's almost out of juice. I left both our chargers in the hotel the day before."

She sounded carefree; love had made her younger. Listening to her light, happy voice, Jin Mingcheng almost couldn't bear it. The contrast was too stark—all-consuming tragedy on one side, bliss on the other—especially when you thought how joyous she must have been, all the while spreading the virus on her journey. He quickly explained the situation, and she exclaimed, "Smallpox? That's not possible. When I left America, the outbreak had just started, and I was with my adoptive father the whole time, I barely saw anyone else. My God . . ."

A few moments of silence, during which he heard her murmuring something to her husband. When she picked up again, she was back to her habitual calm and efficiency. Unhurriedly, she said, "I remember now, I might indeed be a carrier. The one social activity I took part in while I was there was an independent forum. There was a man called Zia Baj who gave a bloodthirsty speech, and he mentioned that three of his Native American friends would be embarking on a tour of remembrance. It was these clues that made me call Homeland Security and report a biological attack. Now it seems my report was incomplete. Zia Baj must have infected the attendees with smallpox."

Jin Mingcheng's heart sank. Hearing this, he had no doubt about the nature of this disaster. "Oh, I see."

"Jin, we'll drive through the night to get back as soon as we can."

Jin was silent a moment. "It might be better to get to the nearest big city, and admit yourselves to the isolation ward. I'm afraid that along the way . . ."

"Don't worry, from now on we'll keep the windows and doors tightly shut, and won't go near anyone until we reach the quarantine zone. That'll be safer than stopping in any city. As for the people we've already come into contact with"—a pause, then in a low voice—"I can only pray to God for help."

Jin thought about it, and decided she was right, it was probably safer this way. "All right, let's do that, come back as quickly as you can, but drive safely. Be careful! I mean it! I don't mean to jinx you, but if there were an accident, with a whole load of rescue workers, that really would be the end."

"We'll be careful. We'll take turns driving."

"If this case is verified as smallpox, we'll immediately declare an epidemic and seal off the quarantine zone."

"We'll head straight into the sealed area, and stay there till the epidemic is over. The children need me. Don't worry about us, we haven't shown any symptoms yet, so we must have some resistance."

"When you get back, will General Manager Sun also stay in the quarantine zone?"

"That's the only way. We've been together for so much time, he's definitely a carrier too. But don't worry, he can manage the business over the phone."

"Fine. Thank you, on behalf of the children."

In a small voice, she asked, "What are you thanking me for? If only . . ." But she didn't finish.

After hanging up, Jin Mingcheng told his secretary to hold all calls and visitors; he needed to calm down and think about the situation. The town's anti-infection measures were comparatively strong, and the most worrying factor was the ten-day journey of Mei Yin and her husband, who'd turned this infection from a point to a line. Hopefully it hadn't expanded farther, into two dimensions! Still, he had confidence. After all, China had already been through the SARS crisis, when they'd had no previous knowledge to draw from and the initial stages were much more confused, but they'd quickly found a sense of order. Through that outbreak, they'd gained precious experience.

Suddenly, he thought of another problem: Mei Yin had said they wouldn't go near anyone on their way back, but they'd have to pass through toll booths and gas stations, and at the very least would need to hand over cash. He'd have to warn them, and try to come up with a plan. When he called, there was no answer, just a well-modulated robotic voice: "Sorry, the cell phone you are trying to call is switched off." They surely wouldn't have turned off their phones at a time like this, which meant their batteries were dead, just when it was most urgent to get hold of them. Deputy Mayor Jin kicked himself: When he gave Mei Yin that Lifan, why hadn't he thought to have it fitted with a car phone?

He could get in touch with them through one of the toll booths, but this method could only be used after news of the outbreak was public. Now, all he could do was wait for the Anti-Infection Unit—Yang and the rest—to come up with a result.

Yang Jicun took some samples of pus from the blisters on Patient One, Mei Xiaoxue, then scraped some skin cells from the blisters, swabbed her throat, and took some blood. Back in the CDC's lab, he dyed the pus-smeared slides and blister cell samples using the Bazin method, and studied them beneath an oil-immersion microscope. Holding his breath, he slowly adjusted the lens until the virus came into focus, brick-shaped rather than the icosahedral form of chicken pox. The virus was arranged in a chain, in pairs or clusters. A textbook image of the smallpox pathogen. He yielded his place to Unit Head Lin, standing beside him, who looked through the microscope and silently nodded.

Of course, the proper course of action would be to cultivate the virus, then run some serological and fluorescence antibody tests. But the former would take too much time, requiring four days to run; the latter required costly immune blood-serum or fluorescent antibodies, neither of which the Nanyang CDC had in stock. They were prepared to send the specimens to the national CDC for these tests, but before that they would need to inform Deputy Mayor Jin. According to the epidemic rapid-response rules, any diagnosis of a high fever with a suspected Category A disease (smallpox had been removed from the Category A list by now, but only because it had been "eliminated") ought to set this apparatus in motion, let alone now, with confirmed lab tests.

Unit Chief Lin immediately phoned Deputy Mayor Jin, who was at that moment in a meeting with the Health and Infection Department, the Animal Infection Department, the Traffic Department, Public Security, the Civil Affairs Department, the Citizens' Militia commander, various major hospitals . . . In short, any organization under his jurisdiction that had anything to do with responding to this epidemic had been summoned. Only the Armed Police was absent, as they didn't come under his command. The meeting had been going on for three hours now, and he'd already announced that a Category A infection had been discovered in Nanyang, which could mean the plague, anthrax, cholera, or smallpox, and he wanted to get everyone together right away to decide how to set their defenses in motion. His bearing was stern—even though everyone believed this was just an exercise, they took it seriously and managed to agree on a plan.

The discussion was over, but Deputy Mayor Jin hadn't dismissed them, instead asking them to remain in their places and take a little break. The smokers were beginning to get desperate, and now quickly got their cigarettes out, and after a bit of polite to-ing and fro-ing at the door, plumes of smoke were rising outside the room. Director He from the Central Hospital said to his neighbor, the head of the Traffic Department, "Our new deputy mayor has quite a talent for acting. Did you see how he kept a straight face for three or four hours, as if there really was an epidemic?" Department Head Guo laughingly replied, "If there really was an outbreak, he'd have sent us out, rather than keeping us here kicking our heels! Besides, if this was for real, would the epidemic department head really be absent? We'd be letting him call the shots."

The only person in the meeting who knew what was going on was the epidemic department secretary—the unit head and Yang were off carrying out their tests. But Jin had made it clear that until there were confirmed results, news of the real infection was not to be revealed, so the secretary could only listen to the discussion without saying a word, now and then exchanging a long and meaningful glance with the deputy mayor.

It was just past noon, and the civil servants were done for the day. From the conference room, they could be heard chatting as they clattered down the corridor. Deputy Mayor Jin kept a poker face, and still did not dismiss them—the room began to grow restless, the conversations grinding to a halt, as everyone stared at their leader. The deputy mayor looked calm, but his heart was on fire. They were just waiting for a call from the Anti-Infection Unit, and if it was good news, he'd laugh and tell everyone, *Thank you for taking part in today's exercise, you're free to go now!* Thus avoiding any unnecessary panic. But if it was bad news, they'd have to put the plan they'd just agreed on into action right away. Finally, his cell phone rang. He stepped out of the room before accepting the call. Hearing Unit Chief

Lin's report, he went back inside, and said with a grim smile, "You must all be thinking that what happened today was just an exercise, and I wish that were the case too. Unfortunately, it isn't. The Health Department's Anti-Infection Unit, I should say the CDC, has just verified a smallpox outbreak in Nanyang, originating at an orphanage within the city limits. The virus might have been brought back from America by its director, Ms. Mei."

There was a painful silence, broken only by a slight cough that was immediately muffled. Deputy Mayor Jin exchanged glances again with the secretary, and went on levelly. "Emergency measures will be taken right away, following the plan we've just decided upon. Each department knows what to do. I'll inform the Armed Police now, and they'll coordinate with our activities."

Mei Yin and her husband weren't home yet, and he still couldn't get through to them, but their route was already under surveillance by HQ by means of the toll booths that littered the whole country. Through the State Council, the Command Center had been able to send an urgent notification to all toll booths and gas stations: if you see a black Lifan, registration R-C5360, give them free passage and gas, and notify the Nanyang Epidemic Control Center immediately. Not long after this bulletin was put out, a report came in to say the car had passed through a toll gate in Sichuan, its windows shut, the tinted screen on the left window ripped off, and the passenger holding a piece of paper ripped from a notebook, on which were scrawled some words in large ballpoint writing: "Highly Infectious Patient." The toll attendant's first reaction was that these people were trying to get through without paying, with an unusually inventive trick. But then she saw that the two people in the car appeared wealthy, and it seemed unlikely they'd wreck that expensive window shade just to evade some tolls. After a moment's hesitation, she decided to give them the benefit of the doubt. Collecting ten yuan more or less was no big deal, better not to risk getting some awful illness. And so, reluctantly, she raised the barrier.

Hearing this news, Jin Mingcheng couldn't help cracking a smile. Mei Yin and Jingshuan were being smart about this, so he could stop worrying. After this, everything went smoothly, reports coming in from toll booths and gas stations, making it clear the car was speeding toward Nanyang and had made it as far Xiangfan, not quite a hundred miles away—they would be here within an hour. Deputy Mayor Jin urgently looked forward to their return, partly so he could understand more about how this had happened, and partly because Mei Yin was a first-rate virologist, and he'd feel more secure having her around. There was one other consideration: if Mei Yin could return to the orphanage, it would benefit the children's emotional state, since he knew what affection they had for her.

Deputy Mayor Jin had no way of knowing that one other person was also hurrying toward Nanyang at the moment, and his arrival would cause an even greater storm.

At seven o'clock on the second evening of the epidemic, after nightfall, Mei Yin and her husband arrived back in Nanyang. The city was under lockdown, with police cars parked across the roads, their lights flashing, and masked officers blocking oncoming traffic and sending it away without exception. Two armed policemen stood on alert by the roadside. Mei Yin stopped and rolled down her window. An officer had already taken note of her registration, stepped forward and bowed, then passed a walkie-talkie into the car, waving them on. Mei Yin started the engine with one hand, pressing "Speak" with the other. "Hello, is this Deputy Mayor Jin? We're back in the city, heading to the orphanage."

"Jin here. Good journey?"

"It was fine. We didn't come into contact with anyone, just ate the food we already had and drove through toll booths all the way."

"How are you both feeling?"

"No symptoms. How are things in the zone?"

"Fairly positive. Only two serious cases, including Mei Xiaoxue at the orphanage. More than a thousand suspected cases, but symptoms are mild. Experts from the Anti-Infection Unit are puzzled by this."

"Is Mei Xiaoxue . . . Forget it, we're almost at the orphanage."

The car zoomed past the second ring of defenses, a more forbidding barrier than the outer circle, the air filled with the thick scent of carbolic acid, and the police there were dressed in thick white cotton-padded protective gear, with face masks, looking like a group of astronauts. The streets were desolate, without a single pedestrian, and if not for the flashing police lights and stiff-looking officers, they could have been entering an abandoned city. Seeing the car approach, the police waved them on from some distance away. The Lifan was able to pull straight into the orphanage courtyard, where two guards were holding two sets of protective gear for them. Mei Yin opened the door and declined with a smile. "Thank you, but we won't be needing those. If we were going to be infected, it would have happened long ago."

One of the astronauts was Dr. Zhou from the Anti-Infection Unit. His voice muffled behind his full-face mask, he insisted, "At least wear something over your mouths."

"No, there really is no need."

Sun Jingshuan emerged from the passenger seat, and also politely declined. "Yes, we don't need these. We're resistant. Now please take us to see the patients."

Dr. Zhou led them in, explaining that of the thirty-four people in the orphanage, fourteen hadn't been affected, and they'd been taken away once that was verified. The other twenty were past the incubation period, but their symptoms were fairly mild, which caused them some puzzlement, because the strain of smallpox spread by the terrorists in America had been virulent.

Mei Yin said nothing to this. They entered a dorm, where Mother Liu was staying with sixteen of the girls, while Mother Chen and the boys were in another room. It was obvious that no one told them that Mei Yin would be arriving, and everyone froze as she entered, only reacting a few seconds later: "Director Mei!" "Mommy Mei!" "Mommy Mei's back!"

The children rushed toward her. Mother Liu screamed, "Don't come in! Director Mei, put on your protective gear!" But it was too late, and Mei Yin smiled and waved her concerns away as she pulled the children to her bosom. Jingshuan was also beaming, hugging two little girls, kissing them on the cheek. Mei Yin studied their symptoms. Blisters on the head, but fairly sparse and shallow. The fever had abated after symptoms appeared, and they were in good spirits. The orphans were gabbling away nonstop, all trying to push forward and squeeze into Mei Yin's hug, wanting her to stroke their faces too. Mei Yin's eyes were teary, and she said, over and over, "You're all fine, I can stop worrying. You'll all be better soon, don't be afraid. Until you're well again, Mommy Mei will stay here and keep you company, all right?"

The children whooped and cheered.

Then they visited the boys in the next room. Mei Yin said to the two mothers, "It's been hard on you."

"We can deal with it. It's worse for the children, especially Xiaoxue."

"Where is she? I want to see her."

Mother Liu led them to the room that had once been their bridal chamber. When they were alone, she carefully asked, "Director Mei, did you really bring the virus back with you from America?"

Mei Yin turned to look at her, and said calmly, "Quite possibly. I wasn't in the infection zone while I was in the States, but I did bump into someone at a meeting, and only later found out that he was the mastermind behind this terror attack. He might have . . ."

She didn't finish. Mother Liu sighed and asked no further questions.

Xiaoxue, isolated in her room, had heard the cheers from outside, and by the time she saw Mommy Mei walking toward her, was in a frenzy of anticipation. The nurse caring for her barred the door, and warned her to stay in the room. Now she cried out, "Mommy Mei! Mommy Mei! Uncle Sun!"

The couple hurried over and hugged Xiaoxue tightly. The girl buried her head deep in her Mommy's embrace, and when she looked up again, tears were streaming down her face, soaking Mei Yin's chest. Her symptoms were indeed severe, with red welts all over her body, some already swelling into blisters, and while her temperature was lower now, the earlier high fever had left her pale and unsteady, her eyes uncertain and her voice weak. Mei Yin clutched her face and sobbed. "Xiaoxue, how you've suffered. Don't worry, you'll definitely get better. Mommy Mei will stay with you until you're well."

Mei Xiaoxue's eyes brightened. This had been her secret desire for many years now, though she'd been hesitant to tell anyone—just sleeping in the same bed as Mommy Mei, leaning on her bosom, all the pleasures she'd never enjoyed as an actual child. And if this illness could bring her such happiness, then she'd think it was worth it. Timidly, she asked, "Mommy Mei, will you stay here tonight?"

"Yes, I'll sleep here beside you."

"Ah, no, you'll get infected!" Suddenly remembering this point, she quickly squirmed out of Mei Yin's embrace and said anxiously, "Mommy Mei, why aren't you wearing protective clothes? You'll get sick!"

Mei Yin smiled, and wrapped her arms around the girl again. "Don't worry about it. Mommy and Uncle Sun have immunity. Really, it's the truth."

Xiaoxue relaxed, and only now turned her attention to the neglected Uncle Sun. Tilting her head to one side in thought, she said, "Mommy Mei, you can keep us company during the day, but at night you ought to be together with Uncle Sun."

Jingshuan tweaked her little nose. "Clever little devil, trust you to think of that. But Mommy Mei can keep you company, and I'll stick with Mei Xiaokai and the other boys."

Only now did Xiaoxue let herself believe that the happiness she'd longed for was about to descend upon her. Enchanted, her eyes sparkled brilliantly.

That night, Mei Yin hugged Xiaoxue as they slept, the girl's face pressed against her Mommy's chest. Xiaoxue was almost drunk with happiness, and stayed silent for a long time. Suddenly, she looked up and said, "Mommy Mei, I want to ask you something, is that all right?"

"Of course. Ask away."

Xiaoxue summoned her courage. "Mommy Mei, are you my real mother?"

Mei Yin paused. "Just treat me as if I am, all right?"

This wasn't enough for Xiaoxue, who sighed with disappointment. Once again, Mei Yin felt a jolt of pity, and held the child tighter, quietly worrying for her. Xiaoxue's red blisters were now appearing, and soon her temperature would shoot up again, and the blisters would become sunken pockmarks; then her fever would rise even more, and the blisters would fill with pus, which might lead to sepsis. The vaccine had come too late, and the antibodies wouldn't do her much good. She'd only be able to rely on her own natural resistance, the immunity granted by the Creator to every living thing. Death was unlikely, but she wouldn't escape without severe scarring. Of course, these days you could get extremely effective plastic surgery, with special dermabrasion to get rid of the pockmarks. The results would be good, though her face would never again be her own. Now, Xiaoxue snuggled contentedly into Mei Yin's bosom, under the wing of her mother love, still unaware of the tragedy that was to come. Poor Xiaoxue.

Mei Yin was the cause of Xiaoxue's sickness. She'd anticipated that this epidemic would have a few serious cases, and even a few deaths, which was unavoidable. Although she understood all this from a theoretical standpoint, she was still filled with guilt about Xiaoxue. At this moment, she made an important personal decision. Turning Xiaoxue's face toward her, she looked straight into her eyes and said,

"Xiaoxue, I have a plan. When you're better, I want to put in the adoption paperwork. I want you to live with us, as my and Uncle Sun's daughter. Will you agree?"

Xiaoxue was stunned into silence at the unexpected arrival of such good fortune. "Real—really?"

"Of course. Would Mommy Mei lie to you? I haven't said anything to Uncle Sun yet, but I'm sure he'll agree."

Xiaoxue was in shock for a long time, then suddenly flung her arms around Mei Yin's neck, floods of tears streaming from her eyes. She cried so ferociously that Mei Yin was scared. Touching Xiaoxue's face, she said, "Stop it, Xiaoxue, don't cry. I know, you're sad because you don't want to be my daughter. All right, then forget I said anything, how about that?"

Her teasing forced a tearful giggle from Xiaoxue, and she murmured, "Mommy. Mommy."

Already she was calling her by a different name. Mei Yin happily stroked her back, crooning, "Good girl, the most beautiful daughter in the world, the loveliest daughter."

They whispered together for a long time before Xiaoxue snuggled against her Mommy, and with both tears and smiles slipped into dreamland.

It was eleven o'clock at night. Having set off from Wuhan in a taxi after dinner, Xue Yu was just reaching Nanyang. The news was out that it was an infection zone, and with SARS still fresh in everyone's memory, no driver had been willing to take him there. He'd had to resort to pleading and offering a huge amount of money before one took pity on him, but even then the driver would only take him as far as the first barrier. The TV said this smallpox epidemic had been brought to China by a traveler who'd been visiting family in America.

It was Mei Yin. She'd brought back the virus. Yet from the instant he heard the news, Xue Yu felt a sharp worry in his heart. He had to tell Ms. Mei his suspicions—that the source of infection wasn't America, but General Manager Sun's facility—otherwise all their preventative measures would prove useless. He phoned her frantically, but couldn't get through, and Sun's cell seemed to be off too. These worries weren't anything he could share with the authorities, as they could only get Ms. Mei into trouble. Finally, there was nothing he could do but get a taxi to Nanyang, trusting that she would be heading back there as well.

The taxi dropped him off at the boundary and immediately sped off in the opposite direction, the driver unwilling to linger even a moment. Xue Yu spoke to the police guard, and learning that Ms. Mei was back in the city, was able to momentarily set down the burden in his heart. He asked to see her, only to have the officer scold him. "Are you suicidal? You see what's going on, and you want to barge into a quarantine zone?"

Xue Yu protested that he really did have urgent business, and if they wouldn't let him in, they should at least give him Ms. Mei's current phone number. The officer said he didn't know and couldn't help. Xue Yu flew into a rage. "Listen, I might be able to stop the epidemic. This is important! If you won't let me in, will you take responsibility when things get worse?"

In the face of his stubbornness, the officer phoned his commander, then started a police car. "Get in, I'll take you there."

The guard didn't take him to Ms. Mei, but to the commander of the infection zone. The HQ had taken over Mei Xiaoxue's middle school, not far from the orphanage. At the moment, a meeting was going on in a lecture hall, with several prominent officials including Deputy Director Zhang of the CDC—the youngest member of the director-level cadre in the whole of China, an intelligent and capable man who was expected to do well; an expert from the WHO—Noriyoshi Matsumoto, a courtly older Japanese man; the Nanyang council secretary and Mayor Tang; and Deputy Mayor Jin Mingcheng, who was chairing the meeting, as he held the Culture and Public Health portfolio. There was also a huge group of reporters, Chinese and foreign—far outnumbering the actual participants of the meeting—neatly seated in the back rows of the hall. It was an internal meeting, without simultaneous translation, so the various agencies had mostly sent along their best Mandarin-speaking reporters.

It was Director Zhang who'd decided to announce the epidemic to the foreign press at the same time as the domestic press, and the central government had approved. During the early stages of SARS, the Chinese had kept certain things from the press, which later affected their ability to fight the infection and led to international criticism for their role in worsening the situation. Director Zhang said that this time around, they wouldn't be so foolish.

Now Yang Jicun of the CDC was reporting on the current state of the outbreak. On the whole, the situation was good, far better than the epidemiologists had predicted. There were 343 confirmed cases and another 1,345 suspected, but their symptoms were relatively minor. Smallpox came in severe and mild strains, but China wasn't in the mild-strain infection zone. Yet the American epidemic had evidently been one of regular smallpox. So if they accepted that Director Mei had brought the virus back with her from America, this contradiction was impossible to explain. Only two of the victims were ill enough to be in a life-threatening state, namely Mei Xiaoxue at the orphanage, and Dr. Ma, who first reported the outbreak.

At the moment, the scenario most feared by the CDC was that smallpox would have spread along the route taken by Mei Yin on her honeymoon, so they'd asked her to provide a detailed itinerary, and were keeping a close watch on all the areas she'd passed through. So far they'd discovered a dozen suspected cases, again with mild symptoms. As the couple had been on their honeymoon, they hadn't spent much time in any one place, and even if they had spread it, the virus—being airborne—would have quickly dissipated. As far as they could tell, the spread of the disease had been effectively halted.

At this point, a staff member approached Jin Mingcheng and whispered in his ear, at which Jin turned to the mayor and said, "A young expert from the Wuhan Institute of Virology has arrived. He says he has something urgent to tell us." Then he hurried out of the meeting.

Jin Mingcheng left the room and shook hands with Xue Yu. "What's so urgent?"

Awkwardly, Xue Yu said, "It's just a suspicion. I'd like to first ask Ms. Mei for her opinion."

The deputy mayor's face sank. "Does it have something to do with the epidemic? If not, you should go back to Wuhan, we don't have time for this."

"Of course it has to do with . . ."

"Then out with it! I'm the commander of the infection zone, and I have the right to hear anything about the outbreak first. If you really do need to speak to Ms. Mei, I can make it happen later."

Xue Yu briefly described what he'd seen in that lab at Heavenly Corp. He said, "If it really is as Ms. Mei said, then the white pox virus could also cause an infection, with symptoms very similar to smallpox, and we have to consider that. It may be that this outbreak wasn't smallpox brought over from America, but a mutation of white pox from the lab that accidentally leaked out. Ms. Mei brought me there to visit before all this happened. Could she have unintentionally come into contact with the white pox virus?"

Jin Mingcheng's heart sank. His first, rather ignoble, response was to consider what effect this would have on his career. Before being transferred away from Xinye, he'd made a point of inspecting the new workshop space at Heavenly Corp., and he'd suspected that there was something odd going on there. Unfortunately, he hadn't looked at the lab in question. He'd walked right up to the door, but hadn't gone in. How careless. But then, even if he had gone in, he probably didn't know enough about virology to understand what he was looking at. He felt an enormous resentment toward Mei Yin—she'd broken her word to him when he invested, saying that the facility would have nothing to do with viruses; meanwhile, she had secretly created a lab to study viruses. She'd gone too far. Who did she think she was? His rise had begun with the successful clinching of this deal, but Mei Yin might also be responsible for his downfall.

He shook his head, pushing these feelings away. Right now, all that mattered was the outbreak, and a moment's hesitation from the commander could lead to tens or hundreds of additional victims. He didn't have the luxury of being distracted, nor could he try to bury Xue Yu's revelation. He said, "Thank you for your sense of duty, and for your sharp eyes. I know nothing of this field, so just let me confirm something: When you said the white pox virus could mutate into something like smallpox, becoming infectious—is that really possible?"

Xue Yu hesitated. Jin Mingcheng guessed what he was thinking, and said in a gentler voice, "Just tell me frankly, don't keep anything back, all right? I want to get to the bottom of this, even if it means digging my own professional grave. Whether as the deputy head of the county government's chamber of commerce or the Xinye County chief, I'll need to take responsibility for this secret lab. But I have to do this now."

Xue Yu could hear his sorrow and hurt, and flushed red. This wasn't the time to let considerations of personal loss get in the way, even if it did mean getting his beloved Ms. Mei into trouble. He said honestly, "If we're talking about a natural mutation, the chances are minuscule. Current medical consensus is that the monkeypox virus, including its mutation white pox, could occasionally infect someone, but without the possibility of further contagion, that is to say, human-to-human infection is impossible. This couldn't possibly lead to an outbreak as widespread as what we're seeing now. Unless—there were a human hand in this."

156

Jin Mingcheng, stunned, pressed him. "Turning a harmless virus into a deadly one on purpose? Why would anyone do that?"

Xue Yu hurriedly explained. "It's not as simple as you're thinking. Scientists might be perfectly justified in doing this for preventative reasons. And studying the process by which it goes from harmless to harmful can help us learn to combat viruses. Of course," he admitted with difficulty, "such research comes with certain risks, and there should be ample public consultation and official permission before it goes ahead. It can't just be carried out privately."

His tone was as conciliatory as possible, but it was clear he was passing severe judgment. Jin Mingcheng looked at this former student of Mei Yin's and said nothing. He'd always had a great deal of respect for Mei Yin; he'd almost regarded her as a perfect human being. She was generous and kind, prudent and rigorous in her work. She treated people gently as spring breeze, regarded the orphans as her own children, and had little interest in money or wealth. He'd never have thought, in his wildest dreams, that Mei Yin would do something as imprudent as this. He nodded. "Come on, back into the meeting room. You'll tell them what you told me, and we'll deal with it right away. Xue . . . thank you."

When he came back in, Secretary Qi and Mayor Tang stared at him silently, their eyes full of questions. The press corps grew agitated, turning their combined gaze on him and the young man who entered the room behind him. Someone stood to take Xue Yu's picture. The bailiffs went over to stop her, but the journalist had already gotten the shots she needed and sat back down with a smile, hands spread wide. Xue Yu found an empty seat in the front row. Jin scribbled a note for Qi and Tang, who read it quickly and exchanged a few quiet words, then handed it to Director Zhang of the CDC. Zhang read it expressionlessly, staring at the scrap of paper motionlessly. Everyone grew preternaturally quiet, and even Yang Jicun, who was giving his report, felt the strangeness and paused, looking questioningly at Mayor Tang. By then, Director Zhang had made his decision, and waved at Yang Jicun to stop, gesturing for the microphone to be placed in front of him.

Director Zhang smiled. "An unexpected situation has come up. Before anything else, I should make it clear that this isn't verified, and could well be a false alarm. But as we have promised the press and media that they will be kept apace of new developments as they occur, I'll announce this publicly now, and we can confirm it later. Though I must insist that the assembled journalists report this just as it stands, without exaggeration. Don't blow it up as if it's established fact. The contents of this note are rather technical, and might not be easy to understand, so I'll go slowly."

He cleared his throat, then began reading slowly from the note:

"A student of the researcher Mei Yin, one Xue Yu, says, 'Please consider another possibility about the origins of this epidemic. Mei Yin is the director of Heavenly Corp. in this city, in which there is a research lab where she has been studying the infectious white pox virus, a mutation of monkeypox and very similar to smallpox. This is an individual research project.'"

This was a bombshell of an announcement, and the meeting attendees listened, riveted, while the reporters scrambled to record all this, those who didn't speak Chinese frantically asking their colleagues for help. The Japanese expert, Noriyoshi Matsumoto, had an interpreter next to him who swiftly translated what was going on, from time to time exchanging a quick word or two.

Director Zhang went on. "This is to say, Comrade Xue Yu—Mr. Xue Yu—believes it's possible that the culprit in this epidemic isn't smallpox, but a mutated white pox virus that could induce the same symptoms. Is that right?"

158

He looked at Xue Yu, in the audience. Xue Yu stood and answered simply, "Yes."

Director Zhang, who had a technical background, gently shook his head. "As I understand it, the likelihood of this is low, but we still have to listen to what the experts think. Could Mr. Matsumoto of the WHO respond?"

Matsumoto stood. He was an old man with a full head of white hair, of medium height, with fine, thin features. Bowing to the room, he spoke a few words. The interpreter said, "Mr. Matsumoto believes the likelihood is small, unless it has undergone induced directed mutation. Even so, it would also need to go through a long period of filtering. But Mr. Matsumoto also says there is no need to waste time on this point— once the virus is amplified, DNA sequencing or probe hybridization should be able to separate them. The Institute of Microbiology of the Chinese Academy of Sciences ought to be able to do this."

He added a sentence or two, and the interpreter said, "Mr. Matsumoto doesn't think it's very likely to be white pox, but the symptoms here are clearly much milder than in America. This seems to indicate that the epidemics have different sources, which accords with the suspicions of Mr. Yang from the Nanyang CDC."

Director Zhang called Yang Jicun to the lectern and murmured a couple of questions to him, then said into the microphone, "Prior to this, the Nanyang CDC had sent samples to Beijing for DNA testing, and should have the results by tomorrow. But we have an even more direct method." He turned to Jin Mingcheng. "Our chair contacted the Chinese American researcher Ms. Mei Yin, director of Heavenly Corp., and foreign specialist at the Wuhan Institute of Virology, and she interrupted her journey to come straight back here. She's been assisting with our work within the infection zone. We could just question her directly."

Jin said nothing, but allowed a staff member to fetch a walkie-talkie and hold down the "Talk" button. Director Zhang's words had given him a chill: it was a bad sign that he kept emphasizing Mei Yin's status as a foreigner. He knew where this was going. If Mei Yin had indeed been carrying out a secret research project, if she had indeed caused this epidemic, then she would have to take full responsibility, and no one could save her. Throwing her under the bus at the first opportunity would reduce international speculation that this was some kind of national program—there'd been far too much of such irresponsible rumor-mongering in the past from the West. At this moment, Jin Mingcheng was both furious at Mei Yin for her reckless behavior, and worried about her future. He handed the walkie-talkie to Director Zhang, who said equably, "Is this Researcher Mei Yin? Zhang Shiyuan here, from the National CDC. I have something to ask you."

Her voice was calm too. "Mei Yin here. Please go ahead, Director Zhang."

"You ought to know the significance of the following questions, and I trust you'll answer honestly."

"Of course."

"Your student Xue Yu has just suggested a possibility to this meeting: the source of the epidemic might not have been America, but the white pox virus you're researching. Could you please tell us whether you've been experimenting with white pox mutation in a lab at Heavenly Corp.?"

A pause, not a long one, but enough for everyone present to notice it. Then, still calmly, "Yes, I have."

In order for the journalists to follow both sides of the conversation, Director Zhang had turned the volume to its highest level. Now, these three simple words had the explosive force of a bomb, stunning the room into silence. In this extreme stillness, the reporters craned to hear every word coming from the speaker, swiftly taking notes.

Director Zhang asked, "In that case, in your opinion, is there any possibility that Xue Yu's hypothesis is correct?" His tone remained level, but there was now a heavy chill to it.

The reply came. "It's possible. I've confirmed that the viruses I was working with are indeed pathogenic."

She didn't say "the white pox virus" but chose a more ambiguous form of words. No one present noticed this small discrepancy, though, not even Xue Yu, who was most familiar with the situation. It was only after the truth came out that he understood how careful she'd been with her phrasing.

Mei Yin went on. "It'd be easy to uncover the source of this outbreak. The CDC can come get a specimen from the lab for DNA sequencing, then compare it against the virus in the infection zone. That ought to do it."

This other disclosure—that her viruses were pathogenic—set off another bomb, and the press corps couldn't help smiling at the big fish they'd just landed, even if their satisfaction took place against a miserable backdrop of mass infection. Of course, they had questions too: If this Mei Yin truly was the author of this infection, how could she be so calm? Why would she be the one to suggest DNA testing?

Director Zhang was furious, and no longer bothered hiding the harshness in his voice. "Who organized and approved this research project?"

"This was a personal experiment, no one approved it. Even General Manager Sun of Heavenly Corp. had no idea." A pause, then she added, "I'm willing to take full responsibility for my actions."

Director Zhang softened his tone a little. "We can talk about blame another time. Right now, the most important task is to deal with this epidemic. I'll send someone right away to pick up specimens from your lab. Thank you for your cooperation."

"Just go ahead, you don't need me there. The virus is preserved in liquid nitrogen, with live specimens in the reactor. By the way, if our lab does turn out to be the origin, our present preventative strategies will remain effective, including the cowpox vaccine."

Her words were a little too confident, giving the impression that she was suspiciously clear about the situation, and had known all along that a leak from her lab caused this outbreak, but kept it under wraps. Director Zhang suppressed the anger bubbling up in him and said icily, "Thank you."

"No need to thank me, I'm just doing what I can." Then, a little abruptly, she said, "It's my student Xue Yu you ought to thank, for his civic-mindedness. I knew I was right about him."

Everyone turned to stare at Xue Yu, who blushed, the eyes of the crowd burning him like needles. He'd been forced to denounce Ms. Mei, with absolutely no personal consideration. His conscience was clear. Still, that knowledge didn't lessen the guilt he felt toward his mentor, especially if he was responsible for getting her into trouble with the law. Ms. Mei's praise felt like the cruelest sarcasm. But he knew that couldn't be—Ms. Mei wasn't a cruel person. Then he heard Deputy Mayor Jin calling him. "Xue, why don't you take Department Head Yang there, you know the facility best."

So the traitor was about to be exposed to the crowd. He'd have to face the despising stares of everyone at the facility. Clenching his teeth, he thought, *Damn them to hell, it's not like I've done anything wrong.* "Fine, I'll bring you there, I know the place well, I was the student Ms. Mei trusted most—she once asked if I would take over this research project."

Director Zhang could tell from his rambling how confused his state of mind must be, and said sympathetically, "Xue, I really have to thank you for your sense of responsibility. I think everyone will be grateful. Come on. You too, Mr. Matsumoto. And the reporters, if you like. Let's go."

When the call came from Director Zhang of the CDC, Mei Yin and her husband were in Xiaoxue's room. Her pockmarks had become blisters, filled with pus, and her temperature was rising. She was showing signs of sepsis, her mind confused, sometimes agitated. She'd been on a drip for days now, with high-potency gamma globulins to treat the smallpox and prevent lung inflammation. Although she wasn't always lucid, she insisted that Mommy was by her side at every moment. Mei Yin felt as if knives were slicing through her heart. Even with a weaker strain of smallpox, there was no way to prevent especially sensitive individuals from having an adverse reaction. She'd understood this from the start, but there's always a gap between rational understanding and actual experience. Seeing the demon torturing Xiaoxue, she couldn't help blaming herself.

After the conversation with Director Zhang, she said to her husband, "I really am grateful to Xue Yu. He set me free. Now they just need to get the specimens from the lab, and the truth will come out."

Her husband pressed her hand to his own palm. "I've been set free too."

"Don't be silly, we're sticking to the plan. Don't try to be some knight in shining armor. You can't take the fall for me."

"It's not like I can get away scot-free. They'll never believe I didn't know anything about this."

"Who cares what they believe, the law is based on evidence. As long as you keep denying it, at the very worst you'll get a light sentence. The facility needs you, and you'll have to take over my work at the orphanage too. And—our daughter. We can't let her become an orphan again, after she's just gotten a father and mother."

Jingshuan nodded. "I know. I'll do my best to deny everything in court. And if you get sent to jail, I'll wait for you."

Mei Yin said placidly, "I might not make it. I'll probably get twenty years."

"It doesn't matter how many years. I'll wait for you."

They dropped the subject and looked down at Xiaoxue. Her whole face was red, the blisters covering almost every surface of skin, the few clear patches blotchy and swollen. Her eyes were shut, their long lashes trembling from time to time, and her lips were moving too, as if praying to some god through the gloom. Mei Yin said painfully, "Everything Xiaoxue's suffering now, I caused."

"Try not to blame yourself. Mr. Dickerson was right, illness is an evil mankind will never be free of. And he said God loves the species, not the individual, and that's what his great love means. You taught me these ideas."

"I know. I don't regret what I did. It's just, seeing Xiaoxue like this . . . Jingshuan, my period came yesterday," she said abruptly. "I'm so sorry, I won't be able to have a child for you and Granny. There isn't enough time."

Jingshuan let out a breath. "Let's not force it, then. We'll obey our fate."

Xiaoxue suddenly sat up in bed, manic again. Mei Yin quickly held down her left arm, which had a drip line sticking out of it. Xiaoxue mumbled, "Mommy, take me home."

Her eyes were shut, and this was obviously the fever talking. Mei Yin stroked her face, her heart aching. "Xiaoxue, get better soon. When you're well, Mommy will bring you home. All right?"

"Mommy, bring me home. Don't go to prison."

The couple were shocked. Wasn't she delirious? Yet she must have heard and understood what the two of them had been talking about. They studied her, but her eyes were shut and her face blank, and she had obviously sunk back into unconsciousness. Mei Yin's eyes reddened as she murmured over and over, "Xiaoxue, get well soon, when you're well, Mommy and Daddy will bring you home, to our home. All right?"

Xue Yu led Department Head Yang of the Nanyang CDC to the lab at Heavenly Corp. to collect a sample. Along with them were Director

Zhang, Mayor Tang, and Deputy Mayor Jin, as well as Mr. Matsumoto from the WHO and a dozen journalists, both Chinese and foreign. The collection took place as everyone watched (safely behind a glass window). Three specimens were taken, one for the Institute of Microbiology of the Chinese Academy of Sciences; another for the CDC in Atlanta, Georgia; and the third for the WHO lab in Geneva. This arrangement was Director Zhang's idea, and everyone familiar with the unspoken rules of Chinese bureaucracy worried he was putting himself at risk by involving so many parties. But China had been accused of insufficient transparency during the SARS incident, and if they tried to keep things under wraps this time, made-up headlines would surely be on the Internet by that evening: *Chinese Army Manufacturing Biological Weapons in Secret Nanyang Lab, Recent Leak Causes Smallpox Outbreak!*

Director Zhang took a certain amount of confidence in knowing that China in fact had no such secret labs, that this had been Mei Yin acting alone (he thought furiously how reckless this American woman was!), so what was there to hide? Far better to allow the WHO representative and the foreign journalists to report the truth of the matter. The three labs would all be very cautious, and not make any announcements for three or four days at least. He felt reassured because the reporters who'd witnessed the collection process didn't seem in a hurry to manufacture news items, but confined themselves to careful reports on whether there'd been any progress or not.

When the three organizations simultaneously revealed their findings five days later, it caused an enormous public controversy.

Mei Yin and Jingshuan had known all along what the results would be—the virus in the lab wasn't white pox, but the smallpox she'd brought back from Russia—but before the announcement, they avoided the topic altogether, focusing on caring for Xiaoxue and the other children. The orphanage had been divided by a quarantine line across the courtyard, on one side the children with mild infections, taken care of by Mother Liu and Mother Chen, while on the other were Mei Xiaoxue, Mei Xiaokai, and Little Niu, looked after by the newlyweds. The mothers worried endlessly, and kept shouting across the dividing line, asking how Xiaoxue and the rest were doing.

Another piece of bad news emerged: Dr. Ma, the first to report the outbreak, had died. So far, he was the only fatality. Though Mei Yin and Jingshuan knew that "disease is an evil mankind will never get away from," it was still hard to bear a death that actually touched them. Dr. Ma's death also meant Mei Yin would get a heavier sentence, though this wasn't her main concern.

Ever since joining her adoptive father's Crucifix Society, she'd been prepared for this ending.

Xiaoxue's symptoms weren't improving, and now several doctors and nurses in protective gear busied themselves by her bedside, bringing in an oxygen tank, a respirator, and other emergency equipment. The smallpox infection would be at its most contagious when the blisters erupted, but Mei Yin cared for Xiaoxue without any protective gear, not even a mask, turning her over, wiping away the pus, hugging her. She seemed completely unworried, but the medical professionals watching her "go into battle unarmed" shivered. They urged Mei Yin to take some precautions, but she refused with a smile.

On the thirteenth day of Xiaoxue's infection, her symptoms began to stabilize, her temperature fell, and the blisters began to scab. She grew more lucid too. Mei Yin put down the pain she'd been carrying with her all these days, and silently intoned "thank the Lord"—meaning, of course, not the God of religion, but nature itself. She knew that the doctors had done all they could, but at the bottom of it was Xiaoxue's young body that had done the work of fighting the illness. This defensive ability, in turn, was the product of nature, and four billion years of evolution. Nothing was more effective, exquisite, or elegant. No medical procedure came anywhere close to this, even within the majestic tower of modern medicine.

The doctors and nurses departed, leaving the recuperating Xiaoxue in the sole care of Mei Yin. The girl slept soundly for a good long time, and opened her eyes at dawn, looking around her with unclouded eyes. The sun had risen, and a sunbeam slanted through the window, countless motes of dust dancing within it. The room was full of the fragrance of carbolic soap. Beyond the window was a square of blue sky, and a falling leaf drifted past it, sticking to the window for a second before reluctantly sinking to the ground.

How good life was. She'd escaped the claws of death, and could enjoy her existence anew.

Mei Yin, on the other side of the bed, was startled awake. "Xiaoxue, are you up?"

"Mu . . . Mommy," she called weakly. Mei Yin hadn't so much as changed her clothes in ten days now, and appeared fragile, particularly the few strands of white hair Xiaoxue noticed in the sea of black. Moved, she said, "Mommy, you have white hairs, these few days must have worn you out."

Mei Yin smiled. "I've had those for some time now. Mommy is more than forty years old. Xiaoxue, you'll be completely recovered soon. You're scabbing now, and when the scabs come off, you can be discharged."

She thought about telling Xiaoxue about the pockmarks, about plastic surgery. But it seemed better to reveal these things slowly. Xiaoxue had something else on her mind. Softly, she said, "Mommy."

"What is it, Xiaoxue?"

Xiaoxue said, in some torment, "Mommy, when I was sleeping, I heard some bad news. But I can't remember what it was. Are mean people coming to catch you?"

Mei Yin paused. So the words she'd spoken during her delirium hadn't come out of nowhere, Xiaoxue actually had overheard their conversation, and held it in her memory for a moment. But how had she, in her delirium, only picked out words to do with her mother? Mei

167

Yin found it hard to bring her emotions under control—when she said good-bye to Xiaoxue now, it might well be forever. Stifling a sob with difficulty, she steadied herself and smiled. "That was a nightmare. Why would nasty people be coming to catch me?"

When Xiaoxue thought about it, it did seem unlikely, so she too smiled and pressed her cheek contentedly to her Mommy's palm.

The walkie-talkie beeped. Mei Yin pressed the "Speak" button. "Is that Granny? Granny, don't worry, things are much better here. The last patient, Mei Xiaoxue, is almost recovered."

Granny didn't answer her, only asked, "Is Shuan there?"

"Yes, I'll get him." Mei Yin had noticed a bone-chilling iciness in Granny's voice. Smiling grimly, she shook her head, and called out from the doorway. Sun Jingshuan dashed in and took the walkie-talkie. They went outside to prevent Xiaoxue from hearing.

"Granny, it's me. Where are you?"

"I heard some news and was worried, so I decided to come into the city. The checkpoint wouldn't let me pass, they say the quarantine hasn't been lifted yet, and gave me this thing to talk into. Shuan, our facility has been taken over by the People's Army. Did you know about this?"

"Yes, I did. And it's not the People's Army, it's the civil militia and the Armed Police. It's part of the quarantine zone, same as here."

"Before that they sent people to the facility to get some virus specimens?"

"Yes, I knew about that too."

"They say Mei Yin was making viruses there, and this whole mess was her fault?"

Jingshuan smiled humorlessly as he nodded to his wife, meaning, *You're about to become Public Enemy Number One, and even I will have to turn my back on you.* He said, "Granny, I heard about that too. Honestly, I don't know anything about the lab, Mei Yin was in charge of that. She said she was researching white pox, which is harmless."

"If it's harmless, why would the People's Army take over the building? People are saying some ugly things. That your wife is an American spy."

Although they'd agreed that Jingshuan would create some distance between himself and his wife, he couldn't stop himself from rebuking his grandmother now. "Granny, are you mad? Don't listen to this wild talk. You must know by now what kind of person your granddaughter-in-law is. She's a good person, one hundred and twenty percent good, as noble as Mother Teresa. If she's made a mistake, I'm sure it was well meant."

A fairly long pause followed, then, "Shuan, you're right. Put your wife on the phone."

Mei Yin took the walkie-talkie. "Granny, it's me."

"I was rude to you just now. Don't be angry at me . . . but if you really did make a mistake, just admit it honestly to the government, and they'll be lenient. Remember that."

"I will. Granny, don't worry. Oh yes, there is one thing I need to ask for your help with. Jingshuan and I are about to adopt Xiaoxue from the orphanage as our daughter. She's a very good girl, and I'm sure you'll like her. If I had to go away for a short while, could you take care of her, please?"

Granny didn't say anything for quite a while, and was sobbing when she finally spoke. She knew what Mei Yin was hinting at. "Don't worry, I'll take care of her, as long as my old bones still hold up."

She hung up. Jingshuan's eyes were red too. Mei Yin shushed him, gesturing back toward Xiaoxue's room, whispering, "Stay calm. No matter what people say, you can't defend me. Have you forgotten your promise?"

Sun Jingshuan nodded, not saying a word.

The orphanage had no computers, and there was no way to get online. With the quarantine, they had no way of getting news from the outside world. The test results had surely been out for some time now, but no one notified them, probably deliberately keeping the information from them. Deputy Mayor Jin, who'd once been so close to them, hadn't gotten in touch at all. It was the silence before a storm, and Mei Yin knew what was coming. But she didn't dwell on it—there was no use thinking about it right now. Instead, she chose to put all her energy into Xiaoxue. The girl was more or less recovered, the scabs now coming off bit by bit. She'd been ill more than a month now, and hadn't bathed once, leaving her sweaty and stinky, with matted hair. The clothes she'd changed into the day before were already sour smelling. She still couldn't shower, so Mei Yin changed her again, then carefully brushed her hair, braiding it into little plaits. Now Xiaoxue was beautiful again, she said. These little scars were no big deal, plastic surgery was so advanced these days, they could make her look as good as new. Her interest aroused, Xiaoxue said, "Mommy, could you bring me the mirror? I want to look at my braids."

Mei Yin looked at the desk. "Where could the mirror have gone? I haven't seen it for days."

"It should be on the table."

Mei Yin kept searching. "It's not. Someone must have taken it away."

Xiaoxue was in good spirits, snuggling into her Mommy's bosom, chattering away like a little mynah bird. She asked her Mommy, "When can we do the adoption paperwork?"

"Very soon, I'll take care of it after you're well."

"The scabs are so itchy, I can't stand it, let me scratch," Xiaoxue said.

"Try not to. Here, Mommy will scratch a little bit for you."

"After I leave the orphanage, will I live in Wuhan, or in Xinye with Daddy Sun, or will I stay here in Nanyang to go to school?" Xiaoxue asked.

Mei Yin said, "We've decided that to start with you'll transfer to a school in Xinye, and live in your daddy's house. When we're at work, Granny will take care of you."

Then Xiaoxue thought of another question. "Mommy, how come you're not afraid of the sickness? The doctors and nurses were all wearing suits, and you didn't even have a mask. You even dared to hug me when we slept."

Mei Yin said, "I'm immune. And Xiaoxue, after this illness, you'll be immune too. You won't have to worry about smallpox again in this lifetime."

"Really?"

"Of course, really."

She explained in detail how the immune system worked in humans, and how to build up immunity. Vaccinations usually only lasted four or five years, but a bout with smallpox conferred lifelong immunity. Xiaoxue said, "Mommy, you know more than anyone in the world. When I grow up, I want to go to medical school, and learn as much as you."

Mei Yin said joyfully, "That's good, with your Daddy and I teaching you, you'll surely do better than us."

In this happy atmosphere, Mei Yin prepared to break the news about Xiaoxue's pockmarked face. She knew what this meant to a girl who was used to being beautiful. But, that's just how the world is. Mankind will never be free of illness. God hates perfection. Parasites can prevent hay fever, and a pockmarked face means precious immunity against smallpox. Xiaoxue was still young, and would come to understand these things when she was older. Mei Yin said, "Xiaoxue, Mommy's going to tell you something. I know our Xiaoxue is a smart and brave girl. Am I right?"

Xiaoxue said anxiously, "Mommy, what's wrong, is it bad news?"

She was so sensitive. Mei Yin realized she couldn't be too direct, and tried to think how best to be tactful. She never got the chance to finish this conversation, though, because just then there was a tramping of feet, and a policeman in a mask and protective suit jogged in and bowed. "Director Mei, Deputy Mayor Jin has sent me to summon you and General Manager Sun to an important meeting at the command center. Please come at once."

Mei Yin knew that the sky, overcast for so many days, would now break upon them, and the sword of punishment was about to fall on her head. "All right. General Manager Sun is in the room opposite; we'll leave at once."

Kissing Xiaoxue's scarred face, she said, "Mommy has to go to a meeting. I think Uncle Deputy Mayor wants me to do something for him, and I don't know when I'll be back. Keep getting better, and listen to what Mother Liu and Mother Chen tell you. Will you do that?"

Xiaoxue nodded with difficulty. Now Mommy was saying good-bye to her, then to the mothers and other children. Now she was walking out the orphanage gate with her husband. A police car was waiting for them. Two officers held the door open, politely but coldly asking them to get in.

The couple looked back longingly at the orphanage, the autumnal old city, the sky with its white clouds. A V-shaped line of swans flew overhead, heading south, reminding them that it was late fall. Exchanging a mournful glance, they got in the car.

The police brought them to a meeting room in Xiaoxue's school. Around one side of an oval table sat Director Zhang of the National CDC, Deputy Mayor Jin, and Mr. Matsumoto. A large number of journalists sat in chairs against the wall. The other side of the table was empty, with spaces left for Mei Yin and Jingshuan. It looked like an interrogation. The couple took the seats of the accused.

Xue Yu sat behind Deputy Mayor Jin. Mei Yin smiled at him and nodded a greeting. Although he had no reason to feel guilty, he still found it difficult to look his mentor in the eye. He'd already guessed at her coming downfall.

The three "interrogators" nodded at the couple. Director Zhang and Deputy Mayor Jin gazed at them, cold-faced. When they'd discussed the investment back in the day, she'd sworn to Jin that the facility wouldn't have anything to do with viruses, and now he could see that was a pack of lies. She'd turned Nanyang and Xinye County into disaster zones, broken Chinese law, and no one could save her now. But the thought of her spending the rest of her life in jail was still hard for Jin to bear. They'd known each other more than ten years, and Heavenly Corp. had been such a success. Then there was the orphanage . . .

Director Zhang smiled. "Director Mei, General Manager Sun, we have some good news for you. Forty days after the first case of infection, every patient has now recovered, and we're lifting the quarantine zone. All this while, you've been taking care of the children at the orphanage, where the outbreak was most severe. It's been hard on you. We're especially grateful to Ms. Mei, as an American, for pitching in when our country was in trouble. That is rare indeed. On behalf of the Chinese government, I thank you sincerely, and you, too, Mr. Sun."

The couple said they'd just done what they ought to, and there was no need to thank them. Smiling guilelessly, Mei Yin added, "I might be American by nationality, but I'm Chinese by blood. I was born in this country, and spent more than half my life here. And now I've married a Chinese husband. So really, you should count me as Chinese. Please don't regard me as an outsider."

Director Zhang knew he was being mocked, and he flushed red before continuing. "We've carried out tests on the samples obtained from the Heavenly Corp. laboratory, and the results of all three tests have been publicly announced. Are you already aware of this?"

Mei Yin said, "My husband won't know this. He was completely in the dark about the lab. But I can guess. The results were: they weren't mutated white pox viruses at all, but smallpox."

Jingshuan blurted out, "What are you saying? Smallpox?" He turned and looked in shock at his wife. Silently, Mei Yin praised him: excellent, this was a pretty good performance. Out loud, she said apologetically to him, "I'm sorry, I've kept all this from you. The mutated white pox I was researching was actually three different varieties of smallpox: West African, Asian, and South American."

Though they already knew the truth, Zhang, Jin, and Matsumoto hadn't expected such a frank confession from Mei Yin. She had to know that she was admitting guilt! The two Chinese men's faces fell, and Director Zhang asked coldly, "Then you can also guess at the other conclusion drawn by the report?"

"Yes, I can. The smallpox virus that caused the epidemic in China didn't originate in the States, but was accidentally leaked from my laboratory. I remember about forty days ago, when I told my student Xue Yu about the lab, I showed him around. That must be when it got out."

Director Zhang looked at Xue Yu, sitting behind him, who nodded with certainty. Jingshuan was staring with his mouth open in shock.

Mei Yin sighed. "Actually, once the outbreak started, I considered two possibilities—I'd brought the virus back with me from America, or else it had leaked locally. But by that time, we were busy dealing with the infection, and there was no time to think. It seemed likely that the source was local, because the epidemic was so much milder than in the States, and it was improbable that the same strain was responsible for both. There was no rush to verify this, because in either case the treatment would be the same."

The journalists were scribbling away at lightning speed. Director Zhang's voice grew sterner. "In that case, could you please tell us where the smallpox in your laboratory came from?"

Mei Yin said calmly, "I'm unable to disclose that at present."

Director Zhang smiled coldly. "Perhaps there's someone who can help you remember. Mr. Miguel de Las Casas, please come forward." He ushered one of the journalists behind him to the table, introducing him to the room. "Mr. Las Casas is a reporter with the Spanish newspaper *El País*. Three days ago, he wrote an article containing a rather important tip-off. The next section of the interview will be carried out by Mr. Las Casas, though the rest of the press is welcome to join in."

It was a risky maneuver, but Director Zhang's hand was forced. The article had been fairly truthful and objective, but contained a hint that the smallpox virus Mei Yin smuggled back from Russia might possibly have been a "national activity," part of a Chinese military plan to manufacture a biological weapon. Director Zhang knew how easily that story would spread, and how hard it would be to dispel the rumor—even the most serious official denial would be treated as a cover-up. And so he'd decided on a dangerous move. The person who tied the bell to the tiger's tail was best placed to remove it; he would ask the author of this accusatory article to defuse it. The day he saw that essay, he'd sent a message inviting Mr. Las Casas to visit China and interview the suspect in question. In the e-mail, he said, "I trust you're an upright journalist, and that in accepting this invitation, you'll report the facts you see objectively to the world, whatever those facts might turn out to be."

Miguel de Las Casas was a skinny middle-aged man with black hair and dark skin, and eyes blazing with spirit. Seven days previously, he'd suddenly had a visit in Madrid from a Russian official, and from that moment he'd been at the center of the global conversation. He'd written an explosive article, based on information given to him by the Russians, that had caused quite a stir worldwide. What he hadn't expected was an invitation from the director of China's CDC to visit China. He was grateful, and respected this Chinese official for taking the initiative—it demonstrated broad-mindedness on the part of the Chinese. Yet he was also on his guard: Was this "transparency" in fact a cunningly designed trap?

Sitting down in front of Mei Yin and Sun Jingshuan, he began with a question. "Ms. Mei Yin, may I ask, Mr. Zhang said you and your husband have been confined to the quarantine zone, taking care of patients for some time, and haven't read my article. Is this true?"

Mei Yin nodded. "Yes. There are no computers in the orphanage so I couldn't go online."

"Can you read Spanish?"

"I'm afraid not."

"That's all right, I've printed out an English translation. I do apologize, but there wasn't enough time to prepare a Chinese version. I don't know if your husband understands English?"

"Oh yes, my husband's English is excellent."

"In that case, could you please read this article together?"

He handed over a few sheets of paper. The headline on the first page was *Did China's Smallpox Outbreak Come from Russia?*

Mei Yin went through the article quickly, taking in ten lines at a glance, handing each page to her husband as she finished. It described an anonymous Russian official seeking out a meeting with Mr. Las Casas in Madrid, wanting to talk about a perfectly ordinary death in 1997, connected with the Vector Institute in Russia. The Russian police had investigated the matter, cutting the cocoon and unraveling the silk, following the threads back one by one, and in the end they led to a Chinese American woman named Mei Yin. She was an ambitious individual, skilled in martial arts, and she'd had an affair with the deceased, a Russian virologist named Stebushkin, before his death. The most logical explanation was surely that Mei Yin's journey had something to do with the Level-Four viruses at the Vector Institute, where Stebushkin worked. Now three separate strains of the smallpox virus had been found in Mei Yin's secret lab, and when placed in conjunction with her trip to the Vector Institute in 1997, only an idiot would think it was a coincidence.

Mei Yin was absorbed: it was an odd sensation, seeing her own history through another person's eyes. The Russian agents had reconstructed the sequence of events fairly accurately, though for whatever reason they didn't mention the means Stebushkin had used to kill himself. It seemed likely that the Russians might have leaked this information as an alternative way to get at the truth of the case. The choice of a Spanish newspaper was also a cunning one, as Spain was relatively neutral toward all the nations involved.

The article ended with a quote from the nameless Russian officer:

> *Ever since Stebushkin's death, the Russian intelligence agencies have been watching Mei Yin's every move. Lacking sources inside China, we've been unable to verify whether she indeed illegally obtained Level-Four viruses in order to create a biological weapon for the Chinese military. Of course, it stretches credulity that she stole the viruses for personal reasons, not at the direction of the Chinese government.*

It was this hint that caused such ripples across the world.

Mei Yin quickly finished reading it and sat, sunk in thought. The essay brought her back to that year, the little stream with no traces of humankind anywhere near it, the Russian man she'd had an affair with. Stebushkin was the first man she'd slept with. She'd seduced him not out of love, but on the orders of her adoptive father. Yet she came to hold him in her heart as her husband, and remained single ever after. A silent form of penance. Then she'd met Sun Jingshuan, who'd freed her from guilt.

She turned to look at her husband. He'd finished reading too, and his heart was lurching—when she'd first refused his proposal, she'd said she'd had a lover in Russia, and that she'd placed him on the altar of her heart. Yet the article presented a different story altogether—her relationship with the man had, at least in its early stages, only been a pragmatic affair. Now he saw another side of Mei Yin: the ruthless, resolute side, which would unhesitatingly cast aside morality for the sake of her beliefs. In the midst of his admiration for her, there was now also a little fear.

The couple were clearly deeply affected by the article, and the Spanish journalist waited until they seemed to have calmed down before asking, "Ms. Mei Yin, could you comment on the accuracy of the article?"

"Its contents are basically accurate."

A shocked murmur rose from the press corps. Smiling, she teased them. "Apart from the bit about my martial arts prowess. I wish I were that good, but unfortunately, I only spent two years learning tae kwon do, and never had any special spy training, neither from China nor America."

Miguel de Las Casas pressed her. "So you're saying you infiltrated the State Research Center of Virology and Biotechnology, in Novosibirsk, and obtained smallpox and other viruses from Stebushkin, in order to manufacture a biological weapon?"

"I'd say that's right, if you remove the words 'and other.' I got the smallpox virus from Stebushkin, three strains in all. Just smallpox, no other viruses."

Mr. Las Casas pursued. "And can you tell us honestly what your motive was for doing this? Patriotism? Money? Misanthropy? Please forgive these ugly speculations, but I really can't imagine any other reason you'd do what you did."

A few dozen pairs of eyes were now fixed on Mei Yin, waiting to see what astonishing answer she'd come up with this time. Perhaps most anxious was Director Zhang, who'd only dared make this play because he was confident that China had indeed never had any such biological weapons. But the situation might spin out of control if, for instance,

Mei Yin had some kind of vendetta against the Chinese government, and insisted that she was indeed carrying out a mission on behalf of China. They'd likely be able to unravel her story, eventually, but even so, it would put them on the defensive. Deputy Mayor Jin and Xue Yu were holding their breath, as well. No matter what she said now, the self-possessed woman in the defendant's seat was no longer the gentle, loving person they'd thought they knew.

Mei Yin made a decision: concealment was now impossible, so she might as well go with the flow, and reveal the whole truth about the Crucifix Society. On her last trip to America, she'd often debated the point with her adoptive father: They'd kept a low profile, focusing on recruiting like-minded individuals, but now they were fully fledged, surely they should go public? But the Godfather disagreed, saying they should wait until the last possible moment, in order to keep her safe. Alas, at this moment Mei Yin was unable to ask the Godfather's advice.

She smiled at the Spaniard. "Unfortunately, all three of your options are wrong." She turned to her husband. "I'm sorry, I've kept so many things from you, and now I've gotten you into trouble."

She was reminding him once more to stick to the plan they'd agreed on, to keep his distance from her. Jingshuan looked at her with an expression of very genuine conflict, and murmured, "I don't blame you. I believe that your motives must have been pure and unselfish."

Mei Yin said sadly, "Thank you for your trust. With those words, I'll have no regrets no matter what happens." To Jin Mingcheng, sitting opposite her, she said, "I'm sorry, Jin. I abused your trust when I first came to Xinye County. But you'll find in time that it wasn't a malicious act."

Deputy Mayor Jin could say nothing to this, so kept silent.

Mei Yin said to the crowd, "I went to Russia to get the virus on the orders of my adoptive father, Walt Dickerson. A group of like-minded friends have organized themselves around him, and we all wear a crucifix around our necks." She held hers up for the reporters to see. "This doesn't represent Christianity. The cross has been used as a cultural symbol in many indigenous societies, and its fundamental meaning is a fearful respect of nature. Life in the natural world wasn't created by God, but from simple genes coming together, and from the basic rules of biochemistry. Life formed and developed out of a random process of trial and error. The errors led to death, successful trials to life. It really is that clear and simple—four billion years of natural selection created today's boundless universe, with all its beauty and variety, exquisite efficiency and uniqueness. If, within the gloom, there really were an eternal, limitless, loving, incorporeal, omnipotent, all-knowing God, and he could see how life had spontaneously arisen in today's world, he'd only be able to applaud in admiration, and sigh at his own unworthiness.

"After four billion years of unforgiving trial and error, every living thing that has survived till today is a winner, an irreplaceable treasure. And together, they make up the circle of life on the planet, and all have the right to continue living within the circle, be they coyotes, hyenas, mosquitoes, roundworm, 'dog pee' fungi, horsetail grass . . . or a virus. Human beings are only one part of this circle, and what's more, they are latecomers to it, so what right have we to pass a death sentence on other life-forms? Does the rabbit have the authority to declare the coyote illegal?

"I accepted the teachings of my adoptive father, more for pragmatic reasons, because of humankind's selfish nature. The circle of life is the result of four billion years of progress, and has reached a high degree of stability. Yet man is like a five-year-old child who's just learned to use a screwdriver, and immediately runs around tearing apart every appliance in the house. As for whether he can put these complicated devices back together again, or if there's any danger in unscrewing a high-voltage switch, none of that enters his consideration. Humanity has only been civilized for, at most, tens of thousands of years, so how deep could our understanding be of this four-billion-year-old circle of life? Take the smallpox virus. It's the first virus that humankind completely eliminated from the natural world, leaving samples only in laboratories in America and Russia, which were due to be destroyed too. Yet the extinction of smallpox might cause the spread of AIDS, by vacating its ecological niche. This is just a hypothesis I'm looking into at the moment, and while I haven't been able to prove it yet, it hasn't been disproved either. If the smallpox virus specimens were to be completely destroyed, when the day comes that humanity wants to vindicate the virus, there'd be no way to bring it back to life!"

Las Casas asked, "So you, or rather your adoptive father, set up this organization, dedicated to stealing samples of this virus before the global community eradicated smallpox altogether, and secretly kept it alive?"

"That's right. Kolya Stebushkin of the Vector Institute was my comrade. But he had doubts about our plan, and once said to me, 'I don't know whether I'm doing the work of the angels or the devils.' Later on, the contradiction became too much for him and he killed himself. He's a martyr for the cause, and I respect him a great deal."

As Las Casas listened, he was running Mei Yin's words through a rigorous mental filter. He was inclined to think that her version of events fitted reasonably well with the account given by the anonymous Russian, all the loose threads joining up, narratives dovetailing. She was probably telling the truth. The Russian scientist killing himself out of guilt also sounded psychologically plausible. And it was far more likely that the whole thing was orchestrated by this Crucifix Society, and not by the Chinese military.

After going through her testimony thoroughly, he still had a niggling doubt:

"So you admit that the source of this epidemic wasn't the American infection, but a leak from your laboratory."

"I believe so."

"Don't you think that's a bit too much of a coincidence?"

Mei Yin shook her head. "I have nothing to say to that. Coincidences truly do exist in the world, otherwise the word wouldn't exist in so many languages."

Las Casas turned to look at Director Zhang. "I have no more questions. I'd like to see the laboratory in question. Is that possible?"

"Of course, I'll make the arrangements at once. The other reporters already visited when we collected the samples, and since that time the building has been sealed. If the rest of the press corps wish to visit a second time, they're welcome to."

Las Casas went on. "Ms. Mei Yin, could you please provide us with your adoptive father's address? After seeing the laboratory, I'd like to travel to America to interview him, in order to complete my report about this incident."

The request seemed to indicate that he believed Mei Yin. "Of course," she replied. "I'll give it to you later."

Director Zhang was satisfied with how things were going. His bold tactic of full transparency had paid off, and the journalists would have difficulty sustaining the "China's secret biological weapons program" story. He felt differently toward Mei Yin too: hatred and anger were now tempered by a grudging admiration. She had, in a sense, behaved unselfishly, and you could even say she'd made an enormous sacrifice. Like Stebushkin, she was a martyr. But his admiration was grudging because, no matter what, her behavior had been rash, and she'd almost caused a deadly epidemic that could have swept over all of China's people. Fortunately, the danger had passed, and the storm was all but over now. He asked, "Mr. Matsumoto, do you have anything to add?"

The Japanese man was cautious by nature. On this visit, he'd listened and watched intently, but had barely expressed an opinion. He hadn't said a word at this meeting so far, and only when Director Zhang asked him directly did he carefully speak. "I'd like to say that I don't condone Ms. Mei Yin's behavior. Even if she were right in her belief that smallpox should not be destroyed altogether, this isn't something anyone should do on their own. It's too important, and requires the cooperation and agreement of an international effort, with many countries working together and proceeding with caution, otherwise . . . we might not be this lucky next time. Still, I should also make clear my personal opinion. Even among the WHO experts, there are factions for and against the destruction of the remaining virus stocks. I count myself among those against it, and strongly oppose the extinction of this virus."

He nodded at Mei Yin, in silent support. She responded with a look of gratitude.

Director Zhang then exchanged a few quiet words with Deputy Mayor Jin, who nodded. Having heard Mei Yin's testimony, Jin's anger at her had mostly dissipated. No matter whether her beliefs were right or wrong, she'd given up everything in pursuit of them, and this alone was worthy of respect. She'd sacrificed so much for her faith, both in terms of money and her personal life. She was a kind of devout ascetic. In this world, and in Chinese society, such martyrs were few and far between. Even so, her actions had gone against the law, and the Nanyang Prosecutor's Office, after consulting with counterparts in the county and national offices, had decided to bring charges against her. A warrant had been issued, and immediately after this meeting, she and Sun would be arrested and brought to the detention center, to await their hearings. Still, she was a good person—her work with the orphans alone ought to have brought her a better reward that this. Jin Mingcheng's heart was full of doubt, and he found himself unable to meet her eyes.

Director Zhang said to the rest of the press corps, "If any of you have further questions, please feel free to ask them."

A reporter from the Xinhua Agency, clearly disgusted by the unspoken sympathy for Mei Yin welling up in the room, asked with some passion: "Ms. Mei Yin, you might well believe in your own account of your motives. But regardless of that, your actions have led to catastrophic consequences. Never mind the economic damage, let's look at the personal loss. The first person to report the epidemic, old Dr. Ma, has passed away. Some of the beautiful girls in the orphanage are now scarred for life. And as Mr. Matsumoto said, China managed to swiftly handle this outbreak through sheer luck. Hundreds of thousands, even millions of people, could have died. Would you have the courage to face these people and their families in court?"

Mei Yin shivered visibly. She'd never met Dr. Ma, and while she felt guilt over his fate, she hadn't directly experienced that loss. Mei Xiaoxue's image, though, was branded in her mind. She'd been the most beautiful girl in Nanyang: clear features and sparkling teeth, fine blushing skin and a smile that radiated purity. Now that face was covered in hideous scars. Of course, amid the vast flowing river of human civilization, one person's pockmarked face was less than a fleck of foam on a single wave. But for that individual, particularly a young girl who'd once been beautiful, it could ruin her entire life. With some pain, she said, "I'm to blame for that. I'm willing to accept the punishment of the law."

The reporter hadn't expected such a thorough admission of guilt, and had nothing to say in response. The rest of the press corps had other questions, but none as pointed as the first one. They'd been touched by Mei Yin's strength of character, and from a rational standpoint also had to admit that her argument made sense in some ways. The main outline of the case was clear now, and they were just filling in some gaps.

A journalist from Hong Kong asked, "I have a question for Mr. Sun. Did you know anything about Ms. Mei's actions?"

Sun Jingshuan shook his head. "Not at all. When Director Mei asked me to build her this lab, she said only that it was for private research into mutated white pox viruses, which should have been harmless to humans. I had no idea she was actually working with smallpox. I should be punished for my gullibility and negligence. But having heard her argument, I should also add that—if I had known at the time, I would still have supported her."

He turned to look at Mei Yin, who nodded in gratitude.

Several reporters obviously didn't believe in Sun's ignorance, but none of them pursued this line of questioning. Mei Yin's eyes swept the room, lighting on Xue Yu in the back row. Smiling, she called out to him, "How are you doing, Xue? Do you remember, I once asked you to take over my research? If you'd agreed then, I'd have told you the whole truth right away. But it's just as well you didn't, otherwise you'd have been implicated too."

His heart a tangle of emotion, Xue Yu could only smile grimly.

"Xue, I have a favor to ask you. If both my husband and I were to . . . I'd like you to take care of Mei Xiaoxue. She has the worst scarring of all the children, and must be suffering a lot."

Xue Yu knew what she was asking, and replied with sorrow, "Don't worry, I'll take care of her."

Director Zhang said, "Fine, then that's all for now. The two of you can go." The couple stood and nodded their good-byes as they left the conference room. When they were almost at the door, Mr. Matsumoto confounded everyone by striding ahead so he could respectfully bow to them, a full ninety degrees at the waist. Mei Yin was a little flustered by this overt show of deference, and hastily returned the bow. Matsumoto didn't say anything to her, but returned to his seat.

When they were gone, Director Zhang made an announcement. "Even if Ms. Mei acted from the very best motives, even if she was only putting her own beliefs into practice, she has broken Chinese law, and the law has no flexibility. As of now, the Nanyang Prosecutor's Office has issued a warrant for their arrest, and they'll soon be arraigned in the municipal court. Before this happens, we'll be sure to notify all of you, and you're very welcome to be present there too." To Miguel de Las Casas, he said, "Especially you. You said you wanted the whole story—you'll have to attend the trial for that."

Director Zhang was now completely at ease. The curtain had come down on this nail-biting play, and his bold move had succeeded. There was no further danger. Even if he somewhat regretted Mei Yin's downfall, there was no way to help her. It was worth sacrificing her if it meant the country could clear its name. Las Casas, sharp-eyed, could see the happiness in this official's heart, and a wave of displeasure surged up in him. As an official of the CDC, Zhang's conduct had been irreproachable, even outstanding, but he shouldn't be so callous with an individual like Mei Yin. After a moment's hesitation, he said tactfully, "Ms. Mei is only a suspect at the moment. Should we be so quick in stating that she's broken the law?"

Director Zhang blushed, and quickly said, "Of course not. I misspoke."

"Mr. Zhang, I'll come straight back after I've interviewed Mr. Dickerson in the States. At that time, would I be able to visit the Meis? If they agree, I'd like to engage a good foreign lawyer for her."

Zhang shot a glance at him. He was observant enough to know that Las Casas was unhappy with him. This was quite a reversal; three days ago, this journalist had still been reporting that Mei Yin was China's "Dr. Germ"—a reference to Rihab Taha, the Iraqi scientist in charge of Saddam Hussein's biological warfare program—and now he was firmly on her side? But that was good too, at least it meant Mei Yin had convinced all of them, which meant the "Chinese biological weapon" narrative would go away. Plastering a smile on his face, he said, "Thank you, on behalf of Ms. Mei and her husband, I'm grateful for your concern. But you may not be familiar with the Chinese judicial system, which stipulates that lawyers cannot operate in this country unless they are qualified and certified to practice law in China. You can certainly engage a foreign lawyer, but they'd need to hold these documents. China has many very good lawyers, in fact—as competent as those from any other country. We're just as concerned for Ms. Mei Yin's fate as you are."

"Are you? I'm glad to hear that," said Las Casas dryly.

The police car sped to the municipal station, where the actual arrest paperwork would be processed. The officer in charge would read them the charges, which the couple would sign. Before their trial, they'd be held in a detention center. The officers confiscated their personal effects, and issued a receipt. Their belts and penknives were taken away too—a suicide prevention measure. Even their shoes were removed, replaced by slippers. All of this was carried out skillfully and respectfully. Jin was present throughout the processing. The police had never seen a deputy mayor accompanying suspects to the station like this and understood that this couple were no ordinary criminals. When they tried to take away the crucifix hanging around Mei Yin's neck, she held up a hand and said politely, "This is a symbol of my faith, please let me keep it."

This put the officers in an awkward position. They looked at Deputy Mayor Jin, who was well aware that Mei Yin was no Christian. But he didn't expose her, just waved his hand so the police didn't push the matter. Afterward, the couple's hands were put into shiny handcuffs. Xue Yu, looking on, felt a weight in his heart, and couldn't stop the tears gushing from his eyes. He was the one who'd blown the whistle on them. At the same time, he hadn't done anything wrong—his conscience should be clear. All these thoughts swirled together in his mind, and he couldn't disentangle them, only weep. Mei Yin brushed away his tears with her cuffed hands, and said warmly, "Xue, don't cry. You're twenty-eight now, a grown man, people will laugh at you. I don't blame you, really, I don't blame you at all." Then she repeated, "Help me take care of Xiaoxue, and I'll have nothing to worry about."

Still crying, he nodded.

The couple got in the car and were driven off, lights flashing. Deputy Mayor Jin and Xue Yu watched the police vehicle disappear into the distance. On their way back, Xue Yu stopped the car at the orphanage. Jin patted him heavily on the shoulder, then drove on alone. Drying his eyes, Xue Yu went in to look for Xiaoxue, the little girl he still remembered looking like the most delicate flower, in order to carry out his mentor's wishes.

Many years later, when Mei Xiaoxue thought back to this day, she would understand that she'd already known of the two great tragedies awaiting her, but had deliberately closed her eyes in willful blindness. The future described by Mommy Mei had been too bright, too glittering, and she'd been dazzled.

She'd stayed in her room, lost in daydreams, not noticing the confusion engulfing the rest of the orphanage, like a beehive that had been struck with a pole. Mei Xiaokai and Xue Yuanyuan barged in, shouting in a panic, "Xiaoxue, Xiaoxue, why are you still here? Something's happened! Something big."

Xiaoxue said, "Hey, what are you two doing in here? Get out, Mommy Mei and Mother Liu both said I'm a serious case, you should stay away from me."

Xiaokai told her Mother Liu had announced the quarantine was lifted. Xiaoxue saw faint pockmarks on both their foreheads, and her heart trembled. Just running her hand across her face, she could feel the indentations. But never mind, Mommy Mei said surgery could make her skin smooth again. Breathing hard, Xiaokai said, "You still don't know? Mommy Mei's been taken away by the police! They say our smallpox didn't come from America, but from some secret smallpox lab Mommy Mei had in the Heavenly Corp. building. The virus somehow escaped! It was at that birthday celebration. She spread it to us."

Xiaoxue stared at them, openmouthed. Something perfect in her heart was slowly, unstoppably crumbling. She screamed hoarsely, "No! That's all lies! I don't believe you!"

Yuanyuan was crying. "We didn't believe it either, but—so many people are saying this. You know why Mother Liu and Mother Chen aren't here? They've gone to visit Mommy Mei, to bring her clean clothes. They were afraid you'd be too sad, so they didn't dare tell you."

"No, I don't believe it!"

Xiaokai said, "Do you remember Uncle Xue Yu who came that day? He was Mommy Mei's student, he was at that birthday party . . ."

Yuanyuan interrupted angrily. "Don't call him 'Uncle,' he's a traitor!"

Xiaokai said, "He was the one who accused Mommy Mei, and he personally brought people to the Xinye lab. Uncle Sun was taken away too. I heard that when Granny Sun learned about her grandson being arrested, she screamed and collapsed on the ground. It was a stroke. They might not be able to save her."

Xiaoxue finally believed what they were saying. Now she suddenly recalled that strange expression in Mommy Mei's eyes when she'd said good-bye, earlier that day, when the police came to summon her to a meeting. She'd been puzzled then, and now she understood that Mommy Mei had been saying farewell. She burst out crying, sobbing so hard it choked her. The seven or eight other kids who hadn't already been taken away heard the weeping and came running, crowding into the doorway, terrified to see their big sister in such floods of tears, and of course they started howling too. Xiaokai and Yuanyuan could only leave, coaxing them all away.

That left Xiaoxue alone in the room, crying, looking around her with tear-blurred vision. On the bed was the blanket her Mommy had slept under. By the bedside were her medical books. On the desk were some basic makeup, a wooden comb, and a hair clip. In the two weeks

Mommy had spent with her here, the orphan had enjoyed true mother's love for the first time in her life. Mommy had said she would bring Xiaoxue home and become her real Mommy, but that beautiful bubble had burst in an instant.

She was worn out from weeping, and now slumped on the foot of the bed, sobbing. Her hand landed on something hard and round. It was Mommy Mei's mirror, stuffed under the mattress. Xiaoxue fished it out, and looked at herself. In that instant, the second disaster crashed cruelly onto her—she'd felt a pang seeing the faint marks on Xiaokai and Yuanyuan's faces, but she was so much worse off than them. They only had light scars, whereas her whole face was covered with deep pits. She'd become a scarred woman! An ugly, scarred woman!

No wonder Mommy Mei had hidden the mirror, and kept talking about plastic surgery.

No wonder Mommy Mei, Xiaokai, and Yuanyuan, not to mention Mother Liu and Mother Chen, found it so hard to look directly at her, their eyes skittering from her face.

The smallpox virus from Mommy Mei's lab did this to her!

Xiaoxue could no longer cry. At moments of deepest sorrow, human beings move beyond tears.

It was late. Time flowed calmly on. For a long while, Xiaoxue's mind was blank, empty of any thoughts, leaving only the sense of destruction that engulfed her, body and soul. Then she heard someone speaking in the courtyard, a man asking: Where is Mei Xiaoxue? And the kids cursing at him, "You're looking for Sister Xiaoxue? Traitor! You're the one who betrayed Mommy Mei!"

She looked out the door, and there was Xue Yu. He looked embarrassed, besieged by the kids, uncertain what to do with himself. Mother Liu led the children away, but had no kind words for him, only pointing coldly at Xiaoxue's room.

Ashen-faced, Xue Yu walked over, only for the door to slam hard in his face. He tapped and called gently, "Xiaoxue, please open the door. Mommy Mei sent me. She wanted me to take care of you, and to send you for plastic surgery. Xiaoxue, it really was Mommy Mei who sent me."

The door remained tightly shut, no sounds behind it. Xue Yu spent a whole half hour trying to persuade her, but behind the door was only the silence of the grave. Eventually he called toward the door, "Xiaoxue, I'll come again tomorrow."

That night, dinner was very late at the orphanage. The two mothers had spent all day dealing with the chaos, first visiting Director Mei at the detention center, where they hadn't been allowed to see her. Then they'd come back to check on the unruly mass of children, while trying to work out where the money would come from to continue taking care of them. Director Mei had always supported this place out of her salary, which she wouldn't be getting in prison. It was eight or nine by the time they got the evening meal on the table, and the starving children refused to say grace, grabbing their bowls and wolfing down their food.

Mother Liu said, "Xiaokai, go call Xiaoxue to dinner. She's not under quarantine anymore."

Xiaokai left, but was soon back. "Mother Liu, Xiaoxue's not in her room or the courtyard."

"Where could she have gone? Continue with the meal, I'll look for her."

A moment later, they heard Mother Liu's tearful cries outside. "Xiaoxue! Xiaoxue! Where have you gone, child? Xiaoxue, I hope you haven't done something foolish."

She couldn't find the girl anywhere, and began to worry that Xiaoxue had succumbed to despair. Mother Chen and the other seven or eight children couldn't bear to keep eating, so they came out too, looking over the entire grounds and neighboring streets, but she was nowhere to be found.

Finally, Yuanyuan discovered the note under her pillow:

Mother Liu, Mother Chen,
I'm sorry, I'm going far away. I'll never come back here.
Don't come looking for me.
 Xiaokai and Yuanyuan, please take care of the
younger kids for me.
 Mei Xiaoxue

Mother Liu burst into tears when she'd finished reading.

"Xiaoxue, you silly child, how will you survive all on your own? Xiaoxue, how will I explain this to Director Mei?"

In the months after that, Mother Liu and Mother Chen searched everywhere for Xiaoxue, but there was no sign of her at all.

CHAPTER FOUR
SENTENCING

Spring 2017—Nanyang, China

Mei Yin's case was formally brought to trial three months later, as spring was just beginning to arrive. The outbreak that had come so abruptly and left so quietly now seemed like no more than a wisp of smoke, and even many of the locals had all but forgotten it. It was still in the world's consciousness, though, and people still remembered that peculiar "virus-smuggling case." The trial attracted international attention, and the various big media organizations sent their best reporters.

All the good hotels in Nanyang were packed, and they were running out of rental cars. The court could hold a thousand people, but with so many turning up, they decided to allocate seats by a system of vouchers, which quickly became sought-after, hard-to-find items.

As the case opened, the audience included Xinhua News Agency, TASS Russian News Agency, Kyodo News, the Associated Press, Al Jazeera, Reuters, ANSA Italian News Agency, Agencia EFE, Phoenix

Hong Kong . . . over a hundred reporters in all. There were also representatives from the Wuhan Institute of Virology. Though the leak had nothing to do with the institute, Mei Yin had been their employee, and they needed to have a presence. They deliberately kept a low profile, sending two low-ranking employees who listened in silence, rebuffing all press queries with a smile.

Xue Yu was there too, but he'd taken leave and was present in his personal capacity. He was terribly anxious about Ms. Mei's fate, and had been determined to come hear the case for himself. Three months had been long enough for everyone to calm down, and no one yelled *traitor* or *snake* at him. At the end of the day, Xue Yu's denunciation hadn't been for personal gain or unworthy motives, and people understood this. Still, he felt a certain amount of personal guilt, and kept to himself, sitting quietly in the back row, not talking to anyone, not even his own uncle, Professor Zhao Yuzhou, who'd come after reading about this online and discovering that Mei Yin opposed the elimination of the smallpox virus and the strong-arming of nature by science, which filled him with righteous anger. He hated these people who'd been nurtured by science then turned and bitten the hand that fed them, and hoped to watch her burn at the stake of justice with his own eyes. He was retired, anyway, and had far too much leisure time, so he was able to hurry here on the next train.

Mother Liu and Mother Chen had to take care of the orphans, so they were taking turns being present. Mei Yin might not be a believer, but after fourteen years of friendship, they regarded her as closer to them than sisters in the faith. When Mei Yin was arrested and the orphanage lost its source of financial support, the government had picked up part of the tab, while Heavenly Corp. dealt with the rest, allowing them to stay open.

Five more notable individuals were in attendance: University of California materials science expert Scott Lee (who'd designed the Society's crucifixes, including their concealed blades), WHO expert

Noriyoshi Matsumoto, Cambridge University "scienceology" authority R. M. Williams, Moscow Technical University cybernetics specialist Arkady Labsky, and Swedish mathematician Auer Lendl. They had come into the country quietly, on tourist visas, but they were some of the most renowned scientists in the world, and were still bound to arouse the media's interest. The press guessed that they were here to present a united front for the Crucifix Society. They came in quietly as the trial began, sitting in silence in the back row, identical silvery crosses sparkling around each of their necks. Of this group, Matsumoto was the most recent recruit, having only joined a few days ago. They left two empty seats in their midst, one for Mei Yin's adoptive father, the Godfather, Mr. Walt Dickerson. The eighty-six-year-old Walt was supposed to travel with them, but his heart had given him some trouble the day before the journey, and he'd had to postpone his departure. The American scientist Susan Sotomayor had stayed behind with him, and the pair would come over when he was better.

Also in the audience was the Spanish journalist Miguel de Las Casas, a gleaming crucifix around his neck. He was an impulsive man, and had undergone a complete reversal of his attitude after interviewing Mei Yin, now worshiping at her altar. Although he hadn't agreed with her point of view at first, he had the utmost admiration for her. After traveling to America and interviewing her adoptive father, he'd taken the next step, and completely surrendered to the gospel as preached by father and daughter. He did two things in America: first, he joined the Crucifix Society, and second, he kept his promise to Mei Yin and hired a first-rate Chinese American lawyer, Mr. Du Chunming, who was bilingual and certified to practice law in China. Before leaving America, Walt Dickerson, Du Chunming, Miguel de Las Casas, and several other members of the Crucifix Society had held a long meeting, in which they'd hammered out the principles and tactics that would govern their defense; they had to use the opportunity to promote the Society's point of view vigorously, while preventing Mei Yin from being found guilty. Du Chunming had come up with an ingenious plan, which they thought was sure to succeed.

The two defendants and their individual lawyers entered the courtroom separately, taking their allocated seats. Under Chinese law, defendants in the same case couldn't share a lawyer, so Sun Jingshuan had hired his own, a young man named Li Yan. The couple wore tokens of mourning, Granny Sun having died two months previously, following a massive stroke. Mei Yin greeted her husband before taking her seat next to him. This was their first meeting in three months, though in the detention center they'd been on opposite sides of the same wall.

Mei Yin looked around the courtroom, noticing Mother Liu, Xue Yu, and the six foreigners wearing crucifixes, and nodded to each of them in turn. She knew the two empty seats were meant for her father. Through Du Chunming, she'd urged him not to come, but he'd insisted he couldn't possibly be absent, that he'd be there as soon as his health allowed him to travel. Suddenly, she saw Zhao Yuzhou in the crowd and froze for a moment, uncertain why the old man had put in an appearance. Then she saw the glee in his eyes, and knew he was here to satisfy a thirst for righteousness. No doubt he was "self-funded" again. Would he brag about it this time too? She smiled at him, but he stared coldly back at her.

The clerk called for order, and everyone stood as the three judges entered, single file. The chief judge somberly announced, "Court is in session. The case of Mei Yin and Sun Jingshuan, on the charge of disseminating an infectious disease."

Inspector Tong Guangwu of the Nanyang Prosecutor's Office stood to read the charges. Two months previously, Beijing had sent a party leader to Nanyang, summoning the police, prosecutors, and judiciary for an unofficial discussion. Worried that, during the course of the case, rumors would again begin to fly that the Chinese government had been behind Mei Yin's actions, he had given the prosecutors strict instructions that failure in the case was not permissible—they had to make sure Mei

Yin got the stiffest possible sentence, in order to demonstrate China's innocence. Tong Guangwu was feeling the pressure. The problem lay in the first section of the story, the part where Mei Yin went to Russia and smuggled smallpox back, for which no evidence existed. She'd confessed it to the press corps at the earlier meeting, but that wasn't any good; she could recant that testimony at any time. Besides, her lawyer was a formidable litigator. Du Chunming had taken on quite a few big cases with an international dimension, and hadn't lost a single one. He was especially skilled at cases involving a high-tech element. He had said in private that the law was a stiff carapace, but science was expanding every second, splitting the carapace of the law, opening cracks through which a skillful lawyer could wrest successful verdicts.

Du Chunming was a tall man with gold-rimmed glasses, refined in appearance, a warm smile always on his face. But those eyes, concealed behind glasses, would flash from time to time, revealing something very sharp, enough to see right through anyone in his path. Now he looked around the room, and when he met the prosecutor's gaze, he smiled and nodded in a friendly manner.

Tong Guangwu smiled back, thinking, *Let's see what tricks you have up your sleeve.*

He finished reading the charge sheet. ". . . this court believes that the accused, Mei Yin, has violated the People's Republic of China Penal Code, Statute 331, disseminating viruses and/or bacteria. The accused Sun Jingshuan has violated the People's Republic of China Penal Code, Statute 397, negligence. Pursuant to the People's Republic of China Penal Code, Statute 136, we will charge both defendants jointly. Please rule in favor of the law."

From his place in the audience, Xue Yu grew more and more agitated. The crime Mei Yin was being charged with carried a sentence of ten years or more, with the possibility of life imprisonment or even death. And it looked like the prosecutors were going to push for a harsher sentence, in order to prevent suspicion of government involvement. It was obvious that leniency was being shown to Sun Jingshuan, who would probably get away with a year's jail time and a year's probation.

Next was the judges' questioning of the defendants. Mei Yin's statement was very simple: "The prosecutors have accused me of illegally transporting the smallpox virus from abroad. I deny this."

There was a furor. Three months ago, in front of many reporters, Mei Yin had admitted to obtaining smallpox specimens from Russia's Vector Institute, and had even specified there were three different strains, but she was now recanting her previous testimony.

In fact, Mei Yin was now following a strategy laid out by the Godfather and Du Chunming. The lawyer had told Mei Yin that their strategy, if successful, was likely to get her off altogether. This being the case, "rescue Mei Yin" would become their primary objective, and "spread the word about the Crucifix Society" could take a backseat.

For his part as the second defendant, Sun Jingshuan briskly pleaded guilty to negligence. Next came the cross-examination. The prosecutor provided the judge with the results of the analysis carried out by the WHO in Geneva, the CDC in America, and the Institute of Microbiology of the Chinese Academy of Sciences. "The specimens provided are the smallpox virus, comprising three different strains, namely West African, Asian, and South American. There's a high degree of correspondence with samples taken during the Nanyang smallpox epidemic."

The chief judge asked if the defendants wished to dispute the evidence, and Du Chunming smiled. "These three organizations are the most authoritative in the world when it comes to analyzing viruses, naturally we have no doubt they're right. But while accepting these three reports, we do have a clarification that we will make at an appropriate juncture. Please carry on."

The prosecutor admitted the second piece of evidence, a deposition from the police force in Klaznov, Novosibirsk. The deposition was just a list of facts, without any significant conclusions. The document stated that the Chinese American Ms. Mei Yin had, between the twentieth and twenty-fifth of September, 1997, entered Russia via Kazakhstan, and she'd spent three days in Klaznov, where she'd come into intimate contact with Kolya Stebushkin, a scientist at the State Research Center of Virology and Biotechnology. The police found Mei Yin's fingerprints in many places around Stebushkin's apartment, and the long black hairs on the bed were verified as likely to be hers through DNA testing. Stebushkin killed himself the day after she departed.

It was strongly hinted that Mei Yin and Stebushkin's relationship had been sexual. The listeners grew restless, and all eyes swiveled to the couple. Du Chunming said equably, "My client doesn't deny she had a Russian lover. In a way, you could call him her first husband. She did indeed travel to Russia in 1997 to see him. But please note that nowhere in the deposition is a transaction involving viruses mentioned."

Next came the questioning of witnesses. First to be called was Zhang Jun, a trader operating on the Russian-Chinese border.

"Please state your name and profession."

"I'm Zhang Jun, from Harbin, general manager of Ancheng Border Trading Consortium in Urumqi."

Glaring at Mei Yin in the defendant's seat, Zhang Jun swelled with hatred. She'd actually tricked him into bringing the virus into China. Did she want to kill a million people in China? She had Chinese blood flowing through her veins! And even at this moment, she was shameless enough to smile and wave at him.

Scowling at Mei Yin, he said to the judge, "On September twenty-sixth, 1997, this Mei Yin asked me to carry a small box. We crossed the border at the Dzungarian Gate in Xinjiang. According to her, she was carrying frozen Ferghana horse sperm obtained in Turkmenistan. I believed her, and thought how great it would be if Ferghana horses could be brought back to China once again, so I helped her to smuggle this over, and didn't collect a penny. If I'd known the box contained the smallpox virus that could kill or hurt millions of people, I definitely wouldn't have helped her!"

Du Chunming said, "Objection! All you can prove is that she brought a box across the border. You can't be certain that it contained the smallpox virus. That's misleading."

"Sustained. Witness Zhang Jun, please confine your answers to known facts."

The prosecutor continued. "Could the witness please describe the box?"

"It wasn't large, about the size of my fist, and the outer shell was stainless steel. Mei Yin told me it was a cold-storage box, with liquid nitrogen inside. It was freezing when I took it from her."

"Did the defendant say this was a cold-storage box?"

"Yes, I'm sure of it."

"No further questions."

"Any questions from the defense?"

Du Chunming smiled. "No. Like the prosecutor, I believe this was a cold-storage box. And making use of such a box suggests storage of some biological matter, whether viruses, bacteria, frozen sperm, or many other things." He emphasized the last three words.

The next witness was a lab worker from the secret lab at Heavenly Corp., a woman of forty or fifty. She was awkward in front of the court, and kept her head down, though she shot a glance at the accused from time to time, then looked back down, as if guilty. She had obviously respected Mei Yin a great deal in the past, and even now couldn't shed her old habits.

"Please state your name and profession."

"I'm Hu Cuihua, I do odd jobs at the bosses' lab at Heavenly Corp. We call it 'the bosses' lab,' because it's only used by Director Mei and General Manager Sun."

"How many workers are there?"

"Five."

"What do you all do at this lab?"

"Manual labor, moving things around, cleaning up, bringing cells from the other labs, usually in pails, ready to be added to the biological reactors."

"Have you seen the output of the biological reactors?"

"No. Professor Mei did that herself. General Manager Sun handled it when she wasn't around."

"Do you know what was in the biological reactors and liquid nitrogen cold-storage containers?"

Hu Cuihua looked timidly at Mei Yin, and said a little stiffly, "I didn't know. When the orphanage had smallpox and the police came to the lab, I heard them say it was smallpox virus. I know that's very dangerous, you'll die once you get it."

A disturbance rippled again through the crowd. Mei Yin had placed five workers in a position of danger, and kept them ignorant of the truth. "Thank you," the prosecutor said. "No further questions."

Du Chunming sensed the hostility in the room, yet he pushed for more details. "Could you tell me what safeguards Ms. Mei had you take against infection? For instance, protective clothing, an airtight face mask, disinfection on entering and leaving the lab?"

"No, nothing at all. We all thought it was strange. Other people would get sick at the slightest touch, but the five of us were there all day without so much as a mask, and never got ill."

"Did Ms. Mei and General Manager Sun wear any protective gear?"

"No, not once. When people said bad things about Director Mei, I'd defend her by saying she spent even more time than us in the lab. After the workers left, she'd be there alone working late into the night. And she wasn't scared of getting infected."

"Thank you. No further questions."

The court summoned the next witness.

"Name and profession, please."

"I'm Xue Yu, I work at Wuhan Institute of Virology. I was once Mei Yin's doctoral student."

"Before the epidemic, the defendant told you this lab contained a mutated, possibly infectious white pox virus, correct?"

"Yes."

"And the defendant took you to see this lab before the outbreak?"

"Yes. She asked me to work there and take over this research project. I didn't agree."

"Could you tell the court why you didn't agree?"

"The project was important, but it was fairly dangerous, and ought to have public oversight rather than being carried out privately. Of course, I later found out that Ms. Mei hadn't told me the truth. The infectious virus she'd mentioned wasn't mutated white pox, but smallpox."

"That day, did she open the liquid nitrogen containers or the biological reactors?"

"I was in the lab for a very short time, and only have a vague impression of the visit. I think she did open them."

"No further questions."

The court heard more evidence, by which time the outlines of the case were fairly clear. It was time for both sides to give their concluding speeches.

The prosecutor said, "The defendant secretly stored a Level-Four virus in an open-plan laboratory, where improper storage procedures caused a leak, which led to an epidemic. The evidence on this point is incontrovertible. As for the defendant illegally smuggling the smallpox virus from Russia into China, only Stebushkin, now deceased, could have provided conclusive testimony. But we believe that the depositions of the Klaznov Police, Zhang Jun, Hu Cuihua, and others, added to the fact that the laboratory did indeed contain the smallpox virus, constitute a complete chain of evidence, from which a logical inference can be made about how the virus was transported into this country."

He glanced at Du Chunming. The defense lawyer's case was largely on the ropes, yet he still appeared unruffled, as if he had something up his sleeve. This was crunch time. Could he be holding something in reserve?

As it came to the defense's turn, the audience heard a disturbance. An elderly Caucasian man, unsteady on his feet, was being led into the courtroom by a middle-aged woman. He was silvery haired, with a wispy white beard, his features withered but his eyes bright, a crucifix hanging around his neck. He looked like a fasting, meditating prophet from some religious painting. The five crucifix-wearing foreigners hastily ushered him to his place. In the defendant's chair, Mei Yin's eyes moistened as she saw her adoptive father arrive. When she shot him a worried glance, the old man waved and nodded reassuringly.

After the audience had quieted down, the sense remained that something had changed. There seemed to be a vortex around Dickerson, demanding attention, like a magnetic field or black hole. This invisible center seemed to quietly alter the energy of the court.

Mr. Du's attitude seemed to change as well; his eyes blazed as he began his rebuttal.

"My client does not dispute much about the prosecutor's account, apart from one crucial point—the cold-storage box she brought back from Russia did not contain the smallpox virus. As for what it did contain, I can explain that now."

Not smallpox? The audience had thought this point decided, and now pricked up their ears. Perhaps most apprehensive was Xue Yu. He'd had the most contact with the lab, and thought there was no doubt in this matter. Why was Du Chunming denying it?

The lawyer went on unhurriedly. "In order to present the facts, I first have to introduce Mei Yin's adoptive father, Mr. Dickerson, from America, and the Crucifix Society of which he is the head. My client has already acknowledged that she went to Russia to carry out a task for her adoptive father. I'm curious as to why the prosecution hasn't brought up the instigator of the purported crime? I will now help this court to do that job, though it's a little like I'm switching teams." A ripple of laughter spread through the audience. The prosecutor and judges had indeed chosen to keep Dickerson out of this case, partly to keep things simple, partly because he was in far-off America. But such an omission was, legally speaking, hard to explain. "I'd like to take two minutes of the court's time to introduce some beliefs of the Crucifix Society, because these viewpoints will be significant in what I'm about to say."

The judge said, "Please confine yourself to the facts pertinent to this case."

"All right. I'll bear that in mind. The Crucifix Society is a loose-knit group formed by like-minded scientists. There are nine members present here today. The note I'm about to read is jointly authored by all of them."

He read from a piece of paper. "All living things are legal members of the circle of life on earth, and all have the right to exist. Human beings may not judge whether a species should live or die, not even if they are harmful beasts, parasites, or pathogens. When humanity tries to use the tool of science to revolutionize nature, we ought to also maintain a sense of respect for the natural world, preserving the balance of nature as far as possible, rather than wantonly interfering. Some farsighted members of the scientific world could no longer keep silent or merely sit and pontificate, but had to take practical action to stop man's rape of nature.

"Looking specifically at the smallpox virus, we believe the current decision to completely eradicate it needs to be revisited. Although the eradication has brought a halt to more than a thousand years of suffering, which of course is an enormous step forward, it has also created an extremely dangerous vacuum, one that could be exploited at any moment—the terrorist attack on America proves this. Smallpox itself has advantages, as well: for instance, it can be used to suppress

AIDS. The best strategy is to suitably lower the virulence of smallpox, and then allow it to continue to exist in the natural world."

Du Chunming lowered the paper and continued speaking.

"Let's now turn to the facts of the crime before the judges. As a result of the Crucifix Society's aforementioned opinions, or should I say, beliefs, a Russian member, the distinguished virologist Stebushkin, took advantage of his position at the Vector Institute to cultivate a weakened form of smallpox. That's right, my client subsequently leaked the smallpox virus by accident, but did you wonder why the outbreak was so mild? Why the lab workers, including Mei and Sun themselves, spent long periods in contact with it but had no signs of infection? The reason is this: the object my client transported across the border and stored for a long time in her lab wasn't the smallpox virus, but"—he paused after every word—"a weakened smallpox antigen!"

The room grew very quiet. Everyone was working hard to digest this new interpretation of the case. Prosecutor Tong Guangwu felt as if he'd been clubbed over the head. He wasn't a medical expert, and couldn't describe the difference between a virus and an antigen—perhaps there was no clear dividing line—but the fact that they were called different things would have a big impact on the magnitude of Mei Yin's guilt. Scrambling to regain his footing, he retorted, "Counsel for the defense seems to have forgotten the analyses of three august bodies? When the reports were read earlier, the defense raised no objections."

Du Chunming said calmly, "And I still raise no objections—a weakened smallpox antigen is, in the broadest sense, still a smallpox virus, not white pox or chickenpox. But the main distinction between an antigen and the original virus is that an antigen is not infectious. When you provided these institutions with samples to analyze, you instructed them to identify either smallpox or white pox, and all three organizations came up with the right answer. But if you'd asked them to test for a live virus versus an antigen, I'm sure their reports would have said something different. Viruses become antigens after being weakened, and can be differentiated by their DNA structure. Many viruses, including rabies and polio, are treated by using their attenuated antigens. In the past, the treatment for smallpox didn't use antigens, because of a coincidence in the natural world: the cowpox virus, very similar to smallpox, is relatively nonpathogenic while inducing immunity to smallpox. Thus, research into smallpox antigens has been completely neglected—until now. Stebushkin and Mei Yin successfully developed the smallpox antigen, using a combination of the West African, Asian, and South American strains.

"I'd like to respectfully inform the court that we've commissioned a second analysis, and the results arrived two days ago: Mei Yin's lab was producing a smallpox antigen, not the virus itself."

The prosecutor smiled coldly. "Yet the antigens you speak of infected a thousand people with smallpox, killing one and disfiguring many others."

Du Chunming replied levelly, "In fact, far more than a thousand people were infected. My client estimates the true figure to be over ten thousand, most of whom experienced such mild symptoms that they weren't included in the tally—but they too will have quietly acquired immunity to smallpox. Do you think there were no victims with cowpox? Let me give you a figure. When America was using cowpox inoculations nationwide, seventy-five thousand people died each year as a result, and one in a few hundred thousand patients suffered from gangrenous vaccinia, allergic purpura, encephalitis, and other complications. Seventy-five thousand!

"As for my client's antigen, it was not completely attenuated, so it remained somewhat virulent and lead to one death and several disfigurements. My client expresses deep guilt over this. But I have to cite another figure: even if we accept the official count, this leak has resulted in at least one thousand people having immunity for life. The outbreak in America, even with access to the best medical treatment in the world, still resulted in 143 deaths, and left tens of thousands disfigured."

The prosecutor found this line of attack hard to rebut. It would seem the defendant had indeed weakened the smallpox virus, and as to whether the result counted as smallpox or an antigen—that was a linguistic problem. Yet it could lead to a large gulf in sentencing—it was a crime to disseminate viruses and bacteria, but not antigens! And with this little space for maneuver, Du could keep muddying the waters, until the accused was cleared of the main charge. Heaven knew if the virus she'd smuggled in from Russia had been weakened. Stebushkin was dead, and the dead give no evidence.

All eyes were focused on the prosecutor. With little time to think, he could only say, "Counsel for the defense, you claim what the defendant brought in from Russia wasn't smallpox, but a weakened antigen. Please produce your evidence for this."

Smiling breezily, Du said, "Oh, I don't know. Everything I've just said is only a hypothesis. As for whether the cold-storage box that was brought across the border contained smallpox, antigens, or a man's sperm—for all we know, my client planned to have a baby with her Russian lover through artificial insemination—I have no idea at all. As the prosecutor has charged my client with the criminal act of 'illegally transporting an infectious pathogen,' please let him produce his evidence."

The prosecutor blushed from ear to ear. In his panic he'd committed a major error—the burden of proof was indeed on him. Yet this wouldn't be easy. The smuggling case was already weak, relying on the presence of smallpox in the lab for the chain of circumstantial evidence to be convincing. But now, with the contents of the lab shown to be antigens, the whole chain came crashing down. He conferred tersely with his assistants, for the moment unable to answer.

In the audience, Xue Yu was delighted. His understanding was that Ms. Mei had been cultivating an attenuated version of the virus for all these years. That was beyond question. Why hadn't he thought of that himself, to help Ms. Mei prove her innocence? Du really was a clever lawyer. He looked set to help Ms. Mei escape the net of the law altogether. The only thing that made him uneasy was something Las Casas had said: *"Wasn't it too much of a coincidence that the Chinese epidemic took place right after the American outbreak?"* This doubt, however, was no more than a tiny cloud on the horizon, and Xue Yu didn't pay it much attention. It would be a few days later that he'd realize the small cloud had expanded into a full-blown storm.

The prosecuting team still hadn't thought of an effective comeback, and Jin Mingcheng was becoming embarrassed for them, so much so that he turned to study the audience instead. The most prominent members were, of course, the seven foreigners—particularly the old man in the middle, with his weathered features and upright spine, his silvery hair and beard, looking like a biblical prophet. The seven individuals sat in silence, not even talking among themselves. Their mere presence, though, was an imperceptible threat. After years of acquaintance, Jin was well aware of how much Mei Yin respected, even worshiped, her adoptive father, which gave him an enigmatic air. Jin had never seen a picture of the man, and here he was, stepping out of mystery into reality.

Mei Yin, in the defendant's seat, actually hadn't paid much attention to the discussion in court. Instead, she kept her gaze fixed on her adoptive father. He was sitting bolt upright in the back row, like a statue, reminding her of a trip they'd taken to Africa almost forty years ago, during the Ebola outbreak in Zaire. The day he'd finished dealing with the epidemic, her father had sat just like this, bolt upright beneath an acacia tree, all through the night.

Jin Mingcheng had noticed Mei Yin's focus on her father. A short time later, he also noticed Mei Yin's expression change, then she whispered something to her lawyer. He swiftly glanced into the crowd, then wrote a note to the judge. The judge looked in the same direction, then summoned a bailiff and murmured an instruction. The bailiff hurried to the back row of the audience, and spoke to the outermost of the seven foreigners. That person leaped up in shock, then leaned over to Walt Dickerson, in the center of the row, prodding him and calling his name. Dickerson didn't move. All six foreigners were now flustered, screaming in English, "Quick, call an ambulance!"

Susan Sotomayor, his companion, stroked the old man's hand, checked his nose for breath, then pulled up his eyelids. She shook her head. "No use."

Jin Mingcheng's English wasn't good enough to follow what they were saying, but it was obvious what had happened. Mr. Dickerson had passed away. Like a Buddhist monk, he'd died while seated. Judging by rigor mortis, he'd been dead some time already, but maintained his upright posture, so even his colleagues sitting beside him didn't notice. Jin walked to the entrance and called an ambulance from his cell phone. After a moment's thought, he summoned a hearse too.

Mei Yin knew her fears had been realized. She moved to stand, then looked imploringly at the chief judge. He hesitated, then conferred with both his colleagues before standing to announce, "Due to an unfortunate incident, we'll end here today. Court is adjourned."

He nodded at the defendant. "Go ahead." Mei Yin and her lawyer rushed into the audience. By this time, most people were aware of what had happened, and the courtroom was in chaos, the bailiffs vainly trying to restore order, shepherding the onlookers out as quickly as possible. Those being forced out kept twisting round, standing on tiptoe as they looked back, some reporters holding cameras over their heads in an attempt to get a shot.

Fewer than twenty people were left in the room. Apart from the six foreigners, there were Mei Yin, her husband, and their lawyers; the two bailiffs; Deputy Mayor Jin, Las Casas, and Xue Yu. Walt Dickerson remained seated, his expression peaceful, his body still not completely stiff, though his hands and feet were already cold. His eyes were halfway shut, and still seemed to be squinting at the world. Mei Yin gazed sorrowfully at her adoptive father, her eyes red, but holding back the tears. Sun Jingshuan came over and embraced his wife. The bailiffs moved toward them, hesitated, then finally decided to leave them alone.

The ambulance and hearse arrived together. The paramedics ran over with their stretcher, then saw the posture of the deceased, and looked to Mei Yin for how to proceed. She sighed and said, "Let's take him directly to the crematorium." She turned to the six foreigners. "I'll have to trouble you to deal with his remains. The ashes can be scattered anywhere you like. My father didn't believe in concepts like nationality or territory. Jin, I may have to leave this to you . . ."

"Not to worry. The two of you will be able to attend the funeral, I'll talk to the detention center and make it happen."

"Thank you."

She looked at Xue Yu but said nothing. He knew she wanted to ask about his search for Xiaoxue. It had been three months since she'd disappeared, and he'd done his best, even getting the police to put out a bulletin, but hadn't turned up a single clue. "Ms. Mei, I'm still trying my best to look for Xiaoxue," he said, guiltily. "I'll find her no matter what. Don't let it trouble you."

"Thank you."

Walt Dickerson was hefted onto the stretcher, and carefully carried to the hearse. The back doors slammed shut, separating him forever from the world of the living. Mei Yin and the others watched the hearse until it was gone, then she got into the patrol car with Sun Jingshuan.

The couple got special treatment at the detention center, where they had their own rooms. Like the other cells, these contained a large bed frame, wide enough for seventeen or eighteen people, with a space all around the bed about the width of a single person. Normal inmates were forced to squat in that space in an orderly line anytime they weren't sleeping. The ceiling was very high, and a dull yellow lightbulb hung from it, like the murky eye of an old man, staring at Mei Yin all night. Attached to this room was a balcony half open to the sky, to provide some fresh air. A sturdy steel net covered the opening. Against the wall were a sink, a faucet, and a toilet bowl. There was nothing else. No tables, no chairs, no lamps.

Conditions might be basic here, but Mei Yin didn't mind. She'd been used to deprivation since childhood, even after Walt brought her to the States. He'd often taken her traveling to the poorest countries in the world as part of his work. They'd been places where a bed frame as large as this would have been a luxury. He'd hoped to train her in his profession, which meant getting used to these conditions.

She was allowed one other special privilege: the door between the cell and the balcony was never locked, so she could go in and out as she pleased. That night, after tossing and turning, unable to sleep, she pulled on her clothes and went into the open-air section, sitting cross-legged on the icy cement floor, looking up at the night sky through the wire mesh. She remembered the trip to Africa, the day of her adoptive father's "enlightenment." He'd done this too, sat cross-legged outside the tent, looking up through the sparse acacia leaves, staring for a long time at the profound dome above him.

She seemed to hear footsteps from the neighboring cell. Was her husband also suffering from insomnia? Although the couple had been right next door to each other these past three months, they might as well have been separated by an entire galaxy. She walked to the wall, intending to knock on it, but then noticed the surveillance camera in a corner of the ceiling, smiled at it, and gave up the idea. She was being treated very well here, and didn't want to abuse the privileges she'd been given. Jingshuan loved her a lot, but it wasn't clear if their marriage would survive. She would have to harden her heart to spread the teachings of her father—how else could she deal with the unavoidable suffering and death, including Dr. Ma's misfortune, Xiaoxue's ruined face, the passing away of Granny Sun and her adoptive father? And there was no avoiding attaining noble goals through despicable means, but Sun Jingshuan's heart was too soft, too conventional, especially since Granny's death had all but crushed him. He was sunk deep in guilt. She couldn't put her husband through such torture.

So she'd tell him to go away, to leave her. To come down off this cross.

The security panel in the door slid open. Nighttime inspection. A female guard saw her sitting on the balcony, and knowing she must be devastated at the loss of her father, said softly, "It's late, you should rest. My condolences."

Mei Yin replied quietly, "Thank you. I'll go to bed now."

She returned to the bed frame, but sleep continued to evade her. Her mind kept churning back to Xiaoxue. Where was the girl now? Mei Yin herself had grown up in an orphanage too, and she was more than ten when her adoptive father took her away, all the way to America. She understood Xiaoxue's thirst for a family, for parents. And now her wishes had been destroyed, and her face ruined. These blows might have been too much to take. Mei Yin worried if she'd survive.

Hopefully Xue Yu would find her very soon. Hopefully.

1979—Africa

When Mei Yin was ten, her adoptive parents finally finished the last of the paperwork in China, and brought their orphan girl to America, a new and glamorous vista for her. Later, Walt Dickerson brought her on a voyage to Africa, opening yet another landscape before her: undeveloped, beautiful, ravaged by bone-deep poverty and awful epidemics, yet imbued with such strong life . . . All of this, in the end, would sublimate itself into her philosophy of life.

It was the summer of 1979, and her father brought her to the Serengeti National Park to see wild animals—but they found themselves on a very different kind of adventure. The pair took a plane to Wilson Airport in Nairobi. As soon as they reached the gangway, an officer in his forties came over. "Professor Dickerson from the Atlanta CDC? I'm Mr. Smith, the American ambassador to Kenya."

Her father smiled. "Yes, I'm Dickerson. I didn't expect a welcome from the embassy—this is just a private vacation."

Mr. Smith smiled grimly. "I'm afraid your vacation will have to be postponed. The CDC's just sent a telegram, asking me to pass it to you."

This message read:

> *Deadly epidemic in Yambio, South Sudan. Suspected Ebola. CDC and WHO sending teams ASAP. Prof Dickerson and daughter traveling in Africa. Please inform him necessary to obtain virus specimens from Yambio. Prof knows where to get supplies. Thank you.*

Dickerson did indeed know how to find the necessary supplies. Three years earlier, during the first outbreak of Ebola in Africa, he'd been part of the medical team sent here, and on that occasion they'd left behind equipment, including syringes, glass plates, specimen bottles, hand-operated centrifuges, and so on. They were all stored at a nearby Belgian church, in the church refrigerator (which operated on kerosene, the local electricity supply being none too reliable), along with some blood plasma from recovered victims. The team thought it likely that they'd need these things again before too long, and unfortunately they were right. Dickerson didn't have a current visa to Sudan, but that wasn't a problem. Epidemics frequently cross borders, no visa required, and by convention medical response teams were often allowed to use their yellow cards—the WHO's international certificate of vaccination—to get through immigration. Dickerson paused for a moment after reading the telegram. As an epidemiologist, he was duty-bound to obey, but he had to consider what to do with Cassie.

Mr. Smith said, "Your daughter is welcome to remain at the embassy, where I will be responsible for her. Is she here to see the wildlife? I can send someone to take her on safari, so her vacation won't be interrupted."

Mei Yin protested. "Dad, I want to go into the epidemic zone with you."

Before Dickerson could say anything, Smith exploded in shock. "The epidemic zone? A young girl like you? You don't know what it's like there—hell on earth! Even the airlines are refusing to land there, and no drivers are willing to go."

Mei Yin said nothing, only looked at her adoptive father. In the few years since she'd arrived in the United States, she'd more or less become an American girl, though the marks of China would never completely fade. She'd never forgotten her biological parents, for instance, and the fact that they'd died of plague had made up her mind to be an epidemiologist like her adoptive father. Dickerson knew this was her ambition, and so said, after another pause, "All right, come with me." Then, to the stunned Mr. Smith, he said, "My daughter wants to be an epidemiologist, and this is a rare chance for her to get some practical experience. Besides, I could do with an assistant. Don't worry—the so-called Level-Four viruses are terrifying, but they can be defended against, and we know how."

Smith argued with him for a long time before finally giving up and arranging plane tickets. The three of them sat in the airport lounge, waiting for the next flight to Khartoum. Smith asked Dickerson what he thought the outbreak might be—Lassa fever, green monkey disease, yellow fever, Crimean-Congo hemorrhagic fever, or Ebola, only just discovered in 1976.

"That's what I'm going there to find out. But I'd guess it's Ebola."

Mei Yin knew that all the illnesses Smith had mentioned were extremely deadly, particularly the last one, which was both airborne and spread through contact. During the 1976 outbreak in Zaire, the death rate was 90 percent. A vaccine had still not been found, and there was no treatment.

Smith asked, "Mr. Dickerson, you're an expert, perhaps you can tell me why pestilence is so fond of Africa? This continent has almost all the diseases of Europe and Asia, including leprosy, smallpox, tuberculosis, rabies, and so on. It also has quite a few of its own, such as Lassa fever, green monkey disease, Crimean-Congo hemorrhagic fever, Ebola, the sleeping sickness, all of them particularly virulent viruses. Conditions in the New World were exactly the opposite. When America and Australia were discovered, the natives only gave the colonizers syphilis, a relatively benign illness; the colonizers brought them smallpox and the flu in return."

Smith's question gave Dickerson pause. "I don't know. I'd guess it might be because this is the 'Old World.' Humankind had its start here, and it's quite possible that so did all pathogens. The long process of evolution would have created many different varieties of illnesses."

"That can't be right! I know in the medical world they say pathogens and human beings, in general, have a cordial relationship. One the one hand, humanity slowly develops immunities; on the other, extremely virulent pathogens die along with their hosts, which doesn't help them at all. So in the course of evolution, pathogens generally grow milder. If you look at how smallpox and the flu have changed in various continents, Europe and Asia, Australia and the Americas, this theory is borne out. Yet it breaks down in Africa—why? This continent was the cradle of humanity, yet it's also where viruses are strongest."

Dickerson was silent for a very long time, and finally had to admit, "I don't know. The experts don't have any answers for that one. Let me think about it, and see if I can come up with a convincing explanation."

The plane to Khartoum was boarding, and Mr. Smith tried one last time to dissuade them. "It really is terribly dangerous to head into an epidemic zone. Why don't you let the girl stay behind at the embassy?" Mei Yin smiled and shook her head, and Dickerson said, "Thank you for your concern, but she's coming with me."

Mr. Smith sighed and patted Mei Yin on the shoulder. "All right, then. Bon voyage, brave girl. I salute your courage."

At Khartoum, they needed a connecting flight to Nzala, but just as Smith had said, no one would fly there. Dickerson, who had experience in this area, went straight to the American embassy, and got them onto a police plane that would bring them directly to Nzala. On the flight, he whispered to Mei Yin, "Don't mention the epidemic in front of the pilots."

"They don't know they're flying into an infection zone?"

"From the way they're talking, it appears not, or at least they don't know how serious things are. But if they did, they might not . . ." He shrugged.

Mei Yin felt this way of doing things was a little dishonorable—tricking unwitting pilots into entering an outbreak region. But her father spoke very calmly, and clearly believed that if it meant saving thousands of suffering, near-death victims in the area, God would forgive him a few small lies. They landed at dusk. Nzala Airport was just a bumpy tarmac runway, and the arrivals hall a tin shack next to it.

The pilots learned about the severity of the epidemic in short order, and were desperate to leave. Unfortunately, the plane couldn't be serviced and refueled until the next day, which meant they'd have to spend the night there. Dickerson quietly rejoiced: now he could collect blood plasma samples overnight, make some hasty analyses, then have the returning plane bring them straight to the American embassy at

Khartoum, where the samples could be delivered to the CDC for closer study. In 1979, no detailed research had been done into Ebola, and they could only use indirect immunofluorescence to identify antibodies. It would take more time and specialized equipment to separate a particular virus from cultivated tissue or cells. Reaching that point a day earlier might save hundreds of lives.

The pilots spent the night at the local government rest house. Father and daughter headed to the Belgian church to pick up their supplies, after which they drove through the night to the hospital at Yambio. Although Mei Yin had spent more than ten years of her life in China, she'd never seen such grinding poverty. The hospital was a row of mud huts with thatched roofs, each with small kerosene lamps throwing flickering light over two dozen dying patients lying on straw mats on a dirt floor, their bodies rigid, wheezing deep in their throats. There was only one doctor here, named Adi—the rest of the medical staff had abandoned their posts and fled. Some patients had their families with them, though most awaited death alone. Even Dickerson, accustomed to terrible scenes of infection, was shocked by the desolation. Family ties were important here, and the sick usually received very good care. Flocks of relatives would usually descend on hospitals to tend to them, and after death, they'd be ritually washed, inside and out, and the entire tribe would hold a wake, wailing and smearing ash on their faces. The funeral rituals would last more than ten days. Unfortunately, these customs often led to even more infection, and in the past medical teams had tried hard to dissuade families from visiting, but to no avail. It was unheard of for patients to be left in such isolation like this. Apparently, the virulence of this epidemic had shaken the very foundations of traditional African society.

Adi was a kind-hearted doctor with curly black hair, a fondness for palm wine, and an optimistic outlook on life that allowed him to focus on the big picture. Dickerson learned from him the source of the outbreak: a few tribespeople had contracted the illness while eating chimpanzee meat, but it was this hospital, with its poor hygiene and untrained staff, that had turned an infection into an epidemic.

He helped Mei Yin put on a white plastic protective suit and mask. Dickerson himself wore no such thing, finding the gear unbearable in the high summer heat of Africa, and restrictive to his work. Ebola might be terrifying, but experience told him a mask alone would be sufficient to prevent airborne infection. The main thing was to avoid accidents such as getting pricked by a syringe. Still, for the sake of precaution, he insisted his daughter wear full protective gear.

Dickerson knelt to examine each patient, while Mei Yin held the kerosene lamp for him, her eyes round as she watched her adoptive father at work. Going by the symptoms, this was very likely a second outbreak of the dreaded Ebola. As Dickerson carried out his inspection, he told Mei Yin how to make a diagnosis. Mild internal bleeding was a classic early symptom, but it was difficult to see the telltale red or purple spots on the dark-skinned patients, particularly in such poor light. Instead, he pried open their eyelids, searching for blood in the whites. Or else he opened their mouths, looking for blisters on the palate, checking if their throats were inflamed. Among twenty-one patients, he found seven confirmed cases of Ebola, the rest highly likely. He told Adi to inform the relatives, and to move the seven definite infections to a quarantine room, where blood plasma could be drawn from them. All this had to be done very fast, because the plasma and red blood cells would need to be separated. In the absence of electricity, this could only be done with a manual centrifuge, a process that took a good half hour.

Adi had been working for five days straight, and was near the point of collapse. After the initial examination was complete, Dickerson insisted he go home to rest. Father and daughter had been on the road for more than twenty hours, and then come straight to the hospital to work. They were so exhausted they could barely keep their eyes open. Dickerson urged his daughter to rest, but she shook her head and pushed away the fatigue. Her voice blurred by her mask, she said, "I'm not tired. I'll help you finish."

Dickerson pitied his daughter, but also needed an assistant, so he nodded. "All right, you can sleep when we've taken all these samples."

Now it came to the taking of samples, which Dickerson did while Mei Yin held down the patients—many of them weren't lucid and couldn't follow instructions. They began to draw blood from the suspected cases. One of them was an old woman with loose skin and prominent bones. She had a high fever, and was incoherent. There were no obvious marks on her body, but she'd definitely come from the Ebola zone, and her high temperature made Dickerson suspect she was infected too. Mei Yin held down her arm while her father stuck a needle into a vein, and began extracting the blood. The old woman suddenly reared up, with surprising strength. Perhaps Mei Yin was too tired to hold the arm in place—the needle slipped out and stabbed through Dickerson's left glove.

He immediately ripped the glove off. At the base of his thumbnail was a bright drop of blood.

In 1976, during the first outbreak, Dickerson had been in a lab in London when his colleague Bradley, who was working on animal experiments, was nicked by a needle. Even though Bradley immediately flushed the wound with disinfectant, he fell gravely ill and almost died. Fortunately, the accident took place in England rather than Africa, and he'd had access to first-rate medical care. During the subsequent inquiry, an official at the British Department of Health asked why he hadn't taken more decisive action, and sliced off his thumb right away? It wasn't a joke; losing a thumb would be far preferable to contracting Ebola. If Dickerson didn't try, it was likely because he didn't want to frighten his daughter.

Mei Yin's face drained of blood. Her clumsiness might have cost her father his life! Tears fell from her eyes, leaving two streaks inside her mask, and her shoulders trembled. Dickerson rushed to comfort her. "Don't, don't be frightened. I'll disinfect it right away. It'll be fine."

He soaked his hand in antiseptic. There was no cure for the Ebola virus, apart from an injection of blood serum from a recovered victim, which contained the necessary antibodies. He did have samples of such blood serum on hand, and while they weren't fresh, they'd been through a thorough filtering process to remove impurities. An injection would provide at least psychological reassurance. He filled a syringe with the antibody-rich serum and asked Mei Yin to inject him with it.

Now they could only wait. It was two in the morning by the time they'd finished with the seven confirmed cases. Apart from praying that the old lady didn't actually have Ebola, they also prayed that the antibodies would be effective. Although Dickerson's mood was dark and his body exhausted, he still had to finish the task of separating the blood. Mei Yin brushed her tears away and said, "Dad, you rest, I'll crank the centrifuge."

Knowing he couldn't talk her out of it, yet not trusting her to work on her own, he sat to one side, directing her as she separated out a dozen blood samples, storing them in the dry ice they'd brought from Khartoum. The centrifuge was exhausting to operate, but Mei Yin refused to let her father take a turn. It was almost dawn by the time the job was done, the last stars twinkling in the dark blue sky, the wide grasslands shrouded in fog. Dickerson forced his daughter to rest, though he still needed to carry out a luminescence test for antibodies, the first step in confirming the nature of the epidemic.

Pulling off her protective gear, Mei Yin lay on the straw mat next to her father, and in a short while was fast asleep. Dickerson put a portion of the infected blood serum into a small jar, having already prepared glass slides fixed with Ebola-affected cells. When he dropped the blood serum onto the slides and shone fluorescent light onto them, a twinkling light would mean it was positive for Ebola antibodies.

Dickerson left the old woman's test for last. Six of the earlier tests were definitely Ebola, seven death sentences pronounced by a gleam of light. When Dickerson got to the final slide, he adjusted the microscope particularly slowly. On the slide the cells came into focus, revealing their outlines and nuclei, gray and green and black, with patches of brightness—but no twinkle.

Dickerson let out a long breath. It didn't definitely rule out Ebola, as the patient might have been in the early stages of infection, before antibodies developed. At the very least, though, his death sentence had been postponed. He longed to tell his daughter the good news, but she was sleeping so soundly he couldn't bear to wake her. But at this moment Mei Yin lifted her head and asked blearily, "Dad, did you do the fluorescence test? Was it negative?"

Even in her dreams, she'd been worried. Dickerson wanted to kiss her, but stopped himself with the thought that he wasn't completely in the clear yet. Instead, he lightly said, "Yes, negative."

Mei Yin was wide awake in an instant. She jumped up and hugged her father, cheering, her eyes shining. Dickerson quickly put his hand over her mouth, lest she kiss him in her excitement.

In the morning, father and daughter rushed to Nzala Airport. The pilots were itching to depart. Dickerson handed over the packed blood serum and cell samples, and asked the pilots to deliver them to the American embassy as quickly as possible. The pilots had no medical knowledge, and no idea that their cargo contained the very Ebola virus they were so desperate to flee. The lead pilot only asked in passing, "What's so urgent?"

Deadpan, Dickerson answered, "Just my papers. They're almost out of date, and I need to rush them to the embassy for a new visa."

Cheerful now that departure was imminent, the pilot smiled and said, "Don't worry, I'll get it to them pronto."

The broken-down police airplane wobbled down the bumpy runway, looking for a moment like it might not take off, before finally rising and disappearing into the northern sky. Mei Yin sneaked a glance at her father's face. He looked peaceful, not in the least bit guilty at having just told a lie. Of course, the specimens were all sealed up, and the pilots shouldn't be at any risk of infection—though if they got curious and decided to have a look inside, or if the plane crashed and someone else stumbled upon them, that would be a different story. This was Mei Yin's second lesson in her father's way of doing things, and an important one: in the pursuit of a noble goal, it may be necessary to use ignoble tactics.

It was a lesson Mei Yin took to heart.

Days later, when the follow-up team from the WHO arrived, father and daughter said good-bye to Dr. Adi, then went to see the old woman one last time. She had more or less recovered, and was sitting up in bed, running her fingers through her tangled hair, chatting to her neighbor in a language they didn't understand. She naturally had no memory of the blood-drawing incident, and no idea that her own recovery had signaled someone else's salvation too. Mei Yin and her father looked at her and laughed, their hearts full of unspoken joy.

It was only in 1986, a full five years after AIDS had been discovered, that Dickerson suddenly thought of the six hundred blood samples he'd taken in Zaire back in 1976. They'd all been tested for Ebola, but could the AIDS virus have been present too? Mei Yin had graduated early from the University of North Carolina by then, and was working at the CDC's new AIDS laboratory. Dickerson proposed revisiting the samples, and with the CDC's agreement, retrieved them from cold storage. The blood specimens were old and degraded, but Mei Yin finally succeeded in cultivating cells from them, and achieved a result—0.8 percent of the samples were from AIDS victims.

The virus isolated by Mei Yin was the original form of the AIDS virus, and proved very helpful to subsequent researchers looking into its later mutations. Later, the CDC carried out a large-scale investigation into several countries in Central Africa, finally proving that AIDS had had a stable presence in the villages of Central Africa for quite some time, with an infection rate of about 0.8 to 0.9 percent, a comparatively mild transmittable disease. What's more, until the late eighties, it maintained this comparatively low rate of infection in these villages. In the cities, however, it suddenly became the scourge of an entire era.

Fortunately, the vial of serum Dickerson had injected himself with ten years before hadn't been among that 0.8 percent, otherwise he'd have had the distinction of being the very first AIDS patient in America.

After leaving the infection zone, Mei Yin and her father hurried to the Serengeti grasslands, on the border of Tanzania and Kenya. In the tribal language, this area was known as the "eternally flowing land," though it wasn't the grasslands that moved, but the animals on them. Every summer, millions of wildebeests and zebras would migrate northward to the Maasai Mara wetlands, only returning during the dry season.

Mei Yin had watched the wildebeest migration on TV and felt drawn to it—perhaps the idea of returning to one's ancestral lands resonated with her. After watching this program, she couldn't stop thinking about it, and kept asking her father: When can we go to Africa to see it? And now, her wish was finally granted.

Dickerson rented a Jeep and drove to the Grumeti River, which intersected the migration route diagonally and, as the only water source along the way, was a guaranteed spot for seeing the wildebeests. Their driver/guide was a Maasai tribesperson. He spoke a little French, but Dickerson's grasp of the language was only enough for the most basic conversation. In the end, they simply handed over the task of navigation to him, since discussion was essentially impossible.

They stopped by the river and spread out a blanket as a simple bed. They ate their dry rations and drank river water, which tasted like nectar as far as Mei Yin was concerned. In Zaire, they'd used iodine to make the water potable, which gave it an awful flavor. That night, they were so worn out they fell asleep right away. The next day, soon after the sun rose, there was a faraway sound like drumbeats. The driver pressed his ear to the ground, then pointed into the distance and yelled in delight, "They're coming! They're coming!"

Great plumes of dust rose from the horizon, and the morning light fell on a sheet of moving life, a great tide of flesh. Millions of wildebeests appeared majestically from the south, charging toward the Grumeti River. Around the herbivores were lions and cheetahs, keeping pace with them, keeping watch for the young ones, launching sneak attacks under cover of dust clouds. The wildebeests accepted these losses with equanimity, though occasionally a mother would tussle with the lion prides, usually to no effect. When a death was inevitable, the mothers howled with grief, then returned to the herd and continued the journey. Now they were at the river, and at the foot of the steep banks was the water they longed for, though instinct told them there were deadly enemies within—crocodiles. The lead wildebeest tottered toward the bank, sniffing every few steps, calling out and retreating, a back-and-forth dance with death. The ones behind could smell the water and pushed impatiently ahead, inexorably forcing the lead animals into the water. Finally, one of the herd tumbled in, then immediately reared up, scrambling back to shore, panicking the rest. The crocodiles began to attack, and with a flash of teeth a wildebeest was caught around the neck, its throat ripped open an instant later. A few more wildebeests were bitten to death in quick succession and dragged underwater, fresh blood spreading through the river, dyeing it red. But fear seemed to leave the others now, and they boldly roared, stepping on the bodies of their companions and even of the crocodiles, surging to the opposite shore. The vast majority of the animals made it across, shaking off water, and without a moment's pause continuing their stampede across the grasslands.

The Maasai guide laughed at the sight, so familiar to him. Mei Yin was deeply moved, however, and could barely hold back her tears. It was a true battle of life and death, the fate of the species in the balance. The bodies left behind became a river of life, individual sacrifices exchanged for the survival of the species. It was a play that had been acted out for billions of years.

One wildebeest escaped from a crocodile's jaws, and tottered its way up the shore. Its wounds didn't look fatal, but after swaying a little more, it tumbled to the ground not far away. Dickerson said to Mei Yin, "I think this one might be ill. Let's take a look."

The two of them went over and knelt for a closer examination. Sure enough, tears and saliva were streaming from its face, the mucous membrane of its mouth unnaturally flushed, and when it fell, foul-smelling bloody stools seeped from its rear. Seeing the humans approach, it struggled to stand, but didn't have the strength. A leopard had been eyeing this animal and now slowly approached, snarling and snapping at the two of them. The guide quickly pulled them back into the Jeep.

As the Jeep pulled away, Dickerson said, "That leopard was doing a good deed. The wildebeest had cattle plague, and couldn't have been saved. By eating it, the predator makes it less likely that the disease will spread to the rest of the species."

Mei Yin listened carefully, not saying a word. Only later in the evening, when they were eating dinner, did she suddenly ask, "Dad, you said cattle plague was highly infectious, so why wasn't that wildebeest herd wiped out by it? They're mammals, like humans, so their immune systems should be similar too. And they migrate in such a tight pack, squeezed together, diseases should spread between them even more easily than between humans in cities. Besides, there aren't any wildebeest doctors, no vaccines or inoculation, and no stupid protective suits or masks."

Dickerson laughed. She'd hated having to wear all that protective gear over the last few days; she'd refused to put it on during their last day, and he'd been forced to give in. Now, he said, "That's right, imagine a million wildebeests all in protective masks, that'd be quite a sight. Actually, there is a kind of medicine among the wildebeests—God's medicine, that is, natural selection. Those susceptible to illness are eliminated, whether by the sickness or predators, so that leaves only the individuals with good immunity. Of course, this isn't workable with human beings. Ever since the time of Hippocrates, medicine has been inextricably linked with humanism. Medical science is built on the foundation of individual lives, and its objective could be summed up as one single golden rule: save the individual, not the species."

"Huh, at least these wild animals live naturally. Look at the wildebeests, so strong and full of energy! Seeing them run across the plains, I feel like they're not animals, but flying spirits. So, the way I see it, God's medicine is every bit as good as human medicine."

This statement stunned Dickerson. Thirty years in medical research, yet never noticing the most obvious truth. The standard of human health was no better than the wildebeests'—perhaps worse. Now, God was staging a great drama in the African wilderness, and the actors were millions of beasts, brimming with the energy of life. These creatures instinctively knew God's instructions, and were a living demonstration of these rules—and it was a child who'd first understood this. He sighed. "But it's not the same."

Mei Yin wasn't buying it. "Why not?"

"God's medicine actually seems more effective. The way he does it, the individual is perpetually in danger of death, but the balance between the whole species and the pathogens is stable. Even when there are ups and downs, they're not too violent, so the species won't suddenly collapse. Whereas in human medicine, the individual gets complete protection, but as a species we have a most unstable relationship with pathogens, and the whole system becomes susceptible to a crash. Truly, scientists should seriously consider your question. Speaking of which, I have an answer to Mr. Smith's question, from the Wilson Airport in Nairobi."

"Yes?"

"There's nothing wrong with the theory that, on the whole, pathogens and their hosts find a stable balance. African viruses have a long history, so there are more strains than on other continents. And among their original hosts, such as the green monkeys or gorillas, they are indeed a benign presence. It's only the growth of modern civilization that's disrupted the original balance too much. Add that to the many varieties of African viruses, and that's what makes them so deadly to humans."

Mei Yin said thoughtfully, "Oh, I see."

That night, several large herds of wildebeests remained by the riverside. Having eaten and drunk their fill, they were sauntering along the banks, the calves squirming playfully around their mother's legs. The lions, also full, rested nearby at the river's edge. The wildebeests, zebras, and gazelles ignored the lions, even daring to frolic quite close to them, instinctively knowing that if the predators' bellies were heavy with food, they wouldn't need to kill. The shroud of night lowered over the plains, and a peaceful stillness lay on the riverside, as if the daytime slaughter had never happened.

They decided to sleep in the open air, as before. National Park guidelines forbade this, but if a baby wildebeest wasn't afraid of the lions, why should they be? The Maasai guide was even less bothered, his tribe having historically viewed both lions and wildebeests as part of the family. He spread out the blankets, and quickly fell asleep. Mei Yin and her father sat cross-legged on the grass, gazing at the dome of the sky, watching the twilight clouds grow dimmer, as the first stars appeared and a new moon rose. Their surroundings were slowly swallowed by darkness, not a glimmer of light, not a hint of civilization. Nature had been forging its own path for billions of years, and would continue to do so, indifferent to the ups and downs of a certain intelligent species.

Resting her head on her father's knee, Mei Yin slipped into sleep. She woke again late in the night, and saw he was in the same position, still gazing up at the sky, his eyes glittering. She murmured, "Dad, why're you still awake?" In a moment she was asleep again, but Dickerson stayed up almost till dawn. The Crucifix Society and its teachings came into being that night. He came to understand that the living world had reached a point of natural equilibrium through billions of years of evolution. Humans were now disturbing that equilibrium. They couldn't return to the natural condition of wildebeests—it was too late for that. *Homo sapiens* could only continue along the road, and seek a new equilibrium.

In the morning, he shook her awake and said, "Get up, look at the sunrise over Africa, how beautiful it is!" The scenery was breathtaking, animal silhouettes swirling in the distance as the mist rose around them, like spirits in a dream. Her father's smile was just as radiant, seeming to come from deep within his heart, his face mysteriously glowing.

Spring 2017—Nanyang, China

Dickerson's funeral took place three days after his death. Deputy Mayor Jin gave his personal assurance to the detention center, so that the two defendants were able to attend. Several members of the Crucifix Society were there, of course, as was Xue Yu, but no one else. The cavernous hall that could have held a thousand felt empty. The cross around his neck had been taken off and presented to Mei Yin. His body was turned into a pile of warm ashes on foreign soil. Mei Yin scattered half of them into the nearby river, and gave the other half to Susan Sotomayor to bring back to the States. Her adoptive father was a citizen of the world, but if he had such a thing as a soul, it would feel closer to home there.

The trial resumed the next day. Xue Yu arrived very early and saved a place for Deputy Mayor Jin. It was Mother Chen's turn to come watch, and she sat on his other side, muttering anxiously. "What'll happen to Director Mei? Will she be jailed? It never rains but it pours: first her granny dies, then her dad, and now she and her man are both going to prison. How much can one person take?"

The deputy mayor was early too. Recognizing him, Mother Chen quickly leaned over and repeated the whole speech. Jin reassured her. "It's up to the court whether or not she goes to prison, but the way things are looking, it should be a light sentence."

"That's good, that's good."

The day before, there'd been a meeting between the city's legal committee leaders, the city council, the municipal government, and the prosecutor's office. They all agreed they'd met their main objective—demonstrating the nation's innocence—and so could afford to go easy on Mei Yin. If her lawyer managed to get her off altogether, then why not allow her some leniency. Her actions, after all, had shown her to be on the side of humanity, even if her opinions and behavior were somewhat extreme. Besides, the most serious charge—smuggling the smallpox virus from abroad—lacked persuasive evidence. The prosecutor's attitude had softened.

The foreigners were in court too, sitting in the same place, an empty seat in the middle for the deceased. The journalists in the back row recognized Deputy Mayor Jin and pointed at him, whispering. Then the defendants, prosecutor, and judges had all arrived, and court was in session. The judge said, "Previously, the defense said it had conducted its own analysis of the virus specimens from Heavenly Corp. Please produce your results."

The defense lawyer smiled mirthlessly. "No need for that. My client wishes to change her plea to guilty."

The audience couldn't believe their ears. Xue Yu stared in shock at Ms. Mei, but from where he was, he could only see her profile. Next to him, Mother Chen was asking doubtfully, "Xue, what did that lawyer say? Director Mei says she's guilty?" The journalists were buzzing in their seats. The commotion grew too loud, and the bailiffs came over to ask everyone to hush. The other defendant, Sun Jingshuan, appeared as shocked as everyone else, and stared at his wife uncomprehendingly. Mei Yin's lawyer appeared helpless, his expression seeming to say, *This is the defendant's own decision, nothing to do with me, this isn't my fault.*

Jin Mingcheng was perhaps more baffled than anyone. When they'd called a halt to proceedings, the trial had been going favorably for the defendants. The city had been in touch with the prosecutors, and the day before, he'd met with Du Chunming to secretly inform him of how the wind was blowing. As far as he was aware, Du Chunming had then met Mei Yin. Why was she suddenly admitting to her guilt now?

The chief judge, also startled, said, "Defendant, you're pleading guilty?"

Mei Yin said calmly, "Yes. I did indeed transport the smallpox virus into the country from Russia. Stebushkin, who provided me with the samples from the Vector Institute, hadn't attenuated the virus. So what I brought in was the virulent form of a Level-Four virus."

"What was your motive in doing so?"

"I was carrying out the teachings of my adoptive father, Walt Dickerson—taking practical action to alleviate the smallpox vacuum created by science. Later, I spent more than ten years cultivating and weakening this virus, not to turn it into antigens, but to create a mild strain of the virus that could exist in the natural world. That's a new medical concept. Should I explain a little more?"

The judge nodded.

"Let me talk about the antigens first. Compared to inactivated vaccines or other forms of inoculation, antigens have a great advantage: as they are alive, they can multiply within the patient's body, meaning the immunity they confer lasts much longer. Yet this 'living advantage' isn't fully exploited with antigens, which still need to be first cultivated in laboratory conditions, then stored and disseminated by human means, so they are relatively inefficient, limited by the human factor, unable to become part of the balance of the natural world. For instance, if a war were to cut off production of antigens, interrupting our stocks and supply chains, disease would proliferate again. Mild viruses are different. They're able to exist in the natural world, and can squeeze out the original, more virulent strains, becoming the dominant variety, conferring immunity against the original virus in everyone they infect. All in all, cultivating a mild virus and setting it free in the natural world was a way of inducing a small epidemic now, to prevent a potentially much worse epidemic later."

This was a fairly technical speech, and the audience seemed to be having trouble following it. Xue Yu, however, felt a shock wave pass through him. This was a completely new concept. If Ms. Mei had actually done it—and from the way the Nanyang epidemic had played out, it would seem that she had—it would be a historic revolution, akin to Jenner's invention of the cowpox vaccine, or Fleming's discovery of antibiotics. At the same time, he was shattered by the words "setting it free," a phrase that carried terrifying implications. The judges and audience were evidently still catching up, and hadn't realized the import of what she'd said.

Finally, the chief judge asked in puzzlement, "You're telling us—the smallpox virus in the orphanage was deliberately planted by you?"

Mei Yin looked him in the eye. "Yes. The mild strain of the virus I mentioned was in the shared birthday cake."

Another silent thunderclap. Her explanation slashed through a fog in Xue Yu's mind. He'd suspected for some time that it was too much of a coincidence for the virus leak to have taken place so soon after the American attack—the Spanish journalist had seemed similarly suspicious. But if it was a deliberate act, that explained everything—Ms. Mei had made use of the confusion after the American incident to put her own plan into action. This would make it harder to detect, and reduce opprobrium toward her, perhaps even saving her jail time. Her scheme had more or less succeeded. What he couldn't understand was, why would she choose to come clean at this point?

Mother Chen hadn't understood most of Director Mei's speech, only the last sentence. She turned to Xue Yu, her eyes frozen, and stammered, "Xue, what did Director Mei say? She put the smallpox in the birthday cake? I must have heard wrong. Xue, I heard wrong, didn't I?"

Xue Yu couldn't look at her. He turned the other way and exchanged a grim look with Deputy Mayor Jin. Mother Chen knew from his expression that there was no mistake. The Holy Mother of her heart had put a virus in the children's birthday cake. Unable to take this blow, she sat stunned for a moment, then ran from the courtroom.

The chief judge was mystified. He asked, "Does the defendant admit to deliberately releasing the virus in the orphanage, leading to Dr. Ma's death, and the disfigurement of Mei Xiaoxue and others?"

The question chilled Deputy Mayor Jin and Xue Yu—they hinted at a charge of murder. Sun looked sadly at his wife. Mei Yin's lawyer was now helpless, and could only look on as his client slid toward her fate.

Mei Yin replied, "The consequences weren't deliberate, but I was aware when releasing the virus that they were possible. In order to activate the antibodies, the virus had to possess a certain level of virulence, harmless to most, but dangerous to a very small number of sensitive individuals. In addition, the attenuated smallpox virus could possibly mutate into the more virulent strain in the natural world. It's a very small chance, but not impossible. God hates perfection. No one and nothing could ever be flawless. There's nothing to be done about that." She looked straight at the chief judge. "I'm not trying to talk myself out of guilt. I take full responsibility for Dr. Ma's death and Mei

Xiaoxue's disfigurement, and I'm willing to accept the punishment of the law."

The chief judge understood that his question could be construed as leading in the direction of a murder charge, and quickly backtracked: "I'd like to ask the defendant about Mr. Dickerson's research into attenuated smallpox viruses." He was careful to emphasize the word *research*, a quiet retreat from his previous certainty. "Why not carry it out in America? The environment there ought to be more suitable."

"No, it wouldn't have been suitable at all. Our new concepts need to be accepted by society as a whole in order to be put into practice. Western medical principles are built upon individualist foundations, and ignore the advantage human beings gain in grouping together. Mr. Dickerson believed that Chinese culture is built upon respect for the collective, and that China is a rare society with no national religion, so we would meet fewer theoretical barriers. China was our strategic choice as a base to carry out our work."

A subtle change came over the courtroom. This speech had appealed to the self-esteem that lurks within the Chinese subconscious, and had left the audience a little better disposed toward her. Mei Yin went on. "I have one request: Could Mr. Matsumoto of the WHO please read his deposition as to the good and bad points of using an attenuated virus?"

Mr. Matsumoto, who had been entered on the list of witnesses, but who hadn't spoken a word so far, entered the witness box with an interpreter.

"Please state your name and profession."

"Noriyoshi Matsumoto. I work in the World Health Organization's Special Pathogen Department, and I'm a member of the WHO Committee of Medical Ethics."

"Go ahead."

"I'm naturally unable to express an opinion on the legality of Professor Mei Yin's actions with regard to Chinese law. I can only represent eleven of the WHO's senior experts in calling on the Chinese government to preserve Professor Mei's research laboratory and the attenuated smallpox pathogens she cultivated. As for whether her proposed plan is medically valid and acceptable, that will have to wait for the test of time. But at least it's now certain that the danger to human beings is so slight as to be negligible. Preserving the smallpox pathogen in this form will do more good than harm, and weighing up all the considerations, this research project should be allowed to continue."

He read out the names of the scientists who'd signed the deposition. "The eleven of us are working hard to convince the WHO to extend long-term funding to this project."

He bowed to the judges and audience, and left the witness box.

This speech changed the atmosphere in the court, moving the focus from "criminal investigation" to "scholarly research." The chief judge asked the prosecution and defense to deliver their closing statements, then adjourned the court so the judges could confer on their verdict.

The courtroom buzzed with tension until the three judges returned. Everyone stood, and the chief judge began reading.

". . . It is the opinion of this court that the actions of the defendant, Mei Yin, are sufficient to find her guilty of disseminating a virus or bacteria, and negligent homicide. These are the charges brought by the prosecution, and we concur. Pursuant to the People's Republic of China Penal Code, Statute 331, governing the dissemination of viruses and/ or bacteria, we find the defendant Mei Yin guilty, and sentence her to six years' imprisonment. Pursuant to the People's Republic of China Penal Code, Statute 233, governing negligent homicide, we find the defendant guilty, and sentence her to five years' imprisonment. The two sentences will be combined into a reduced sentence of eight years' imprisonment, beginning today, less time already served. Total sentence will run from October twelfth, 2016, to October twelfth, 2024."

Mei Yin's lawyer let out a sigh of relief. The verdict was far worse than what he'd hoped for when he began the case—though that was entirely Mei Yin's fault—but her confession could have landed her on death row. The audience, including Xue Yu and Jin, also seemed satisfied. Perhaps the most relieved was Mei Yin, who'd helped the Crucifix Society navigate its most difficult step—out of the shadows. From now on, they could face the world openly, and her adoptive father could rest easy in his grave. She'd owed too many debts in the course of her life's work, to Stebushkin, Dr. Ma, Granny Sun, Mei Xiaoxue, and even Deputy Mayor Jin, Xue Yu, and her husband. Now she'd repay them all with interest.

There was little suspense around Sun Jingshuan's sentence. The court had evidently decided to be lenient, and sure enough, he was only convicted of negligence, and sentenced to six months' imprisonment, with a full suspension. Hearing this, Jingshuan immediately looked at Mei Yin. He'd escaped, just as he'd hoped, but his wife would be in jail for eight years. Yet Mei Yin gave him a dazzling smile. Her lips moved, and he knew what she was saying: *Xiaoxue. Help me find Xiaoxue.*

Mei Yin turned and murmured to Du Chunming, "Thank you." He shook his head in bemusement. She also looked at the audience gratefully, particularly at the eight foreigners, Deputy Mayor Jin, and Xue Yu. Just as the court was about to be dismissed, there was a stir in the gallery. It was Xue Yu's uncle, Zhao Yuzhou, who'd kept quiet these few days. Even Xue Yu had almost forgotten he was there. But he'd witnessed the whole case, and now stood suddenly, shouting in rage, "This court has been swayed by personal considerations, and given a light sentence for a heavy crime! I strongly object! I'm going to publish my objection online, and you can wait for the world to condemn you!"

No one apart from Xue Yu and Mei Yin even knew who this old man was, nor why he'd suddenly leaped up and started shouting. They looked at him as if he were mad, which seemed bitterly unfair to Zhao Yuzhou. He had no grudge against Mei Yin personally, his anger was purely unselfish, the righteous fury of a disciple of science against a traitor to science. This horrible woman was a murderous witch, yet the court sentenced her to a mere eight years in prison, and quite a few people even seemed to pity her!

The curiosity of the crowd quickly faded, and in a moment everyone had dispersed. Even the journalists were gone, and not one of them had tried to interview him. Xue Yu thought of going to talk to him, but after a moment's hesitation simply went off alone. Professor Zhao, feeling humiliated, left the courtroom in a huff.

CHAPTER FIVE
NEW LIFE

2023—Bozhou, Beijing, and Nanyang

A vegetable market lay on the fringes of Bozhou, in Anhui Province, where the city met the rural villages. It sprawled around a crude cement platform, on which various vegetables and soybean products were displayed in the open air, alongside fresh meat on hooks. To either side were rows of shops, mostly selling dry goods, staples, stewed meat, noodles, steamed buns, and so on. The open-air portion had a thin black cloth draped overhead against the scorching summertime sun. That noon, many of the men in the market were shirtless, the women scantily clad too. A thick stench of sweat mixed with the sound of many haggling voices.

As Xue Yu strode in, his suit and leather shoes appeared out of place—his unusual attire and handsome features drew attention as he walked. The far end of the market sold live chickens and ducks, live fish, and slaughtered cows. At this moment, the fish stall was crowded, seven or eight people squeezed between the two large fish tanks, some squatting and some standing. The stall owner was a young woman of twenty or so. Now she was on her haunches in front of the tank, nimbly scaling a fish as she shouted, "Live jumping grass carp, three-fifty a pound!"

She spoke crisp, standard Mandarin that cut through the local dialect. Through gaps in the crowd, he could see she was wearing a black plastic apron and a T-shirt that revealed her cleavage as she bent over, which was attracting the stares of many men. Moving his gaze upward, Xue Yu's eyes landed on Mei Xiaoxue's ugly, pockmarked face. Her fine features were at odds with those scars: gleaming black eyes, delicate nose, moist red lips.

He'd finally found her.

Xue Yu didn't join the crowd but stood behind them, looking at her with a catch in his heart. A girl becomes a woman at eighteen, as the saying goes, and Mei Xiaoxue was prettier today than seven years ago—if you ignored the pockmarks, that is. Her loveliness combined with her damaged skin to give her a tragic beauty, inspiring primal awe in the opposite sex. Many in the crowd were not there to buy fish.

Finished cleaning the two fish, Xiaoxue stood to weigh them and collect payment. Smiling, she called, "Next?" A woman pointed at one of the fish in the tank. Xiaoxue glanced over the crowd and noticed a well-dressed man at the back, obviously from a different world, and a little familiar, though she couldn't place him immediately. Squatting again, she quickly cleaned the fish, scales flying to the ground like snowflakes.

Two more men approached, one of them saying, "Which one's the pockmarked beauty, where is she?" The other cautioned, "Shh, she's a fierce one!" But his warning came too late. Mei Xiaoxue had heard him, and leaped to her feet, the scaling knife pointed at the offender as she shouted, "Asshole, come closer if you have balls, I'll give you some pockmarks of your own!" The men fled in panic, diving into the crowd, then bursting into gales of laughter once they were a safe distance away. The blood had drained from Xiaoxue's face, and even her pockmarks were pale. Tears flowed down her cheeks. A middle-aged woman from the neighboring duck stall hurried over and hugged her, urging, "Xiaoxue, don't cry, it's not worth losing your temper over scum like that. Come on, Auntie Guo will get revenge for you. Number Three! Number Three!" she hollered at the man butchering beef. "Someone's bullied our Xiaoxue again. Go curse those bastards to death!"

The butcher ran in the direction the two men had disappeared in, swearing loudly. Xue Yu now keenly appreciated the richness of the Anhui dialect. The swear words flowed from the man's mouth in a vivid stream, varied and bright and sharp as blades. Xue Yu only understood some of the expressions. The two nasty men said nothing in response—apparently they had been cursed to death. Number Three kept the barrage up a little longer. Auntie Guo burst into laughter, and so did several of the customers, all of whom urged Xiaoxue not to be angry—Number Three's scolding was sure to leave them covered in boils. Xiaoxue was clearly used to such scenes, and in a short while had stopped crying, brushing away her tears as she squatted to resume cleaning the fish.

Xue Yu watched in silence, his heart aching as if pricked by needles. After a while, when all the other customers were gone, Xiaoxue fixed her eyes on him. "Are you buying a fish or what?"

"Xiaoxue, it's me."

Mei Xiaoxue realized at once who it was. "Uncle Xue . . . Xue Yu?" Once again, her face went pale. "You traitor, you wolf, what are you doing here?"

Xue Yu smiled. "I came so you could yell at me. It's been so long since you've yelled at me."

Mei Xiaoxue slowly calmed herself. She'd sworn at him impulsively, but actually she'd always been conflicted about Xue Yu and Mommy Mei. She knew that Uncle Xue had been right to denounce Mommy.

But still, he was the one who got her into trouble. On the other hand, Mommy was the one who'd smuggled smallpox into the country in the first place, then brought it into the orphanage and ruined Xiaoxue's life! Her heart was rocked by conflicting emotions. She looked down and was silent.

Auntie Guo, noticing something odd, wondered if this pretty boy was here to torment Xiaoxue too. She stared at him keenly. After a long time, Xiaoxue lifted her head and said awkwardly, "Uncle . . . Xue." She wasn't sure how to address him. "I'm sorry, I shouldn't have yelled at you. I know you're not a bad person."

Xue Yu was also conflicted, longing to reach out and hug her, but stopping himself. Xiaoxue was a grown woman now, not the young teenager of so long ago. He came straight to the point. "Mommy Mei asked me to find you. I've been searching six or seven years, and so has General Manager Sun."

At the mention of Mommy Mei, Xiaoxue was overcome by both hatred and longing, and couldn't stop herself from weeping again, not making a sound, her tears flowing like a fountain, shoulders heaving in waves. Auntie Guo hurried over and embraced Xiaoxue, glaring suspiciously at Xue Yu, saying over and over, "Xiaoxue, what happened? Is he bullying you? Number Three! Get over here, Number Three!"

Xiaoxue hastily stopped crying and said, "No, this is someone from my hometown. My Uncle Xue. He and Mommy Mei have been looking for me for six or seven years."

Auntie Guo was overjoyed. She kept saying, "That's good, that's very good. Xiaoxue has a family now." Xiaoxue asked Auntie Guo to take care of her stall for a while; she wanted to bring Xue Yu to see where she lived, and then she'd take him out to lunch. Xiaoxue lived not far from there, an upstairs room in a farming family's house, small with tattered furniture, but spick-and-span. A wooden chest was covered in a colorful plastic cloth to serve as a dressing table, with cheap cosmetics on it. Xue Yu checked to see if there was a mirror. There wasn't. With a throb, he thought, *Xiaoxue still doesn't dare to face her own reflection.*

Embarrassed, she asked him to step outside for a moment so she could change. Xue Yu went out and stood in the doorway, and in a moment Xiaoxue appeared in a white T-shirt and green shorts that showed off her slim figure. Taking Xue Yu's hand, she said she'd take him to the Tianhe Grand Hotel for a meal, and he didn't try to dissuade her, but went along willingly.

The waiter at the hotel restaurant was well-bred enough to avoid staring at Xiaoxue's face directly as she ordered, though he still glanced at her out of the corner of his eye. Xiaoxue ignored him, she was used to people giving her strange looks. She asked Xue Yu, "How did you find me? I've been to quite a few places these seven years, to Xinjiang, then three or four years in Kyrgyzstan." Xue Yu smiled. "I asked everywhere. This time it was General Manager Sun who got the tip-off, and sent me here."

He wasn't telling the whole truth. True, it hadn't been easy to find her, but she was after all the only person in the whole of twenty-first century China severely scarred by smallpox—much worse than the other orphanage kids—and was beautiful to boot. The two things made such an unusual combination that asking around wasn't quite as difficult as it might have been.

The food arrived. Fragrant fish, spicy boiled pork, lotus-braised pork, stir-fried shredded potato. All very plain dishes, but obviously Xiaoxue's favorites. It was clear from her simple tastes how much deprivation she'd suffered. They chatted aimlessly for a while, Xiaoxue avoiding any talk of Mommy Mei. Xue Yu could understand how she felt, but he eventually brought the conversation back to this topic.

"Xiaoxue, Mommy Mei urged me again and again to find you. She's been in prison all this while, and her health is bad. She has rheumatic heart disease and rheumatoid arthritis, and can only walk with difficulty. Do you—still hate her?"

Xiaoxue looked down, tears flowing. She hated Mommy Mei, and missed her too. But now, pushing aside the surface layer of anger, she found a sturdy foundation of love below. She'd never forgotten Mommy Mei's birthday cake, and the happiness she'd felt during her illness—leaning against Mommy as she slept, inhaling her Mommy scent, a pair of warm hands on her forehead as she drowsed or slept. Yet one scene stood out from the others. That night, as she lay in a feverish daze, Mommy Mei and Uncle Sun had sat watching her, and they'd spoken in low voices. Mommy Mei already knew she was going to prison, and couldn't bear to leave her daughter Xiaoxue. She was telling her husband to bring up their daughter well. Through all the years of her lonely youth, she'd dreamed at night of Mommy Mei looking longingly at her, saying, *Xiaoxue, I have to go to prison, I'll never see you again.* Xiaoxue would weep as she reached out for her mother, but her hands clutched nothingness as she jolted awake.

She sighed. "I don't hate her. Knowing she's been looking for me all this while, I hate her even less. No matter what, it was an accident. She didn't do it on purpose."

Xue Yu shot a quick glance at her. Could she still not know that Mei Yin had deliberately infected everyone with smallpox? But it had been all over the papers and TV news and Internet for years after the case. How could she not know? Perhaps that all happened while she was abroad, the language barrier keeping her in a news-free zone.

Xiaoxue asked him all kinds of details about her Mommy: Did the prison have good doctors? Did they have to pay to see the doctors? How many years had she been sentenced to, and how long was left? Xue Yu answered all her questions, then she asked, "Is Uncle Sun well? Before I left, I heard his granny died."

"Uncle Sun didn't go to prison, he's still the general manager of Heavenly Corp. And now I'm his assistant. Granny Sun died, yes. And Uncle Sun and your Mommy Mei are divorced now."

Xiaoxue was so shocked she almost dropped her chopsticks. "Why? Mommy Mei's still in prison, and he . . ."

"Don't blame him, it was your Mommy Mei who insisted. She said she wouldn't be able to have a child, and didn't want to disappoint Granny Sun. Granny was old-fashioned, and after Uncle Sun married your Mommy, she kept nagging them to produce a great-grandchild for her. Ms. Mei understood this very well."

"Oh, I see."

There was actually more to the story. After Granny Sun suddenly passed away, Jingshuan had never gotten over his heavy sense of guilt and responsibility. He'd been working hard these few years to train Xue Yu as his successor. Perhaps in a year or two, when Mei Yin was out of prison, Xue Yu would be able to run the company himself, at which point Sun Jingshuan could leave his hometown and go far away from that place of sorrow. Xue Yu felt such sadness for this couple, both of whom were so principled and honorable, and so well suited. They ought to have grown old together. But there was a knot in their hearts that was too deep and too heavy to undo, and they'd become weary from it.

But wasn't he the same? These few years, Xiaoxue's disappearance had pressed on his heart too, even though he bore no responsibility for her illness and subsequent disappearance.

After speaking a little more, Xiaoxue seemed calmer, and Xue Yu was able to come to the main reason for his visit.

"Xiaoxue, Mommy Mei sent me so I could bring you to Beijing for plastic surgery as soon as possible. Come with me, today, right away, straight to Beijing. The Chinese Academy of Sciences Medical Cosmetology Center. Let me tell you, five years ago, I made an appointment with Dr. Chen Huanran there. He's the best facial reconstruction surgeon in the whole country, and anyone wanting to go under his knife usually has to wait in line two years. But he promised me that whenever I found you, he'd see you right away."

Xiaoxue, deeply moved, murmured, "I've wanted that too. I've been saving up."

Xue Yu pulled out a card. "I've saved enough for you long ago—don't refuse, I want you to have it, and it's also what Mommy Mei and Uncle Sun want. I'm deputy general manager at Heavenly Corp. now, I earn a decent salary. So take my money and go have your surgery. You can pay me back later, in your own time. How about that?"

Xiaoxue's eyes gleamed. She'd clung to this dream for seven years now, though she'd thought it might be a decade or more before it could be realized. Now it was happening this very day. Uncle Xue seemed sincere, and she wasn't going to say no. Joyfully, she cried, "Yes. But I'll sign an IOU, and when I've saved up enough money, I'll pay you back."

"Of course, of course. If you don't, I'll hound you for the cash. But don't worry about an IOU, a pinky swear will do. When has Mei Xiaoxue ever gone back on a pinky swear? Never, that's when. I trust you. Come on, hook fingers, tug, a hundred years, no take-backs."

Xiaoxue giggled as they linked little fingers. Afterward, Xue Yu folded her small hand within his own. Even her hand, exquisite as a work of art, was covered in scars. Xue Yu looked at her scarred hand, her scarred neck, and his eyes reddened as his emotions slipped out of control. Xiaoxue noticed too, but didn't want to embarrass Uncle Xue, so pretended not to have seen anything. Instead, she playfully said, "But no more calling me a child. I'm twenty-one now, I've been roaming the world for seven years. I grew up long ago."

"That's right, you're an old warrior now. How disrespectful of me!"

The two of them burst out laughing.

After lunch, they returned to the market, and Xiaoxue said good-bye to Auntie Guo and Uncle Number Three, handing the fish stall over to Auntie Guo to look after for the time being, saying she'd be back after her surgery. Xue Yu thought it unlikely that Xiaoxue would return, but just stood to one side, smiling. Auntie Guo and Uncle Number Three were overjoyed that this poor girl had met a benefactor, and was about to move up in the world.

As they were leaving, Uncle Number Three said, "Xiaoxue, have your surgery quickly, then come back and show uncle how pretty you are. And as for this fellow—we'll leave Xiaoxue in your care. I'm an uneducated man, I say what I mean, and if you mistreat her, I'll . . ."

Xue Yu interrupted, using the same intonation as Xiaoxue had earlier. "Stab me full of holes?"

"Yes, that's right, full of holes!" They all laughed.

They boarded the next train, arriving in Beijing the following morning, and went straight to the Plastic Surgery Institute in the suburb of Badachu. Dr. Chen Huanran had seen photos of the younger Xiaoxue, and was delighted to meet her in person. He couldn't stop praising the excellent material he had to work with. "See how broad her forehead is. Her forehead, the tip of her nose, the crest of her lips, the point of her chin—all high. The distance between her eyes, the space between her nose and forehead, the dip of her philtrum, all exactly proportionate! Only slight imperfections in the chin and philtrum, but that's easily fixed. Excellent! I'll sculpt her into a model Chinese beauty!"

Xue Yu and Xiaoxue were delighted by his praise, but also a little confused—Xiaoxue's surgery was meant to be for her pockmarks, why was he talking about all these other things? Dr. Chen saw what they were thinking, and shrugged. "As for her pitted face, that's a minor issue. There are mature technologies for that, I'll just use a special polishing tool to smooth them out, and we can make your facial skin as good as new. Don't worry, Xiaoxue, think of it as if you didn't wash your face this morning and it's gotten smudged. We'll make it lovely again."

"Dr. Chen, I only want to get rid of the pockmarks. As for the rest of my face . . ."

"Not possible! Once you board my pirate ship, I'm the captain. You have such good raw material, I'm going to get you to perfection!" He turned to Xue Yu. "Are you worried about the cost? I can use this operation as a student demonstration, that'll cut the fees in half."

Xue Yu smiled. "Thank you, Dr. Chen, we'll do as you suggest. Everything has to be perfect. Oh, and along with the pockmarks on the face, you'll have to deal with the scars on her body as well, her neck and chest and so on. It doesn't matter how much the fees are, I'll take care of it."

Dr. Chen was still looking Xiaoxue up and down. Like a sculptor, he was now caught up in the spirit of creation. "Of course, that goes without saying. In order to attain perfection, the surgery might have to take a little longer. I suggest the two of you rent an apartment nearby. If you stay there rather than paying hospital in-patient fees, that'll save you a bit of cash. Why don't you go arrange that now, and we can begin the surgery tomorrow."

"All right."

"And another thing, young lady. I only deal with physical beauty, you'll have to take charge of your inner beauty yourself. I know that whenever anyone has physical flaws, especially young women, they have deep self-esteem issues. I couldn't say if that's the case with you. But if it is, then you should handle it as soon as possible. I'll tell you a secret: girls who believe they're beautiful really are more beautiful, at least thirty percent more beautiful than otherwise. If you have self-confidence, your face will blaze and shine!"

Xiaoxue smiled gratefully. "I'll do as you say, Uncle Chen."

After lunch, they asked around and found a nearby one-bedroom apartment to rent, fully furnished. It was small, but clean and in a good neighborhood, just a few stops from the hospital by public transportation. Xue Yu brought her to the supermarket, where they picked up everything they needed, particularly some more expensive makeup. After they were all settled in, Xue Yu gave her a silver cash card. "Xiaoxue, I'm so sorry, but there's a lot of work to take care of back home. I'll need to catch the train back tonight."

Xiaoxue was a little reluctant to see him go, but she knew Uncle Xue couldn't possibly keep her company for the few months this would take. She nodded. "All right."

"That card is loaded with enough money to cover all your needs. Don't worry about spending a bit, you have to be comfortable. When I visit again, you'd better not have got any skinnier."

Xiaoxue smiled and nodded.

"If I have the chance to come here on business, I'll drop by and see you."

"No, don't come. I don't want you to see me until the surgery is done."

Xue Yu knew what she was thinking—to present herself to him with a brand new face. He was gratified. How quickly the wounded, coarse, angry Xiaoxue had gone away. Now she was a girl of sunshine, completely transparent. In fact, that's how she'd always been, until unjust fate gave her a different appearance. Now, the warmth of love had freed her. "Okay. I'll wait to hear from you, then."

As Xue Yu was leaving, Xiaoxue said hesitantly, "There is one more thing."

"What is it?"

Xiaoxue blushed. "I have a request. You have to say yes."

"A request I have to accept? What a dictator! All right, all right, I agree. Go ahead."

"I'm grown up now. I don't want to call you Uncle anymore, that's not fair to me."

He had to chuckle at that. "What strange logic is that? Just because you're grown up, calling me Uncle isn't fair anymore? Don't forget, you may be seven years older now, but so am I."

Xiaoxue grew even redder as she insisted stubbornly, "That's not the same! Seven years ago, you were exactly twice as old as me, so of course

I called you Uncle. Now I'm almost twenty-two, and you're only twelve years older than me, so Older Brother should do."

"How are you twenty-two? You're twenty-one, that was one of the first things you said to me."

"I said almost twenty-two!"

Xue Yu knew what was really behind this request, and felt a surge of warmth to his heart. In truth, he'd been quietly hoping for this too. Solemnly, he said, "Fine, I accept your request."

Xiaoxue beamed. "Big Brother Xue, when you get back, ask after Mommy Mei and Uncle Sun. I can't wait to visit Mommy Mei in prison with you."

"Of course, I'll be sure to pass that on. Little . . . Sister Xiaoxue." He shook his head. "That felt weird. If I'm your big brother, then I'll have to start calling them Auntie Mei and Uncle Sun? That may be fair to you, but it's not to me."

Xiaoxue blushed and giggled. "Not fair to you? Going by age, they ought to be your uncle and aunt anyway." She took Xue Yu's arm and led him to the train station.

Xue Yu returned three months later, after receiving a message from Xiaoxue. On the door he found a note:

> *Big Brother Xue, I've gone to get groceries, I'll be back in a while. Come in and make yourself at home.*

Xue Yu let himself in with his key, to find the apartment looking about the same as before, everything as clean as an eggshell. The first thing he noticed was a large round mirror on the bedside table, the only new item. This detail eased his worries; Xiaoxue was no longer twisted up inside. Her bed and desk were piled high with thick books, which he assumed would be beauty manuals, but upon inspection turned out to be medical texts: epidemiology, virology, cell engineering, and so forth. Xue Yu was glad to see this—he had worried about her interrupted education. He'd been thinking of adult education for her, but now it looked like she'd been quietly working hard on her own, without saying anything to him about it.

Xue Yu wondered if she'd be able to understand these college textbooks, with her level of education. Flicking through them, he saw that she'd at least finished *Epidemiology Studies*, because the back pages were all creased and ink smeared. She'd left her notes out on the desk, and when he flipped through them, they were lists of things from such-and-such a page she didn't understand, some of which had been crossed out, presumably because she'd later filled in the blanks. Then he came upon a page that looked completely different from the others, covered in cramped writing: "Mommy Mei Uncle Sun Uncle Xue Big Brother Xue Mommy Mei Uncle Sun Big Brother Xue . . ." This went on, row after row, the words breaking down into a scrawl, obviously all idle doodling. By the bottom of the page, "Big Brother Xue" had become "Xue Yu," then just "Yu," written with such force it went through to the other side of the paper, showing the strength of her emotion.

The sight intoxicated Xue Yu.

A key in the door. Xiaoxue entered with a few plastic bags, crying out in surprise and joy. "Xue Yu . . . Big Brother Xue!"

He stared at her face, stunned, delighted. Dr. Chen thoroughly deserved his reputation as the "Best Scalpel in the Country." His hands had brought springtime back. The pockmarks had vanished, and while her skin wasn't quite as good as it had been, it was almost as fine. Apart from that, there'd been some changes to her features, though Xue Yu couldn't put a finger on exactly what was different. Regardless, she was a knockout. Her eyes were fixed anxiously on him, trying to read his first impressions. Xue Yu murmured, "My God, I can't see. I'm blinded by your radiance. Too beautiful, far more beautiful than I'd expected."

"Really?"

"Of course! Now quick, come back to Nanyang with me. You don't know how happy Mommy Mei and Uncle Sun will be when they see your new face."

Xiaoxue cheered and tossed down her shopping, flinging her arms around Xue Yu and spinning him round the room. After a couple of rounds, her laughter stopped and soon tears were falling onto his shoulder. She sobbed, "Brother Xue, thank you, and Mommy Mei and Uncle Sun."

Xue Yu turned her face to him and wiped away the tears. "No crying. You ought to be happy now. Oh, and I see you've been reading medical books. How's that going? Do you understand them?"

"Mostly."

"I've made arrangements to enroll you in adult education classes, once you're back. We'll make up for those missing seven years."

Xiaoxue shook her head. "No. I want to work, and teach myself in my free time."

"Why?"

Xiaoxue had made plans for the future. She was of course willing to go back to school, to at least get a college degree, but with her current level of education, that might take five or six years. By that time, Xue Yu would be almost forty, and it'd be too late—too late for marriage and children. She didn't want to slow him down. In her mind, she'd already linked her life to Xue Yu's, though she didn't know what he was thinking. He loved her, of course, she could see that in his eyes, but— she was so much less educated than he was, an ignorant, brutish girl, and she'd been disfigured . . . She could only say, "No matter what, I'm not going to school, I just want to work and study at the same time."

Xue Yu had intuited what she was thinking; he'd always been able to. Xiaoxue was much sunnier after the operation, but even so, there was a patch of self-loathing deep inside her that hadn't been eradicated.

He pulled her onto the couch and, taking a deep breath, said, "Xiaoxue, I have to take my courage in my hands and say something to you."

"What is it?"

"I know a man who, seven years ago, saw a girl as pretty as a flower in an orphanage. That exquisite child left an indelible impression on his heart. Later on, for one reason or another, that man never got married, and his path kept getting tangled up with the girl's, right until she was grown up, twenty-one years old. No"—he chuckled—"almost twenty-two. He could tell her that he loved her. But the man didn't dare. And why? He looked down on himself for being twelve years older than her, a whole zodiac cycle!"

Xiaoxue smiled like a blossom opening. "What's twelve years? I . . . The girl surely wouldn't mind that!"

"It's no good, they were both born in the year of the tiger, and they say one hill can't hold two tigers. If two tigers get married, they're sure to be unhappy."

"Nonsense! All nonsense! I don't believe it . . . you don't believe these superstitions, do you?"

They stared at each other, and suddenly hugged, laughing and kissing passionately. Just like that, they were engaged, as if their hidden destiny had suddenly been revealed. They talked about the future that day. Xue Yu agreed with Xiaoxue's suggestion: she'd study while she worked, with Xue Yu as her teacher, which should shorten the time needed for her education. They'd get married as soon as possible, to make it easier for Xiaoxue to arrange her life, though they'd wait a while to have children, so as not to get in the way of her studies. Xue Yu was living in Sun Jingshuan's old house. Sun had moved when he started his new family, unwilling to stay in the place where his grandmother had died, leaving the existing place to Xue Yu. Xiaoxue understood why Uncle Sun had remarried, but still grieved on Mommy Mei's behalf.

That night, Xue Yu and Xiaoxue slept together. After a shower, Xiaoxue pointed out everywhere the scars had been, her chest, her legs, her feet, everywhere now smooth as new. Xue Yu kissed every inch of his lover's skin. Perhaps because he was twelve years older, as they tumbled together, his body contained not just a man's passion, but also a very deep tenderness. Xiaoxue's beauty had been destroyed, and then restored. He would cherish her, protect her, keep her from any kind of hurt.

The next day, they went to see Dr. Chen together, to thank him. Highly pleased with himself, he proclaimed Xiaoxue his "finest creation." Before they left for Beijing, they first stopped by Bozhou so Xiaoxue could say good-bye to Auntie Guo and Uncle Number Three. They almost didn't recognize her, and kept complimenting her, openmouthed. Everyone in the city who'd known of the "pockmarked beauty" came crowding up to gape and praise her, leaving her flushed as a sunset. When they heard the couple were engaged, Auntie Guo and Uncle Number Three were even happier, and said she should give out wedding candy now, in case they couldn't make it for the big day. The couple agreed, and not only did they give out candy, they also threw a wedding banquet at Tianhe Grand Hotel, inviting everyone Xiaoxue had known in town.

They arrived in Nanyang the next day. First, they went to the orphanage. Most of the kids she'd known were gone; only a few still remembered "Big Sister Xiaoxue." After a moment's shyness, they came over to hug her. Mother Liu and Mother Chen still worked there, and weren't as taken with Xiaoxue's beauty as the Bozhou folk because they still remembered her as the pretty girl she'd always been. Mother Liu took her hand and wept. "Xiaoxue, your Mommy Mei is still in prison. She's not well, poor thing."

Xiaoxue's eyes reddened. "I'll visit her tomorrow."

That night, they headed to Heavenly Corp., where General Manager Sun was waiting for them in his office. He'd aged a lot in the last seven years. Xiaoxue got out an "Uncle Sun," but could say nothing more. She'd remembered that moment in the orphanage when she'd said, "I'm going to stop calling you Uncle Sun, you're Daddy Sun from now on." She'd once thought Mommy Mei's marriage was perfect, and now they'd been parted! Though she knew Uncle Sun was a good person, something at the bottom of her heart couldn't forgive him.

Uncle Sun looked at her closely, and said with satisfaction, "The surgery was a success. That's a weight off my heart."

They described to him their plan for the next few years, and he approved. "Xiaoxue can come do work-study at a research lab here, and in three to five years she'll be a lab manager. I'll arrange that with HR tomorrow. Now go back home and get some rest."

They left the facility and walked home along the small path through the pine forest, treading on soft pine needles, watching little squirrels poke their heads out from the branches. Xiaoxue had never been here, and looked all around her with curiosity. Deep in the woods was the former Sun household, the large courtyard full of all kinds of plants, a wisteria trellis in its center, sheltering a round stone table and chairs, and a garage on the east side. The house itself was a little worn down on the outside, but refurbished and thoroughly modern on the inside, particularly a charming bedroom, decorated in warm colors and all kinds of little feminine touches, including an ivory-colored dressing table.

Xue Yu said, "This is for you, your little kingdom. Of course, when I put this together, I wasn't expecting that our relationship would develop so quickly." He smiled. "Now I'm hoping you'll move into the master bedroom with me, that's the rightful place for the mistress of the house."

She looked in delight at the house, but didn't answer directly. "So many rooms!"

Xue Yu said there were indeed a lot of rooms, and he'd hired a woman to come clean them twice a week. Xiaoxue said, "Don't bother, I'll do it myself, all my operations must have put you into debt, we should clear what you owe as quickly as possible."

Xue Yu smiled. "It's paid back already—most of it, anyway!"

He was referring to his debts of conscience, rather than cash. Seven years ago, he'd denounced Ms. Mei, and that left him owing a great deal. Now that he'd helped Ms. Mei find Xiaoxue and gotten her the surgery, he felt he'd paid it off. As for Xiaoxue becoming his wife—that was an unexpected windfall.

Exploring her new home, Xiaoxue felt her exhaustion from the journey slide away. She wanted to see every corner of every room. Xue Yu gave her a bunch of keys and let her go explore. Meanwhile, he put on an apron and started making dinner, listening to her childlike exclamations as she raced up and down the stairs, outside and back inside. After a while, he called her to dinner and she exclaimed, "It's lovely! I've never seen such a big house and such a spacious courtyard. Mommy Mei could come live here if she wanted. Yu, take me to see her tomorrow."

The next day happened to be visiting day at the prison. The visitors' room was divided by a thick pane of glass, and all conversations had to take place through a telephone. Guards looked on from the far side of the glass. The prisoners came in one by one. Xiaoxue watched anxiously; Mommy Mei came last. She was in a wheelchair, pushed by a female guard. Xiaoxue froze, then turned back to look at Xue Yu. He sighed. "Her rheumatism has gotten worse. I bought her the wheelchair before leaving for Beijing."

Xiaoxue worked hard to hold back tears, not wanting Mommy Mei to see her cry. Mommy was at the glass by then, her body frail, her hair white, but her eyes as full of life as ever, her clothes and hair immaculate. She studied Xiaoxue's features, and said happily, "Xiaoxue, you're even more beautiful than seven years ago. Xue, thank you."

Xue Yu said, simply, "I only did what I should."

"Xiaoxue, where did you run off to for seven years? Mommy missed you."

"Mommy, I . . . missed . . . you, too." Just one sentence, and she was all choked up.

"Mommy made you ill. She made you suffer for seven years. Mommy let you down."

No, Mommy, I forgave you long ago. In fact, I never really hated you. Xiaoxue shook her head, unable to get the words out. She knew that if she opened her mouth, the tears would stream out too.

Mei Yin said, "Let's not talk about that. We should be happy to meet again. Before leaving for Beijing, Xue Yu said to me he was going to pluck up his courage to propose to you. How about it? Did he do it?"

Xiaoxue smiled tearfully. "Mommy, he's so pathetic. I don't want to say yes, but I feel bad refusing. I'll let you choose for me."

Mei Yin laughed brightly. "Hear that, Xue Yu? Your happiness is in my hands!" She turned back to Xiaoxue. "Say yes. He's a good man, and you'll do well together."

They chatted for a long time, until visiting hours were almost over, then Mei Yin suddenly thought of something. "Xiaoxue, these few years, what day did you celebrate your birthday? Still the first Sunday in September?" Xiaoxue said nothing. What had there been to celebrate, in the last seven years? Guessing this, Mei Yin said to Xue Yu, "It's Xiaoxue's birthday soon. Don't forget, that's your first test. Xiaoxue, let Xue Yu celebrate your birthday on Mommy's behalf."

On the way back from the detention center, Xiaoxue no longer tried to hold her tears back, but wept to her heart's content. She said to Xue Yu, "I want Mommy Mei to come home with us. Can we do that? Can she apply for medical parole? Big Brother Xue Yu, will you help me bring her home?" Xue Yu didn't reply at once, his hands on the wheel, looking at her in profile, something strange in his eyes. Xiaoxue could feel it, but didn't know what the strangeness meant. Anxiously, she asked, "Won't you do it? Do you still have some grudge against her?"

Xue Yu parked the car by a stream and told her to come with him, then hugged her as they sat on the grass. The water flowed placidly; now and then a little fish leaped from the water.

"No, I don't have any grudge against Ms. Mei. In fact, General Manager Sun and I are sorting out the paperwork for getting her paroled on medical grounds, and should have a result soon. Although—there's something I'd hoped to keep from you, but if Mommy Mei's going to be living with us, I think I'd better tell you."

Xiaoxue had an uneasy feeling. "What is it? Tell me."

"It's not really a secret; you might be the only person who doesn't know. Xiaoxue, seven years ago, the smallpox outbreak was no accident. Mommy Mei did it on purpose. She put the virus in your birthday cake."

"Wha—what?"

"That's right. She did it deliberately. Of course, she didn't mean to harm you, she was acting on a medical theory that's a little difficult to explain."

Xiaoxue didn't hear a word of what came next because her blood was roaring in her ears. She'd done it on purpose! In the orphans' birthday cake! In an instant, fragments of memory had linked together, showing her the unmistakable truth. Mommy's guilty expression; the conversation she'd half overheard; Mommy Mei's sudden desire to adopt her; Xiaoxue's despair at the first sight of her pockmarked face in the mirror; seven years of hostile looks . . . yes, it was true, and she, the victim, was the last to find out. It was too cruel.

Xue Yu watched painfully as she passed through these torments. "I know it's difficult to hear this. But there's an even deeper truth behind this truth, a deeper kind of love. Listen to me."

He patiently explained everything. "In fact, before this outbreak, Ms. Mei had already carried out experiments on her own body. Do you remember how she didn't even wear a mask when she was taking care of you? Yes, she and Uncle Sun both had lifelong immunity. They knew that this strain was fairly safe, although even the safest variety may have outliers, and your body just happened to be especially susceptible. You suffered a great deal, but you gained lifelong immunity to smallpox too, and that's a very precious thing.

"Did you know? I've taken over Mommy Mei's research. This field of study is heavily debated in medical theory circles, and the government can neither openly acknowledge it nor ban it outright. The Chinese government is being circumspect about it, they're using a 'double negative' strategy—neither saying it's legal, nor that it isn't. Putting Ms. Mei in prison on the one hand, allowing her research lab to stay open on the other, and not asking any questions. The research project's been allowed to slip between the cracks, until it's been proven or disproven. General Manager Sun and I have arranged for you to work there, to research attenuated smallpox viruses and other pathogens. The WHO's been funding us.

"I've told you the whole truth now. Do you still want to bring Mommy Mei to live with us? If you do, then that's wonderful. If you can't accept it yet, Mommy Mei and I will understand, and I'll arrange for her to stay somewhere else when she gets out."

Xiaoxue didn't hesitate. "Of course she should come live with us. No matter what has happened, her love for me is real. You couldn't fake mother love like that. And I'll love her back in the same way."

"Excellent. I'll make the arrangements as soon as possible."

A month later, Sun, Xue Yu, and Xiaoxue went to the prison together, to bring Mei Yin home. The high metal gates slowly rolled open, and a female guard wheeled her to the exit. Mei Yin pushed herself the rest of the way, her smile as bright as a child's. In that instant, as if someone were slicing onions nearby, all their eyes filled with tears. Jingshuan rushed over to lift her from the wheelchair, but Mei Yin declined with a smile, saying, "I can walk a few steps—I can." Jingshuan ignored her, and she didn't refuse again, very naturally wrapping her arms around his neck and allowing herself to be bundled into the car. They got back to the house in the pine forest, and installed Mei Yin in the room that had been meant for Xiaoxue. Jingshuan busied himself serving tea, but in this place, his old home, facing his ex-wife, his heart was a jumble of emotions: melancholy, guilt, and hurt all competing for room. He tried not to show any of this, but nevertheless seemed downcast and quiet. Mei Yin guessed what he was feeling, and kept the conversation light. She smiled. "Are He Ying and Jiaojiao well? You should bring them for a visit someday soon."

Xue Yu laughed. "General Manager Sun keeps his wife tucked away like a treasure. Even I hardly ever get to see the family."

Jingshuan let this pass, and said to the couple, "From now on, I'll leave Ms. Mei in your care."

Xiaoxue said, "Don't worry, Mommy's living with her daughter, she'll be taken care of."

Xue Yu said, "General Manager Sun, stay for lunch? There are two bottles of aged Maotai wine—you left them behind when you moved out."

Jingshuan stayed, and drank a little too much. Now that Mei Yin was out on parole, and Xue Yu could assume the burden of Heavenly Corp., he felt a weight lift from his heart. He could leave now. He could take his wife and daughter, the ancestral portraits of his grandfather and grandmother, his guilt and his longing, and seek a new life elsewhere. He said, "Mei Yin, do you remember the *Romance of the Three Kingdoms*, how Xu Shu brought Zhuge Liang to Liu Bei?"

"Of course. I still know the classics—do you think I'm still that much of a foreigner?"

"That happened here, in Xinye. Cao Cao had captured Xu Shu's mother, forcing Xu Shu to leave Liu Bei. Before going, he said, 'In the past, General Liu, I helped you to victory by listening to my heart. But now that my heart is muddied, what use is there in staying?' Then he said to the crowds who'd come to say good-bye, 'I couldn't end as well as I began. Gentlemen, don't follow my example.'"

The other three knew what he was saying, and could sense his sorrow. Mei Yin tried to stop him. "Jingshuan . . ."

"Let me finish. Xue Yu, Xiaoxue, the truth is always cruel. Holding fast to the truth isn't easy, and living it is even harder. My psyche was too weak. I couldn't end as well as I began. Don't follow my example."

They realized he was saying farewell. Mei Yin didn't try to change his mind, knowing he'd stand firm. "Jingshuan, remember us, come and see us often."

"I will, I'll come back."

After lunch, the two men went back to work, and Mei Yin wheeled herself to the door to see Jingshuan off. When Xue Yu got back that night, he said, "Mother Mei, General Manager Sun has done all the paperwork for the handover of the company. He wants to leave tomorrow, but he won't come to say good-bye, so he asked me to give you this crucifix in remembrance."

Mei Yin took the gleaming silver cross, and clutched it tightly. Neither of them said another word about Jingshuan's departure. Xiaoxue could tell her mother's heart was heavy, so she smiled. "It's a shame Uncle Sun couldn't stay for our wedding. Mommy, you came back just in time, you can help us organize the wedding. We're thinking of doing it in a month's time."

"We'd planned to wait two or three years to have children," Xue Yu added awkwardly, "but there was an accident. That's fine, it just means Xiaoxue won't start work yet. She can use this time to hit the books, and take up the job when the baby's a year old."

"That's wonderful news. In fact, I've never liked the way women are having their first children older and older, it's bad for the body. Twenty is the most natural time for a first pregnancy." She was silent for a moment. "It's a pity I never had a child. If I could have my life over again, I'd make sure to have a baby early on."

These words were soaked with sadness, but she had brushed them away a moment later, and happily began making plans. She said, "I'll take care of the child when it arrives; Xiaoxue, I'll be in charge of your studies too. I think you can take an accelerated syllabus—in two or three years you'll be an exemplary lab manager." She scribbled down a reading list, mostly college textbooks, and told Xue Yu to order them as soon as possible. "Xiaoxue, your life as a student starts tomorrow."

The next morning, Xiaoxue got up and went to the bathroom, then Xue Yu heard her calling, "Xue Yu, where's Mommy??" He leaped out of bed, only to find Mei Yin in the courtyard, her wheelchair pushed up against the wall, enthusiastically admiring the plants around her. Xue Yu and Xiaoxue watched, smiling, from the doorway, then went back in to get breakfast ready.

At breakfast, Mei Yin said, "Xiaoxue, I was looking at the sponge gourd plants earlier. Do you know how the creepers climb up the wall? They have tendrils that stick into the cracks, then the endings swell so they get fixed in there. It's the same way mountain-climbers' crampons work. What an amazing design!"

Xiaoxue put down her bowl and went out to look, and it was as she said. The sponge gourd's tendrils bloated into little green balls once they were in the cracks, wedging them in so tightly you couldn't pull them loose. They were commonplace plants, but she hadn't noticed their little trick until Mommy Mei told her that. Now she stealthily studied her Mommy. Gray-white hair, scrawny frame, but brilliance in her eyes, full of life. She thought, with joy, *Mommy Mei's new life begins now.*

The next day, both mother and daughter started new routines. After Xue Yu went to work, Mei Yin started teaching Xiaoxue. During the three months of surgery in Beijing, she'd gulped down quite a few books on epidemiology, in order to stay connected to Xue Yu's life. With only a seventh grade education, she was separated from this professional knowledge. Now, with Mommy Mei to teach her, she found the gap easy to bridge. Studying with Mommy Mei made her realize what a masterclass was. A true master is able to turn the hardest knowledge into easily graspable concepts. A master's knowledge is complete and organized, touching on neighboring topics, and personal. Mei Yin was happy that, though Xiaoxue was uneducated, she had a sharp intelligence and a lively mind, and she often came up with unusual ideas—shallow, perhaps, but original. Maybe this was precisely due to her lack of schooling? Her native intelligence hadn't been stifled by force-feeding. As she encouraged her mind to run free, Mei Yin was also quietly indoctrinating her in the beliefs of the Crucifix Society. And like a sponge, Xiaoxue absorbed them steadily, growing all the while, seeming to change every day.

One day, Xiaoxue sat staring at a book, when suddenly she slammed it shut and said, "Mommy, I don't dare study anymore. The more I learn, the less sure I am about science."

Mei Yin was interested. "Really? Why?"

"I used to think science was all light, no shadow; that it could do anything, it was even more powerful than God. There were still flaws, tragedies, and pain in the world only because science hadn't gone far enough yet. A day would come when human existence would be a perfect paradise. For instance, people in the future would live free from disease. Now I know that was just a fantasy."

"You're right. Science will never completely eliminate disease."

"Science invented antibiotics—and that led to drug-resistant bacteria, which are evolving faster than humans can come up with new medicines; science eliminated smallpox—which led to a dangerous smallpox vacuum, which Zia Baj and other wicked people took advantage of; science allows even people with hereditary illnesses to live till an old age—but that just means bad genes are allowed to proliferate, setting time bombs for the future. Science invented human cloning—but if that leads to asexual reproduction, so men and women don't love each other anymore, how awful that would be!" She sighed. "God's got a strange personality, both kind and nasty, holding on to our ankles, pushing us two steps forward then pulling us back a step and a half."

Mei Yin laughed. "That's right, he's a true eccentric. But in the end, he's not too bad, he still let us advance half a step."

"Mommy, now I'm worried for all the animals in the world, like wildebeests, lions, and dolphins."

"Why?"

"They've evolved an equilibrium with their own pathogens, but now human beings are creating so many superpathogens, what if one of them turns out to also cause infections in wild animals? The animals would be in trouble then! They haven't evolved to resist them, and they don't have our modern hospitals!"

Mei Yin smiled and nodded, but didn't answer. These were exactly the thoughts she'd had at the age of twelve, watching the great wildebeest migration. And now she'd planted them in Xiaoxue's consciousness too.

"Mommy, I think your point of view is right. Humanity needs to live in harmony with nature, rather than fighting it."

Mei Yin thought gleefully that perhaps in a year or two, she'd be able to hang her ex-husband's crucifix around Xiaoxue's neck. She had no idea that in a few months' time, Xiaoxue's beliefs would undergo a massive reversal.

Two months after Mei Yin was released on medical parole, Xue Yu and Xiaoxue got married. They didn't dare delay any longer, because her pregnancy was starting to show. People were more open-minded these days, but there was still something embarrassing about being a big-bellied bride.

The celebration combined city and country customs. They had the reception in the courtyard, which was uniquely suitable, because where could you find a courtyard big enough for thirty tables in any city these days? The dinner was catered by Nanyang's Jinjue Hotel Restaurant, which sent two chefs and several dozen helpers. Xue Yu's parents traveled from Wuhan, and adored Xiaoxue from their first sight of her. Such a beautiful, young, cheerful, and virtuous girl, and their son had caught her, the lucky rascal. Later on, when they learned she was giving them a grandchild, their affection knew no bounds. This was a good place to live too, not like Wuhan, where houses were all crammed together and you could hear your neighbors playing mahjong all the way across the next building. When they retired, they said, they'd come to live with them. Xiaoxue smiled and said they were very welcome, there were more than thirty rooms, plenty of space for them. The old couple were a little uneasy about Mei Yin's status—a convict out on medical parole. But Xue Yu explained the situation to them. Mei Yin was sent to prison for her unconventional beliefs about medical science, and because she'd tried to put these beliefs into practice. He said she could be considered a "scientific political prisoner." That set the old couple's minds somewhat at ease.

Xiaoxue had invited Mother Liu and Mother Chen of Nanyang's Sacred Heart Orphanage, who showed up with all the children in tow, aged two to ten, taking up three whole tables. The kids clutched Xiaoxue's legs and hollered, "Sister Xiaoxue, we want wedding candy," making so much noise they sounded like a pond full of frogs. The two mothers hugged Mei Yin and Xiaoxue, weeping tears of joy. "The saying is right, happiness comes after great misfortune. Xiaoxue's been through so much, and now you've finally come through the other side."

Of the orphans who'd been there at the same time as Xiaoxue, she'd lost touch with all except Xiaokai and Yuanyuan. Both of them had left for school, but took time off to come back. Xiaokai was embarrassed, feeling uncouth and awkward, while Xiaoxue had blossomed into beauty, graceful and elegant—a proper lady. Yuanyuan gasped. "Xiaoxue, you're so beautiful. All those fashion magazine editors must be blind, not to put you on their covers! Did you know, Xiaokai's had a crush on you for seven or eight years now. Even when you had your pockmarks, he still liked you. It's a shame you lost touch for so long, and now you've been nabbed by Mr. Xue."

Xiaokai blushed. "What nonsense, Yuanyuan!"

Yuanyuan pouted. "You told me yourself!"

Xiaokai's face was bright red, but he didn't dare answer back. Moved, Xiaoxue took his hand and generously said, "Xiaokai, thank you for your affection."

Then Yuanyuan noticed Xiaoxue's figure and whispered, "Pregnant?" Xiaoxue nodded shyly, and Yuanyuan rapped her on the forehead, giggling. "You don't waste any time, do you? That's good, I get to be an aunt soon."

Mayor Jin had been invited too, but didn't show. After the scandal, the municipal government had been very cautious about Mei Yin's company, carefully sticking to its "double negative" policy, not budging an inch either way. On one hand, they'd sent Mei Yin to prison, refusing to cut her sentence despite granting her parole, because they had to make their official stance clear to the world. On the other hand, the WHO was allowed to fund the research project, and the city adopted a don't-ask-don't-tell policy about the company's illegal experiments. Jin had been promoted to mayor, and if he were seen attending the wedding of the Heavenly Corp. general manager, it would damage their carefully cultivated ambiguity. He sent a handsome gift and phoned Mei Yin. "A public servant's life is not his own. Sister Mei, you'll understand."

Mei Yin said she understood very well, and thanked him for the present.

There was one other important guest at the wedding: Xue Yu's uncle, Zhao Yuzhou. He'd always had time for his nephew, and naturally turned up on this occasion. According to local custom, the bride's uncle was always the guest of honor, and had to be served well. If he wasn't happy with his treatment, he could give everyone a hard time. But Xiaoxue had no family, so Mommy Mei represented the whole of the bride's side. Mommy Mei teased Xue Yu, saying, "Maybe Mr. Zhao should play the part of the bride's uncle." Zhao Yuzhou thought his new niece was wonderful, and gave the couple a very expensive present. But he had a bone to pick with them. How could they let Mei Yin stay with them after she got out of prison? It was outrageous. She had refused to eradicate smallpox, then sneaked the virus into the orphans' birthday cake! Yet here she was, allowed a peaceful life like some dowager. But it was his nephew's wedding day, and he had no intention of making a scene. Fortunately, local custom dictated that the bride's parents weren't allowed to take part in the ceremony, so there was no danger of them locking horns. She would have a separate celebration later—traditional wedding ceremonies always culminated in games around the wedding chamber, and if the pranks got out of hand, it would be embarrassing for the bride's parents.

This wedding was comparatively tame, though—the guests only played a few token tricks, such as making them kiss in public, try to take bites from a suspended apple, light everyone's cigarettes, and so on. The wedding ended early, as many of the guests, including the chefs and orphans, had a long drive back to Nanyang. The local guests began drifting away too, the courtyard lights went out, and all was still again. The newlyweds, Xue Yu's parents, and Zhao Yuzhou went into the living room, where Mei Yin was waiting for them. As everyone sat, she smiled. "Now that the ceremony's over, I have a little ritual of my own. Xue Yu, turn off the lights."

Xue Yu wasn't sure what was going on, but did as he was told. Mei Yin wheeled herself out of the room, then in a moment, sailed back in with a blaze of light. Mei Yin had a tiny birthday cake on her lap, twenty-two candles flickering merrily on it. Her face bathed in the warm golden light, like a golden sculpture. She laughed. "The wedding just happened to be on Xiaoxue's birthday. I knew everyone would be full from dinner, so I just got a little cake. We can have a bite each."

Xue Yu scratched his head. They'd both been so busy preparing for the wedding that they'd completely forgotten about Xiaoxue's birthday. "I'll need to be a better husband," he said. "I guess mothers and daughters are always closer! Xiaoxue, make a wish."

Looking at her mother's withered legs, Xiaoxue silently wished her mother better health, then blew out the candles and gave everyone a slice of cake. Mei Yin saw Zhao Yuzhou was sitting coldly to one side, and reached out to him. "Mr. Zhao, it's been seven years since we met in America. Do you still remember that man, Zia Baj?"

Zhao Yuzhou replied frostily, "That Afghan American scientist? I remember him."

"Who knows where he's hidden himself. I keep thinking he's vanished into some dark cave like a vampire bat, and someday he'll fly out and start harming people again."

Furious, Zhao Yuzhou barked, "Why do you think so badly of him? Was it what he said that day? In my view, he was absolutely right to criticize the hypocrisy of the West, ripping open the syphilitic sores of the white people. Of course, his proposals went too far. I advised moderation to him."

Mei Yin stared at him, aghast. "You don't know?" But she realized he had no idea. People only remembered the terrorists who'd appeared on TV, while Zia Baj had remained below the surface, and his name hadn't registered with most people. "Zia Baj was behind that terrorist attack."

Zhao was shocked, and obviously disbelieving. Mei Yin went on. "There's no doubt about it, I have firsthand information. I informed US Homeland Security of his links to some terrorists; they called to thank me and to say they'd confirmed my suspicions. Don't you remember, at that meeting, Zia Baj said he was leaving America right away? He *did* leave that day, and then vanished, and still hasn't been arrested."

Xue Yu knew who they were talking about—even Xiaoxue did too. Mei Yin had first lied about deliberately sowing smallpox in the orphanage, saying that Zia Baj must have infected her at that meeting. Even when her lie was later revealed, no one forgot his name. Xue Yu's mother was a little embarrassed for her brother—he still obviously supported this terrorist mastermind's opinions. And how supercilious to say he'd "advised moderation." Zhao could only simmer in shame and rage, his face alternating white and red.

Seeing how awkward the conversation had become, Mei Yin tried to change the subject. "Xiaoxue, your uncle's finished his cake, get him another slice."

That presented Zhao with an excellent target, and he grabbed Xiaoxue's wrist, sneering, "No, I won't have any more. Who knows what viruses might lurk in that cake."

And with that, he quit the room in a huff, heading to bed. The direct reference to Mei Yin's past "crime" left everyone uncomfortable. After a while, Mei Yin smiled. "The old man has quite a strong personality. Come on, let's eat. More cake, anyone?"

Xue Yu's parents nodded like chickens pecking at grain, eager to show they weren't worried. "Yes, let's have another slice." As they ate, Mei Yin said, "It's getting late. Xue Yu and Xiaoxue must be exhausted. Let's all get some rest."

◆　◆　◆

By breakfast the next morning, the awkwardness of the day before had been forgotten, and only Zhao Yuzhou was still sullen. Xue Yu's parents loved the surroundings—"like a fairy kingdom"—and decided to stay a few more days. Zhao Yuzhou was flying back to Beijing that day. After breakfast, he called his nephew into his room for a chat. A little later, Xue Yu emerged and said to Xiaoxue, "I have to see how things are going at the office. Could you take Uncle to the airport?" Then, sotto voce, he said, "Actually, he was the one who asked for you to drive him. I guess he has something to say to you."

Xiaoxue did as he asked. She had a good impression of the uncle, although he was a little hot tempered. He was still a very frank old man; his likes and dislikes were all heartfelt. They spoke of this and that on the way, and got to the airport very early, so they found a quiet place to sit. The uncle said, "Xiaoxue, there's something I want to warn you about. I know you won't listen to me, but whether or not you pay attention, I have to do my duty."

"Please go ahead, Uncle."

"You know the role Mei Yin played in that epidemic seven years ago?"

"Yes."

"No, I don't think you do. That outbreak was no accidental leak. She spread the virus on purpose."

"I know. Xue Yu told me."

The uncle was stunned. "You know? In that case, why would you . . . She killed a man. She disfigured orphans. It's wickedness."

Although she'd made her peace with all this, it still made her sad to hear it said this way. She replied quietly, "I know, I know all that. The dead man was Dr. Ma, from the alleyway by the orphanage. He got sick because I went to see him. The most disfigured child in the orphanage was me. It was only a few months ago that Xue Yu brought me to Beijing for reconstructive surgery."

He was even more shocked, and studied her features carefully, to confirm that she had once been pockmarked. Now he was in a frenzy of rage. More things Xue Yu had kept from him. So he'd brought her to Beijing for this surgery, and hadn't thought to visit his uncle? And he still didn't understand: Xiaoxue ought to loathe Mei Yin. Why recognize this "mother"? Why bring her from prison to their home? Xiaoxue had pulled herself out of her sadness, and smiled. "Uncle, Mother Mei is a good person, she only did what she did out of medical principles, not to harm anyone. We all understand."

The uncle snorted. "I don't understand at all! Xiaoxue, I'm advising you both to stay far away from this woman. She's bad news. Her whole body stinks of death! Don't think I'm simply bad-mouthing her, you have to hear this now or you might regret it later on. Remember, stay far from her, don't let tragedy land on you both, and especially not on your child!"

Hearing him mention the child, something clenched in Xiaoxue's heart. She forced herself to smile. "Uncle, thank you for your concern, I'm truly grateful. And I'll think about what you said."

Zhao Yuzhou knew he'd gone too far, and there was no use pressing his point. After they'd sat in silence for a while, it was time for him to go. Xiaoxue didn't leave right away after the plane took off, but stayed in the departure lounge on her own for a long time. Of course she would never turn against Mommy Mei on his say-so, but his confident prediction of disaster—he'd sounded like a sorcerer, setting a curse—still plagued her heart.

He'd mentioned her unborn child!

Back home, she didn't let her worry show. Xue Yu was back from work, and seemed as cheerful as always, joking around. When they'd retired to their room, Xue Yu asked with a laugh, "Did Uncle warn you? That we should stay away from Mother Mei? Because she's bad luck?"

"Yes, he did."

"That old busybody. Once he sets himself against someone, he never lets it go. Too bad Mother Mei got on his bad side. But to be fair, Uncle's saying all this because of a difference in political opinions, not because of some personal grudge. You have to understand him."

"I do."

Xue Yu could tell something was troubling his wife. "What's wrong? You seem unhappy." He had to ask a few times before she told him, "Uncle warned me that if we didn't keep our distance from Mother Mei, disaster would fall on our son's head. I don't believe his nonsense, of course, but I don't know, it just stuck with me."

"That old man and his inauspicious mouth. He said some bad-luck things in front of me. Now you too! We can't let Mother Mei know about this."

Xiaoxue murmured, "Of course not."

Mother Mei only let the newlyweds rest for three days before urging Xiaoxue to start her lessons again. She said they'd already delayed seven years, there was no more time to waste. Xiaoxue was suffering from morning sickness; unable to eat, she was growing thinner by the day, and had no energy. Xue Yu was worried, and kept urging her to eat something, bringing home all kinds of fruits and foods for her to try. Mother Mei worried too, but her method was completely different. She said to Xue Yu, "Don't bother forcing her to eat, just let nature take its course. Evolution created 'morning sickness,' so it must have some function. There are errors and omissions in evolution, but they're usually small details. With something as important as reproduction, evolution usually gets it right. Scientists have hypothesized that pregnant women throw up to protect the fetus at its most vulnerable, by ensuring minimal contact with potentially dangerous foods—don't forget, plants evolved to keep herbivores away, often by developing toxins in their fruits."

Xue Yu had always trusted Mother Mei, and so, though it hurt him to see his wife listless and limp, he stopped trying to make her eat. After some time, Xiaoxue noticed that Xue Yu and her mother seemed to be reaching a deeper rapport, apparently based on their continuing work.

When her husband came home from work, he often went to Mommy Mei's room first to exchange a few words with her, never very much, a few quick statements. Sometimes, she didn't even reply, just nodded, but the depth of their shared knowledge was palpable. One day in bed, Xiaoxue mentioned this to her husband, in mock jealousy, and he replied, "What a thing to say! Mommy loves you so much, and you're still not satisfied. I ought to be the one who is jealous!"

After teasing her a bit more, Xue Yu put his head on her belly to listen to the fetus's heartbeat, that intoxicating rhythm. Later, when its little hands and legs started moving, he was even more enchanted, calling out at each little kick, "It moved, it moved again, the little thing's saying hello to me."

At the start of summer, the pomegranate tree in the courtyard was aflame with blossoms. Five visitors arrived that day, each from a different country, to see Mother Mei. They were Mr. Joon Cheol Choi from Korea, Mr. Rajaratnam from India, Mr. Clausen from Norway, Mr. Schmitt from Germany, and Madame Izmailova from Russia. Mother Mei was delighted, talking animatedly with all of them. Xue Yu took the day off work to keep them company. Mother Mei introduced the now heavily pregnant Xiaoxue to the guests. "This is my daughter, I'm going to be a grandmother soon!" The visitors all said, "The child will surely be as beautiful as her mother."

The conversation in the living room took place in English, and Xiaoxue couldn't keep up. After a little small talk, she went off to her bedroom alone, thinking that five foreigners were unlikely to have all shown up for social visits at the same time by coincidence. After a while, Xue Yu came in and said, "The visitors said the pine forest is so lovely they want to take a walk in it. Mother Mei and I will go along."

Xue Yu pushed Mommy's chair, and the seven of them set off, chatting and laughing. After an hour, they still weren't back. Xiaoxue thought she ought to start preparing lunch for the guests. There wasn't much in the fridge, so she'd have to go get some takeout from the shop at the facility gate. Hands supporting the small of her back, she walked slowly down the path through the pine woods. In the distance, she saw her husband and the rest among the trees, huddled around Mother Mei's wheelchair, their backs to her. They seemed to have been joined by someone. Xiaoxue walked toward them, and saw that the additional person was Xue Yu's new chief engineer, Mr. Lin. Something seemed odd about them. They were standing in a straight line in front of Mother Mei, gazing respectfully at her, while she sat in her wheelchair like the pope on his throne, charitably bestowing blessings upon true believers. It was gloomy beneath the trees, and they spoke in whispers.

Now Mother Mei pointed at Xue Yu, who stepped forward. Mother Mei said, "Speak the motto of the crucifix."

"Be in awe of nature."

Mother Mei held out a cross, and said clearly, "This is the cross once worn by Mr. Dickerson, inscribed with his initials. I've asked Scott to add yours. I trust you will live up to it."

Xue Yu said gravely, "Godfather, I will not be unworthy."

He lowered his head and allowed Mother Mei to hang the cross around his neck, then stepped back. Hiding behind a tree, Xiaoxue was in shock. Had Xue Yu called Mother Mei *Godfather*? How could she be a godfather? Xiaoxue was some distance from them, and maybe had heard wrongly. Now Mother Mei pointed at Chief Engineer Lin, and he too stepped forward.

"Speak the motto of the crucifix."

"Be in awe of nature."

"This is the cross once worn by my former husband, Sun Jingshuan. He made an enormous contribution to the cultivation of the attenuated smallpox virus, but unfortunately he left us in the end. I've asked Scott to carve your name on this cross. I trust you will live up to it."

"Godfather, I will not be unworthy."

He lowered his head, and Mother Mei put the cross on him. Xiaoxue had heard clearly this time. They were definitely calling her "Godfather." Now the five foreigners went through the same ceremony, accepting their crucifixes and swearing to the Godfather. The only difference was these five crosses were newly made.

Afterward, Mother Mei said, "After twenty years of research, our lab has reached our goal, a stable version of the mild smallpox virus. We have reduced the virulence of this strain so it only produces slight symptoms in humans, but has cross immunity with regular smallpox. This mild strain is strong enough that, if placed with regular smallpox in a natural environment, it would quickly become the dominant strain. We have decided to set this strain of smallpox loose in the wild. The work will begin in China, and later, when we've completed the higher levels of work, we'll send the pathogens to you all via the WHO."

Everyone nodded. Xue Yu smiled. "Let's go back, it's almost lunchtime."

He pushed the wheelchair, and the other six followed, heading in Xiaoxue's direction. With some resentment, she thought that all that stuff about going for a walk in the woods had been just to avoid her. Mother Mei didn't seem surprised to see Xiaoxue, she merely looked back and gestured at Xue Yu. He put someone else in charge of the wheelchair, and hurried over. Afraid her husband would think she'd been spying on him, she said defensively, "I was going to get some food, now we have an extra five, no six, guests for lunch."

He smacked his head. "Right, I forgot to tell you, I've already gotten take-out lunch for all of us. You needn't have bothered. Let's go back in."

Back in the house, Xue Yu didn't let Xiaoxue lift a finger, as usual, but put on his apron and began bustling around the kitchen. The visitors sat around Mother Mei, chatting vigorously, not at all like the solemn mysticism of the pine wood. Madame Izmailova hugged Xiaoxue, and asked how the child was doing. Between Xiaoxue's rusty English and some hand gestures, they managed to get quite a good conversation going. A while later, Xue Yu appeared with a dozen or so dishes, and everyone sat down for lunch. They kept talking animatedly all through the meal, but using medical jargon that Xiaoxue couldn't follow.

The visitors left after lunch, and when the house was quiet again, Mei Yin resumed her lessons with Xiaoxue, though Xiaoxue found it hard to focus. Afterward, she immediately went in search of information about smallpox. The information online didn't go very deep, and when she searched her husband's bookshelves, only the older textbooks contained what she wanted. Mei Yin could tell something was bothering her, but only watched her, saying nothing.

That night, the couple lay in bed, and as always took great pleasure in talking about the child. Xue Yu loved pressing his ear to his wife's naked belly, listening to the fetal heartbeat, or carefully feeling for its legs and hands with his fingers. Xue Yu said, "What an active little baby, I bet it's a boy." Then a while later he said, "Or maybe a girl would be better, a girl would be like her mother, the prettiest creature in the world; a boy would take after his dad, and with my looks that'd be a tragedy." They'd decided to keep the baby's gender a surprise.

Today, though, Xiaoxue wasn't her normal self. Xue Yu spoke to the baby for a while, then lay down next to his wife, asking cheerfully, "I can tell you've got something on your mind. Tell me. Are you worried about my uncle and his bad-luck prediction again? Don't believe a word of that."

Xiaoxue didn't believe it, though it was true that something about that prediction—if the disaster doesn't land on your head, it'll land on your child's—had lodged in her heart, leaving her constantly on edge. She explained, "I heard you calling Mommy 'Godfather.'"

"That's just the name we use. The Crucifix Society is a loose collective of scientists, not a religion, and definitely not a cult. But old

Dickerson looked like Pope John Paul II, so his colleagues joked that he was their godfather, and the name got passed on."

"So Mommy is the current godfather?"

"Yes. While she was in jail, the Society took a vote and elected her to the office. Everyone acknowledges her strength of character."

"Yu, today I happened to overhear your conversation. You're planning to spread the mild smallpox virus. And of course, I'm afraid you're going to start here."

"Yes."

"Today, I looked up the impact of smallpox on a fetus."

"Mother Mei told me you'd been looking through my books. Did you find an answer? You could just have asked me."

"More or less. The books say after coming into contact with the virus, a healthy immune mother will temporarily become a carrier. The possibility of passing the disease on to her baby isn't high, but can't be eliminated altogether. It also might infect the mother's amniotic sac, then the baby through the amniotic fluid."

"Yes, women infected in the late stages of pregnancy might indeed pass it on through the blood or amniotic fluid. But if the woman isn't infected herself, just in an environment that contains a mild strain of the virus, the possibility is even lower. And if infected with this weaker variety, the chances of developing serious symptoms is lower yet. A small probability times a small probability is practically zero."

"Practically zero isn't the same as zero. No matter how much research you do, how many precautions you take, you'll never be able to guarantee a death rate of zero. Correct?"

"Yes. You're right, and actually that's the fundamental standpoint of the organization."

Xiaoxue was silent for a very long time, before saying, "These few months, I've come to understand the Crucifix Society's point of view—medicine shouldn't focus only on the individual, but also on the group. And when the interests of the group and the interests of the individual clash, the group should prevail. Logically, it makes perfect sense. But put into practice, it would be so cruel! You're disseminating the smallpox virus for the good of humanity as a whole, in order to fill the smallpox vacuum, which could lead to a dangerous disequilibrium. That's a noble goal. But, if, just if, the one-in-a-million chance happens, and our baby gets smallpox, and I have a miscarriage, or it's crippled, or it dies, then that'd be everything to us! If that happened, and if I'd done nothing to stop the possibility, then my conscience would never let me rest, not in this lifetime."

Xiaoxue had stayed calm and reasonable throughout this speech, but Xue Yu knew his wife, and knew that she was actually taking a stand: she had to stop the spread of this virus, at least until the child was born, and she wouldn't hesitate to pit herself against her mother and husband to do it. Even a young girl, on the verge of motherhood, can tap into a mother's strength, the most powerful force on earth. Xue Yu thought about it, and said, "Let's play a game. If you haven't changed your mind by the end of it, I'll do as you say. Okay?"

Xiaoxue eyed him suspiciously. "What kind of game?"

"It's very simple, but there's a sort of cruelty in it. Prepare yourself, because once we start, we'll have to finish. There's no stopping halfway."

She hesitated. "All right."

Xue Yu found a sheet of stiff card, and cut it into ten coin-size pieces. With his back to Xiaoxue, he scribbled something on each one, all the while saying, "This is how it works. Imagine there's an evil demon in the sky, and the mortals have offended him. This demon decides to kill a million people, and not one less. He begins the killing. Every day, people drop dead out of the blue. Thousands die. This is hell on earth. Entire families are wiped out. There are too many corpses to deal with. The workers sent out to collect the bodies fall dead next to them. The later bodies aren't even buried. Rich folk get in their carriages and leave the infection zone, but that only seems to draw the demon's claws after them."

Xiaoxue knew what he was hinting at. The history books of Europe, China, and India recorded many such plagues that occurred during the Middle Ages.

"Then a holy person decides to save the people from this tragedy. It doesn't matter who this person is, but let's give him a Nanyang name, let's call him Zhang Zhongjing. The doctor-saint Zhang Zhongjing passes through all kinds of hardship and danger to get to the demon, and pleads for him to spare the innocent. The demon laughs. 'I've heard of you, and for your sake, I'll spare a million people. But God hates perfection, so out of the million, I'll have to pick ten at random to kill. These ten people's deaths will redeem the rest.' The saint keeps pleading, and the demon roars. 'If you don't shut up, I'll kill a million people like I planned, and not spare a single one!' So Zhang Zhongjing can only agree. The demon says, 'And let me warn you, the ten sacrifices might include you.' The doctor-saint says, 'If it spares innocent lives, why would I be scared to die?' And so, the demon picks ten people to kill, including the saint himself. And after that, there's peace on earth."

Xue Yu paused, and looked at Xiaoxue. She thought this story was a little simplistic, and there wasn't a game at all, so she waited curiously for him to continue.

"If that were all, this game wouldn't be so cruel. Exchanging ten lives for a million is quite a bargain. But there's actually a different version of the ending, and it goes like this—the demon laughs coldly. 'If you want me to save a million people, that's easy enough. Here's a list of ten names. For each name you pick, I'll kill that person, and spare a hundred thousand lives. If you choose all ten names, I'll kill them all, and save the full million lives. And let me warn you, the list of names includes your own. Will you do it?' And the doctor-saint says, 'I'm not afraid to die; it will be as you say.' And so the demon hands him a list of ten names."

Xue Yu passed her a charcoal pencil and the stack of cards. "Here, you're the saint, and these are the ten names. Pick one, draw a cross on it, and that person's dead. You'll save a hundred thousand lives with each one. Go ahead. And remember what we agreed: once we start, you have to play till the end, no stopping halfway! Begin."

Xiaoxue unfolded the pieces of paper, and her face turned pale as snow. The ten names were Granny Sun, Dr. Ma, Xiaokai, Yuanyuan, Mother Liu, Mother Chen, Xue Yu, Mei Yin, Mei Xiaoxue, Xiaoxue's baby.

Xue Yu said quietly, "This is just a game. Even if you cross out a name, that person won't really die. But it's important that you do this. Quick, go ahead, a million people are waiting for you to save them."

He was pressing her mercilessly. Xiaoxue couldn't go back on her word, so she hardened her heart and drew a cross through Granny Sun's name. Those black lines seemed to slice her heart open. Xue Yu took the piece of paper, saying, "We're saying for the sake of the game that Granny Sun hadn't already died; now you've just killed her. But, after all, she was an old stroke victim, her death isn't the greatest tragedy. Right, that's a hundred thousand lives saved. Next."

Xiaoxue steeled herself again, and struck out Dr. Ma's name. Xue Yu said, "Dr. Ma was the hero who first reported Nanyang's smallpox outbreak, and because he treated you, he was infected and died. Now you've killed him once again. But he was old, so let him die. Xiaoxue, you've saved another hundred thousand people. Continue."

Next, she picked Mother Liu and Mother Chen. They'd been good to her back when she was at the orphanage, but now she was condemning them to death. Even though this was just a game, it still felt like a knife through the heart. They were two of the oldest on the list, though, so she had no choice.

"Another two hundred thousand saved. Continue."

Xiaokai and Yuanyuan. "Two hundred thousand lives. Continue."

She couldn't bear it any more. Tears covered her face, but Xue Yu said coldly, "We agreed, no stopping this game. You have to go on till you're finished. Continue. Why not pick me next? A child needs its mother more. Go on."

Her eyes blurred with tears, filled with sorrow and anger—hating her husband for tricking her into this cruel game, she violently crossed out Xue Yu's name.

"A hundred thousand people saved. Xiaoxue, you'll have to pick Mother Mei next. She's older, and in bad health. If you kill yourself instead of her, she'd find it hard to bring the child up alone."

Xiaoxue was sobbing so hard she could barely catch her breath, and tried to refuse. Xue Yu had no mercy, but grabbed her hand and forced her to scrawl a cross over Mei Yin's name, and toss the piece of paper aside. Now even his voice had started to tremble, but he clenched his teeth and went on. "Another hundred thousand people. Continue. There's still the last two hundred thousand waiting for you to rescue them. Xiaoxue, you can only choose the baby next, he or she is still so young, even if you spared it, it wouldn't survive without its mother. Animals will abandon their young when death threatens—it may be heartless, but it is entirely correct. Not according to human morality, but to natural morality."

Xiaoxue howled, flinging aside the last two scraps of paper and pummeling her husband's chest. "I hate you! Cold-blooded animal!"

Mother Mei heard the commotion, and quickly wheeled herself over. Xue Yu hugged Xiaoxue and shot a glance at his mother-in-law—so she silently retreated. When Xiaoxue was calm again, Xue Yu continued. "I don't feel good about this either. It's just a simple game, but it still feels like being stabbed ten times in the heart. And actually, it's not a game, it's the reality of existence, it's a fable for the history of life on earth. Caring for the herd rather than the individual is the guiding principle of God. We might rationally be able to accept this rule, acknowledging its truth and necessity. But if it leads to the death of your loved ones, especially if you're personally responsible for those deaths, then that would be more than most could bear. Now do you understand why Kolya Stebushkin killed himself, why Mother Mei was so filled with guilt, and why Uncle Sun decided to abandon the journey halfway?"

After that game, Xiaoxue stopped asking about the plan to release mild viruses. In all likelihood, her husband had already done it, and the smallpox virus was now swirling round their home. She didn't want to know. She tried to comfort herself with the thought that it had been the right thing to do, rationally speaking, and that the chances of their child contracting smallpox were "virtually zero." She once again appeared happy, but Mei Yin's sharp eyes could see the lingering fear in her heart, and it caused her pain. Xiaoxue was nearly a mother, but she was still only a girl of twenty-two.

When her time came, Xue Yu drove Xiaoxue to the maternity ward of Nanyang Central Hospital, and Mei Yin hired a helper to look after her. Since she'd been released from jail, Mei Yin's legs had gotten much better, and she could walk short distances without the wheelchair. Xue Yu was very busy with work, but as soon as he had a bit of spare time, he would drive to Nanyang to be with his wife. Xiaoxue's labor pains were much worse than most people's, and they tormented her for three whole days and nights.

Those three days of torture slowly worsened Xiaoxue's state of mind. She gradually became certain that a great tragedy would befall either herself or her child. This idea took deeper and deeper root until, after yet another wave of pain, she abruptly said to her husband, "Yu, if anything should happen, save the baby first."

Xue Yu froze. "What nonsense are you talking? Every checkup has indicated this will be a normal labor. And if anything goes wrong, a C-section should sort it out. That's just a small procedure."

Xiaoxue didn't seem to hear her husband's comforting words. After a while, she said, "I'm worried our child will have cowpox."

Actually, she meant smallpox. Xue Yu said, "More nonsense. We've had all the tests, the fetus is absolutely normal."

Xiaoxue said nothing more, but there was still terror in her eyes. Xue Yu and Mother Mei exchanged a look, and changed the subject. Xue Yu silently cursed his uncle for having planted such seeds of fear.

As Xiaoxue finally went into the delivery room, the doctor said to Xue Yu, "You can keep her company, she'll find that reassuring." He stood at the head of the bed and held her hand. Xiaoxue's fingernails pressed into his palm. Her eyes shut, and she clenched her teeth, moans slipping between them. The doctor said encouragingly, "Push, go on, use some strength, the head is almost out!" At this moment, Xue Yu truly understood what he'd read in books, that women suffer for evolution. Compared to other animals, every human baby is premature, and every human birth tests the mother's limits.

A resounding cry came from between Xiaoxue's legs, and the doctor cheered. "Wonderful, a plump little boy!"

The nurses rushed to cut the umbilical cord, wipe off the blood, and take impressions of the baby's feet. Xue Yu murmured into her ear, "Xiaoxue, everything's all right. It's a boy."

After so many days of agony, Xiaoxue had no strength left at all. She struggled to say, "Let . . . me . . . see."

Xue Yu knew what she was thinking, and as soon as the nurses had swaddled the baby, he held him up for her to look. "Don't worry, all is as it should be, no blisters, lesions, or anything else abnormal. A perfectly healthy child."

Xiaoxue finally let herself stop worrying, and was soon sound asleep.

They named the boy Jiji, and he soon became the angel of the household, a little heartbreaker. Mei Yin adored him all the more for never having had a child herself. After he came home, she was always running around doing things for him, and soon her legs had recovered completely. He was her lucky star, she said. Xiaoxue grew cheerful again, and the house filled with the laughter of both mother and son. Sometimes Xiaoxue thought back to the sorrow and terror she'd felt in the days before the birth, and wondered how she'd come to have such strange ideas—they seemed inconceivable now.

CHAPTER SIX
NEXT TARGET: TOKYO

Winter 2029—Tokyo, Japan

Situated in Tokyo's Kinza District, Hanako Advertising was Japan's largest ad agency. It was almost the New Year, and the gray twenty-story building had been decorated with colorful lights trailing from the rooftop, along with a *kadomatsu* at the main door, a traditional decoration made of pine and bamboo. Masashi Sasaki, head of marketing, was receiving an important client that day, and as a result of this meeting, the company would be plunged into a frenzy over the New Year holiday.

The young Chinese man's business card introduced him as He Zhichao, general manager of Beijing's Heavenly Fragrance Cosmetics Inc. He was thirty-five years old and dressed in a designer suit, not a speck of dirt on his leather shoes. Speaking flawless American English, He Zhichao exuded an air of competence. The minute he came in, he apologized profusely for disturbing them so close to the New Year, he was truly sorry, but he had no choice, because—

"We want to export our cosmetics to your country, and we only received authorization from the Ministry of Welfare's labor minister this morning. As soon as I got the paperwork, I came straight to your office."

He pulled the papers from his briefcase to show Sasaki, and said jokingly, "I'm almost regretting choosing Japan over Europe as our breakout market. Turns out Japan's requirements for imported cosmetics are even stricter than the European Union's! But no matter, I've got the approval now."

Sasaki knew he had a major client on his hands. A few months previously, this Mr. He had gotten in touch with Hanako to say he wanted to conduct an "earth-shattering" advertising campaign in Tokyo, and he'd be in touch with the head of marketing as soon as he got the necessary permissions. Given China's new towering world status, Hanako would be sure to treat this tycoon with great care.

Smiling, Sasaki said, "No need to apologize. It would be our honor to work with you. Please go on."

Mr. He took six identical little vials from his briefcase and arranged them in a row on the desk. They were opaque and unlabeled. "Before we get down to business, I'd like you to try these perfumes so you'll have a better understanding of my company. Of these six perfume samples, three are from the classic Christian Dior Poison series—Pure, Original, and Hypnotic, all excellent names that worked insidiously in the minds of men and women. The other three are my company's Heavenly Fragrance series, Numbers One, Two, and Three, otherwise known as Soul-Capturing, Spirit-Catching, and Life-Taking." He wrote out the kanji for these words, and smiled. "The names might seem overboard, but the quality of the product will bear them out. And now, would you like to test these, and say which are superior? Maybe you have some female employees who might be willing to try them out?"

Mr. Sasaki thought about it and made a couple of calls. A moment later, two women walked in, both natural beauties, their makeup as exquisite as a crystal sculpture. As they passed by, a faint scent lingered in the air. They bowed to the visitor. Mr. Sasaki gave them some instructions in Japanese. They nodded and opened the six bottles, sniffing carefully, then dabbing each one on a pulse point, wafting the aroma with tiny movements. This took a very long time, but Mr. Sasaki waited patiently, and He Zhichao didn't seem in a hurry either. When they were done, they discussed it a while, and finally, with some hesitation, presented Mr. Sasaki with three of the bottles.

Mr. He said, "Made your choice? These ladies believe these three bottles are the superior blends? I can't tell from the outside which product they've chosen, so I'm a little nervous too. Mr. Sasaki, would you peel the adhesive paper off the bottom of the vials?"

Sasaki did as he asked. The names on the bottoms of the bottles were Hypnotic Poison, Soul-Capturing, and Life-Taking. He Zhichao laughed and ripped off the other three: Pure Poison, Original Poison, and Spirit-Catching. Satisfied, he said, "Thanks to both experts for your opinions. You've judged that two of my company's scents are superior to Dior's, in which case I have even more confidence in your business." He took six exquisite larger bottles from his bag, handing three to each woman. "These are our Heavenly Fragrance series, Numbers One, Two, and Three, a gift for you. Please accept them. And if you're satisfied with them, please recommend them to your friends. Thank you."

The women smiled as they took the presents, bowed, and departed. He Zhichao said, "Mr. Sasaki, you see the evidence. Of course, one trial sampling isn't conclusive. But I will say that we can give Dior a run for their money. Unfortunately, the world of cosmetics is too focused on designer labels, and no matter how excellent our products are, we're closeted away from the common taste. So what we need now is to grab the attention of fashionable women with a well-designed, explosive ad campaign! That's why I've come to you. I believe your company's superb work will help us enter the high-end Japanese market."

"We can definitely get you the results you want. Do you have any initial thoughts about the direction of this campaign?"

"Actually, I do. How about if, in Tokyo and other major cities, we had heavenly maidens scattering flowers? That is, we'd drop paper flowers like these from airships."

He produced a stack from his briefcase. They were small, about half the size of a sheet of tissue, the paper soft and spongy, covered with something similar to the dust of butterfly wings, slick and delightfully scented. On each one was a haiku, written in kanji, as Japanese custom dictated the most elegant writing should be:

Flowers from Heaven
Small Petals Of X-tasy
Breeze wafts to mankind

He asked Mr. Sasaki to pinch a flower, and when he did, a mist of fragrance rose from it. He Zhichao explained, "The powder on the paper contains tiny sacs of our perfume, which preserve the scent. When someone picks up the paper flower and squeezes it, the perfume is released. I'm thinking that on an important holiday, perhaps New Year's Day, airships could scatter these over Tokyo and other big cities, which could reach hundreds of thousands. This would be done when most people are outdoors, maybe in the evening. Imagine, glittering airships appearing out of the twilit gloom, scattering clouds of blossoms. Absolutely gorgeous. How about it? The campaign will need careful organizing. It won't be easy to get clearance to use the airspace over Tokyo."

"We can deal with the technical difficulties, don't worry about it."

"We don't need to know the details of how you arrange everything, but we do have an additional requirement that at least a hundred thousand people are exposed to the ad—and we'll hire a third party to evaluate that."

"No problem."

"As for the fee, I trust in your company's business ethics, so I'm proposing an unorthodox payment method." He pulled out his checkbook, and signed a couple checks. "This first check is for ten million American dollars, as payment in advance. The second check is blank, already signed. After the event, you can fill in whatever figure your actual expenses turn out to be, and we'll honor it, as long as the number doesn't exceed Heavenly Fragrance's registered capital!"

Sasaki laughed too as he accepted both checks. "Thank you for your directness. I believe we'll be very happy working together."

In the time that remained, the two men hammered out the details of the campaign, fixing the date for the third of January, the final day of *sanganichi*, the first three days of the New Year. That was when most Japanese would be out visiting friends and relatives, and the streets would be thronged. The greater difficulty was getting permission to use the airspace, particularly because it was less than a month in advance. Hanako would need to hurry to get the paperwork finished in time, and if it really couldn't be done, they'd have to postpone till the next holiday. Heavenly Fragrance would manufacture the paper flowers in China, though they'd only be coated in perfume granules at the last minute, when the date for the campaign was certain. The scented flowers would be sent to Narita Airport on the morning of January 3, and even allowing for the customs inspection, they would arrive in time for the evening's activity.

After discussing every aspect of the campaign, the two men signed the contract. Sasaki saw his Chinese visitor to the main entrance, where they said good-bye. He Zhichao had to hurry back to China to get the flowers and perfume granules ready, as well as all the necessary paperwork—time was tight on their end too.

He Zhichao returned to the Yaesu Fujiya Hotel, and immediately phoned the Riyadh-based chairman of Heavenly Fragrance, Mr. Bin Talal, to say the ad campaign would be carried out as planned, on January 3. Bin Talal asked, "In the evening?"

"Yes, as you suggested."

"The weather?"

"I've checked. Clear, somewhat overcast, no rain. Perfect flying conditions."

"Did you emphasize how important it is that we reach those numbers?"

"Yes, and they will be verified by an external auditor."

"You've done well," said Bin Talal flatly.

He Zhichao quickly checked out and got on the next plane back to Beijing from Narita. He secretly admired Bin Talal for his calm. The ad campaign was a huge gamble, and if they won, they could begin expanding into Western markets; if they lost, the company would surely fold. Heavenly Fragrance's registered holdings were just $200 million, though He Zhichao knew there'd been a certain amount of creative accounting and they actually only had forty million on hand, half in cash and the rest in fixed assets. Enough to pay for an ad campaign, though not for production afterward. But Bin Talal had told him not to worry about the money, just make sure the ad campaign was a success.

He Zhichao had been working at a different Chinese cosmetics company, God of a Hundred Flowers, as the chief technical officer, until a year ago, when a friend named Zhang, who worked as an engineer in Riyadh, had introduced him to Bin Talal. They'd seen each other once in Beijing's Great Wall Hotel—though that wasn't quite the right term, as Bin Talal was blind.

Right after introducing them, the friend left the two men alone. Bin Talal wore a kaffiyeh, a long Arabic robe, and large dark glasses. Like many blind people, he didn't face the other person when conversing, but kept his face turned to one side in order to hear better. His English was fluent, and he spoke with an American accent. As soon as they began talking, he said crisply, "Mr. Zhang said your technical skills were excellent. I'm investing forty million in a cosmetics firm, and I want you to be the general manager. You'll invest your technical skills as capital stock, holding forty-nine percent of the shares. What do you think?"

He Zhichao was startled at this offer, which was on the high side. According to China's Company Law, technical shareholders generally only got a 20 percent stake in a business, and any more than that would need special approval from the government. The Saudi man was being generous. Bin Talal smiled. "Other people have said to me that's a high proportion. But the way I see it, a technological expert can earn me billions, so why grumble over a mere twenty million? I like the environment in China, and I want to plant a seed here that will grow into a mighty tree. Don't miss this chance to get rich."

He Zhichao was worried that if he left his company to do a similar job for a rival firm, it might be a conflict of interest and leave him open to a lawsuit. But still, $19.6 million in shares, and even more if the business did well . . . For the sake of that much money, he was willing to take a bit of a risk with his future.

He bit the bullet and agreed on the spot. Bin Talal said happily, "I admire that in a man, being able to take the plunge. I'm sure we'll enjoy working together. I'll wire over forty million as soon as I get back to Riyadh. We might not see each other that much after this. I'll leave you to take care of things here. I have absolute faith in you, and trust you won't disappoint a blind man. Ha-ha!"

And that was settled. Next, He Zhichao talked about his plans for the future: how to bring his current company's technology with him without getting caught. He also suggested that Bin Talal inflate his declaration of the company's holdings, thus easing their way into overseas markets. This would be unthinkable in most other countries, but was a normal practice in China. In fact, there were companies that specialized in these deceptions, providing a sum of capital that, for a fee, would spend a week in your firm's bank account. Bin Talal agreed to all these suggestions, and gave He Zhichao authority to put them into practice. The meeting had lasted under an hour, and afterward it felt like a dream to He Zhichao, as if the whole discussion might come to nothing. But a few days later, right on schedule, the forty million from Bin Talal arrived.

The amount of trust Bin Talal placed in He Zhichao was touching, and he would give Bin Talal the best of the Chinese work ethic in return. During the following year he'd tirelessly worked to bring the company into being. Six months ago, Bin Talal had suggested the business plan of attacking the Japanese market first, and come up with the concept of the midair advertising campaign. He Zhichao agreed with all of this, and had then spent half a year making Bin Talal's vision into reality.

Hopefully this explosive ad campaign would take the Japanese market by storm, and usher their firm to the next level. On board the Boeing jet from Tokyo to Beijing, He Zhichao wished fervently for success.

Winter 2029—Tibet, China

As the S-70 Black Hawk helicopter slowly descended, Xiao Yan, a reporter from *Technology Daily*, shouted, "Stunning! Tibet is so beautiful. Paradise on earth!"

Commander Zhang, who was piloting the craft, turned back to smile at her, nodding in agreement with this young woman who hadn't seen much of the world. There were three others on board: Director Xue Yu of the Center for Environment Control at China's CDC; his wife, Mei Xiaoxue; and his mother-in-law, Ms. Mei Yin. All three were smiling too, though silent. Tibet's scenery was indeed lovely, but they'd already been there more than ten times to study the marmot plague. Besides, it was overcast, which made it harder to appreciate the landscape's beauty.

All around them were mountains in white snowy hats, circled with pale gray clouds. A northern goshawk glided past, while inky-feathered choughs settled on the enormous rocks, looking curiously at the visitors. The vegetation up here was different than in the plains, being an especially deep green, and the purple flowers amid this dark green looked especially bright. The Qinghai-Tibet Railroad ran past not far from here, and some of the topsoil had shifted to reveal naked patches of earth, the tangle of roots and vegetation giving way after about ten inches to loose pebbles. This was a textbook example of highland vegetative cover, created over tens of thousands of years, an extremely fragile ecosystem.

Xue Yu and the others got out of the helicopter. As had become their habit after so many visits to Tibet, the first thing they did was scan their surroundings with binoculars, looking for marmots or highland pikas. Sure enough, there were some marmots in the distance, squatting on their haunches and eyeing the humans alertly. A little earth mound behind them was the entrance to their warren, and they could vanish into its safety at any moment. Xue Yu handed his binoculars to Xiao Yan, pointing in their direction. When she got them in her sights, she shrieked, "Ah! So many marmots!"

Xue Yu said, "Yes, there's been an increase in their population this year, perhaps because of a decline in their predators—hawks and foxes. Or it may have to do with the reduction in the plague. The Tibetan herders have been educated, and now they pay attention to the plague warnings. As soon as they see a dead marmot or pika, they'll cover the body with stones, then report it to the epidemic station so they can come and disinfect it. This has made plague less likely to spread between animals. And once we've sprayed this place with the mild plague bacillus, the symptoms will be brought completely under control, which might mean these two animal populations will keep increasing. That's not necessarily a good thing, because they could cause quite a lot of damage to the vegetation cover on this plateau. We've suggested human intervention to increase the numbers of their natural predators too. The natural world is so interconnected that tugging at one strand is sure to disturb many more."

Three lightweight Z-11 helicopters landed nearby. A dozen workers in white uniforms jumped out and began measuring wind speed, temperature, humidity, and brightness. Xue Yu and Commander Zhang ran over too. Xiaoxue stood to one side with her arm around Mother Mei, away from the air currents streaming from the helicopters. Today they would commence the first large-scale open-air dissemination of pathogens ever to be carried out in China, and indeed the world. Walt Dickerson's idea of half a century ago would finally come to fruition. Before this, the dispersal of mild smallpox virus in Nanyang had been a success, but on a small scale, and it was never made public. Thinking back to those times, Mei Yin, now sixty-two, felt something stir inside her. They'd accomplished so much . . .

Xiaoxue's cell phone rang; it was Uncle Sun Jingshuan. He was calling from Beijing Airport. He and his wife, He Ying, were taking their daughter, Jiaojiao, to Japan on vacation, and Jiji was going with them. Uncle Sun said, "We're taking off soon, I'll have to turn my phone off in a minute. I wanted Jiji to say good-bye to you."

Jiji said good-bye to his mother and grandmother, and Xiaoxue couldn't help nagging him a little. "Be careful, listen to the grown-ups." Jiji said impatiently, "Yes, yes, I know." Then Uncle Sun called for Jiaojiao to say good-bye as well, but there was just a long silence, after which he chuckled. "Jiaojiao's too shy to talk on the phone. She says she and Jiji are like brother and sister, so how could she call Xiaoxue 'Sister'? I said, 'If you call her Auntie Xiaoxue, then what does that make me?'"

Mei Yin and Xiaoxue both laughed at this, thinking it really was a puzzle—given that Mei Yin and Sun Jingshuan had once been married, Jiaojiao was technically a generation older than Jiji, but in fact she was only two years his senior, so they could hardly ask Jiji to call her "Aunt." Xiaoxue laughed. "Don't give her a hard time, we'll answer to anything. I can be Jiaojiao's big sister, and she can be Jiji's big sister. Doesn't that work?"

Only now would Jiaojiao take the phone and say good-bye to "Sister Xiaoxue" and "Auntie Mei Yin."

He Ying asked after them too, chatting with her husband's ex-wife for a while. It was a happy phone call, but Xiaoxue couldn't help feeling sorry for her mother. Now Uncle Sun had his cozy little family, but Mother Mei was all alone. Her daughter, son-in-law, and grandson were all with her, but none of them could replace a husband. How her Mommy had suffered in this life.

Xiao Yan and a cameraman came over, wanting to interview the two of them. Xiao Yan faced the camera and said, "And now, as we prepare to spray the attenuated plague bacillus over the infection zone, I'm reporting live from the scene. As we know, plague is a highly contagious disease, with a very high death rate. After smallpox was eradicated, plague took its place as one of the most feared infectious diseases. In the fourteenth century, the plague caused the deaths of one in three people in Europe; and at the moment, plague is present in nineteen of China's provinces, in 286 counties—that's 444,017 square miles, or twelve percent of the country's land. The Qinghai-Tibet Railroad cuts through this plague zone, and in order to ensure the train doesn't help spread the disease, the central government has established epidemic observation stations in Nagqu, Damxung, and other areas. But that is purely a preventative measure, whereas today we're going to actively attack the source of infection."

She held the microphone in front of Mei Yin. "Ms. Mei, this is a historic moment. Everyone knows that you're the driving force behind this innovation, and that you spent almost eight years in jail for it. At this moment, do you have anything to say to the public?"

Mei Yin said calmly, "This isn't really that historic. We're only spreading the plague antigen, which modern society has had for a long time. All we did was strengthen it so it would be able to survive in the wild. We've gone from injecting it into people to disseminating it in the open, so it can thrive and take the place of the original virulent strain of the bacillus, leaving long-lasting immunity in its hosts. If we succeed, this one dose ought to control the plague in this territory forever. This is only the first step in reforming the Qinghai-Tibet plague zone. The large-scale program of outdoor testing has also been successful; both China and the international community will extend the program to cover anthrax, Ebola, Lassa fever, and so on."

"Ms. Mei, in recent decades, natural sources of infection seem to be rapidly expanding. Many scientists have advocated direct measures to stop these pathogens."

"I'm afraid that's just an idealistic dream."

"Why?"

"As modern society spreads itself into wilderness regions, the growth of infection zones is inevitable. In the past, geographical divisions meant that many ecosystems were completely isolated. After civilization broke down these barriers, though, the ecosystems began to collide. The big outbreaks throughout history, such as smallpox, the plague, Spanish flu, Ebola, yellow fever, Lassa fever, syphilis, and AIDS, were all the result of these collisions. The clashes weren't all bad, however, and the smaller ecosystems combined into a larger one, a global one, within which human beings and pathogens reached new, higher degrees of equilibrium. The process is irreversible. All scientists can do is monitor it and try to reduce the violence of the collisions, so all life-forms can coexist within the same circle, harmoniously. That's what we're trying to accomplish here today."

"When you talk about a global, unified ecosystem, in which human beings and pathogens will find new equilibrium, does that mean there won't be any more serious human epidemics?"

"No, in the natural world, disequilibrium is absolute while equilibrium is only relative. We'll never get rid of infection altogether, but when human beings and pathogens coexist in the same environment, they can evolve in concert, and the outbreaks that do take place will have minimal impact."

"But wouldn't it be better if science eradicated all pathogens, just like we got rid of smallpox?"

Mei Yin and Xiaoxue exchanged a wry look. Xiaoxue said, "Xiao, your thinking is twenty years out of date! The cost of such a victory would be far too high, so we've given up seeking it."

Commander Zhang came running over. The spraying was about to start. Although Mei Yin had no official designation beyond being a member of Director Xue's family, the commander knew how important she was to this project. He gave an exemplary salute, and said, "Professor Mei, we're ready to start. Please give the order."

Mei Yin was a little uneasy at this show of deference, and quickly replied. "Please, go ahead. You don't need me."

Commander Zhang saluted again and jogged back, setting off a signal flare. The three Z-11s set off together, flying at the same height, dispensing the aerosol containing the mild plague bacillus. Such sprays would usually be colorless and odorless to prevent enemy detection, but this was, in a sense, the opposite of biological warfare, and the mist had been dyed a bright red to make the results more obvious. There was one other difference in this scenario: none of the people on the ground wore protective suits, only masks.

Behind the helicopters trailed three long red dragons, which twisted lazily in the wind, wriggling and stretching, their tails mingling, diffusing, growing pale, and finally vanishing into a faint red fog that covered almost four hundred square miles of plateau grasslands.

Xue Yu once again looked at the marmots through his binoculars. Their heads were arched upward, their front paws hanging down, watching the three helicopters intently, but the pinkish mist that enveloped them seemed of no interest to them. They had no idea that the cloud was protecting them from a virulent plague.

The three Z-11s had finished their task, and flew straight back to base. The Black Hawk prepared to leave too. Before Xiaoxue boarded, she got a phone call from Uncle Sun. Their short flight to Japan was over, and the four of them had already landed in Tokyo, where they were staying at the Yaesu Fujiya Hotel. Uncle Sun said he'd told the two kids to have a shower and go to bed early, so they'd be full of energy for sightseeing the next day. Xiaoxue replied, "We're going to finish up here, and should be back in Beijing tomorrow. Hope you have a great time in Tokyo."

Then He Ying took the phone and said, "We'd planned to come back before New Year's Day, but the kids wanted to see a few more places. So we'll celebrate the New Year in Japan. I'll wish all of you a Happy New Year in advance. Tell Sister Mei."

"Thank you. Don't spoil Jiji, he's born in the year of the monkey, so he's very mischievous. Thank you for taking care of him."

"No need to thank us. He and Jiaojiao are having a great time together. All right then, good-bye."

Winter 2029—Pakistan-Afghanistan border

He Zhichao stepped up his preparations when he got back to Beijing. They had enough supplies of perfume, and the paper flowers would be easy to make. The main issue would be the granules of scent, made of a nanotech material able to absorb several times its weight in perfume, then release all of it when crushed. He'd done all the groundwork for this beforehand, and this too would be quickly prepared.

Hanako Advertising was very efficient, and a few days later Mr. Sasaki called to say their request to use the airspace had been approved for the evening of January 3. The airships were arranged too, as Japan led the world in dirigible technology, and they'd found it easy to hire three from the Japan Aerospace Exploration Agency and the Japan Agency for Marine-Earth Science and Technology. Each airship was 154 feet long and 40 feet wide, and weighed over a thousand pounds. They'd all arrive in Tokyo in a couple of days, to be decked with colored lights and put through a trial flight.

As for the scattering of the paper flowers, their tests showed it would be easiest to do manually. According to Japanese airspace regulations, however, the airships couldn't have any foreigners on them as they flew over Tokyo. He Zhichao said this was no problem—Hanako could hire Japanese workers to throw the flowers from the ships. Sasaki asked the weight and volume of the blossoms, so they could provide a dummy cargo for the trial flight.

Then Sasaki said, "I have a suggestion. Would it weaken the efficacy of the scent if the flowers were delivered a day early? We'd be in less of a rush."

"I don't think that would be a problem. Let me check with my boss and I'll get back to you."

He Zhichao phoned Bin Talal. No one answered the Riyadh number, so he tried his cell. When Bin Talal answered, He Zhichao said, "Sorry, I tried your other line but couldn't get through. Give me the number of where you are and I'll call that."

"Don't bother, we'll talk on my cell. I'm in Afghanistan now, not Saudi. I have a perfume factory here too."

He Zhichao reported on the progress in Japan, and Bin Talal said, "Very good. I'm satisfied with your work."

"Hanako asked if we could send the paper flowers to Japan a day early. I said it shouldn't be a problem, the materials are all ready."

Bin Talal hesitated. "I'm afraid that won't be possible. I was going to talk to you about this. You know how crucial this advertisement is to the company's survival. I wanted to add a special ingredient to the perfume, which I'm manufacturing in Afghanistan. I need you to send the flowers and granules to Kabul by December twenty-fifth, so the special ingredient can be added before shipping them back to Japan. It'll be tight, but I guarantee they'll get there by the third."

This sudden change in plans left He Zhichao dumbfounded, and he groaned inwardly. Why ship everything all the way to Afghanistan for some "special ingredient"? He was sure Bin Talal had some technological secret he wanted to keep to himself—and to think He Zhichao had gone the extra mile for him. Besides that, he had a strong suspicion that this had been the plan from the start, and Bin Talal had been lying to him. Still, he had to obey the boss, and could only ask, "Is this necessary?"

"I believe so. You know very well what was in those samples we gave Hanako."

He Zhichao blushed. Having been the chief technological officer at God of a Hundred Flowers, he'd been able to design a world-class scent for Heavenly Fragrance, but still not one quite as good as Dior's. In order to make an impression on Hanako during the negotiations, the samples of their product that he'd given them had actually been Dior Poison. Unaccustomed to such tactics, the Japanese had never suspected him. But when the flowers showered down during the ad campaign, of course, they would be using Heavenly Fragrance's actual perfume. Chastised, He Zhichao only said, "Mr. Bin Talal, what's the special ingredient? I'm not trying to steal any trade secrets, I just want to remind you not to get into any other trouble. I know Afghanistan is the world's leading opium producer, but I hope it's not that." He was teasing, but there was a barb in the joke.

Bin Talal said, "It's legal, don't worry about that. And don't forget, I hold fifty-one percent of the company's stock."

This woke He Zhichao up. That's right, the company was Bin Talal's private firm, and he wasn't going to play around with his own $40 million. As for himself, if Heavenly Fragrance went bankrupt, he'd stand to lose $19.6 million—cash that was really Bin Talal's. He'd only be losing a gift promised by Bin Talal. This calmed him down, and he said, "Okay, I'll make the arrangements. I'll get everything to you by the twenty-fifth, and expect the goods to arrive in Tokyo by the third of January." After a moment's thought, he added, "We said they'd be coming from Beijing, and now suddenly they're being sent from Kabul. Do you think Hanako will mind?" Bin Talal seemed to consider the question too, and he quickly answered, "I'll find a Kabul-to-Tokyo flight that goes via Beijing. I'm guessing they won't pay too much attention to the origin."

He Zhichao smiled coldly. Bin Talal was smart, but why this insistence on sending the goods to Afghanistan? What was his blind boss playing at? Damn him, it was his money, anyway. In a level voice, he said, "As you wish."

At the other end of the line, Bin Talal smiled as he hung up. The Chinese man was clever, maybe too clever for his own good, but in this show he was destined to play the part of the clown. The secret ingredient in these paper flowers would be neither perfume nor opium, but something far worse. After this strike, Heavenly Fragrance Cosmetics Inc. would no longer exist, and He Zhichao's $19.6 million in shares would vanish into thin air.

It was getting late, and the cave was growing dark. His cell phone would be out of power soon. He left the inner cave, ordering an underling to start the generator. Someone answered in the darkness, and the sound of a motor started up. The lights on the cavern roof came on, shedding a faint yellowish light that slowly grew brighter, revealing the biological reactors, centrifuges, and freezers lined up in the center of the cave, as well as four white-haired crippled men. Zia Baj returned to his inner cave and plugged his cell phone into its charger, then walked toward the four men.

This cave was the same one that Abu Hamza and Mohammad had met in decades ago. When Zia Baj left America, he'd fled to several countries in Central and West Asia, changed his appearance through facial surgery, pretended to be blind, asked various village elders for help, and in the end managed to evade the pursuing US intelligence forces. He eventually came to this cave to lie low, and Bin Talal was born. He was far from civilization here, with no electricity, telecommunications, or roads, so everything had to be transported by mule. He had four people working for him: Ahmed, who was blind in one eye; Ismail, who'd lost his left arm; Jamal, whose testicles had been smashed; and Tamala, whose right leg was missing—this last was the shorter tour guide who'd led Mohammad here, all those years ago. Their loyalty was beyond question. All four had been fierce warriors, back in the day, and now that they were old and had sustained injuries on the field, they'd put down their rifles and come to serve him for poverty wages. They were uncultured men, elderly and slow-witted—from an intellectual standpoint no better than four mules. And yet, from such unpromising material, Zia Baj had built a crude biological weapons factory. Given the conditions, he'd only been able to use the simplest method of cultivating the smallpox virus—starting with natural animal blood serum, and adding low-concentration chemical mutagens during the process. The smallpox virus couldn't be tested on animals, which only left themselves as test subjects. They'd all been immunized, so they could test the virulence of each batch by exposing themselves, and measuring the level of antibodies in their blood.

In the end, he'd created vast quantities of the smallpox virus. All in all, biological warfare was an excellent weapon for the poor man: affordable and simple to make. Mass production was possible even in the impoverished hills of Afghanistan.

The four henchmen had heard their boss's phone call, and came over to ask, "Is the time set?"

"Yes, the Chinese man will send the paper flowers to Kabul by December twenty-fifth at the latest. We should set out tonight."

They loaded the smallpox virus onto their mules. It was a five-day journey to the house Zia Baj had rented near Kabul, where they'd be able to mix the smallpox with the scent granules before scattering them on the paper flowers, then repackage them and put them on a flight to Tokyo. And then—there'd be quite a spectacular show to watch.

He asked, "Are all the mules loaded up?"

"Yes, they're outside the cave to stay cool."

In winter, this high above sea level, it was about ten degrees below zero, a natural freezer. Considering that the virus would spend five days in the open air while being transported (there was no possibility of a freezer van in this area), Zia Baj had chosen winter for the attack. One-eyed Ahmed chuckled. "The Americans have it coming to them again, another 9/11!"

Zia Baj hadn't told them any details of the plan. "No, not America. This is for Tokyo."

"Japan?" Tamala was puzzled. "Americans deserve to die more than anyone else. Why not infect New York or Washington, DC?"

"Americans are on their guard, and we'd never get this stuff through customs. Besides, they've already had a smallpox attack, they've stockpiled lots of the vaccine. I decided on Japan this time."

Tamala said anxiously, "What about Japanese immigration? Won't they inspect the goods?"

"No, I've looked into it carefully. They only test plant matter for infection, or people and boats from infected areas. Paper flowers or other manufactured products aren't on their radar."

"All right, so we'll kill a few hundred thousand Japanese, that's not bad either. Who asked them to be so friendly with the Americans, always sending them troops and ships?"

Ismail said, "What a coincidence, the last two test subjects were Japanese, too."

All five of them turned to look in the same direction, a deep crevice within the cave, where the bodies of the two test subjects were buried. A year ago, Tamala had casually asked, *"So, do our viruses work or not?"* That was precisely what Zia Baj wanted to know. The original smallpox pathogens he'd brought with him were powerful, but would this virulence have been maintained after more than a decade of production? He'd tested them on himself, and they'd induced a satisfactory antibody reaction, but needed to try them on someone without immunity before he could really be sure. Fortunately, that would be relatively straightforward. Zia Baj made a call to a friendly organization, and before long they sent over an elderly Japanese couple who'd been abducted while sightseeing in Kabul. They spoke no English, and no one there spoke any Japanese. They could only gape in terror, babbling nonstop, probably asking their kidnappers for mercy and saying they'd be willing to pay any ransom. Zia Baj grew tired of their babbling, so he got his men to hold them down while he injected a syringe of smallpox-infected blood serum into them. The incubation period was usually two weeks, but after just four days they started showing symptoms—high fever, delirium, pustules—and soon they'd reached the dangerous stage of sepsis. Zia Baj didn't wait for the disease to kill them. The strength of the virus was no longer in doubt; the test could stop. Since the victims' bodies were full of the virus, which could be preserved and used for the next step of expansion, he got his underlings to tie them up so their blood could be drained and put in cold storage. The old man was in a frenzy, probably realizing what his fate would be. Suddenly breaking free from Ismail and Tamala, he charged toward Baj and bit his left wrist hard. Tamala ran up from behind and knocked the old bastard to the ground.

He'd broken the skin on Baj's wrist, which glistened bloodily. He laughed coldly, and did nothing about the wound. He and the four others had all had the pox, and then deliberately contracted smallpox—the immunity from cowpox was shorter, whereas full smallpox more or less conferred immunity for life. The old Japanese fool was wrong if he thought he could drag Baj down with him. He was held down, and his blood drained. The man thrashed, his skin growing slowly paler, his body weakening till it was over, and he was motionless.

They did the same thing to the woman, then left the bodies in the deepest part of the cave, covering the opening with a rock. Then Baj separated their blood with a centrifuge, freezing the virus-rich blood serum. Tamala, assisting him, suddenly burst out laughing. "Mr. Baj, why bother using machines and electricity growing these viruses? This method isn't bad. Get a few hundred infidels, stick them full of germs, and when they're almost dead, suck out their blood. That's recycling, making use of rubbish. No need to waste electricity, no need for these machines, and no need to keep buying animal blood in the village."

The other three called out their agreement. Baj chuckled and said this was indeed a good method, and Western virologists would never think of such a simple, effective way of doing things. They never did put that into practice, though. Not because their consciences forbade them, but because they worried that if too many infidels went missing on the Pakistan-Afghanistan border, it might attract international attention and expose their secret lair. Not a risk worth taking.

That night, they left the cave, leading four mules and a donkey. The mules carried a load of crude smallpox virus that they'd manufactured in the last few years. One-legged Tamala couldn't come, so he said good-bye at the cave entrance, probably forever. Baj had given each of his men five hundred afghanis, which wouldn't even cover travel expenses. Tamala was almost sixty and only had one leg. It was easy to imagine what the rest of his life would be like. Zia Baj would have liked to have given him a little more money, but that simply wasn't possible. The cash he'd gotten from Hamza was almost all gone, some spent on that farm in Idaho, some on setting up Heavenly Fragrance, and the rest on funding this attack.

Anyway, Tamala didn't seem too sad, smiling as he said good-bye. Twenty-eight years ago, during the Afghanistan War, a rich man calling himself Mohammad had given him two valuable diamonds, but he'd rejected the gift because he'd known he didn't have many days left to live. Yet Allah had taken special care of him, and he'd made his way through forests of guns, hails of bullets—and although he'd lost a leg on the way, he'd held on to his life. Which is to say, those twenty-eight years had been a bonus. Of course, when he thought of the fortune he'd turned down, he couldn't help regretting it.

The four mules and donkey disappeared into the distance, leaving Tamala at the entrance, waving to his comrades. He lit a piece of wood and tossed it into the cave, which they'd doused in gasoline, so a plume of smoke immediately rose from its entrance, high into the night sky.

Tamala stumbled away on his crutches, hopping against the backdrop of the raging fire. He could see four people leading pack animals, carefully walking down the steep path, heading toward Kabul. When everything was settled there, the other three would say good-bye to Baj; this would likewise be forever. All these years they'd lived together in resistance—suffering, murdering, fleeing—with no friends, no family, their one goal in life to become martyrs and enter paradise. But paradise hadn't taken them yet, and now the war no longer needed them, so how would they live? They all felt a little empty, a little sad.

There was no light anywhere around them, apart from a sliver of new moon shining on the uneven path ahead. Jamal and Ismail walked in front, and Ahmed brought up the rear, with Zia Baj in the middle. Baj could sense the heavy hearts of his three companions, but he was in the same boat. This was without a doubt his last mission for the cause, and whether or not he succeeded, his life would probably end here. Right now, the only spiritual strength keeping him going was not so much faith as hatred. He loathed the cocky, bullying Americans, the complacent Japanese and Europeans, the wealthy Chinese and Indians. He hated that man who went by Mohammad—he and his leader had chosen submission and pleasure while handing over the virus and letting him toy with the infidels' lives; he hated Hamza—who'd once been his spiritual leader, but changed sides after being captured by the Americans; and he hated the instructors at the camp he'd trained at—they'd plucked young Zia Baj from regular life and turned him into this thing, destroying his chance to ever be normal. But it was too late now, at fifty-four years old Zia Baj could only follow the path he was on till the end.

The journey was smooth, and even though they had to pass through some army checkpoints on the way, a trading caravan comprising five animals and three disabled men aroused little suspicion. Now they just had to get through the Ayal Pass, and Kabul would be very close. Baj got another call from the Chinese man. The signal wasn't good, and he bellowed, "I'm traveling, you'll have to talk louder!" Amid the static, He Zhichao said that he'd sent the goods to Kabul, and was about to get on a plane to Tokyo himself, to personally oversee the campaign. Baj paused a moment before answering—on the desolate Ayal Pass, amid a caravan of mules, he worked to summon the persona of the wealthy Saudi Bin Talal—and finally said in a smooth, cultured voice, "Very good, everything's going to plan here. I'll leave you to handle the Tokyo side of things."

January 2030—Tokyo, Kabul, and Beijing

Sun Jingshuan, his wife, and the two kids spent more than ten days in Japan, traveling to Tokyo, the Heian Shrine, Mount Fuji, Yokohama's Chinatown, and Disneyland, and enjoying some hot springs. On New Year's Day and the next few days, they spent some more time in

Tokyo, again at the Yaesu Fujiya Hotel. This stay was partly to rest and regroup—even Jiji, the most energetic, was asking for a break—partly to experience how the Japanese celebrated New Year's. The hotel was nicely decorated, with a *kadomatsu* outside the main entrance; there were organized trips on New Year's Eve to a shrine to hear the traditional tolling of the bell one hundred and eight times; and on New Year's morning, the hotel served *toso sake*, *o-zōni*, and other New Year foods like herring roe, black beans, little fish cooked in soy sauce and sugar, and so on. The manager of Fujiya Hotel even led his workers in paying New Year's visits to the guests and handing out greeting cards.

On the third day of the new year, they did more exploring in Tokyo, visiting a shopping mall in Ginza and watching a song and dance performance, wandering through the Akihabara electronics emporiums Laox and Akky, picking up some of the latest gadgets as gifts for friends back home, buying so much they had to arrange for the purchases to be sent back to China. It was dusk by the time they left the mall, and red clouds were slowly fading into darkness in the west. As the night thickened, neon lights flashed on above all the shops. Nikko Street was full of people, every bit as crowded as Beijing's Wangfujing. As they moved through the throngs, looking for a restaurant, Jiji suddenly pointed at the sky and shouted, "Jiaojiao, look, airship! Three huge airships!"

"Dad, Mom, they really are airships! They're huge, and so pretty."

The three white dirigibles had risen in the sky behind them, and were heading steadily in their direction. They looked a lot like spaceships, and blotted out almost half the night, squeezing the sky into the gaps between them. Lights glittered all around the airships, illuminating them in silhouette, with swiveling lamps beneath shooting beams of multicolored light into the air. The two kids screamed with delight, and the adults were exclaiming too, everyone tilting their heads back to look. Then, from the tail of each airship, long white dragons suddenly appeared, their bodies twisting and disintegrating into snowflakes that drifted down and scattered over the crowd. Everyone reached out to grab at them. Sun Jingshuan got hold of a few, which turned out to be delicate paper flowers, so light and soft they might have been made of silk, covered in something like the powder on butterfly wings. Squeezing them released a delicious scent. On each flower was Japanese writing in kanji, a haiku and an advertising slogan. Jingshuan noticed the brand name beneath: China Heavenly Fragrance Cosmetics Inc. He had to laugh at that, chuckling to his wife and the children. "It's a perfume ad! A Chinese company. They know how to hustle—ads in Tokyo, and so creative, too."

He Ying and the kids were grabbing at the flowers too, the kids sniffing delightedly and saying how good they smelled. "Our Chinese perfume is even better than those Italian ones." They squinted, trying to decipher the words, and Jiji looked up, confused. "Uncle Sun, why is the airship dropping smallpox? Look, it says here."

Before Jingshuan could answer, Jiaojiao butted in. "Idiot, that's not what it says, can't you read? It's petals of . . . something. Flowers from heaven, anyway."

Jingshuan looked at the row of words Jiji was pointing at. He'd only picked out the capital letters in "SMALL Petals Of X-tasy" and read "SMALLPOX." Jingshuan stifled a laugh. Jiji was Mei Yin's grandson and Xue Yu's son, of course he'd immediately think of smallpox— virology ran in his blood. He ruffled Jiji's hair. "Your sister's right, it's referring to the heavenly lady dropping flowers from above. Anyway, the Japanese word for 'smallpox' is completely different."

He Ying scolded her daughter. "How can you call your little brother an idiot? That's not how a big sister should talk!"

Jiaojiao pouted. "That's just what we call each other, it's not bad language. He calls me an idiot too."

He Ying laughed, because Jiji indeed used the word a lot. Still, she insisted. "Even if he does, you're not allowed to."

Meanwhile, Jiji wasn't satisfied with Jingshuan's explanation. "But Uncle Sun, the heavenly lady dropping flowers from above is a Chinese legend. Do the Japanese have the same story?"

"Yes, it came over here from China."

Only now did Jiji believe him, and so he bent down to gather a pile of flowers. All around them, Japanese pedestrians were grabbing flowers too, having decided they were a sign of good luck for the new year, sniffing them and stuffing them into pockets. The airships sailed into the distance, still dispensing flowers, and disappeared into the night. The Suns had dinner and got a taxi back to the hotel. In the Fujiya lobby, a man in his thirties, seeing Jiji and Jiaojiao with their arms full of paper flowers, asked in Chinese, "Are you from China?"

"Yes," Jingshuan said. "You here on vacation too?"

"No," he said jubilantly. "I'm here for an ad campaign. Those flowers your kids are holding are advertising my company's perfume."

Sun Jingshuan and He Ying praised his work, calling the campaign a masterstroke, then said good-night.

They went to bed early, since they were leaving for home the next day. In the middle of the night, He Ying was roused by her husband tossing and turning. He turned on the bedside lamp, and when she saw the look on his face, she asked, "Are you all right? Worried about something?"

"This might be nonsense. But what Jiji said—about the airships distributing smallpox—made me really uneasy. I'm thinking . . . what if there was something in that?"

"But it was a Chinese perfume company doing the ad. That General Manager He we met tonight doesn't seem like a terrorist."

Jingshuan shook his head. "Don't forget, when Zia Baj organized that tour of remembrance attack more than ten years ago, he made use of that Native American guy who had no idea what was going on. That's how he operates."

He Ying wasn't convinced, but still felt a chill. If her husband's suspicion was right, then smallpox was in their bodies at that very moment, multiplying in the dark, quietly feasting on their flesh. But more importantly—the children! Jiji might be all right, Sister Mei had said something about him having been exposed to "mild smallpox," so he'd have some immunity, but Jiaojiao had no such protection. If . . . but it was too terrifying, she couldn't complete the thought. "So . . . what should we do?"

Jingshuan had no answer for her. After thinking about it, he made a decision and picked up the phone, asking the operator to place a long distance call to China. From more than six hundred miles away, Mei Yin's sleep-filled voice answered, "Who is it?"

"Sorry to disturb you. It's Jingshuan. Something urgent's come up. I remember Mr. Matsumoto from the WHO moved back to Tokyo after he retired, is that right? I need you to give me his number."

Immediately, Mei Yin was wide awake. She knew he must have a good reason for calling her in the middle of the night with a request like this. "Yes, he's in Tokyo, and I have his number. Why are you—"

Jingshuan briefly explained about the airborne ad campaign. "It might be nothing, but I do sense the whiff of that terrorist on these paper flowers. He's skilled at making use of a patsy to do his dirty work. And not long ago, you said that Zia Baj wouldn't just vanish quietly, that he'd pop up again sooner or later."

There was a rustling sound, and then she gave him Matsumoto's number. "You're doing the right thing—considering the worst-case scenario. Whatever happens, tell me as soon as you know."

Jingshuan didn't waste any time in calling the Matsumoto residence. Up to now, He Ying had been skeptical, but seeing how seriously he was taking this, she couldn't help becoming anxious too. Quickly getting out of bed, she went to check on the kids, who were sleeping soundly. She touched their foreheads. No fever, and no blisters. That meant nothing, of course—there'd be an incubation period of several days at least. She went back into the main bedroom, where Jingshuan was on the phone to Matsumoto. He kept repeating, with some embarrassment, that this might be no more than a hyperactive imagination, that he had no proof.

Matsumoto assured him. "Don't worry about that. It won't hurt to do a test and be sure. I happen to have some of those flowers—picked them up while saying good-bye to my guests this evening. I live in Shibuya, which is quite some distance from where you were, in Akihabara. I'm afraid that means these flowers might have scattered over most of the city. Two or three hundred thousand people might have come into contact with them."

"I hope this is a false alarm."

"Let's hope so. But if it's real—even if Japan responded at once, with such a large area to cover, I'm afraid . . . As far as I'm aware, we've only stockpiled a hundred thousand doses of cowpox vaccine. But let's not think about that for now. I'll get in touch with some colleagues at the University of Tokyo, and analyze the flowers as soon as possible. Stay in touch."

"Thanks. You too."

He hung up. He Ying said, anxiously, "But our flight's tomorrow."

"We'll have to postpone—we can't risk bringing the virus back to China. Let's go back after the test results are in."

Meanwhile, Mei Yin had continued to worry, only letting herself relax after Jingshuan called again to say he'd been in touch with Mr. Matsumoto, and they were delaying their return.

In the morning, Jingshuan woke the children, and told them they'd be staying a little longer. There would be no discussion; the grown-ups had made up their minds. The kids didn't mind spending an extra couple of days in Japan, anyway. When they headed into the bathroom, He Ying couldn't help following them and urging them to use extra soap on their faces and hands. Jiaojiao protested impatiently. "Mommy, why're you nagging so much today?"

Jingshuan dragged his wife out and whispered, "It's no use. If it's true, they were already infected yesterday."

After breakfast, the kids played indoors. Jiji suddenly remembered the paper flowers from the day before. He'd carefully put them away in the nightstand, and now he couldn't find them anywhere. He looked everywhere. "Sister Jiaojiao, have you seen my paper flowers? Uncle Sun, Auntie He, have you seen them?"

Jiaojiao cried out, "Mine are gone too!"

He Ying told the kids that the flowers might have germs on them, so she'd flushed them away. Jiji was unhappy about that, but since it was a grown-up who'd done it, he could only sulk.

A little later, Mr. Matsumoto called and came straight to the point. "The test results are in, and you guessed right. The powder on those paper flowers does indeed contain the smallpox virus."

Jingshuan looked at his wife, who'd gone pale as snow. Matsumoto continued. "The density of the virus is very high. We're still carrying out antibody and other tests, but the initial results leave no doubt. Mr. Sun, please stay where you are, I'm sending someone to your hotel with the cowpox vaccine for your family. Also, there'll be a cabinet meeting this morning, to deploy an emergency response to the outbreak. The prime minister has asked if you will attend."

"All right, I'll be there."

"The Ministry will send a car to your hotel. Once you've had your inoculation, it'll bring you to the meeting."

"I don't need a shot, I have lifelong immunity. Just take care of my family."

"All right, they'll be there soon. Another thing," he went on solemnly. "The prime minister asked me to convey his thanks, and the deep gratitude of the Japanese people."

"He's very welcome. Oh, that's right, the Chinese businessman who paid for this campaign is staying at our hotel, we bumped into him yesterday, and he mentioned that he was responsible. I doubt very much he's the mastermind—probably a pawn. But you could let the police know to detain him."

"The police are already aware of him. We traced him through the Hanako Agency."

Jingshuan hung up, and He Ying took his hand, her eyes full of fear. He reassured her. "Don't worry too much. We discovered this early, so it shouldn't be too bad. The smallpox vaccine is still somewhat effective if taken four to five days after first infection. Mr. Matsumoto said he'll send someone to give us shots right away. Smallpox is no joke, but Mei Yin, Xue Yu, and I figured it out long ago. There's no need to be frightened."

He Ying seemed a bit reassured. The kids, playing in the living room, had heard the grown-ups' conversation and now rushed over. Jiaojiao asked, "Is it really smallpox? Did Jiji actually get something right?"

Jiji said smugly, "What's so surprising? That's my sixth sense at work. Jiaojiao, don't be scared, I'm immune, there are antibodies in my blood. If you get sick, I'll give you some blood and you'll be fine."

"That depends what kind of blood you have. If you're type O and I'm type A, how would you do that?"

"Idiot, you only need to transmit blood serum, it doesn't have anything to do with blood type."

They argued happily, without a hint of fear. Jiaojiao didn't know much about smallpox, while Jiji, for whom it "ran in the blood," had no real awareness of the awful nature of infection. He Ying's eyes reddened as she watched them. Jingshuan hastily pulled her aside, signaling her to leave them alone.

Soon, an ambulance arrived, siren blaring, and two paramedics in white raced up the stairs, swiftly giving all four of them cowpox injections. Jingshuan and Jiji protested that they were immune, but the paramedics smiled, shook their heads, and insisted. As soon as the job was done, they hurried off. That day, after the prime minister's cabinet meeting was done, all of Tokyo's doctors and nurses would be thrown onto the front lines, and they didn't have a moment to waste! As the ambulance pulled away, two police cars arrived, one to bring Sun Jingshuan to his meeting, and the other to detain the Chinese man, Mr. He. A short while later, he emerged from the elevator surrounded by four officers, his face white as paper. Jingshuan shook his head as he watched the poor man being taken away, then got in the second car himself.

Yaesu was close to the prime minister's office, and Jingshuan was there in ten minutes. Mr. Matsumoto was at the entrance to greet him with a deep bow, and to usher him into the meeting room. More than twenty people were already there. At a glance, Jingshuan quickly identified Prime Minister Miki, whose face was often on TV and in the newspapers. Seeing Mr. Matsumoto lead a Chinese man in, the prime minister came over and bowed deeply too, in the Japanese manner, and said in English, "Thank you, Mr. Sun. You're the savior of Tokyo."

Jingshuan quickly bowed back and said awkwardly, "Oh no, you're too kind." There was no time for small talk, so they returned to their seats right away. A middle-aged man began his report again, a quick narration interspersed with one deep bow after another. Matsumoto explained in English that this was the general manager of Hanako Advertising, and he was telling them how this ad campaign had come about, while begging for forgiveness.

Prime Minister Miki interrupted and said a few words, and Matsumoto interpreted. "The prime minister says, 'Let's talk about accountability later, right now we have to take action.'" He sighed. "Hanako might have been negligent, but in the eyes of the law they're completely guiltless—they did all the paperwork. They have permits from the Labor Ministry to promote Heavenly Fragrance, from Homeland Security to use the airspace, and from customs to import the paper flowers. We can only blame the terrorists for being too cunning, or Japanese society for being too inflexible."

Next, someone spoke from the Emergency Task Force, clearly an expert who knew the field inside out, and cut straight to the essentials. "According to Hanako's own estimates, at least three hundred thousand people will have come into contact with these paper flowers. To be safe, we'd need to assume the whole of central Tokyo, about a million people. There are two things we need to do right away. First, declare the center of Tokyo a quarantine zone and seal it off. Second, get hold of more vaccine and make sure everyone in the infection zone is treated. The difficulties are time and our limited vaccine stockpiles. There are only a hundred thousand doses in the whole of Japan, so we can only appeal to the international community for more. We need to consider that quite a few countries will want to keep some for themselves, in case the infection spreads to them. But no matter what, we need to put out an appeal to every other country immediately, gathering as much of the vaccine as possible, and prioritizing the people in the infection zone. All that's fairly straightforward, but the main issue is time! Smallpox has an incubation period of fourteen days, while the antigens typically take eleven to thirteen days to build up strength. Which is to say, if the cowpox vaccine isn't administered within three or four days of first contact, it'll be much less effective. We have to get the inoculations done within that window, which won't be easy, but we'll just have to do our best."

Sun Jingshuan and Matsumoto exchanged a look—each knew what the other was thinking, but there wasn't time to talk now. The meeting continued in an atmosphere of tension. It had been sixteen hours since the first contact with the virus, leaving them only two or three days' time. Decisions were quickly made, and the work delegated. Just before the prime minister dismissed them, Matsumoto stood to speak. "There's another way to deal with this threat. Could I ask the prime minister, the minister of welfare, and the homeland security chair to stay behind for a few words with me and Mr. Sun? The strategy we've just discussed should be put into action at once, without delay. It won't interfere with this alternative plan."

Prime Minister Miki looked puzzled, but agreed. When everyone else had gone, Matsumoto said, "This would take too long to explain from the beginning, so I'll be brief. Within the scientific world, there's a semisecret group known as the Crucifix Society. In Nanyang, China, they came up with a rather unusual way of dealing with viruses, by releasing attenuated strains into the wild. They've now reached the stage of industrial testing, and have released the smallpox virus and plague bacillus into certain areas of Nanyang. The WHO is funding their research, but the theory behind the technology is still disputed, so they're keeping a low profile."

Miki exchanged a few words with the welfare minister, then said, "We're aware of this technique. Is it reliable?"

"Fairly. Back during the sensational Mei Yin incident, there was only one fatality. The WHO has verified that the mild smallpox virus cultivated by Professor Mei Yin not only has a lower virulence, but can activate the human immune system in as little as ten hours, causing the body to produce large quantities of antibodies far more effectively than a vaccine—as long as you can accept a death rate of one in a hundred thousand, which is itself an upper theoretical limit. We could dispense the mild smallpox virus in an aerosol spray from a plane, and within an hour the seeds of immunity would be planted in a million people. We're so close to China, we could get it here quickly. The only problem is whether there are enough stockpiles of the attenuated virus in China for a million people. I'll leave Mr. Sun to speak about this. He's one of the originators of this technology."

Miki and the two ministers turned their gaze to Sun, who said, "I did help to originate this, yes, but I abandoned the cause later. I don't know too much about recent developments. Let me ask."

He called Mei Yin on his cell, and after a quick exchange, turned back to the prime minister. "By chance, it happens that the organization was preparing to carry out a spraying exercise on the whole Nanyang region, with a population of eleven million people, so they have more than enough for us. Last night, when they learned about this epidemic—I reported it to them—they began preparations. As long as the two governments can reach an agreement, the virus can be here within twelve hours."

"Excellent!" the prime minister exclaimed. "I'll get in touch with China at once."

He led the four men into a soundproof room, where there was a direct line between the two powers. Picking up the red telephone that connected him directly to the highest levels of Chinese government, Miki expressed a sincere wish that China lend a helping hand to its neighbor. The Chinese side hesitated and didn't answer right away, saying they'd have to check with the CDC first. Miki put down the phone, confused and worried, and the two ministers were obviously unhappy—in such a clear-cut case of humanitarian need, China ought to have readily agreed. Matsumoto was puzzled too.

Sun Jingshuan understood the Chinese better than they did. "You know why our side is hesitating? It's not because they don't understand the technology, or that they'll ask you to pay the earth for it. The problem is that the technique doesn't guarantee a death rate of zero. Particularly susceptible individuals could contract full-blown smallpox and die. The risk is low—one in a hundred thousand at a conservative estimate—and China could accept using it on its own people. But to deploy it abroad, particularly in Japan . . . that might cause problems. Japan has quite a large right-wing faction—even today, an inscription on the Yasukuni Shrine still claims that the Second World War was instigated by America and China. Now imagine if a 'Chinese virus' leads to the deaths of a dozen or more Japanese—those right-wingers would be baying for blood! They might even claim this was a biological weapon manufactured by China."

He said all this in English. Miki and the others understood, glancing at each other in silence. The scenario envisioned by Mr. Sun was entirely possible. Japan had a free press, so he wouldn't be able to promise the Chinese premier that such opinions wouldn't be broadcast in the future. Not only that, if they administered the smallpox he'd obtained from China and it caused a few hundred deaths, his prime ministership would be over.

They said nothing, and the red telephone in front of them stayed silent too. When Noriyoshi Matsumoto could stand it no longer, he said, "Prime Minister, and the rest of you, at such a moment do you still have time to consider these surface matters? Even the ancients knew that a single life saved is worth more than a seven-storied pagoda!"

At that moment, the phone let out a shrill ring. Miki immediately picked it up, and after hearing what the other party had to say, his face split into a grin, and he nodded nonstop. "Yes, I agree completely with that plan. See you in Tokyo!"

He hung up. "Thank God for Chinese political acumen. You know what they've come up with? It's ingenious: The attenuated virus will be shipped over right away, and disseminated by the Japanese air force. At the same time, a delegation from the Chinese government will come for a visit, and appear in public while the spraying is taking place, breathing in the same viruses as the Japanese people. That way, if there really is some sort of accident, no one will be able to say it was a plot."

Everyone sighed with relief. "There really is no danger at all," Sun Jingshuan reminded them. "The technology is fairly mature, and the Chinese delegation can take a little medical precaution by having a dose of cowpox beforehand. That way, their chances of contracting smallpox fall to zero. I do respect their ingenuity."

He couldn't hold back a smile, having also realized there was a deeper layer to this—if the Chinese delegation arrived with some issue that required negotiation, mightn't the Japanese be a little more generous than usual, under the circumstances? But then he remembered Matsumoto and thought, *Don't be so cynical, have some faith in humanity!*

News of the Tokyo smallpox attack spread to the rest of Japan, then the world. Tokyo was in a state of panic, but still managed to respond in an orderly manner. All flights in and out of the city were canceled, and the police sealed the roads leading to the center. The available vaccines were distributed, first to the doctors and nurses who'd be on the front line of this battle. More stocks were flown in from elsewhere in the country, and would be ready for use the next day. Urgent requests were sent to America and Europe for spare vaccine stocks, though that would still take a day or two.

The people of Tokyo had some good news in the late afternoon: their neighbor had sent a faster, more effective remedy. That evening, only a day after the three airships had scattered smallpox over the city, three C-130 Japanese military transport planes roared overhead. Behind them were three long red tails that dispersed, mingled, and slowly descended in a faint pink mist that enveloped the whole of Tokyo. Residents had been told to come outdoors and breathe in as much of the colored air as possible. The Chinese delegation had arrived too, and the timing was carefully arranged. After the welcome reception, they arrived at Hibiya Park near the Imperial Palace to "meet the people," and the Japanese prime minister embraced them as the red fog descended, then embraced his people too. For a moment, the normally reserved Japanese were practically Spanish or Brazilian in their enthusiasm: a singing, dancing, frothing sea of humanity.

Sun Jingshuan and He Ying were there too, with their two kids. Mei Yin, Xue Yu, and Xiaoxue had also arrived along with the goods. Amid such a commotion, there was hardly room for a quiet chat. Jiji hugged his parents, howling at the top of his voice everything that had happened over the last two days. He Ying respectfully hugged Mei Yin, whom she was meeting for the first time, quietly thinking that her husband's first wife could practically be his mother. Jiaojiao came over and warmly flung her hands around "Granny Mei's" neck. As the seven of them mingled, two plainclothes officers found their way to them: Chinese and Japanese security personnel who, with difficulty, escorted the seven people to the center of the park. Dressed in kimonos, representatives of both countries wanted to shake Mei Yin's hand firmly. The Chinese official said, "Sister Mei, thank you. Your lifetime of hard work brought us to this point!"

Mei Yin's eyes were moist. "Thank you. It's all worth it, just for those words."

"Thank you, Mr. Sun, and you too, Xue. And your families, especially you, Jiji, I hear you were the first to realize the paper flowers contained the virus?"

Jiji smiled foolishly. "I just read the words wrong, I thought they said 'smallpox' but actually it was something about heavenly flowers."

His frankness made everyone laugh. The Chinese minister said, "Well, you still get the credit, even if it was a lucky guess."

Prime Minister Miki came over to shake hands with each of them, then he scooped up Jiji and posed for a group photo. Finally, the leader of the Chinese delegation said, "We'll be heading home in a couple of days, but would the rest of you be able to stay in Japan a little longer, until the infection is completely dealt with? Legally, a smallpox quarantine zone requires forty days to clear. I know that's on the long side."

Xue Yu answered on behalf of everyone. "That's fine, we were planning to do that anyway."

Prime Minister Miki added, "And the two children can stay too. I'll make all the arrangements personally. You won't be able to leave the quarantine zone, but there's plenty to do in Tokyo. I can get you invited to the Imperial Palace and the prime minister's office."

Jiji and Jiaojiao were overjoyed. "Really? Thank you." Then Jiji thought of something. "But our winter vacation is almost over. If Mom, Dad, and Granny aren't going back, then who'll tell the school?"

The Chinese leader smiled. "Don't worry about that, I'll take care of it personally. How about that?"

"That's great, if you ask for permission, the teacher won't dare say no!"

They all burst out laughing again.

Two weeks later—Kabul

The fighting in Kabul had finally ended two years previously, but the place was still an open sore, most noticeably in the way the air was constantly full of dust. After so many years of neglect, and damage from heavy military vehicles, the roads were a complete ruin. The city's buildings were also scarred and broken, so the slightest breeze, or a passing car, would leave the city shrouded in dust.

Amid the poverty and destruction, many were forced to furtively slip into the world's oldest profession.

Salma was one of them. She was only twenty, and her grandfather and father had both been rabid anti-American fighters. Her father was dead, and her grandfather had only just returned home after vanishing for many years without a word. He was missing a leg when he showed up again.

She'd just spotted a new customer, and was hurrying toward him. The man was in his fifties, neatly dressed, looking like a Westerner or at least a Westernized Afghan. He held a briefcase and looked coldly over her and the other women on the street. Salma went up to him and said, in English, "Sex?"

He paused, then sneered, "Sex."

In her painful English, Salma said, "Whole night, two hundred afghani. One time, hundred fifty."

"All right, I'll pay two hundred."

Salma led him home. Walking behind her, the man stayed alert for any signs of movement. After the terror attack in Tokyo two weeks ago, Interpol would have questioned He Zhichao, and should have been able to narrow down his whereabouts. Who knew how many dogs were prowling Kabul right now, trying to pick up his scent. He had to be careful. They arrived at Salma's house, tiny as a pigeon coop, her room only big enough for a bed and small table, and heated by a coal stove. A shabby home, but the man was satisfied. It was precisely a space like this he needed in order to carry out his plan.

Salma lit the stove, and the icy room thawed a little. Pulling some condoms from the table's drawer, she said in English, "Protect. AIDS."

He shook his head. Seeing as he didn't have much more than ten days to live, AIDS was no threat to him. Salma didn't insist, but simply said, "No condom, five hundred."

She studied his face carefully as she named her price, prepared to lower it quickly if he seemed angry. But the man was exceptionally generous, and nodded woodenly. "Fine."

Salma beamed. It wasn't every day that she came upon such a good prospect. Five hundred afghanis! Her grandfather had sold his whole life to the Taliban, and only got a payout of five hundred at the end. After being out of touch for many years, he'd suddenly shown up twenty days ago. Salma's mother had sent word for her to come visit. Grandfather had lost a leg and was dressed in rags, his eyes shrinking from his daughter-in-law and granddaughter, clearly aware he wasn't welcome. Salma didn't want anything to do with the man. When had he ever done his duty by the family? Later, he'd pulled five hundred afghanis from a pocket and handed it to his granddaughter. Her mother told Salma that this was the payout he'd received at the end. He'd begged for food all the way back, not touching any of it. Salma's heart softened, and she agreed with her mother that he could stay with them, though it would put even more pressure on her.

She swiftly removed her clothes and slipped beneath the covers, cooing, determined to show her customer a good time. The man stripped too and lay on top of her. Gradually, Salma sensed something was wrong. He was full of rage, and possessed an enormous sexual drive for his age. He thrashed about, bucking and thrusting, and after he climaxed, his whole body went limp. Yet not long after, he was enthusiastically climbing back on top of her. He was determined to get his money's worth, Salma thought ruefully.

It was late at night before he finally calmed down, sleeping in Salma's bosom like an infant, one of her nipples in his mouth, his lips clamped around it. Salma found this uncomfortable, but didn't dare push him away. Sometime later, she felt something cold on her breast, and when she reached down, she realized he was silently weeping, his tears soaking a patch of blanket. She felt a stab of sadness for whatever unspeakable torments this man was holding inside himself, alongside a fear that he might be unbalanced, maybe even a madman.

He didn't do anything else after that, just slept quietly. Having been put through the wringer, Salma was exhausted, and soon drifted off too.

It was almost dawn when Zia Baj woke. He looked around the room, and at the sleeping Salma. He was about to bid the world farewell; he'd had a moment of weakness the night before. If he could turn the clock back twenty-six years, he would not choose this path again. Looking back, he saw no family, no happiness, no joy—nothing but murder, murder, so much killing that his heart had grown thoroughly hard. Yet this was the road he'd taken, and he would end what he had begun.

After leaving America, he'd spent more than a decade cultivating smallpox pathogens, using up all his financial and mental resources on this terror attack on Tokyo. Although the Japanese anti-epidemic measures were effective, they should have been overwhelmed by such a large-scale attack. If he could have killed two hundred or even one hundred thousand, he'd have died happy.

Yet half a month had passed, and the news made it sound as though a hundred thousand had been infected in Tokyo, but all with mild symptoms, no worse than cowpox. There were only two deaths, both weak and elderly victims. Later on, he learned the reason for his defeat: a virologist named Mei Yin and her technique of inoculation using an attenuated virus. Zia Baj was stunned. He'd once been a world-class virologist, but after so many years out of contact with the profession, it seemed he'd been left behind. He hadn't even heard of this new invention.

Now he recalled that his previous attack in America had also been foiled by Mei Yin—she and another American investigator had sounded an early warning, speeding the response of the American government by a few days. He and Mei Yin had met once, at an open forum, and he could still remember her appearance: not too tall, elegant, fragile on the outside but steely within. It seems he'd found his nemesis.

Zia Baj had begun to lose his appetite for the fight. But he couldn't leave this world without leading one last charge. When he'd been given the viruses all those years ago, there had been a virulent Ebola specimen among them. Since then he'd cultivated huge quantities of smallpox, but done nothing with the Ebola—with no effective vaccine, it was too dangerous to work with. To someone determined to die, though, that was actually an advantage. Ebola had no cure: *Let's see how the Japanese, and Mei Yin, deal with it!*

The Ebola virus had been in cold storage close to thirty years, and had been allowed to breed in that time, but never tested. It was easy to find a test subject, though. He'd chosen a woman with her own room for precisely this purpose. She was sound asleep now. He rose quietly, got some tape from his briefcase, and nimbly bound her hands and legs together. When she woke, she stared at him in terror, screaming hoarsely, "What are you doing? Help—"

He grabbed her underwear and stuffed them into her mouth.

Salma struggled fruitlessly on the bed. Zia Baj ignored her, removing the syringe and distilled water from his bag, breaking the seal on the virus vial, plunging it into the water, then filling the syringe with it. He intended to inject her with it, then wait a few days for the symptoms of Ebola to appear, to judge the strength of the virus. Salma's eyes were fixed on the needle. She didn't know what was in the syringe, but she knew it couldn't be good, and would likely cost her her life. So scared she forgot to struggle, she looked pleadingly at the man, tears rolling down her cheeks. Baj glared coldly at her, ripped off the blanket, grabbed her arm, and prepared to inject her. But suddenly—he stopped, brow furrowed in thought. Just before he'd gagged her, she'd called out in a familiar language. He'd thought it was English, but now it struck him that it wasn't. It was . . . Pashto? That would mean the woman was from the same tribe as he was . . . He lowered the needle and asked in Pashto, "You're Pashtun?"

Seeing a chance to save herself, Salma nodded frantically. Baj thought about it, and pulled the underwear from her mouth, murmuring, "No shouting! Tell me quietly, where are you from?"

Salma obediently lowered her voice and answered in Pashto, then continued gazing piteously at him. So she really was of his tribe. This wouldn't have meant a thing to him, before, but now he decided to spare this prostitute's life. He was planning to turn himself into a human bullet, anyway, and head to Tokyo with the Ebola, so perhaps the test was pointless. He put the syringe to one side, untied the woman, and commanded her, "No shouting! One sound from you, and I'll kill you at once."

Knowing her life had been spared, Salma nodded vigorously.

"Quick, get dressed."

Staring at him, she did as he said.

"Now come over here and stick this in me."

Shocked, she shook her head, and said in Pashto she didn't know how to inject someone. He said in a hard voice, "Do as I say! I'll teach you."

She could only take the syringe, both hands trembling, and under his guidance, stick it into the bend in his arms a few times, finally finding a vein. Baj told her to pull the plunger back, sucking a little blood into the chamber, then pressing all the liquid in the syringe into his vein. As she pushed, he stared silently at the chamber, his expression peaceful. Salma grew calm too, thinking she'd been worried about nothing earlier. It didn't look like the syringe could have contained poison. Perhaps it was some kind of aphrodisiac? With that in his veins, who knew what demands he'd make of her next. Still, it was better than losing her life. The strange thing was, after the injection, the man had no reaction, but sat on the side of the bed, looking at her despondently. After a while, he got dressed, took five hundred afghanis from his wallet and placed them by the bedside, then picked up his briefcase and departed in silence.

Salma watched curiously as he shuffled out. She was certain she'd just had an encounter with a madman, though his five hundred afghanis were real enough. She picked up the banknotes and spent some time happily admiring them, then carefully put them away and went back out to find more clients.

Zia Baj didn't dare delay, but went immediately to buy a ticket to Tokyo. After his plastic surgery, he'd gotten a fake passport with his new appearance, and used that to apply for a Japanese visa. Ebola had a short incubation period, and at its quickest could strike a person down in two days. Within five days his skin would be falling off and he'd be leaking blood from every orifice. It was important to get through customs before any symptoms appeared, or he'd be in trouble. He himself would be the vector of Ebola's spread in Tokyo. This single point of transmission wouldn't create too large an outbreak, but he'd do his best, and if before his own death he could drag a few dozen others down with him, it would be enough.

Six days later—Tokyo

Jiji and Jiaojiao ended up having the most decadent winter vacation. The infection was completely over after twenty days, but for the sake of caution, Mei Yin and the Xues decided they should stay in Japan for forty days, the legally defined period of quarantine. It was forty days of fun as far as the children were concerned, even if they couldn't leave Tokyo. Miki kept his word, and arranged for them to visit the prime minister's office. He personally showed them around, and also arranged for them to visit the Imperial Palace. The emperor didn't put in an appearance, but Prince Akishino welcomed them in person, and walked with them among the lakes and greenery. The Japanese Imperial Palace was completely different from China's Forbidden City, in that it was open to visitors, but the royal family still lived there, so tourists were only allowed access to small areas. Regular visitors could look around the East Garden and Kitanomaru Park as part of a guided tour, but had to walk in a quiet, orderly manner, and could only stop in certain spots, with barely enough time for photographs. By contrast, Mei Yin and the others were treated like foreign dignitaries, and white-haired Prince Akishino led them across Nijubashi Bridge into the palace itself. They saw the royal household's chambers, the imperial meeting rooms, the palace square, and so on. Within the high walls grew an ancient forest, almost three hundred thousand trees from all over Japan. The palace was set in the midst of these trees—all white walls and dark tiles in the Japanese style, a creature with the head of a dragon and the tail of a fish looming over the roof as a figurehead, the emperor's symbol of the chrysanthemum carved on either side. Everyone looked on with great excitement, and Xiaoxue asked her son, "Isn't that beautiful?"

Jiji said honestly, "Very beautiful, but it's not as grand as the Forbidden City."

Hastily, Xue Yu said, "Don't be rude. What nonsense!"

All of this was in Chinese, but Prince Akishino noticed their expressions and spoke softly with his interpreter, then chuckled. "The child is right. Compared to the Forbidden City, our Imperial Palace is much less magnificent. After all, Japan is a smaller country, and our imperial household couldn't put up as big a show. China's feudal society was the most mighty in the world, but that also meant its peasants suffered the most."

Xue Yu and the rest were startled by his words. But it made sense. It was easy to forget that the glories of ancient civilizations—the Forbidden City, the Great Wall, the Taj Mahal, or the Pyramids—were built upon the bodies of peasants. But without those vicious tyrants and the suffering of their subjects, wouldn't human civilization be much duller? A paradox.

Their extended forty-day vacation would be over in two days. Now they said good-bye to their Japanese escorts, and headed to Yoyogi Park to admire the cherry trees. During the cherry blossom season in March, visitors from around the world crowded the place. But now it was colder, and there weren't as many tourists. At the entrance, strangely dressed young people congregated, some doing warm-ups, some throwing Frisbees or practicing acrobatic tricks. In a little square farther on, more young people were practicing street dances. Many others sat around the fountain, hugging their knees, enjoying the peaceful green surroundings.

The park was beautiful, the greenery lovely, and the stillness wonderful. Thick-trunked tall trees blocked out the sunlight, and streams flowed quietly through the dim woods. The two couples sat on the grass chatting, while Jiji and Jiaojiao each took one of Mei Yin's hands, running off among the trees. The adults watched the old woman and her two young companions disappear, and Xiaoxue said enviously, "Jiji's closest to his grandma, even I can't compete." He Ying laughed. "Never mind Jiji, look at how Jiaojiao sticks close to her Auntie Mei, tossing me aside."

Xue Yu sighed. "Mother Mei loves children so much, maybe because she never had any of her own. She's had a hard life, and I know Xiaoxue often feels sorry for her."

Sun Jingshuan said, "Her life was hard, but we shouldn't pity her. She fought hard, and was lucky enough to see her struggles bear fruit. To a scientist, that's the greatest good fortune. You could call it the perfect life. No one with her accomplishments could claim to have regrets when they left this world."

Jingshuan began delving into his memories, telling the other three everything he knew about Mei Yin's life, including what had happened to her in Russia. The stories continued until the sky grew dark, and Mei Yin appeared again with the two children in tow. She called, "Hey, what are you talking about? Looks like a deep conversation."

Jingshuan smiled but didn't answer, and He Ying said, "Jingshuan's telling us that you have a perfect life."

Mei Yin shot a glance at him, and a flash of pain passed through her eyes. But it quickly passed, and she hugged the children to her. "That's right. My life is absolutely perfect. I have a daughter and son-in-law, a grandson, and now I've just acquired a new little niece. Isn't that right, Jiji and Jiaojiao?"

The kids obediently threw their arms around her neck and kissed her, and everyone laughed.

The seven of them walked out of the park. There were two black statues by the entrance, a half-naked one dressed like a Japanese warrior, holding a samurai sword; the other was almost completely nude, a re-creation of Rodin's *The Thinker*. Jiji shouted, "Look, statues! How come we didn't see them on our way in? Daddy, I want a photo with them. Hey!" he yelped in shock. "The statues' eyes are moving!" They were human statues—faces and bodies painted, so still they looked convincingly statuelike. The children happily posed for pictures with them, while Jingshuan placed five hundred yen into each of their bowls.

Outside the park, they stood by the side of the road, waiting for a taxi. One appeared round the corner, but even at a distance there was something odd about it: it was going too fast and zigzagging, as if driven by a drunk person. Xue Yu and Jingshuan reacted first, grabbing the two children and three women and stepping back onto the sidewalk. The taxi zoomed past them and screeched to a halt in front of the human statues, almost colliding into some people taking photos of them. A man dressed in black got out of the cab, lurching toward the crowd. He grabbed a woman's arm and bit hard. She shrieked, too stunned to fight back. Before anyone else could respond, the man in black turned quickly and bit someone else. Finally the onlookers began to react, the men quickly pushing the women and children behind them, others charging the man, ready to fight. The performer dressed as a warrior pointed his sword at the attacker and shouted in Japanese, "Don't move!"

The man ran straight for the sword. It was just a bamboo prop, but the man was moving so fast he actually managed to impale himself on it. The "warrior" looked shocked, and quickly let go of the handle. Seeming to feel no pain, the man pulled the bamboo out of his belly and flung it behind him, barely slowing his forward charge. He flung himself on the warrior, and took a bite out of his shoulder.

Everyone froze. Jiji was the first to react. With viruses on the brain, as always, he shouted, "Rabies! He must have rabies!"

This gave the adults around him a shock. It wasn't impossible. They hastened to push the children safely behind them, and Xue Yu got out his phone to call the police. Only Mei Yin didn't back down—she took a couple of steps forward. Her brain was spinning rapidly; this "rabies" lunatic seemed familiar, and now it was coming back to her. He'd had surgery, but those eyes and the outlines of his face were unmistakable. She knew that dark stare, more crazed than it had ever been before. Taking a couple of steps forward, she shouted, "Zia Baj!"

Zia Baj froze. His brain was being consumed by the Ebola virus, and it had been a very long time since anyone called him by that name. Still, it was his real name, with him since childhood, and he turned to look. An Asian woman in her sixties was shouting at him. She looked familiar, dim recollections stirred . . . Then he realized: it was Mei Yin, his nemesis, the woman who'd crushed two of his attacks. Was it divine intervention, handing her to him, so the two old enemies could meet one last time? Without hesitation, he bared two rows of stark white teeth and dashed toward Mei Yin.

Jiji struggled free of his mother's grip and ran toward Mei Yin, shouting, "Granny, be careful, he has rabies!"

Mei Yin kept her eyes fixed on the mad dog in front of her. No, what he had wasn't rabies, it was Ebola hemorrhagic fever, and his symptoms were severe. The whites of his eyes and his gums were bloody, his exposed skin showed blood clots and was starting to peel off in places, a hideous sight. Mei Yin had seen the condition with her own eyes in Africa when she was twelve, and examined many patients personally. She knew the disease inside out. She'd been worried over the past few days; she had a gut feeling that Zia Baj wasn't going to accept his second defeat so lightly. And it looked like she had been right. He'd turned himself into a vessel from which to spread Ebola.

Baj had almost reached Mei Yin. Shouting, Jingshuan and Xue Yu both rushed to protect her, but they were too far away. Mei Yin was prepared—she waited until Baj had almost reached her, then launched a high kick that landed on his chest. This ought to have knocked him down, but Mei Yin was old, and her legs were no longer as powerful. Zia Baj only staggered back a few paces. He steadied himself, but decided against another assault on the "martial arts expert" Mei Yin. Instead, he made a grab for Jiji, who didn't dodge fast enough. Baj grabbed his left hand and bit down hard. Jiji let out a stifled scream, in such pain he could hardly breath.

Mei Yin's breath stopped too, as if a bucket of ice water had been poured over her. Her brain halted, her mind filled with only one thought: Xue Yu's uncle's curse had finally come true—Mei Yin's sins had been visited upon the child. But even as her brain stopped, her body continued to respond, and she executed a tae kwon do chop-and-parry move. One leg flew upward, connecting with the mad dog's head. Baj's eyes went blank, and he lost consciousness.

The other four adults ran to Jiji. Mei Yin immediately reached out to hold them back, her face twisted in agony. Zia Baj was flat on his back not far away, the symptoms of late-stage Ebola plain as day. Jiji's face was pale, and he clutched his left hand, four fingers glistening with blood. The six-year-old boy was very calm as he turned to his grandmother. "I need to get to the hospital for a rabies shot!"

Mei Yin shook her head, heartbroken. "My child, you don't have rabies. There's no vaccine and no treatment." She shouted at Xue Yu and the others. "Don't touch him! It's very likely he has Ebola."

Everyone, apart from Jiaojiao, knew what that meant—and what it meant for Jiji. Mei Yin approached him and carefully took his left wrist in her left hand, while her right hand lifted the crucifix from her neck, feeling for the secret catch, pulling off the sheath with her teeth to reveal the little blade. Her face was deathly white as she looked at Jiji's parents, then at Sun Jingshuan. Knowing what she was about to do, all three took a step toward her, then halted. They were in Tokyo, and within ten minutes Jiji could be in one of the best hospitals in the world, but it wouldn't do him a bit of good. Mei Yin thought of her adoptive father's story, about the British official asking Professor Bradley: *"Why not take decisive action, and slice off the thumb?"* This wasn't just one finger, but four of them. With a stroke of her knife, Jiji would be handicapped for life.

Xiaoxue swayed, and her body slid to the ground. She was in shock—it was more than a mother's heart could bear. Xue Yu moved quickly and caught hold of her, but his eyes were fixed on Jiji, and Mei Yin's hands. Mei Yin stayed focused, gritted her teeth, and drew the short blade through Jiji's hand. The four severed fingers dropped neatly to the ground. Jiji felt no pain at first, because the knife was so sharp. Jiaojiao shrieked and shut her eyes, unable to watch. He Ying did the same. Jiji's face blanched, but his eyes steadily followed his grandmother's movements. Mei Yin quickly inspected him, and finding no other wounds, ripped a strip of cloth from her blouse, quickly winding it around Jiji's wrist to stop the blood, then another to bandage his finger stumps. "Get him to the hospital!" she rasped.

Hearing this, Xiaoxue opened her eyes and struggled back to her feet. Now she screamed, pointing to the ground. Zia Baj had woken, and was struggling to crawl toward Mei Yin. Still some distance away, he had already opened his mouth, ready to take a bite. Still busy bandaging Jiji, Mei Yin glared at him and roared, "Kick him unconscious! I don't have time for this."

Jingshuan walked over and kicked him viciously in the crotch. Baj yelped and fell unconscious again.

A police van drove up, sirens blasting. Before he'd come to Yoyogi Park, Zia Baj had been biting people in the pedestrian areas of Ginza and Akihabara, and the police were searching the city for him. After Xue Yu's call, the closest squad vehicle came immediately to them. A young officer leaped out and stared at the fallen criminal, then at Jiji's mutilated left hand. Mei Yin snapped in English, "Quick, Xue Yu, get Jiji to the hospital, and the others who were bitten, too. Don't let their blood touch anyone! I'll stay here and take care of things." She turned to the police officer. "Please drive these people to a hospital. That man on the ground is the terrorist who tried to infect us all with smallpox before, and now he's turned himself into a biological weapon. It's almost certainly Ebola, a dangerous hemorrhagic fever."

The officer shivered. Their orders had only been to arrest a lunatic who'd been going around biting people, and suddenly it had turned into a biological terror attack! He recognized Mei Yin from her many recent TV appearances, and knew to trust what she said. He ordered another officer to drive the victims to hospital. Xue Yu and the rest, including the now-revived Xiaoxue, bundled Jiji into the vehicle too. The officer suddenly thought of something and shouted, "Bring the child's fingers too! They might be able to fix them back on."

Mei Yin shook her head grimly. There would be no way to keep the fingers alive long enough to reattach them and also rid them of the virus. But she said nothing, and Jingshuan carefully scooped them up in a handkerchief.

After they'd left, the officer quickly reported the Ebola terrorist attack to the Tokyo Police HQ, which told him to follow Mei Yin's instructions. Mei Yin pointed at Zia Baj, still lying on the ground, and said, "This source of infection needs to be kept strictly controlled. Handcuff him and keep him in quarantine. Be very careful! If you can't get a containment vehicle here, just zip him into a body bag and bring him to any hospital, they should have an isolation unit for Level-Four viruses."

The young officer issued orders to his subordinates, and they immobilized the terrorist, sealing his mouth with tape and calling for a body bag, then calling ahead to a hospital. Mei Yin added, "Has he bitten people in other locations? All the victims should be quarantined and treated for Ebola."

Soon the body bag arrived, and the officers stuffed the still-unconscious Baj into it, then hauled him into their squad car and drove off in a blaze of sirens. Mei Yin now staggered, hardly able to move. Her earlier tae kwon do moves had torn tendons and muscles—she was old, and thirty years out of practice, not to mention her bout with severe arthritis a few years ago. An officer stepped forward to support her, but she quickly motioned him back—having just performed an amputation on Jiji, she worried that her hands might be contaminated with the virus. Painfully, she maneuvered herself into the squad car. The officer said, "Professor Mei, I hope you'll come to HQ first. Would you do that? As we come up with our emergency response to the situation, we could use your advice and scientific guidance."

Mei Yin was still worried about Jiji, but it was more important to deal with the big picture first. "All right, I'll come."

The squad car sped toward HQ, Mei Yin slumped in the passenger seat, her eyes shut. After the day's events, she was shattered. The police officer softly called her name, and her eyes snapped open. "What is it?"

"Professor Mei, we've just had a call to say that including your grandson, a total of forty-three people were bitten today. Your grandson may be out of danger, but as for the rest . . . Can they be treated?"

Mei Yin sighed, and answered bluntly, "I'd estimate at least half of these people will die. At most we can hope that the infection won't spread beyond them."

The officer fell silent. He had guessed at the answer—if Mei Yin thought there was any hope of treatment, would she have sliced off the child's fingers?—but the number was just too high. More than thirty days ago, the city had escaped a major terror attack with only two deaths. The people of Tokyo had escaped disaster, and had the right to savor their victory. Yet today's "handmade attack" would lead to a few dozen deaths, plus the potential for a wider outbreak!

Xue Yu phoned to say they were at the hospital, and Jiji's wound was being bandaged and disinfected. The doctors had carried out a detailed examination, and confirmed he had no other injuries. Only now did Mei Yin calm down. Poor Jiji . . . but he was still lucky. If he'd had any additional injuries, those fingers would have been cut off in vain. As it was, four fingers was an acceptable price to pay for his life—in fact, it was a stroke of great fortune. She said, "Take good care of Jiji. And tell him Grandma will come to see him when she's finished with her work."

The police car stopped at a hospital along the way to completely disinfect Mei Yin's hands and her crucifix blade. She never made it to HQ: the prime minister's office called, and they were diverted there instead. Prime Minister Miki met her at the door, and Mr. Matsumoto arrived around the same time. Miki smiled grimly. "Professor Mei, I hadn't expected we'd need you again so soon. Tokyo has really suffered a lot recently." Mei Yin came in, supported by two officers, and sat with difficulty on the couch. Miki came to the point. "I'm a layman, so I need you to tell me, is it true that Ebola has no vaccine or treatment?"

"That's correct."

"Why is that? To my knowledge, it was discovered more than fifty years ago, even earlier than AIDS."

Mei Yin looked at him and Matsumoto, and said frankly, "Because the disease has so far restricted itself to African countries, and never threatened the West."

Miki blushed—he knew Mei Yin was right. If he received a request for major funding into Ebola research, knowing it wasn't a threat to the Japanese people, he'd very likely turn it down.

Mei Yin said, "Apart from thoroughly disinfecting the victims and putting them on a course of regular antivirals, the only effective cure is blood serum from recovered Ebola sufferers in Africa. As far as I know, there are stocks at the American CDC; hospitals in Nairobi and Kinshasa might have some too. This blood serum would contain antibodies that should be effective if injected into the victims. But it also might—"

The blood serum also might contain other "pathogens of tomorrow." The chances were low, but there were no guarantees—they hadn't screened that blood. On balance, though, it was worth doing. Prime Minister Miki said, "I'll tell the Ministry of Welfare to get on that right away. What else can we do right now? Please tell us."

Mei Yin asked about the condition of the other victims, and was informed that they'd been strictly quarantined. There wasn't much else to be done at this moment. Given Japan's strict health protocols, the infection probably wouldn't spread any further. The difficulty was those forty-two victims, who had no guarantee of survival.

The prime minister asked, "Since there's no cure for Ebola, the terrorist is quite likely to die, is that right? The police want to question him at once."

"Yes, there's no hope for him. From his appearance, he's in the late stages, and only has a day or two left. He must have waited till he was at his most infectious to start biting people. If you want to interrogate him, you should do that as soon as possible." She added fiercely, "Now I wish I believed in Judgment Day, in purgatory and hell. This psychopath is only fit to be roasted in the fires of hell."

As soon as the meeting ended, Mei Yin rushed to the University of Tokyo Hospital, where her family and friends were in a state of anguish and fear. Jiji burst into tears at the sight of his grandmother, and Jiaojiao started howling too. The four adults didn't make a sound, but they were also weeping. Jiji's left hand was elevated, and even though it was thickly swathed in bandages, it was obvious a portion was missing. Mei Yin signaled for Xue Yu and Jingshuan to carry her over so she could hug Jiji, sobbing, "Jiji, don't cry, you're a brave boy."

"Jiji," Xue Yu said, "Grandma's been injured too. Let her lie down for a while!"

Mei Yin quickly shook her head, and insisted on sitting upright in a chair and holding Jiji close, her heart aching as she held his wounded hand. She didn't mention the possibility of reattaching the fingers—it clearly couldn't be done safely. Jiji would have to go through life with a mutilated left hand.

The most sorrowful of them all was Jiji's mother. Xiaoxue wept silently, and when Mommy Mei arrived, she avoided her eyes, refusing to let her Mommy touch her, recalling Xue Yu's uncle's curse: Keep away from Mei Yin, or her sins will bring retribution onto your child's head! Of course, Mei Yin wasn't to blame for Jiji's mutilation, but no matter what, the warning had come true. If she'd listened to him at the time . . . but she had to abandon that line of thought. Still, she couldn't meet her mother's eyes. Mei Yin looked at her and knew what was going on in her heart, but could say nothing.

Jiji's admittance paperwork was done. He would stay here until he was confirmed free from Ebola. A Japanese nurse came in and softly urged the family to leave, saying that only one person could stay with the patient. Mei Yin said, "You should all go, I'll stay tonight." Xue Yu shook his head. "That won't do! You're badly hurt, you ought to go back and rest." It was Sun Jingshuan who understood her, and her ties to her grandson. "Listen to your mother," he said to Xue Yu and Xiaoxue. "Let's go. Everyone can stop worrying, the hospital will take extra good care of Jiji. Xiaoxue, you should go too."

Xiaoxue was very reluctant, but Xue Yu persuaded her. She kissed her son, and told him not to bother Grandma, then finally tore herself away. The room grew quiet. Jiji's hand and Mei Yin's back were both in terrible pain and neither could sleep, so they talked instead. Jiji asked, "Grandma, will my fingers really never grow back? I mean, even with the latest techniques? Don't try to comfort me, I can take the truth."

"At the moment, gene therapy still can't grow back missing fingers—maybe in ten or twenty years it'll be possible. But," she said frankly, "in ten or twenty years, the parts of your brain in charge of those four fingers might have atrophied or moved on to some other use, so even if you did grow new fingers, you might not be able to do anything with them. Besides, organ generation will have its drawbacks. Scientists say it might lead to an increased risk of cancer, and should be used with care. With regeneration, you'd have to reactivate cell growth that's shut down, which is precisely how cancer starts. There's no fundamental difference between the two. Nothing to be done about that. Each step of scientific progress has to contend with such problems. Science is a sharp sword, but it'll always be double-edged."

"Like that crucifix you wear?"

"Yes, like that."

Jiji said sadly, "I guess I'll never be able to play the violin again. Actually, I never liked the violin. Mom made me learn. But now . . ."

"Jiji, do you know about a woman named Helen Keller? She was deaf and blind, but managed to do what many other people couldn't. And did you hear about the Soviet pilot who had no legs? Or the British physicist Stephen Hawking? Or the Chinese writers Zhang Haidi and Wu Yunduo?"

"I've heard of some of them. Tell me about them, Grandma."

Mei Yin called the nurse and asked for another blanket, so she could support her lower back, and wrapped one corner around Jiji. She described those brave souls who didn't allow the disabilities of their bodies to weaken their spirits. As she talked, she told him some other things, things that might have been too deep for a six-year-old to understand: the worship of nature, how tragedy is the flip side of good fortune, how God hates perfection, the bad debts of science, the demands of civilization, and the negation of negation. Much of this went over Jiji's head, but regardless, the child was like a sponge, and what he didn't understand would remain with him, to be recalled and digested as he grew older.

Jiji leaned against her, his right hand toying with her crucifix. He asked, "Grandma, what's this blade made of that's so sharp? Can I look at it? Dad has one too, but he never lets me play with it."

Mei Yin carefully pulled off the sheath, and handed the disinfected knife to him. "Here, just be careful with it."

Jiji cautiously held the crucifix handle, studying the nearly transparent blade. He could just make out the English words *Be in awe of nature* and Mei Yin's own initials. He slithered from his grandmother's lap and began trying it on various objects—medicine containers, drip tubes, stainless steel needles, and so on—enthusiastically slicing them open. The blade went easily through all of them. Jiji was so excited he forgot how much his wound hurt. He knew how much the crucifix meant to his grandma, but in the end he couldn't stop himself from pleading, "Grandma, will you give this cross to me? I'll be very careful. I promise not to lose it or hurt anyone."

Mei Yin looked into his eyes, and couldn't bear to say no. She took the blade and replaced the sheath, then hung the crucifix around Jiji's neck. He exclaimed, "Are you giving it to me, Grandma? Are you?"

Mei Yin patted his face and said tenderly, "Yes, I am. It's yours now. But you have to be careful. It's a very dangerous toy."

"Don't worry, I'll be very careful. Very, very careful!"

Jiji was sleepy now. He crawled back onto his grandma's lap, snuggled against her chest, and soon fell asleep. Mei Yin hugged him, one hand lingering on his crucifix. She thought she might have been a little rash with the gift. Jiji might have promised faithfully, but he was still a child, and it was probably far too dangerous a toy for him. But she'd promised, and couldn't go back on her word. They would just have to be careful. She was tired too, and, still holding the child, soon fell soundly asleep.

ABOUT THE AUTHOR

A master of science fiction, Wang Jinkang won the World Chinese Science Fiction Association's Nebula Award for best novel in 1997 and the International Science Fiction Conference's Milky Way Award in 2010. His books include *Ant People*, *Seven-Layered Shell*, *Life-Death Balance*, *Time-Space Shift*, *Sowing Seeds on Mercury*, and *Human-Like*.

ABOUT THE TRANSLATOR

Jeremy Tiang has translated more than ten books from Chinese, including novels by Zhang Yueran, Yan Geling, and Chan Ho-kei. He has been awarded an NEA Literary Translation Fellowship and People's Literature Prize. He also writes and translates plays, and his own short story collection, *It Never Rains on National Day*, was short-listed for the Singapore Literature Prize.